KU-111-227

Nicholas Searle was a civil servant who spent much of his time working on security matters, before his decision to leave in 2011 in order to become a fiction writer. *The Good Liar* is his first novel.

THE GOOD LIAR

Roy is a con man living in a leafy English suburb, about to pull off the final coup of his career. He is going to meet and woo a beautiful woman. He will swiftly move in with her, and together they will live the seemingly calm life of a retired couple — evenings in front of the television, a little holiday in Berlin. Then he will slip away with her life savings. But who is the man behind the con? What has he had to do to survive this life of lies? And why is this beautiful woman so willing to be his next victim?

NICHOLAS SEARLE

◆

THE GOOD
LIAR

Complete and Unabridged

CHARNWOOD
Leicester

First published in Great Britain in 2016 by
Viking
an imprint of Penguin Books
London

First Charnwood Edition
published 2017
by arrangement with
Penguin Random House UK
London

A catalogue record for this book is available
from the British Library.

ISBN 978–1–4448–3107–8

Published by
F. A. Thorpe (Publishing)
Anstey, Leicestershire

Set by Words & Graphics Ltd.
Anstey, Leicestershire
Printed and bound in Great Britain by
T. J. International Ltd., Padstow, Cornwall

This book is printed on acid-free paper

For C, always

1

Nom de guerre

1

It is, Roy thinks, perfect. Kismet, serendipity, destiny, happenstance; call it what you will. All of these things rolled into one. He is not sure he believes in fate, or whether he believes in anything but the very present. Then again, life has treated him well generally.

He stands and does the walk of his flat, checking that the windows are secure and the appliances are switched off correctly. He pats the chest of his blazer, which hangs on the back of the door: yes, his wallet is there. His keys lie ready on the console table in the hall.

This lady at any rate seems heaven-sent, at least from the résumé he has called up on the screen. At long last. He knows to anticipate the minor alterations, those moments when a slight imperfection is turned by a clever choice of words or a simple ever-so-small fib into a positively positive attribute. This is human nature. He doubts, for example, that her name is truly Estelle, any more than his is Brian. In his view such inconsequential tweaks are to be expected and accepted. They oil the cogs. When they are revealed, he will be suitably tolerant and amused at these minor embellishments. Unlike

1

the rather larger lies you often confront, he thinks as he places the tea bag in the recycling bin, rinses his cup and saucer and places them, upturned, on the draining board.

He takes a breath and powers the computer down, pushing the chair neatly under the desk. He has been here before, hopes held high. With this transitory reflection comes a momentary weariness. Those dreadful meetings in Beefeaters and Tobys around the Home Counties with frumpy old women in whom the bitterness of their long unfulfilled marriages with under-achieving and uninspiring husbands has in widowhood seemingly become the seed of a sense of licence to lie at will. For them there is no legacy of happy memories or the material benefit of platinum pensions in leafy Surrey mansions. They reside in poky terraces that no doubt smell of fried food, eking out an existence on state handouts, cursing Bert, or Alf, or whoever it may be, and contemplating a stolen life. They are out for what they can get now, by whatever means. And who can blame them really?

Quick inspection. Immaculate white shirt: yes. Creases of grey flannels: perfect. Spit-shined shoes: gleaming. Regimental stripe tie: well knotted. Hair: combed neatly. Blue blazer off hanger, and on. Fits like a glove. Glance in the mirror: he'd pass for seventy, sixty at a pinch. He looks at the time. The cab should be here shortly. The train journey from Paddington will take only thirty minutes or so.

For those desperate women, this is an escape.

An adventure. For Roy, this dating lark is something different: a professional enterprise. He does not allow himself to become light entertainment or to let them down gently. He fixes them with his blue eyes before dismantling them forensically. He skewers them. He has done his homework and lets them know.

'I thought you said you were five foot six and slim,' he may say with incredulity, but is delicate enough not to add: rather than a clinically obese dwarf. 'Not much like your photo, are you? Was it taken a few years back, dear?' (He doesn't add the postscript: perhaps of your better-looking sister.) 'You live near Tunbridge Wells, you say. More Dartford really, isn't it?' Or, 'So what you mean by holidaying in Europe is a package trip once a year with your sister to Benidorm?'

If, as planned, he is second to the venue, he will usually conduct a discreet first reconnaissance pass to size things up. When confronted with the familiarly depressing he could simply leave without introducing himself. It is all so predictable. But he never does. He regards it as his duty to shatter their hopeless delusions. They will be the better for it, eventually. Beginning with his usual winning smile and gallant greeting, he will segue rapidly into what has become something of a core script.

'One of the things I dislike intensely,' he says, 'is dishonesty.'

Generally they smile and nod meekly.

'So, with apologies and with the odd unpleasant experience behind me' — another

3

smile, and this is as gentle as it gets — 'let's cut to the chase, shall we?'

Generally another nod, probably no smile, and a shift in the seat that he notices but perhaps others wouldn't.

He is punctilious in splitting the bill when it is over and unambiguous about the future. No insincere pleasantries. 'Not what I was expecting at all,' he will say with a weary shake of the head. 'Oh no. What a shame. If only you'd been clearer. If only you'd described yourself more . . . accurately, shall we say? We could have both avoided wasting our energy. Which at our time of life' — here a brief twinkle of the eye and the hint of a smile to show what they will be missing — 'we can ill afford to do. If only . . . '

He hopes today he will not have to deploy these measures. But if so he will have discharged his duty to himself, to the unfortunate other and to the system that mismatches the hopeless with the delusional and, he believes, is in severe danger of bringing itself into disrepute. All those misspent hours drinking Britvic, all that effort put into stilted conversation over glistening mixed grills and mass-produced microwaved beef and ale pies or vegetable bakes or tikka masalas, all those awkward goodbyes with false promises of future contact. Not for him. Still less, all those doomed couplings in the search for a final day in the sun.

Roy is not a pessimist, though. Brace up, be positive. Each time he starts afresh, hopeful. This time will be different, he tells himself, glossing over the fact that he has said this to himself several times before. But his sense is that it won't be the same.

The taxi is here. He straightens his back, smiles to himself and locks the door before striding to the waiting car.

2

Betty makes her final preparations, careful to keep her excitement in check. Stephen will run her to the pub and wait outside, so she has no practical concerns. No flush of heat as the train runs dangerously late. No undue ache in the hips as she rushes inelegantly up the high street. No risk of a post-meeting sense of discomposure affecting her ability to find her way home again. And Stephen will be there should she feel an unexpected need to terminate the meeting early.

They will have to set off in a few minutes, Stephen has told her as a result of his researches of his Google and his satnav gizmo. She can manage the internet but there are so many things about it that bamboozle her. What, for example, is a tweet? How on earth did we survive without all these devices? Or, more to the point, why do young people so depend on them?

She can hear Stephen padding around the lounge. He seems more nervous than she is; how sweet. While she applies her lipstick she looks at herself in the mirror. There will be no last-minute anxieties. The blue floral dress she has selected will serve perfectly well and sets off her fair hair, which is cut in a bob as fashionable

5

as can be carried off at her age. She will not exchange the delicate silver necklace or its partner brooch for something more obvious like pearls. She will not opt for more — or less — sensible shoes. She will not require a final emboldening cup of coffee.

Betty does not consider herself to be a flutterer. She is calm; realistic too, she likes to think. Once justifiably described as beautiful, she accepts with, she hopes, good grace the effects of time. She prefers to think of them as mere effects, not ravages. Though she retains a certain radiance, she is no longer beautiful. She cannot pretend to be despite the glossies' determined attempts to create and capture a new silver market. Perhaps she is something different, nameless and ageless.

She clicks the top back on the tube of lipstick, rolls her lips together to ensure the correct coverage, fingers the necklace, gently touches her hair and gives herself one final look. She is ready. She glances at her watch: five minutes ahead of time. Stephen greets her with a delicate and decorous embrace when she enters the lounge.

'You look fabulous,' he says, and she thinks he means it.

3

Stephen drives more sedately in the rain than he might otherwise. Even more sedately, that is, since at the best of times he is not a confident driver. He drives slowly for himself, to steady his nerves, and not for her benefit. She is a resilient person, clearly much more resilient than he is despite their respective ages. She has lived a life rather than simply studying how others have lived theirs. A feisty old bird, some might say, but not he. He could not imagine anything less fitting. He would not use such language and anyway it would be inaccurate. She is fragile, though not sparrow-like, with features of porcelain and proportions of fine slenderness. It is her constitution that is strong. Unbreakable, he'd say.

They set off early to avoid any risk of lateness. He noses achingly slowly out of junctions, keeps studiously ten miles an hour below the speed limit and observes the strictures of traffic signs with an exaggerated obeisance. This is an important day, for her, for him.

'You're not at all nervous?' he asks.

'A little,' she replies. 'Not really, though. But it's easier for me, isn't it?'

'Why's that?'

'Because I'm doing it. Not waiting. Watching. I'll be there. You'll be outside in the car. Helpless.'

'But you'll be in there. With him. Who knows what he'll be like? What it'll be like for you?' He smiles.

'That's precisely it. It makes things easier. Truly. You don't see, do you? How could you? I'm past the age when anything really matters, least of all what I say or do. I can be as outrageous as I want with impunity. I'm a dangerous quantity. I'm beyond embarrassment.

If it doesn't work out, it doesn't work out. I'll live to fight another day.'

'You're remarkable,' he says. 'Brave.'

'Not really. What can happen? A drink and a bite with no doubt the perfect gentleman in a busy country pub. With my knight in shining armour waiting outside gripping his mobile phone. What can possibly happen?'

He smiles and turns off the motorway on to the slip road.

4

'Estelle,' she says, extending her hand, and her eyes twinkle as she smiles.

'Brian,' he replies. 'Delighted.'

She has found him. An appropriate ten minutes after the appointed time, owing to some judicious circling of the neighbourhood by Stephen, accompanied by glances at the building, newly constructed to look old, lit brightly in the March midday gloom.

To Roy, she is instantly recognizable. Of medium height, slight, young for her age, something of the gamine about her, an amused, delighted expression and those engaging eyes. Lovely hair. A stunning dress that shows off her figure. A real head-turner in her time no doubt. The photograph on the website did not lie. His slight annoyance that she was not there before him evaporates. He approves. Oh yes. Very much so.

'Now, what can I get you to drink?' he asks.

'I'd love a . . . vodka martini,' she says.

She does not know why; the notion has just slipped into her head. Such impetuousness will not do for the next hour or two. Control and discipline.

'Shaken or stirred?' he says with a smile and a raise of the eyebrow. Rather different from the customary sad small sherry, he thinks.

'Ha ha,' she says.

He orders her drink, suggests they sit and carries their glasses to table number 16.

'How did you recognize me?' he asks.

'I came in, looked around and there you were, standing at the bar. Tall, distinguished, smart, just as you described. Your photograph is very much like you.'

This is not so very far from the truth, she reasons. In fact in a sea of — seemingly — sixteen-year-old thrusting sales executives he was not difficult to pick out.

'Wizzywig,' he says.

'Pardon?'

'What you see is what you get. I do exactly what it says on the tin.'

'Oh,' she says, 'how very disappointing.' She smiles as if to reassure him that she is flirting.

'Ho ho ho,' he booms after a short pause, his shoulders heaving. 'Very good. I can see you're trouble. We're going to get on famously.' He appraises her frankly. 'Oh yes.'

★   ★   ★

They order their food, she a vegetarian pasta, he steak, egg and chips. Between mouthfuls of

9

plastic conchigliette smeared with processed baby-food vegetables and a stringy cheese sauce she considers him more fully. He is indeed tall and broad-shouldered, with a shock of white hair swept back from a florid face on which the tributaries of blood vessels map a complex topography. The hair is tamed with hair cream and plastered down neatly behind the ears. His eyes are striking, alarming almost, the light blue of the irises set in their ovoid milky frames against the sea of reddening skin, watchful, darting even as they focus on her face. Were it not for the watery, diluted quality of age she might be afraid of him; indeed she is a little afraid.

At one point he was a commanding presence, she thinks: tall and authoritative. He still holds himself that way, but at the same time there is an undisguisable physical slump. The shoulders are rounded and the eyes contain a recognition that he cannot, after all, deny mortality. The evidence is now all too compelling and carries disappointment as the decay of physical and mental function accelerates. She knows something of how he must feel, though she has never been imposing: vivacious perhaps, but not infused with that peculiarly masculine vanity whose futility is cruelly exposed in the inevitable waning of virile power. She feels sorry for him, in a way.

The conversation flows easily.

'This is nice,' she says untruthfully, looking up from the mess on her plate.

'Oh yes,' he says. 'You can rely on them here.'

'How is your steak?'

'Splendid. Another drink?'

'Why, yes, Brian. I won't say no.'

'Not driving then?'

'No. My grandson drove me here.'

'Your grandson?'

'Yes. Stephen. He's waiting outside in the car. Immersed in a book no doubt.'

'Close to family, then?'

'Yes,' she says decisively. 'There aren't many of us. But we're very close.'

'Tell me about them.'

This is one of the obvious topics of conversation and she is prepared for it. Her son, Michael, the pharma executive who lives near Manchester, and his wife, Anne. Their son, Stephen, a historian working at Bristol University. Their daughter, Emma, studying English at Edinburgh. She briefly mentions Alasdair, her late husband, but she knows that now is not the time to visit the private sadnesses that have, in part, brought them to this table.

It is Brian's turn. His son, it seems, designs kitchens in Sydney and their contact is infrequent and casual if amicable. No, he has no grandchildren. It is evident that Brian is not at ease discussing his son. Brian himself was the eldest brother of three and his siblings have passed away. And then of course there was his wife, Mary. Poor, poor Mary. He looks down and Betty suspects a tear might be forming.

'You know,' he says, looking up, re-energized, 'one of the things I dislike intensely is dishonesty.' He looks at her and she returns his gaze evenly. 'It seems no one today feels a bit of shame about lying. When they're caught, of course, oh yes. But it seems dishonesty is all right if you can get away with it. I deplore that. Do you understand me?'

She looks at him and smiles, saying, 'Yes. I think so.'

'So I have to confess to you an act of deception on my part. In meeting you.' He pauses and adopts a solemn expression. 'I'm afraid my name is in fact not Brian. It's Roy. Roy Courtnay. Brian was a kind of nom de plume for this meeting. If you see what I mean. One feels so exposed.'

Nom de guerre, she thinks, mildly irritated.

'Oh, that,' she says with cheerful dismissiveness. 'I've never done this before but I more or less assumed it's par for the course. Natural self-protection. I suppose now's the moment where I confess that my name's not Estelle. I'm Betty.'

They look at each other seriously for a moment before laughing in unison.

'I can promise that was the last time I will lie to you, Betty. Everything I say to you from now on will be the truth. Total honesty I can promise you, Betty. Total honesty.' He grins broadly.

Steady on, she thinks, but returns his smile with neither reserve nor equivocation. She says, 'I'm glad to hear it.'

They have crossed a line, each feels privately, and they relax. They chat, talking about young people. It is safe territory and in platitudes they can share bemusement at life these days.

'They're so brave,' she says. 'I'd never have dared do some of the things they get up to.'

'But so casual,' he replies, 'everything's so easy for them. No perseverance.'

'I know. They haven't a care in the world. Not like us. I'm glad they're like that.'

Betty supposes this must be a necessary part of the process, a step on the path to greater intimacy. She believes little of what she is saying; she is making it up as she goes.

She tells Roy that Stephen doesn't even have a telephone in his flat; his mobile smart thing-gummy is all he seems to require. He carries his life in his back pocket. When they were young, they agree, the ultimate status symbol was a telephone in the house. Now it's a social faux pas. Her son owns three cars. And there are only two people in the household now both of the children are away. Or rather he doesn't own them but pays an extortionate amount each month to a finance company and simply cashes each in for another at the end of three years, an abstruse arrangement he has patiently explained a number of times but which she fails to 'get', as he puts it. No one would dream of actually saving up to buy something these days. Her granddaughter is twenty years old and has visited more countries than Betty has in her lifetime. She is burbling, rushing headlong, she realizes, but it doesn't matter. It is all right.

Stephen is duly summoned and approved of. 'A fine young man,' says Roy while said young man is visiting the lavatory. 'A tribute to you, Betty. A fine young man.'

Telephone numbers are exchanged as well as genuine expressions of intent to meet again, very shortly. They offer Roy a lift to the station but he declines. 'Not quite decrepit yet,' he says. 'It's only a short walk.' He stands as they leave and kisses Betty on the cheek. She reciprocates, squeezes his arm and pulls him slightly closer, though not yet to the intimacy of an embrace. Then she extends her arms, holds him there and looks into his eyes.

'Until next time, then,' she says.

'Au revoir, Betty,' he says.

2

Mistletoe and Wine

1

Here they come. The innocents abroad, toddling down the street. The sun has got his hat on and all is well with the world.

They tumble and rush shrilly over the cobbles, ties askew, satchels flying, shirts out of trousers, hair tousled. School shoes clatter on ancient stone as they find their way down cut-throughs from the school towards the pedestrian shopping zone, flowing like liquid, and young voices clamour and vie in excitement.

The girls come more slowly, and more neatly. Well, girls always are better-behaved, more circumspect. Except for the naughty ones. And they can be very naughty. Oh yes.

The Green is bathed in placid sunlight, with its refuges of shade under the venerable trees. This is how it has been for centuries: young people flooding out of the cathedral school with not a thought, brimming with life, eager to resume their dodges and weaves, while old men regard them with ill-disguised envy from their mews cottages and contemplate bitterly their own youth.

With interest but no compassion, he watches them from his chair in the corner of the living room. The girls are particularly fascinating. Boys of secondary school age are mere blustering rhinos, carried on a wave of hormonal surges of which they are the helpless victims and to which they are utterly oblivious. Their female peers have gained an awareness. And with awareness comes uncertainty, expressed in various ways. The plain and studious invest their faith that diligence and intelligence may help them to navigate the horrors, away from loneliness and failure. The fresh-faced, pretty girls of the class — pretty vacuous too, most of them — sense inchoately that their attractiveness may be ephemeral and dependent on the vagaries of their coming physical development. And the little tarts, who aren't especially clever but are smart enough to know that they aren't bright or in the first ranks of prettiness, use cunning, hitching up their skirts as soon as they leave the house, teasing the males. They know that thing called sex lurks somewhere close by; and they quickly learn their power. Oh yes.

Now the older ones. Pimply youths with lank long hair and doleful expressions dance attendance on unattainable girls. Roy likes the girls' disdain, though his scorn for the hopeless male specimens exceeds even the girls'. With flashed mascara glances between them — they tend to walk in pairs — and grins that are intended to appear shy but which Roy knows to be smirks, the girls disguise their feelings.

He cannot see himself in the boys. You fools, he thinks; you fools. I was not one of you. I was bold and handsome. I did not falter or trip.

He is no longer fifteen. Or fifty, or eighty for that matter. But your instincts never change. Once a charmer, ineffably attractive to the opposite sex, always a charmer. He could not help it even if he wanted to.

There she is. The one he has selected for singular attention. Regulation short black skirt and black tights encasing slender womanly legs. The tights are at odds with the school uniform, yet, he thinks knowingly, perfectly congruent given context. Perhaps fifteen, maybe as young as a well-developed thirteen; they grow so quickly these days. Petite anyway, with that wild blonde-streaked Medusa hair that seems never to go out of fashion. Eyeshadow daubed inexpertly but to good effect from where he is sitting. She thinks she is a rebel, an individual, but she is simply treading a familiar path to eventual conformity. If only he were younger he could teach her a thing or two. She might feign haughtiness and indifference, a languorous pretence of experience. She might be enthusiastic as she ventured on the path of discovery, but eventually she would show fear. Roy can deal with fear. Oh yes.

★ ★ ★

Stephen, meanwhile, is running late. Story of his life. He has promised to deliver some books to Betty and then he must be back for a meeting with Gerald at six that is sure to be gruelling. He can predict the questions: Everything on track? All the corners covered? All the boxes ticked?

17

Let's just sit down and make doubly sure, shall we? This project is pretty damned important, after all.

To be honest, the questions are pertinent and Stephen requires supervision. This, not Gerald, is what troubles Stephen. Gerald is all right, though he does revel somewhat in his position. The fundamental issue is, though, that Stephen does not know whether everything is on track. He can't see the track, let alone the corners. He hasn't yet worked out what the boxes are that need to be ticked. This thing seems to have a life of its own.

Project management is not Stephen's thing. Management isn't his thing. Purpose, mental exertion, careful research, the joy of winkling out new facts that change the terrain, a sense of creating something worthwhile, these are the important things, not dry process. Gerald is a necessary evil, he supposes. What would he do without him?

He finds the alleyway between the chemist's and the estate agent's that connects the new town with the old and hastens up it from standard issue high street to centuries-old cobblestones and the Green. The clock is chiming the half-hour somewhere behind the screen of oaks whose leaves rustle in the breeze and dapple the sunlight, casting undulating light and shade over the fine verdant carpet.

It is a gorgeous day in England, one of few so far this summer. The sun is high in a blue sky and pristine white powder-puff clouds skim on the breeze. Children swarm busily from their daily endeavours, the adrenalin of release fuelling their exuberance. At a distance their uniforms look neat and tidy but as he approaches he can see that the demands of the day, as well as sundry attempts to declaim individuality, have taken their toll. Blazers are tossed on shoulders, shirts are crumpled and grubby, shoes are scuffed. And there is the smell of schoolchildren, their sweat and urine and dirt intermingled with heavy-duty synthetic fabrics and that odd faint reek that seeps from the institution itself, combining the almost metallic smell of cleaning fluid and polish with the aroma of dusty wooded age exuding from its parquet floors and the august panelling of the main hall.

There is a cheeriness about the children that bolsters his optimism. He passes through the melee of boys and behind them are the various phalanxes of girls, more cliquey, quieter, more guarded. Older in fact, and more self-aware.

Stephen is careful to be careful about the way he regards the girls, for he knows of the suspicion of every male that must reside in each female heart these days. Was it ever so? He does not know but cannot risk his look being mistaken for a leer.

He is interested in the phenomenon of youth, though not quite sure why. It could be simple curiosity about the human condition, piqued by these young things in that phase of growing, as they observe, mimic, experiment, revise, adapt and finally begin to achieve identity. Perhaps it is because he himself has not yet completed that final phase, despite pushing thirty.

Across the Green he sees a young girl, maybe fourteen, walking on her own, gawky, uncertain, meaninglessly defiant. Her skirt is short, her eyes blackened, her chin juts with attitude, yet she is just a child and in her eyes he sees fear. Her affectation provokes a series of emotions: a flood of something he can only think of as love, an acknowledgement of her vulnerability and a desire, despite his powerlessness to do so and the absurdity of the proposition, to protect. He examines his motives, searching for the shadow of lust contorted into more palatable expressions. He can honestly say that it does not lurk, but it is interesting that he needs to check.

And then he sees him, in Betty's chair by the window. Roy, who has been living at Betty's for two months now. Those lizard eyes are fixed on this girl, acquisitive, hungry. She continues to walk, oblivious as she composes a text. As she passes Stephen, Roy sees him and their eyes lock. Inside a second Roy's expression changes from incredulity to hostility and finally to the sad old man harmlessly passing his days looking out on the world. Roy smiles experimentally and Stephen returns the smile, waving diffidently. He thinks: I know you. However much I dislike you.

2

'I'd be very careful if I were you,' says Roy when Stephen enters the room.

'Sorry?' says Stephen.

'I said you want to be careful,' repeats Roy,

jerking his head theatrically towards the window.

Stephen frowns in puzzlement, opens his mouth to say something, but thinks better of it. Roy's eyes are on his face.

He says, 'Cup of tea?'

'Don't mind if I do,' replies Roy, leaning back in his chair again.

When Stephen has brought the mugs of tea — terracotta-strong with three sugars for Roy, milky-white with none for himself — Roy resumes.

He says, 'Can't be too careful.'

The words hang in the air for a moment.

'Er, yes,' says Stephen finally. 'Pardon?'

Away with the fairies, thinks Roy. Mind off somewhere else. Hopeless. All over the place. Typical academic.

'Misunderstandings,' he says.

'Oh, yes,' says Stephen, inattentive, smiling weakly. 'Yes.'

'Don't patronize me, son.'

Stephen stares at him blankly and says nothing.

'Betty not around?' he comes up with finally.

Roy backs off. Like being cruel to a puppy. Not, necessarily, that that would stop him. But Stephen bores him. Unlikely to be any sport there. 'No,' he says. 'Out meeting a friend for tea.'

'Oh, right. Any idea when she'll be back?'

'Oh no. She's a law to herself, that one.' Roy chuckles. 'I'm not her keeper.'

'No. Of course not.'

'You in a hurry? You seem distracted.'

'A lot on at the moment. I just dropped by

21

with these books I promised Betty.' He holds out the orange carrier bag as evidence. 'She said she'd like to borrow them.'

'Oh yes,' says Roy, looking at him steadily.

Stephen places himself on the edge of the sofa, leaning forward, elbows on thighs, jacket still on despite the heat, ready to leave.

After a pause Roy asks, 'Your work going OK?'

'Fine,' replies Stephen. 'It's going well. I'm on my way to a meeting with my supervisor, actually.'

'Hard taskmaster, is he?'

'He's all right, Gerald. Keeps me on the straight and narrow. I need that.'

'I can see that,' says Roy, and they fall silent.

'What is it exactly you're studying?'

'The Jacobite Rebellion,' says Stephen eagerly. 'Specifically John Graham, his role in the instigation of the movement and his influence on the Fifteen and the Forty-Five.'

'Really?'

'It's a pivotal period in our history, with the Hanoverian succession and the struggle between Scottish Catholicism and Presbyterianism.'

'Very interesting I'm sure. I never was one for history. Not the academic type. What's the point of looking back? I ask myself. What's done is done in my humble opinion. You'll never undo it.'

'But you may begin to understand it.'

'Oh yes. I suppose so. I don't mean to knock it,' says Roy. 'I bow to your greater knowledge. Just not for me, that's all. All that living in the past.'

The clock ticks, measuring the distance between them.

'Oh well,' says Roy, 'each to his own.'

'I'd better be getting on,' says Stephen. 'I said I'd be at Gerald's by six.'

'Righty-ho,' says Roy, and turns to the window again. In his head Stephen has already left.

3

The beginning of autumn, as is customary after a summer whose occasional promise failed to materialize, is perversely fine and warm.

Roy ventures out for a stroll, to get out of the house. Betty has commenced her fussy cleaning routine. The racket of the vacuum cleaner and the disruption of his having to move his feet while trying to sit in peace with the newspaper are usually enough to stir him. She picks up items, sprays, dusts and tidies away the detritus of his existence, splashes water in invisible places and flushes the lavatory, all the while humming with tunelessness and cheerfulness in equal measure. He cannot bear a repeat of the excruciating mini-lecture on the toilet habits of 'little boys' to which she once subjected him. He felt almost sorry for her, she was so embarrassed, poor thing.

So he has mumbled that he will get out from under her feet and leave her in peace, and now shuffles his way across the cobblestones in shambling discomfort. Only once he is out of sight of the house will he be able to pick up his feet and quicken his pace.

It is a real effort, but a necessary one, to convey this message of infirmity. It has demanded thought, planning and occasional self-denial to suppress that reflex urge to vigour. But this way is in his interests, and Betty's too. They know their places. Betty is far better off contentedly managing the household and its quirks, preparing his meals and keeping everything sanitary. This is what he has aimed for.

For the moment. His ambitions range somewhat more adventurously than simply securing the ease of someone else catering to his needs. It's a neat trick to pull, to be sure, but he also wants one last punt, one final heart-stopping session at the roulette table. And he thinks Betty is the one to enable it. The cessation of purposeful activity rankles, and Betty can — inadvertently of course — help him scratch the itch. There will be a series of delicate balances to manage. That is his forte, he thinks fondly.

He is now some distance from the house and nearing the dark passageway that gives on to the pedestrian area. He feels it is safe to move faster. But just as he does so he finds he has to slow again. His heart is pounding, he is breathless and he feels vaguely nauseous and faint. He reflects that perhaps he is not in the tip-top condition he likes to imagine. He is no longer of an age for bravado. He totters on, somewhat disorientated.

In the Little Venice Coffee Shop he orders a cafetière and a slice of chocolate cake smothered in cream. This is his haven. He has few indulgences, but decent coffee is one. Not many places in England, let alone in this small cathedral city lying nicely out of sight and out of mind in the Wiltshire wilderness, have the competence to purchase good Arabica beans and produce something palatable from them. This is one, and it has the gentility of good service too, solicitous but with a spine of efficiency. When the coffee arrives he sighs, closes his eyes and breathes the aroma. If he suspends disbelief sufficiently he can imagine that he is sitting in a cafe in Vienna or in a well-upholstered *Konditorei* in some bourgeois, complacent German town. All German towns are of course bourgeois and complacent, he thinks. He can imagine, but only briefly, and is soon brought back to dog-shit England. Maybe sixty years ago, he thinks; more like seventy, and the rest. He unfolds his newspaper and is at peace.

★   ★   ★

At last he has gone out. It seems the only way to rouse him from that seat in the afternoon is to start to clean. She occasionally has to resort to leaving the house, for fictitious tea with fictitious friends, or an imaginary shopping errand, so that she can compose herself, bring her heart back to near normal and find the right face again.

He has his routine. He rises earlier than she does. Occasionally she is woken by his movements as early as six, as he clatters in the kitchen preparing his cup of tea. Then, after an

25

hour or so, she hears him slide across the floor and clump slowly up the stairs. He remains in bed for a further two or three hours before reappearing.

This is a good thing, since it provides her the opportunity to start her day at leisure. She can go into the small bathroom and, while she is running her bath, clean the toilet and the area of vinyl floor around it. At the outset this task made her gag. How could one elderly man spray his urine so indiscriminately across the surfaces yet apparently be so oblivious? But she has become inured to it. Roy has proved impervious to her requests to develop strategies that either deal with the problem after the event or avoid it altogether. He simply looks at her uncomprehendingly and says nothing.

Still, this is a small price to pay in the greater scheme of things, she tells herself, as is the full range of his idiosyncrasies. Though the idiosyncrasies — altogether too pleasant a term, she thinks — are accumulating into a tidy stack, she continues to put up with them for the longer-term benefit.

She will bathe and take a leisurely breakfast before Roy reappears, having shaved. He will sometimes have laid waste the bathroom once more with his ablutions. She knows to ensure that the newspaper is at hand on the small kitchen table and he will cast a sceptical eye over it while she busies herself with his breakfast. It took several mornings of his opening and slamming cupboard doors cluelessly for her to realize that it is easier this way. He will take the

26

toast from the plate while giving his attention to the broad-sheet he holds deftly in his left, slightly trembling hand at reading distance. From time to time he will make an acerbic comment about the state of the nation, but usually she will be free to carry on with her daily chores.

Now she hums, alternately, themes from Beethoven's symphonies, snatches from Ella Fitzgerald's *Cole Porter Songbook* and the choruses of Beatles hits, as she dusts the bookshelves.

Is this enough? she thinks as a cloud passes across the window. Or perhaps it has crossed her heart. Will this be enough? Can it sustain her and if so for how long? How long before she returns to life on her own? It must endure, she concludes, at all costs. She must do everything she can to accept Roy's less salubrious habits, together with his idleness, for the sake of the satisfaction and security she craves.

Stephen, she knows, is beginning to show a restive reluctance to put up with Roy's ways and to conceal his dislike. An unusual thing for an unusually courteous young man, she thinks; and so far expressed in minute turns of the head, mild facial expressions and marginally infelicitous phrases that, it seems, only she can decode.

Perhaps he has been brought to this. He worships her, she knows. She will have to talk to Stephen. He must understand. He must bear it. He must disguise his feelings. She knows that he cares for her and does not like Roy, but he simply must.

27

4

'Do you enjoy living here?' asks Anne as they sip their sherries some five weeks later.

'Oh yes,' says Roy. 'Oh yes.' He glances surreptitiously at his watch and resists the urge to shake it for fear — no, in the hope — that it may have stopped. But he knows it hasn't. Good God, have they really only been here for twenty-five minutes?

All this for this scrawny, unimpressive man and his blowsy wife. He casts them a smile that might as well be a grimace. Roy has had to spend almost the whole of Saturday exiled from the house while Betty primped and prepared it, spending hours, it seemed, over whether the extravagant bouquet of cut flowers she had bought should sit on the coffee table or the small walnut sideboard. They'll bring flowers anyway, he'd said forlornly; it's a waste of money. And sure enough they have.

This morning he has been subjected to geriatric hyperactivity, a running commentary on the preparations and a lengthy debate over what he should wear. Good God, he knows full well how to turn himself out. He'd had to put his foot down.

So here they sit, drinking sherry, the component parts of this odd gathering, all of them transparently ill at ease apart from Roy, in spite of their quite hopeless attempts to pretend otherwise.

It is cramped in the small living room. There is a real risk that someone will knock over one or more of Betty's knick-knacks. Michael and Anne perch awkwardly on the edge of the small sofa. Their unprepossessing daughter, Emma, with spectacles, lank hair and an unspecified skin problem, sits on a kitchen chair. Stephen sits on the stairs. Roy thinks, where do they get their ugliness from? Certainly not from Betty. Her hubby must have been something to behold, with dominant genes. Michael, Stephen and Emma resemble to him a family of weasels, with their beady eyes and sloping foreheads. Not to mention their snarly, unpleasant Mancunian twangs.

Betty is in continual motion between them, covering the small patch of carpet furiously hither and thither, fussing with nibbles, muttering irrelevancies nineteen to the dozen. Roy leans back in his chair. On one level he is quite enjoying this. Their discomfiture at meeting him for the first time is amusing.

He stifles a yawn and looks outside. At least they have a decent vehicle. Michael's large metallic German car stands at the kerb in the rain. So this nonentity must amount to something despite the evidence.

Someone has spoken to him. The lids close momentarily over his eyes as he contains his boredom and strives for civility. 'Pardon?' he says.

'I said, you've acclimatized to life outside the metropolis all right?' asks Michael with infinite patience but in a voice that suggests he is dealing with an imbecile.

Acclimatized. Yes, that's the kind of word this

bespectacled geek would use. He even calls his mother by her given name. Betty this, Betty that; not Mother or even Mum. No respect. Disgraceful. But it is necessary to hold one's temper in check.

'Oh yes,' he says with a thin smile that even he thinks may not be entirely convincing. 'It's not so hard. I like living here.'

'And you sold your place in London?'

Cheek. Roy knows what he's driving at. But he answers calmly.

'No. Not yet. I'm thinking about it, and considering my investment options.' He looks in Betty's direction and smiles.

'You play the market, then?' asks Michael with a persistence Roy might not have credited.

'Oh no. Not really. No, my money's safe. I have an associate from the old days. A broker who's looked after me for many years. Whatever he comes up with, I'm OK. We'll be all right, won't we, my dear?'

'Pardon?' says Betty, flustered as she is interrupted on her way to the kitchen. 'Oh yes, of course.'

They all smile at one another insincerely and then sip their sherry. You don't like me, thinks Roy. Except Betty of course. You don't like me. And I don't care. He chuckles inwardly, and then starts. It is becoming harder, much harder, as time goes on, to maintain that necessary veneer of politesse and feigned eager, smiling interest. The ageing process. He must not merely try harder; he must do better. For all their sakes he must show himself an engaged and enthusiastic participant, a welcome initiate in the bosom of this complacent coterie, not an interloper.

But it is so very hard. Tolerance has never been his strong suit, he will freely admit — to himself. Disguise of intolerance, yes, but that's a very different thing. It has been entertaining over the years, as well as rewarding, to mask his true feelings with an indulgent smile and a kind word, for the greater good. But now he is short of time and, it has to be said, low on stamina. Yet he must make the effort.

'So you worked in the City?' asks Michael as, shuffling and edging, they gain their appointed places at the table Betty has laid in the tiny kitchen.

There is barely room for the six of them and with difficulty they extend their elbows behind them to place Betty's carefully pressed, ancient linen napkins on their laps.

Roy pauses for a beat to assure equanimity. He says cheerfully, 'At one time. I was in property. Among other things. I've had a few jobs in my time. I can't say that I was one of the big players. The City then wasn't what it is today.'

*　*　*

Stephen thinks: that smile, when he turns it on, is avuncular. Repulsive but avuncular. The ruddy cheeks, the shining eyes, the oozing confidence, it fits perfectly. The smile of the assassin, he thinks, and wonders whether others see it this way, unburdened by his prejudices and the

31

knowledge that he has recently acquired of this man at close quarters. Roy, even in old age, is a fairly impressive act.

He observes Betty, bustling around so far as bustling is possible in such a small space. She is somewhat out of breath, from anxiety, he thinks, as she attends diligently to the needs of her guests, distributing plates, pouring wine, passing bread. The candles are lit and her unaccustomed disarray and nervousness confer a certain glowing radiance. There is a fixed smile on her lips and the soft light draws out the depth of her brown eyes. She has been to the salon and her hair shines and hangs straight and elegant. She is on stage. To him, her performance shines. At the end of the table Roy holds court with his smile. He neither helps Betty nor contributes much to the conversation yet is the conductor of proceedings. Everything refers back to Roy eventually. Which is only natural, since this occasion, postponed from the summer, is intended to introduce him, induct him indeed, into this peculiar family. It is only natural that they should show such interest in him and he deals with their inquisitiveness with a rediscovered bonhomie and energy. He does not, however, display a corresponding curiosity about them.

★   ★   ★

'Christmas,' says Michael apropos of nothing, it seems. They all pay attention and it is implicit among them that the statement is directed at Roy.

32

'Oh yes,' Roy says in response, a wary curiosity infusing its rising pitch.

'It's only a month away. Are you one for Christmas, Roy?'

'Well, put it like this, Michael,' replies Roy. 'Time was, I was as keen as the next man on Christmas. Those were times of austerity, mind you, when if you summoned up an orange for the boy's stocking you were something of a magician. I used to make toys, you know, for my son, from odd bits of wood. Good with my hands, I was. But these days, with all the commercialism and what have you . . . And when you get older . . . ' He pauses for a moment of reflection. 'I was on my own last Christmas. I had two pork sausages and a tin of beans for my dinner and I don't mind telling you I shed a tear or two while I was watching the Queen's Speech.'

Stephen and Emma share a glance, and Roy senses the beginning, quickly quashed, of a smirk passing over her face.

'Well, it doesn't have to be like that this year,' says Michael. 'We were wondering whether the two of you might like to spend Christmas with us. I'm happy to come down on Christmas Eve to pick you up, so you don't have to worry about the train.'

'Well,' begins Betty, smiling, but Roy talks across her.

He says, 'Too kind, too kind. We couldn't possibly.'

'No,' says Michael quickly. 'You must. Betty would normally come to ours anyway and it

33

would be nice to have the two of you.'

'Ah no,' says Roy, looking directly at Michael. 'You misunderstand me. Betty and I have set our hearts on our first Christmas together being here, alone. Haven't we, my dear?'

Betty, looking at Michael, says, 'Oh yes. I was going to mention it. I hope you don't mind.'

There is an awkward moment in the air. Roy can see Michael thinking, battling perhaps with an instinct to vent his annoyance. Come on, man; show some spirit at last; spit it out, he thinks. But no.

'Oh well,' says Michael. 'It was just an idea. A romantic Christmas with just the two of you. Wonderful. Great.'

Is that relief Roy sees shimmering on Stephen's face? Possibly, but then again maybe not. It was there for just a second and he finds these days that his senses are not as finely tuned as once they necessarily were, and his eyesight not so sharp.

5

It's a truism that the older one grows, the more conscious of the seasons one becomes and the separations and transitions between them. Maybe it's just true. Or possibly, Betty thinks, our weather has become more extreme, as the experts say, and the seasons are consequently delineated more starkly.

Whatever. A young person's word that, with its tone of resignation and extinguished hope, signifies the point this generation has reached on the journey from inquiry via bewilderment and disillusion to despondency. Not, therefore, a word for Betty. She rephrases the concept in her mind: it's beyond me. Accompanied by a winsome girlish giggle, it will suit perfectly, she thinks; a suitably little-woman expression.

Roy would know the answer for sure. Which is to say he would be sure he knew the answer, whether or not he did, and would be able to state it with sufficient authority to brook no argument. He is very strong on certainty, Roy, and this is a good thing for Betty.

At any rate the season is currently biting at its coldest, with relentless ferocity. In September she found herself wishing away summer and welcoming in cooler evenings and the march of the night. Better a genuine autumn than the apparition of summer. Strange for her. Since her childhood she has been a creature of the summer: those hot days whiled away in the garden with her sisters, the sounds and cares of the city beyond the high rose-covered brick wall; white dress, bare legs, dipping her toes in the clear pond by the summer house; playing with Elsa, the dog; and those fragrant evenings watching the elder girls through the balustrades of the gallery as they were courted in their ball gowns by dashing army officers. So long ago. Autumn brought gloom and equinoctial winds blowing leaves and dust along grey avenues under grey skies.

Now the moon is full and she watches through the kitchen window as from a leaden sky snow falls in clumpy flakes too heavy almost for their intricate fragility. There is a feeling indoors of cosiness, of protection from cold and misery in this warm centuries-old mews cottage. Perhaps it is another facet of age, she fancies: a greater comfort with the season of winter and its imposed sedentary inwardnesses and reliance on such protections as fluffed-up duvets, strong stone buildings and roaring fires.

Yet she knows this to be counter-rational. In the summer you may at least sit out your dotage on the small patch of lawn under the lilac tree, drink a cup of tea and read a book. You may pretend for a moment that the ageing isn't happening. It is winter that brings arthritis, the inability to venture far, the seclusion that imprisonment at home denotes, the reinforcement of helplessness and uselessness. And she knows that despite the impression of cosy, tucked-up warmth, she may be anything but safe. The wolf lurks, yet his tune is siren-like. She must keep her wits about her.

Christmas has come and gone, a miserable non-event under sodden skies. Still, it was probably better all round that they were on their own. Roy's present to her was a box of supermarket chocolates, the upmarket range admittedly. He accepted the sheepskin coat she bought him with muted thanks but no embarrassment. They ate Christmas dinner in silence and watched television while Roy drank and snored. No walks in the rain. No giggling. No silly games. No friends by the fireside. No family. These are the sacrifices she has chosen to make.

In the evening, while Roy dozed on, she spoke with Stephen by telephone. He was solicitous and concerned, and quietly stricken. Call it off, she could hear him uttering wordlessly down the line in the interstices of their conversation. Call it off. But she knows she will not, cannot.

She sits now at the kitchen table, her laptop unfolded before her, while Roy watches the television at something approaching full volume. The neighbours have complained repeatedly but Roy is hard of hearing and stubborn.

'Shall I get you some more of your ready meals?' she shouts through, but he cannot hear. She goes into the living room and repeats her question. He makes an effort to disguise his annoyance and reduces the volume.

'No,' he says. 'Thank you.'

'Are you sure?' she persists. 'It seems hardly likely we'll be able to get to the shops in the next few days.'

'Oh, all right, then. A couple.'

'I don't know what we'd do without online supermarkets.'

'No,' he says, and is already turning back to the screen.

'In fact I don't know what we'd do without the internet.'

'No.'

'You've never wanted to use it?'

'Oh no,' he chortles, and for a moment suspends his tetchiness. 'Don't trust those things. Wouldn't know where to start. You're braver than me, I must say.'

37

'I don't know. It's not that difficult. I could show you.'

'No thank you,' he replies firmly. 'I'm stuck in my ways. They've always done for me.'

There is a pause filled with the Technicolor flashes of the television.

'But how did you find me?' she asks with innocent curiosity.

'Eh?' he says, irritation simmering again.

'The internet. We met via the internet.'

He glares at her for a moment, as if she has accused him of infidelity. Then he says, lightening perceptibly, 'One of the neighbours. Nice lad. He's hot on all that stuff. I began by using the newspaper. No, he said, that's not the way to do it. Sat me down and took me through it. I'd sit in his flat and he'd press all the buttons. Like magic. But not for me. Can't teach this old dog new tricks.'

He smiles and begins to turn back to the television.

Oh well, in for a penny, she thinks.

'Roy,' she says experimentally. She does not know why she has landed on what she is about to say. Possibly the mention of his old ways.

'Yes,' he says, still — just — with her.

'You never talk about your past,' she says gently.

'Oh, I believe what's done is done. No point in harking back,' he says with an air of finality.

'But there must be so many things you could tell me. So many memories. I'd be interested. I can imagine you have a history.'

'Oh, at our age you're bound to have a

history,' he says, maintaining his good humour, then the smile fades. 'But you wouldn't be interested in anything I'd have to say. My life's been pretty boring.'

'I find that hard to believe. What I find boring is the sound of my own voice wittering on with all of my stories.'

He says nothing and his attention is being drawn by the bright lights on the screen.

'And you have no mementoes,' she says. 'No photos. Why's that?'

'I did have,' he says wistfully. 'Used to keep them in an old suitcase. All those memories. But then there was a house fire in the 90s. All lost. All gone.'

He looks up sadly.

'Tell me about it, Roy,' she says softly.

'No,' he replies, almost brusquely. 'Too painful. All gone. All lost. No point raking over the past. I live for the now, for us and our future.'

He is lost, again, to her. She leaves him to attempt to pick up the threads of his hospital drama and returns to the kitchen to complete the supermarket order. The snow continues to fall.

3

August 1998
London Pride

1

They were gathered here, these brothers in arms, for the purpose of celebrating another glorious victory. Apart from Vincent, for whom Roy had other uses. None was aware, except Vincent, that this was Roy's sign-off. Or kiss-off might have been a more appropriate expression. Nor were the others aware that, strictly speaking, a celebration wasn't really quite the thing. Glorious wasn't the right word either, any more than victory. For them at least. In fact they should be drowning their sorrows, little though they knew it. But they need not worry their greedy little heads about that now. All in good time.

They sat at a window table and watched the Thames sparkle in the sun. There was the usual commotion of river traffic. The pungency of the river, wide and metropolitan, mingled with diesel fumes and the hoppy aroma of their beer. London Pride. It could not get more English, Roy thought. These were the best of times; this smiling bunch were in their prime. The elation of triumph, however illusory. The boys weren't to know. A few beers. Cigars all round. A sunny day

40

by the Embankment watching the world go by and getting pissed. These were the days that, shortly, would be over for him.

He looked at them with affection and a practised air of nonchalance. They were sharp, these boys, but none was as spry as he was. They wouldn't catch him out. He had been there and he had done most of it. Vincent: now he really did have something about him, as well as the letters after his name. Which is why Roy had selected him to be his partner on the final part of this navigation. With all the right checks and balances, of course. Perhaps they would have their own private celebration afterwards, the two of them. He doubted it: Vincent was too serious and, bluntly, Roy was beyond all that.

This motley crew had seemingly formed organically, as if by osmosis, over the years, but in fact Roy had assembled them with painstaking care. Dave was at the bar getting the next round in, while fat Bernie launched yet another telegraphed ribald joke on to the table. Watchful Welsh Bryn, Jones the Eyes, did what he did: he observed, though he too was already two sheets to the wind and cracked a smile. Martin, suave and mustachioed, was in tears with laughter. Tomorrow they would all wake up and ask themselves: why on earth did we think that joke of Bernie's was so funny? Oh, but we laughed.

'Where's that cunt Dave got to?' boomed Bernie, and Martin winced, amused.

Roy had known Martin the longest, had fished him out of the gutter it must have been twenty-five years before. Martin was not bright but he knew the bounds of his limited intelligence, as well as what he was good at. The son of an army colonel and the product of a prematurely terminated public school education, Martin could start a conversation from nothing and keep it going almost indefinitely, exuding empathy and understanding. He was what they called a people person and with his wonderful modulated tones, lovely manners and cut-glass accent he was infinitely credible, however little he knew about the subject at hand. He was biddable, nerveless and ready to be deployed in the trickiest of situations.

'Oh, here he is,' continued Bernie, as Dave, every inch the cheerful ex-copper, approached holding a tray laden with pints, smiling as he dispensed splashes of bitter over the seated customers between whom he weaved in size fourteen boots. Roy could well imagine Dave, uniformed up in dark blue serge, helmeted, red-faced, as the laughing policeman. 'And that fucking bastard Vinny. How come he's not here? What did you say again?'

They turned to Roy. Patiently, above the din, he explained.

'Vinny's down in Sevenoaks tidying up.' The office in Sevenoaks had been their base for the last three months. 'He's the only one who didn't meet the . . . clients.' At this word the assembled party chuckled. 'The chances of that bunch turning up down there are minimal, but it behoves us to be careful.' Sage nods all round.

It was in fact Vincent's nephew, Barry, who had earned a sly £200 to go down to Sevenoaks in his overalls, unscrew the brass nameplate, wash down all the surfaces inside and clear out all traces of their existence. But that was part of another story, yet to reach its piquant denouement.

They drank to absent friends, by which they meant Vinny, and discussed the latest model Range Rovers that they were thinking of buying. They did not touch on their personal lives, their wives or mistresses or children, or their homes. If questioned, they were just mates who met up for a drink and a laugh every so often. Roy presumed that each lived somewhere within the bounds of the M25 but outside the mighty city itself, in that mangled no-man's-land of sub-urbanized villages and towns, industrial wasteland, clusters of prefabricated metal DIY superstores and carpet warehouses. He assumed the others had carved out a small slice of grand comfort in the orbital motorway's ambit, a green and pleasant acre or three topped off by a modest mansion and protected by fences, cameras and on-call 24/7 security.

For Roy, things were somewhat different. He lived alone in a modest flat in Beckenham. His earnings were stockpiled, awaiting the next step. The next leap, indeed.

Roy felt the left side of his chest tingle pleasurably, just on the nipple. This was what he had been waiting for with quiet inner anticipation. In this din others would not have noticed his mobile phone, on silent, vibrating in the pocket of his shirt. He let it buzz and shortly it stopped. He took a calm swig of beer and said,

'Off to the Gents, lads. Got to point Percy at the porcelain. Could be a while. You know me and my bladder.'

He stood and affected a drunken shamble towards the lavatory. Once inside he took a small bottle of mouthwash from his jacket pocket and gargled, splashed a little eau de cologne on his face, straightened his tie and combed back his distinguished white hair. He looked in the mirror and saw a bold, forceful man. He felt a frisson of excitement. This is what it's all about, he thought. He smiled to himself and left the toilet by the other door, the one close by the exit. Outside, allowing his eyes no more than a moment to adjust to the sunlight, he crossed the road briskly, straight and true, to the bank opposite. He had chosen his ground carefully.

Inside he was met by a smiling Vincent and shook hands with the business manager. He was ushered into a private office. He looked at his watch and explained apologetically that he had only a few minutes before he needed to be on his way to his next meeting. Politicians, he said, with a self-deprecating, rueful smile and a raise of the eyebrows. Ministers! No problem, sir, no problem, purred the manager; everything is ready for your signature.

Coffee was offered and politely declined. The documents were laid before Roy and he read them carefully, double-checking the numbers, though he knew well only a few hundred pounds would be left in the account after this transaction. Any two of the company's board could authorize payments, save the company secretary, Vincent. An oddity and an inconvenience, but one on which Vincent had insisted to ensure total propriety when they had all established the company together.

Vincent signed carefully: Bryn Jones. Attaboy. He could do a reasonable approximation that would pass muster against the facsimile held by the bank's City branch and couriered over that morning.

Roy signed and it was done. He shook the manager's hand solemnly, his mind apparently on his important meeting, and thanked him profusely for the convenience of using the Westminster branch. It was, again, not a problem. Roy said goodbye to Mr Jones in formal but friendly tones, every bit the chairman to a board member he did not know especially well. He walked confidently to the door, crossed the road and entered the toilet again to dishevel himself suitably.

'Fuck you been, Roy?' asked Bernie, when he returned to the table.

'Fucking prostate,' he said. 'Bleeding murder.'

'You been a long time.'

'I know. Wouldn't wish it on my worst enemy.'

'Funny,' said Bryn in his insinuating lilt. 'I just been to the khazi for a slash and didn't see you there.'

'Check all the cubicles, did you?'

'I thought you was just having a piss.'

'I was. Fucking try it, Bryn, standing there forever waiting for it to come. You get some funny looks. Besides, might as well take the weight off your feet if you're waiting that long. Feel the benefit.'

Dave was pushing a button on his mobile phone. 'Just had a call from Vinny,' he said. 'He's finished down in Sevenoaks. All tickety-boo and he says have a chaser for him.'

Seat of the pants. Marvellous.

2

It had taken a number of months to bring the project to this point. It was on that pleasurable thought that he luxuriated silently, his smile verging on complacent, in the pub. If asked by one of the others why he seemed so satisfied, he would have answered truthfully, within reason. A job well done, he would have said.

But he was not asked and at length rose to take his leave. The usual male ritual of clamorous bawdy voices proposing one more for the ditch followed, but he refused all blandishments with a modest grin. 'He's a dark horse, our Roy,' Bernie would say once he had left. 'Top man, though,' Dave would add thoughtfully, 'top man.' Martin would drink to that. Bryn would look.

Each had played his role in the drama. Martin had smoothed the way with his mellifluous, effortless interposings, the yin to the yang of Bernie's booming bruiser ready at any moment for an argument. The absent Vincent had been the bespectacled, blinking, i-dotting finance man. Dave and Bryn had, not out of character, been security for the deal. Roy, naturally, had been top dog, content in meetings to smile benignly and twinkle his eyes while Bernie and Martin did the talking; though Roy had given them their scripts at each nightly wash-up so that the transaction could be appropriately nuanced and nudged the following day.

At the same wash-ups Vincent had proffered advice on the legality of the property deal that approached so slowly but had suddenly been upon them. For those aspects where strict adherence to the law was not feasible if this coup were to be pulled off, he had advised on likely detection, severity of penalties and sensible precautions. He had repeatedly emphasized that their stake money gave at least the hope of a defence of acting in good faith. The money in the company account was therefore a kind of insurance policy. In truth most dimensions of the transaction were unlawful in some respect, though repeatedly Roy had reminded his companions that their interlocutors were hardly likely to approach the authorities. Bryn and Dave, meanwhile, observers of the proceedings mostly, had been able to comment on the other side's posture and demeanour, trying to see below the surface of the amicable machismo to any reservations or suspicions. Only Vincent and Roy himself, of course, had known that this was nugatory, if necessary for them to complete their own private supplementary sleight of hand. Would Roy in reality have been so stupid as to tangle with a bunch of Russian oligarchs and ex-KGB hoods? Good God, no; and nor had he been.

The 'Russians' were a group of well-paid Eastern European misfits whom Roy had known when

47

he lived for a time in the Balkans, and whom he'd engaged to take four rooms at the Savoy for two weeks and spend a bit of pocket money supplied by him. They had only to take a few hours out each day to read their lines, carefully scripted by Roy. It was of course rather more complex and demanding than that, but those were the bones of it. These were nimble and wily men too, never entirely to be trusted, who recognized a common interest with Roy and, importantly, knew that he was at least as canny as they were. They did not cross Roy and there was no need for them to. He knew, literally, where the skeletons were buried. Roy was thankful that no one on the home team had any Russian, or certainly not sufficient to recognize that these individuals when they muttered occasionally to one another did not speak the language. He was grateful to good old British ignorant hostility towards foreigners. Innate antagonism neatly obscured the areas in which genuine suspicion should have been vested. I can handle these people, he had told the others; I have the experience.

And for insurance against the event that Bryn might have discharged his responsibilities for security a tad too assiduously, Roy had told him in hushed tones on a strictly bilateral basis that the Russians were 'known' in their true identities and had acquired dodgy passports with sundry Balkan citizenships for their sojourn in London.

Of course he had also had to ensure that the 'Russians' could get nowhere near the real money, the stakes finally delivered to the enterprise by Bryn, Martin and Bernie, which amounted to over £2 million, to match Vincent's and Roy's rather more notional contributions to the enterprise. It was these deposited funds that Roy and Vincent had conveniently transferred elsewhere this afternoon.

So far, so routine. The trickiest aspect had been the process of getting Vincent on board with the more private project. He had known from the outset that the accountant would be required, but a careful management of Vincent's transition to full awareness had been necessary.

Roy had, in a series of drip-fed sidebars, eased Vincent into a position of almost full disclosure. He had confided his suspicions of the Russians and his unease that their aim might be to fleece the syndicate; that his discreet inquiries had shown his disquiet to be well founded; that this might now be turned to their advantage; but that only Roy and Vincent had the deftness of touch and lightness on their feet to bring this home; that it was unfortunate for the boys, but when it came down to it all was fair in love and war.

And, finally, Vincent had said, 'You've planned it this way all along, haven't you?'

Silence. Pained expression.

'Those guys are your people, aren't they?'

Silence. Doleful look.

'It's no skin off my nose. So long as I come out ahead. Substantially ahead.'

This was precisely the conversation that Roy had wanted. He had painstakingly led Vincent to this point, let him be the clever one, let him deduce. He engaged enthusiastically, telling Vincent he had always intended to involve him but that for obvious reasons it was . . . delicate.

Yes. Vincent could appreciate that. And that, more or less, had been that. Allocations of proceeds might have been an issue, but Roy, aware that Vincent alone of the others knew the precise detail, had decided to be generous. Vincent's 50 per cent was, to Roy's mind, an investment.

Now Roy stepped outside to the river path, took stock momentarily of the hubbub and began his walk along the Embankment. The somewhat vacant smile remained on his face and there was a spring in his step, though a spring, he acknowledged inwardly, that might have a little less pert bounce than not so long previously. He was getting older. By most measures he would have been described as an old man, but Roy did not gauge himself by normal standards. He still had more vigour than most thirty-year-olds and much more fire in his belly.

But now was a good moment to finish it and enter a new phase. This would necessitate ridding himself of his Beckenham pad and moving to the genteel Surrey mansion apartment he had prudently secured for himself, abandoning his little flat like the *Mary Celeste* with rent unpaid. Roy Mansion would once again be laid to rest and he would revert to being Roy Courtnay. This was all just housekeeping and, with a little attention to detail, easily accomplished. There was just one last flourish in the final act of this theatrical performance to dispose of himself, so to speak, for once and for all, but that would be elementary. He checked his stride, barely discernibly, and glanced behind him before he reached the steps up to the bridge.

He ambled across Westminster Bridge and paused in the middle, leaning on the balustrade and looking down the Thames towards Docklands, the present-day barometer of London's confidence. Mr Blair will do us all right, he thought. Not like the old days, when his lot spelled disaster. He saw Canary Wharf, that crisp, clean phallic symbol of City bullishness, its tip blinking red in the summer sunlight, and inhaled the rotting green salt stench of the river before continuing his journey, crossing the road carefully and walking down the steps to the water again.

He entered St Thomas' Hospital from the riverside path and accelerated through its corridors, left and right, right again, through doors, up and down stairs, according to a route that he had designed and learned assiduously. Were Bryn — for it was Bryn he believed most likely of this — to have decided that Roy might not be sufficiently trustworthy and have had the temerity to follow him, or have him followed, this should be an adequate countermeasure. An unlikely eventuality, but as Roy knew only too well, you couldn't be too careful these days. And it fitted in very neatly with the legend for the little denouement he and Vincent had devised.

3

A quick dash to a cab, and he was conveyed swiftly to one of the grand hotels along Park Lane where he had a room. Into the room, and he suddenly felt weary, felt his age. He would have dearly loved to collapse into the plumped opulence of the bed and doze. But there was no rest for the wicked and he was on the move once more, to the hotel next door, where he had booked a business room in the name of a company that would soon be discarded.

He waited patiently for Vincent, reliable as ever. Solid as a rock, just what Roy required. He poured three fingers of Scotch into a tumbler — he deserved this — and added ice. The fatigue was extreme but it was a good fatigue. He sighed, and observed his feet for a moment before pulling himself together, standing and stretching his arms and shoulders.

Nearly there. The first day of the rest of his life. How many times had he uttered those words privately? But this time it was for real. He appreciated, if not openly, that his energies were waning: in the very real physical sense that he was perceptibly less capable of accomplishing what no more than five years before had been simple, and in the less direct but equally obvious to him way that mental concentration was difficult to sustain over extended periods. No one else had yet noticed, or at least this was what he believed.

Now was the time to depart, at the top of his game, without rancour. He was in his seventies, for heaven's sake. A good innings, more than good. He could now subside in relative comfort and let his body and mind wind down and tick over to that inevitable day. It was only life, after all, and must be regarded dispassionately. He had always been impatient of those who railed indulgently against inevitabilities rather than examining their own shortcomings, and would not do so himself. When faced with his own mortality he did not intend to become histrionic.

At least now, with this coup, he would be able to manage his decline in some comfort. He would be able to rattle around in his apartment. He would be able to embark on Caribbean cruises in first class and dine with the captain. He would be taxied here and ferried there, enjoy lavish medical care to offset the effects of ageing so far and long as this could be achieved. He could afford the services of visiting top-class, discreet young courtesans — that word had the right tone — at his home and they would be paid well enough to conceal their distaste for his crumbling being as they harvested his remaining virility. Eventually he would be able to lie back while the hired help wiped his arse, fed his quivering face and dabbed the dribble away. Bleak thoughts indeed.

He was interrupted by the arrival of Vincent, with his recognizable hesitant knock on the door. He could remember him as a young man. That shyness, that diffidence, had not changed. But there had been something else, a spark visible seemingly to Roy alone beneath the faltering exterior of the accountant. Roy unlocked the door and let him in.

'You've been careful?' he asked.

'Of course.'

'Drink?'

'Uh, no. I won't, thanks. I'm driving.'

Vincent did not look pleased, either with himself or with the success of their caper. He looked mildly frayed, as if in a state of confused agitation. Roy was not concerned, for this seemed to be Vincent's stock expression. It was, in part, what made him successful in this game. Few would credit that this cautious, conventional bean counter was capable of the necessary deceptions. Vincent brought monochrome stability to the Technicolor of Roy's grand vistas.

'Oh well,' said Vincent. 'It's all done.'

Oh well indeed, thought Roy.

'No problems?'

'None that I know of. Barry rang me to say he'd finished up in Sevenoaks and was on the train back.'

'Nice touch that, you phoning Dave in the pub.'

'Thought it might just add something to the mix,' said Vincent without smiling. 'Been learning from you. Maybe some of the star-dust is rubbing off on to me.'

Roy laughed. 'All the finances sorted out?'

'The transfer's gone through,' replied Vincent. 'The money's in the account. I checked last thing this afternoon. Just need to wait until the dust has settled before moving it on.'

'Fine.'

'And then?'

'Plan A, I reckon. Unless there's any reason to change.'

'Not that I can see. We wrap it all up as soon as possible.'

'That's right.'

'And then?'

'And then it seems I hang up my boots and ride off into the sunset, if that's not mixing metaphors. You get on with a glittering career.'

'Can't see it happening. Surely you're not really jacking it in?'

'Oh, I am. Believe me. I plan to enjoy life while I still can.' Roy smiled.

'Well,' said Vincent, 'I'll believe that when I see it. But then again I won't, will I? Maybe you just want to branch out on your own again.'

'No,' said Roy with feeling. 'If I did anything in the future it would be with you. I'd need your help. No. I'm retiring. Really.'

There was a finality in his voice that deterred Vincent from continuing.

'Well then,' he said. 'Until next time.'

They had a little more business to conduct, but each was aware that the next times would be few.

Vincent left and Roy tidied up to fill in time before his own departure. Habit and prudence, a word coming into fashion, saw him take the precaution of wiping surfaces of fingerprints. He handed the key in at reception and quickly made his way back to his own hotel room.

4

Plan A had been invoked. Vincent rang each of the other members of the syndicate, indicating evenly that they needed to meet as something had come up. Each in turn had reacted with alarm.

'No, no need to worry,' he said. 'It's not that. But I'd prefer not to use the phone.'

They had standing provisions for an emergency meeting. The arrangement was that they would meet at a certain golf club, a neutral, not to say anonymous, venue just outside the M25, over a morning coffee. Bernie and Martin had brought golf clubs and just completed a rather dank round on a cool, misty September morning by the time the others arrived. Bryn had taken the precaution of hiring a car rather than using his own. Dave had booked the private meeting room that doubled as the club's committee chamber.

Vincent was the last to arrive, entering the room in his accountant's grey suit and black tie with a solemn expression that presaged bad news and evoked foreboding in the others. The bustle around the coffee pot ceased. Teaspoons were held mid-air.

'Where's Roy?' interrupted Bernie when Vincent sought to commence proceedings.

'I'll come on to that in a moment,' replied Vincent calmly. 'But first a situation report on the deal. I wanted to reassure you all that everything's on track. There've been no hiccups and it's simply a question of waiting out the agreed period before we access the account and distribute the profits.'

There was a palpable easing of tension in the room. Shoulders relaxed and the darting glances between the principals ceased. Bernie took a sip of his coffee.

'So?' said Bryn.

'So,' said Vincent, taking his time and looking down at the green blotter on the table in front of him. 'So, there is a reason nonetheless for gathering you all together for this meeting. I'm afraid I have some bad news regarding Roy.'

He paused for effect.

'I've pieced most of this together speaking to his wife recently.'

'His wife?' asked Dave.

'Yes. I received a call from her recently. Apparently she found my mobile number among Roy's things. I've had a few conversations with her over the past few days. It seems Roy hadn't been feeling too well in recent weeks. She said she'd been trying to get him to go to the doctor's but he hated anything to do with the medical profession. Besides, he said he was too busy. It must have been the period when we were finalizing the deal.'

They knew what was coming.

'It seems that Roy had a prostate scare in his fifties. He was eventually given the all clear but warned that it required monitoring. Which is why his wife was so insistent on his seeing a doctor when it flared up again. But anyway. One evening — I think it must have been the day we finished the deal — he simply didn't come home.'

'He was complaining about his prostate,' said Dave.

'Was he really?' said Vincent. 'Anyway, she rang round all the London hospitals and apparently he had been admitted to St Thomas'. She didn't get to see him before he died.'

'You sure he's not just done a runner?' asked Bryn.

'Well,' said Vincent drily, 'there is the small matter of the body. His wife identified him. He couldn't have done a flit from the Grim Reaper. And what would be the point anyway? The way we're positioned now, he'd have a lot more to lose than gain.'

'Where does this leave us?' asked Martin.

'Nothing changes,' said Vincent. 'Apart, that is, from what to do with Roy's share of the proceeds. His wife, of course . . . '

They considered for a moment.

'It's our choice entirely,' added Vincent. 'The money still belongs legally to the company and hasn't been paid over to individuals. There's nothing in the contracts to indicate an obligation to pay over to the estate in the event of a death. But we may feel some moral obligation . . . '

There was a pause for reflection.

'Perhaps not,' said Martin. 'It could complicate matters for her.'

'Yes,' agreed Bryn. 'How would we explain it all to her? Let alone to the solicitors dealing with the estate?'

'Way too complicated,' added Bernie.

'Knowing Roy, he'll have left her well provided for,' said Dave.

It was settled.

'Well then,' said Vincent, 'we just wait the prescribed time and meet up again. In the City, I'd suggest, at the branch where the account is held. Any two of you can authorize the transfer. As you'll recall, I can't be one of the two. If you're happy I'll tee it up with the bank in a couple of weeks' time. I have the list of your nominated accounts. Let me know if anything changes.'

They agreed the plan.

'Fine man, Roy,' said Martin. 'He was good to do business with and fun to be around. I owed him a lot. At least he went out on a high.'

'A diamond,' agreed Dave. 'Always brought his mates in on a piece of business. We'll miss him.'

'Sound as a pound,' murmured Bernie in approbation, his mind apparently on other matters.

Bryn and Vincent did not contribute to the eulogy. Vincent was drily businesslike.

'The funeral is on Thursday apparently. Short service in Leytonstone, cremation at Wanstead and then drinks at his home. I haven't got the details yet. His wife and her daughter are trying to piece it all together. She's promised to ring me tonight. Give me a call tomorrow or the day after if you'd like to show your respects.'

They replied, almost in mumbling choral unison, in the affirmative. Vincent knew none of them would call. Like to be there, each would reason to himself, but it'd just confuse matters. Better to leave Roy in peace and his family to grieve privately.

He knew that this would be the last time he saw these men.

5

One final conference was required between Vincent and Roy before it was all wrapped up.

They met in St Albans of all places, in the lobby of an august old hotel.

Roy had rented a car from a limousine service to take him from his flat. The driver waited outside in the car.

Roy was content with his new apartment but felt it was not yet home. Accustomed since childhood to a peripatetic existence, he did not crave a sense of belonging or even, particularly, connection. But a feeling of familiarity short of contempt would, he hoped, come, and be pleasant. After all, he had to accustom himself to a different life.

'Retirement seems to suit you,' said Vincent once they had greeted each other.

Vincent was not one normally given to compliments. Roy looked back at him in initial bewilderment, but then smiled. They went to the bar, which was dark and overdue a refurbishment and smelt of the sour beer of several decades.

They took their coffees, which had the unusual distinction of being at the same time bitter and insipid, to a corner booth. They were brisk in their dealings. They would shortly attend the central London bank branch where their joint account was held. They would authorize the transfer of the money to their respective personal accounts. The appointment had been confirmed. Roy would book his car service once more for the dash into London, have his driver wait outside for the five minutes or so it would take. Then it would be in the car and back to Surrey. Dear old London, he would think. His London, which had sustained him for all those years, even when he was away, waiting for him like a faithful but still glamorous girl. Even before he first came here. Little had he known that his fate would be determined mainly in this great city with its glistering silver artery, the Thames.

In the meantime Vincent would sign the letters that they had drafted carefully months ago and send them to their post office boxes, those grenades that would explode on the breakfast tables of Bernie, Dave, Martin and Bryn.

I'm sorry to inform you, they began. Sadly our Russian clients appear to have been not entirely what they claimed . . . Unfortunate that we failed to discover this earlier . . . Have been confidentially informed of an Interpol investigation into their activities . . . Bank accounts being monitored, according to my sources . . . None of us would want any involvement with criminality or anything remotely improper . . . Our bank will remain rock solid in respect of client confidentiality . . . However, I suggest it would be prudent at present to remain well clear of the joint trading account . . . Need to maintain a low profile for a short period while the dust settles . . . Took the unusual step of writing rather than ringing as thought this was the safest option in the circumstances . . . Probably sensible also not to retain this letter . . . Will call in the next couple of days, however, to confirm receipt . . . Love and kisses, V. Or words to that effect.

Roy and Vincent knew what would happen. Vincent, for form, would call each of their numbers, his script before him. Each of the mobile telephones would have been cut off, the instruments dropped as if on fire, as quickly as the post office box accounts would have been closed. Each would be sitting in his luxury detached, contemplating proceedings and a potential jail sentence. The imperative would be to cut losses, not maximize profits or seek revenge. None would give the others a second thought but would seethe at the loss of his nest egg and his impotence to do anything about it. These were not organized criminals but a bunch of second-rate chancers with hardly an idea between them and no resort to investigative or retributive resources. Their collective competence had resided in Roy alone. They might suspect Roy was not dead, but even if they did there was little they could do. They had no networks other than their pals at their golf clubs or at the Rotary Club and still less could they approach the authorities.

Chapter over, thought Roy as he climbed into his car. Book closed.

4

Academic Integrity

1

Stephen says, 'It's the proximity I find difficult.'

Gerald purses his lips and steeples his fingers. There is an audible intake of breath as he makes to speak but thinks better of it. He must, Stephen supposes, be trying to find a softer way of saying it. Most unlike Gerald, with all his affected asceticism, particularly when both know, more or less, the thrust of what he will say next.

'Proximity. What, precisely, do you mean by the word proximity?' asks Gerald eventually, with evident difficulty.

Oh well, thinks Stephen, that's as good as emollience from Gerald: postponement.

'It's the getting so close,' he says.

'Hmm,' says Gerald, and Stephen can see his impatience grow. 'I'm not sure I needed a dictionary definition, however inexact.'

Stephen grins ruefully; he cannot help it, though he knows it will irritate Gerald further. 'I'm not explaining myself very well, am I?' he says.

'Not particularly, no. But carry on.'

'What I mean is the process of finding out absolutely everything about him. It's the logging and the noting with painstaking care. This is the first time I've ever been involved in such an extensive project about one person. So intense and detailed, getting so close in.'

'The proximity. Yes, I believe you mentioned,' says Gerald drily.

'It's the methodical nature of it. Dissecting him into his constituent parts and laying them out neatly under the lights on the examining table, all stainless steel and clean. They don't seem to fit together. They don't seem to be part of him.'

'That, though, is the job of the researcher. You must surely realize that? Not to rely on assumptions or theories or accepted truths. To go back to original sources and to come up with an amalgam of the facts that better approximates the truth.'

Stephen notes the steel in Gerald's eyes, the sense of purpose that could have seen him, with different choices, as a captain of industry or a prominent politician. Stephen recognizes that he possesses none of that backbone. It is backbone that the subject of his research also possesses in abundance. He perseveres for the moment, however.

'But it seems the closer I get and the more detail I gather, the less I know.'

'Isn't that rather, if I may say so, a rather workaday observation?' says Gerald, striving, it seems, for equanimity. 'The myopia that closeness can induce, the lack of perspective. Isn't it just part of the job to alternate between the microscopic and the strategic?'

64

Part of my job, that's what you mean, thinks Stephen, and he can see Gerald's rising annoyance.

Gerald wraps a delicate hand around the cafetière, flexing his long fingers, and evidently finds the coffee is still warm enough to pour himself a second cup.

'Of course,' he says eventually with a small smile, 'this could simply be a rather unsubtle ruse on your part to divert our session and disguise a certain lack of progress.' And, more gently: 'Let's just see what you have laid out on your examining table so far and whether we will be able to make something coherent from its parts. We did, after all, start out with rather a lot of material. What form will Frankenstein's monster take?'

They sit together at the large table in Gerald's study, illuminated by strategically placed lamps. A masculine room, thinks Stephen, though designed with an aesthetic touch. Gerald is keen to project the face of the high-minded academic, but Stephen knows he is punctilious about appearance and impression.

Stephen lays out his papers carefully, the bundles from his briefcase, transforming them into little piles of facsimiles of original documents, printed commentaries, typescript and his latest handwritten rushes. The piles represent decades of his subject's life, an existence desiccated into dead words on cheap paper. Dotted around the table, they form an irregular oblong; and in the centre, on the polished rosewood, is where Stephen looks in vain for the sum of the parts. Where is he? he thinks. He eludes me still.

'Now then,' says Gerald not unkindly, 'where shall we begin?'

Stephen is mildly irritated at Gerald's didactic tone but says self-deprecatingly, 'I find it confusing. He seems all things to all men at different times; and at the same time several different people in one soul.'

'Aren't we all? Is any of us the epitome of consistency, exactitude and disclosure? Don't worry about the jaggedness. It's in the cracks that we'll find something original to say. Just focus on following your man, capturing him in the net of your mind and pinning him.'

'Like a butterfly on a board?'

'Exactly. That is what we're attempting to achieve, after all, is it not? Now, what do we have here?'

They pore over the documents together. Stephen is aware that he has not come as well prepared as he might have. Gerald sighs and looks at the small pile of images that Stephen has been attempting to verify.

'This is from when?' he asks, extracting one carefully.

'That one's verified. He's in his mid-thirties, nothing more specific than that,' replies Stephen. 'I think it was in Edinburgh.' He picks up another picture, like the rest a poor-quality reproduction. 'We have others spanning the period of his twenties to early forties. They're mostly verified. As sure as I can be, they're all of him. Then we have these other five that I've yet to confirm. They include possible pictures of him as a boy and a young man.'

Stephen studies the photocopied sheets again. To him the images look as if they are of the same individual. The face that stares out has the same features that will later in life mark him out as handsome. More strikingly, he can see in the boy the same superiority and disdain. But he must be cautious, as he knows that it was the convention of the age to produce pictures that both idealized the subject and emphasized his arrogant seriousness. Innocent smiles would not have been customary, even for a child. He looks at the eyes, pixelated crudely, and can derive no meaning.

'Now, what are your largest gaps?' asks Gerald.

'Predictably, his mid- to late twenties. He spent some time in the Low Countries and also in France, with the army. Things are sketchy during this period and it's difficult to keep track.'

'All right. I do think you need to bring more structure to this. I'd like you to take each decade, as represented by these piles, and draw together a series of narratives, each with a summary and of course referenced footnotes. Leave out commentary, emphases and conclusions for the moment. And don't worry about style. Once you've assembled your facts you'll see your whole individual and have to rely less on hunches.'

Stephen accepts the rebuke, delivered drily and with neither sympathy nor annoyance. He knows what Gerald says is true: academic research is about methodical plodding and not intellectual brilliance. Until perhaps, like Gerald, you have served your time and reached the exalted heights from which you can instruct others to deliver the facts, leaving you to add the instinct and the inspiration.

2

Later the same day Stephen sits at Betty's kitchen table.

'Just how can you stand him?' he asks her.

'It's not at all as you imagine,' she replies calmly. 'It's turned out pretty much as I envisaged.'

'But he's repulsive. How can you bear being so close to him?'

'I've experienced worse things. You may not like him. I can understand that. But I make my own choices, thank you very much. I don't require your permission or blessing. You may wish to consider respecting my views.'

She speaks these words not as a reprimand but evenly and firmly as everyday observations.

'I'm sorry. But he's big and he's shambolic and he smells.'

'He smells slightly because he's old. He smells because of his age, seeping from his bones. We die of old age from the inside out, rotting gradually as we get older. It's not something he can necessarily help.'

'You don't smell.'

'I suppose I'm to take that as a compliment.

I'm a woman. And perhaps women are different from men in some regards, however much I dislike generalizations. Do I detect a touch of jealousy here?'

Stephen is aware that his face is ablaze. He finds it difficult to deny.

'But you aren't with someone or apart from them because of the way they smell.'

'Why not?' asks Stephen sharply. 'Why ever not? It's as good a criterion as most.'

'That's not such a ridiculous observation,' she says, smiling. 'But other things come into play, you know. And I must make the odd compromise if I'm to see my way into the future.'

'But is it worth it? With him, I mean? You know enough about him already.'

'I'm quite prepared to talk about it. But I'm afraid you won't budge me,' she says with an implacable gentleness.

'My main concern is for you. Is this really what you want? How can you be sure you're safe? He does have a quick temper and he's still strong for his age.'

'Oh, he has and he is. But I can manage him. As you know, I have a shrewd idea what he wants from this relationship and his needs will act as a brake on his angry impulses. He's very much in control of those impulses, I think. And to answer your question: this is very much what I want. I need this.'

'I'm sorry. I just care for you so much.'

'I know you do,' she says fondly. 'So the best thing is to fall in line with my intentions and to

69

be pleasant to Roy. Not over-fawning; pleasant will do just fine. You should be able to do that, as you're such a nice boy.'

'I'll try,' he says.

'It's Gerald, isn't it?'

'What do you mean?'

'Gerald's being difficult, isn't he? Putting the pressure on.'

'No more than usual. You know what Gerald's like. And we do need to make headway.'

'Can I help at all?'

'I shouldn't think so. But thanks.'

'I'm not decrepit yet, Stephen. I do know how Gerald's mind works, after all.'

'No. I have every regard for your academic expertise. And I know Gerald does too. Your views are critically important, of course. But you've no need to worry about Gerald. I don't think weighing in would do much good.'

'I'm assuming it's his normal refrain on accuracy, attention to detail and verification?'

'More or less.'

'Well, he's right in a way. But he does bore on the subject. Exactly the same when he was preparing his thesis. I think the most important thing in a researcher is a good heart. That's what I used to tell my students, including Gerald. Objectivity is critical of course. But if one sets about with malign intent to mankind, or even indifference or entirely selfish motives, then that way madness lies. Gerald believes this too, beneath the verbiage. He stresses dispassion precisely because he's so passionate himself. He has a good heart and so do you.'

70

3

'What's the matter?' asks Roy as Stephen peers through the windscreen and the car makes its glacial progress towards the bypass. Though not exactly genial, Roy is not aggressively scornful. Maybe he too has had a pep talk from Betty. 'You look as if you've had a hard day. Your face could turn milk sour.'

Prompted by Betty, Stephen has embarked on an excursion with Roy, who needs to go to the garden centre. In the sketchy curriculum vitae that Roy has delivered verbally there is an obscure reference to a former role managing a nursery. He professes, at least, a knowledge of plants and Betty is looking to revitalize the small patch of walled garden she has at the back of the mews cottage. Roy has taken on the project quite happily, but insists that Betty does not accompany him on his purchasing mission. Instead, while he does the job professionally, she may remain at home with the cleaning and ironing. But he requires a driver and this is where Stephen comes in useful.

'Not really,' says Stephen in as placatory a tone as he can muster while concentrating on the journey. 'Just normal stuff. Work.'

'You take it all too seriously if you ask me.'

'It's important to me. I believe in it.'

'It's just work at the end of the day. Your boss giving you a hard time?'

'My supervisor.' Stephen utters the corrective gently. 'Kind of. Well, no. Gerald's always like that. It's just a tricky phase.'

'Sounds like he's a tricky character. And I've known a few in my time. Needs to have his card marked if you ask me. Tell me about this bloke you're researching. What was his name again?'

'John Graham of Claverhouse, later Viscount Dundee. Born in 1648 and a key figure in the early Jacobite rebellions.'

'The Jacobite rebellions? What were they exactly?'

'The revolt against William of Orange and Protestantism and the fight to restore the house of Stuart to the throne. What's interesting is how he goes down in folk history. He was known as Bonnie Dundee to the Jacobites, but the Presbyterians called him Bluidy Clavers because he exacted bloody retribution against their communities. He was a major influence on the Fifteen and the Forty-Five.'

'What were they?'

Stephen reflects that Roy seems to be feigning interest quite efficiently.

'The two Jacobite rebellions of 1715 and 1745. Both crushed by the English. Graham was killed earlier, in 1689 in a battle that his troops actually won. That victory and Graham were vital shapers of the later rebellions. But Graham's death was a critical fault line in them too.'

Roy says, 'What's the point of this work? What's the purpose?'

'Three things really. How John Graham shaped the rebellions. Then there's how the mythology and demonology have persisted. And lastly, what Graham was actually like behind it all. What drove him? What were the actual facts? Was he such a charismatic leader or a cruel criminal?'

'The myth and the man?'

'Exactly. That's the key theme. For instance, a myth persisted at the time that Graham had made a pact with the Devil and was immune to lead shot. According to that, he was killed by a silver button from his own uniform penetrating his heart. That's just one of the legends. Whereas perhaps the most important point really is that, had he survived, the Fifteen might have gone very differently, with his presence and expertise. It could have meant a very different Britain.'

Stephen is surprised how gratifyingly fluent the patter is. Rather more fluent than his stuttering research has proved. Maybe he can do this, after all.

'So why's this Gerald giving you a hard time? You seem to know your stuff.'

'It's mainly technical. He wants me to speed up the validation of sources and data and to begin building a structure. It's fine really.'

'And what's in it for you?'

'With luck, a published paper that's accepted after peer review and changes things, however minutely. With even better luck, a new historical perspective on the period.'

'I mean, where does it get you?'

'Oh, nowhere really, apart from being a major part of my PhD. Any published works will go out under Gerald's name as my supervisor.'

'Sounds dodgy. You want my advice, look after

number one. You don't want this Gerald stealing your glory.'

'My world doesn't work like that. Academics are connected and work on reputation. If I do a good job it'll get round and I'll stand a better chance of securing a good academic position.'

'You want to watch yourself. Life's not a rehearsal. You want to go out there and grab what you want.'

They have arrived at the garden centre. Stephen fusses about Roy, rushing around the car and trying solicitously to help him out of the passenger seat, but Roy is having none of it. Having extricated himself from the vehicle, he looks at Stephen sternly. But their tacit if fragile pact of cordiality holds and he forces a smile.

Stephen pushes the trolley while Roy examines the plants expertly, pondering the labels carefully, feeling leaves, fingering soil. They move together from stand to stand, Roy peering while Stephen looks on, waiting for conversation that does not come.

Eventually Roy, maintaining his equable tone, says, 'Why don't you clear off and let me get on with this? I can manage on my own. I can see you're bored and you're as much use to me as a chocolate teapot.'

Stephen goes inside to contemplate uncom-prehendingly twine, slug pellets, multicoloured reels of hose and garden lights, while Roy continues with his task, examining plants intently before selecting one in particular, transporting it in a shuffle to the trolley that is filling, and moving to the next stand. Stephen will be summoned eventually to wheel the teetering mass of greenery to the tills and then to load the car.

5

Berlin Alexanderplatz

1

'A holiday,' exclaims Betty.

'Oh yes,' replies Roy with enthusiasm. 'I could do with a bit of sun on my back. Spain? Portugal?'

'I don't think so,' she says, 'I need something to stimulate my brain. I thought a city break. And I'm paying, I insist.'

'We'll see about that,' says Roy, not entirely convincingly. 'New York, then. The Big Apple. All those museums. A Broadway show.'

She laughs. 'I may be a woman of means, Roy, but I don't think my budget will stretch that far. Not if we're to do it in style.'

'Very well, then. Barcelona.'

'I was thinking more central Europe. Prague, Budapest, Vienna perhaps.'

'All right, then.'

It is not what he would necessarily wish for, but she who pays the piper . . . And a break will set him up nicely for the summer. There is a chance that there may even be a spot of spring sun. She browses the internet while he sits with his paper and gives his monosyllabic responses to her bright suggestions.

In the end, it is Berlin. He makes a late

counter-bid for Rome, or Venice, or even Bruges. But Berlin it is to be. The city of the thousand-year Reich, of Kristallnacht, Frederick the Great, Checkpoint Charlie and the Brandenburg Gate. There'll be enough history there to last them a lifetime.

2

On a blissful spring morning they walk out of their smart, ultra-modern hotel and into the middle of it all. Unter den Linden rolls away before them towards the Brandenburg Gate, if they can ignore the sundry hawkers and beggars jabbering at them desperately in various forms of German. Roy, despite his years, is still imposing and a glare is all it takes. He wraps his big arm protectively around Betty's shoulder and she smiles.

'It's all here,' he says, waving his other arm expansively.

It is Berlin as imagined, constructed on a heroic scale to convey the national confidence of the late nineteenth century, broad, masculine, frightening, in grey stone. The street, however, is gashed along its sternum as the U-Bahn line is brought to this part of what was once East Berlin. Berlin is being rebuilt and the horizon is dominated by cranes. A new paradigm of German self-assurance is being constructed here, the technocratic new alongside the imperial old.

They spend three hours in the Deutsches

Historisches Museum, which is not exactly how Roy had envisaged it: Betty peering at each exhibit with exaggerated interest while he tags along with an ill-disguised bored impatience to which she seems happily oblivious. Well, she used to be an academic, he reflects as he looks at his watch, and he will shortly be able to sit down to a decent beer.

But no: after a lunch of greasy bratwurst, smeared in garish mustard, bought from a street seller — a surprise, this, for Roy, given Betty's dainty elegance — they are off again. They take the S-Bahn train and the bus to Charlottenburg to look at the palace and walk awhile in the Tiergarten district under budding chestnut trees, taking peeks at the large, silent villas protected by sophisticated security systems that line the genteel wide streets.

'I wonder what it must have been like to live here, in the nineteenth century,' she says, 'or the early twentieth. Or the 1930s. The decadence, the forced fun, the glittering soirees. All that wealth, that confidence. Little did they know what was to become of them.'

'Oh yes,' he says, bored and sardonic at the same time. He is surprised by her energy and that light in her eyes. He thinks of himself as fit for his age but finds his limbs are weary, and craves the privacy of his hotel room and a quiet nap. He can do without this too, all this enthusiasm. He has lived a life long and eventful enough to know exactly how it was and needs no visual cues. He begins to wish he had never agreed to this trip.

'Oh dear,' says, Betty, and his attention returns to the present. 'You look bored. And tired. Have we overdone it?'

'A little, maybe,' he replies with a tolerant smile.

'Let's get you back to the hotel, then, shall we?'

She locates a cab and he dozes as their voluble driver, against the backdrop of talk radio, rails against the fools on the roads as he accelerates and brakes erratically. It is all the fault of reunification and Europe, he says, these people flooding here from the East. Roy feels fragile and hears his heart beating. He can almost imagine himself in another age.

He gets his nap, but there is no time for a leisurely dinner as Betty has fluttered her eyelashes at the concierge and obtained tickets for the Berlin Philharmonic that evening. Roy sits with ill-disguised bad temper in the opulent newfangled hall and, just, bears the flummery and the cacophony of the event: the pomposity of the orchestra and its strutting conductor, and the fat complacent patrons in Hugo Boss with their jewel-bestrewn, elegant, thin accessory wives. The exaggerated finesse of the quiet passages and the fierce attack of the crescendos all meld into one discordant mess in his ears.

At the door of the hotel he says, 'I think I'll take a turn before retiring, Betty. I've had that nap and unless I get a bit of fresh air I rather think I won't be able to sleep tonight.'

Betty says, 'All right. I know all about lost sleep. Shall I come with you?'

'Oh no,' he replies, perhaps a tad too quickly. 'That won't be necessary. I'll only be a minute or so. You get off to bed.'

And so they say their goodnights and she goes to her room.

$$\star \quad \star \quad \star$$

Four hours later, he subsides with relief under the feather duvet in his room. He should know better at his age, he says to himself, partly with a chuckle and partly with an edge of self-pity. But there's no fool like an old fool. He is €500 lighter, for no benefit. He knows where the bad parts of this city are and to enliven his trip he had gone back to the streets near the Ku'damm. Old businesses had died here and new ones sprouted. Plus ça change. After a floor show that in his youth would have been described as exotic he found himself at two in the morning in a soulless, smelly hotel room with a woman he had picked up, unable to perform. Earlier she had been hesitant but had said, when he was insistent, 'OK, Grandpa,' led him to this room and tied him up as he had specified. It was not surprising that he was not up to the task, since it must have been some ten years since he had last been able to bring himself to the point, but he had anticipated some buzz, some illusion of excitement. It was, however, simply fatiguing, in an unpleasant way.

It came as a mild shock, which in earlier times might have been an amusing diversion, that the woman was in fact a man. This became apparent only after his failure. 'I thought you realized, Grandpa,' he said, but at that point Roy dropped off, to find on waking, aching, dry-mouthed and nauseous, that his wallet was empty. Fortunately his binds were untied.

This would not have happened to him even ten years ago. At least he had thought to leave most of his cash and all of his cards and other valuables in his room safe and to secrete his hotel keycard under the orthotic insole in his shoe, but he had to admit he had lost much of his street-sharpness. He gathered up his trousers, pulled them on and made as quick an exit as his arthritic bones would allow.

Fortunately, he was able to hail a cab outside the KaDeWe department store, and the driver clearly regarded him as respectable enough. The car sped through sleek night streets and, despite his experience, Roy still felt a shimmer of excitement. He was living, or approximating living, again. There was the potential for a minor incident back at the hotel, but he was able to prevail upon the night porter to pay the fare temporarily, claiming, with reasonable credibility, absent-minded dotage.

3

It has been an unseasonably hot day in Berlin for April. Betty and Roy are sitting on the terrace of a restaurant in Hackescher Markt, at one time a bustling market near Alexanderplatz and now a bustling hub of eateries. They have strolled

81

through the Hackescher Höfe, once a labyrin-
thine arrangement of grey tenement blocks
lowering over small courtyards with squalid little
shops but now a trendy, multicoloured retail
haven, with funky shops and green communal
areas. Here, Betty has bought gifts to take back
with her. Roy has had no such need.

She sips her sharp green tinder-dry Riesling
while he eagerly quaffs Pilsner beer from a large
glass that is almost a jug. He examines the
remains of his pork knuckle for potential
remnants of fatty flesh that he may yet be able to
harvest. Pink and garish, with startling white
bone, it resembles the aftermath of an autopsy.
He picks but has to content himself with a few
elastic strands of pork fat and the odd tangy
ribbon of sauerkraut, such has been the efficacy
of his attack. He is somewhat revived, and
buoyed by the alcohol.

'All this history,' she says, and he realizes he is
expected to respond.

'Oh yes,' he says. He is surprised she remains
so bright-eyed, so chirpy. For his own part, he
feels oppressed by it all, crushed as if under
these monuments.

'Indeed,' he adds.

'So much suffering, of course,' she says, as if
reading his thoughts.

'Indeed,' he repeats. He does not require a
long exegesis on the Weimar Republic, the Third
Reich or the Cold War from the reading she has
done this afternoon.

'*Dort wo man Bücher verbrennt, verbrennt
man auch am Ende Menschen*,' she says. 'That's

what Heinrich Heine wrote in 1821.'

'Oh yes,' he says.

'I thought you didn't speak German.'

Caught, he decides to confess to inattention with an insolently sheepish grin.

' "Where they burn books, in the end they also burn people',' she says without a quiver in her voice.

'Indeed. And when did he write that?'

'In 1821.'

'Very interesting.' To his mind this is not exactly the stuff of holidays. But just as quickly, her brightness is back.

'Do you like the Germans?' she asks him keenly.

'Oh yes,' he says quickly.

'Why?'

This is rather more taxing a question. He had thought he was simply keeping up polite conversation, not participating in a forensic debate.

'Oh, I don't know. They're very efficient, you know. The hotel is spotlessly clean. And the service is top class. We could use a bit of their efficiency back home.'

They are silent for a moment. Betty consults her menu before summoning the waiter and ordering a coffee in her surprisingly good German. Roy will pass, he says; as she knows, coffee after lunchtime will lose him a night's sleep. Not that there is much danger tonight of him losing sleep, after the previous night's rigours.

'Have you enjoyed it here?' she asks.

'Oh yes,' he says instantly. 'Oh yes.'

'Because you've seemed rather bored at times.'

'Oh no,' he says. 'Simply a bit tired. I can't keep up with you, I'm afraid. I just need some time every so often to recharge my batteries.'

He pauses, and ventures, 'On the other hand, you've simply sparkled, my dear. You've been radiant.'

'Thank you,' she says. 'I find this city so vibrant. It's slightly absurd given all the dark things that have occurred here, but it seems so alive. Some vital force seems to be at work here. It reminds one of when one was young.'

'Hmm,' he says. 'But, as you say, there are so many secrets locked up here.'

'Oh, I know. But you can't blame a place for the inhumanity of the people who've lived here in the past. Or can you?'

'I'm sure I don't know,' he says gently.

It is peaceable among the hubbub. The outdoor heaters have been fired up and have taken the chill off. Blankets provided by the restaurant are neatly folded on the backs of chairs in case that is not sufficient. An Australian woman strums a guitar and churns out passable acoustic versions of pop standards. People toss loose change into her guitar case as they pass. Betty is looking out on to the cobbled marketplace, a smile on her face that conveys contentment. Roy decides that now may be the moment.

'I've been sorting out my affairs,' he says, sidling up to the subject.

She is jolted out of her reverie. 'What? Here?'

'No, no. Before we came out here. Trying to get a few things sorted.'

'Yes?'

'It's a nightmare for us pensioners.'

'What is?'

He thinks: is she being deliberately obtuse? But he maintains his equilibrium.

'The recession,' he says. 'It's hit us pensioners especially hard.'

'I suppose so,' she replies, as if she has never given it a thought.

'Yes. Low interest rates. High inflation. Difficult for your investments to keep pace.'

'Yes, well. I have my occupational pension, which suffices, even if it isn't particularly generous. And my savings. There are trust funds that my husband set up. The rest I more or less leave in a deposit account in the bank.'

'Oh dear. Oh dearie me.'

'What's wrong, Roy?'

'I don't mean to pry, but that won't do. Presumably you have a reasonable amount of capital?' He looks at her expectantly.

'Oh, I'm comfortably enough off. I'm not interested in money. I'm more interested in living,' she says cheerily.

'Goodness me. But having said that, finding a safe place to invest and a decent return is a challenge, I can tell you.' He shakes his head despondently.

'You have some money put away?' she asks.

'A little,' he replies. 'Though no doubt rather less than you, I should have thought. If I sold my little flat I'd have more.'

He pauses before continuing. 'People don't like talking about money, do they? It's a taboo subject, isn't it? Yet it's so important.'

'Like sex,' she says.

'Pardon?'

'Like sex. Critically important but not a subject for polite conversation.'

'Oh, I see, I see. Indeed. But the thing is . . . '

'Yes?'

'You see. I have this man. Accountant chappie. Miracle worker, I call him. He's looked after my portfolio, such as it is, for years.'

Betty does not reply but looks at Roy as if perplexed.

'Yes. I believe you've mentioned him,' she says eventually.

'Name of Vincent. Works wonders. Could sit down with you if you like and go through your holdings.'

6

September 1973
Living in Sin

1

They were living in sin. Over the brush, as she had put it, with her knowing Northern giggle. It seemed that, inexorably and inexplicably, he might be settling down. She was a stunner, this new girl of his, without a doubt. Kenny down the pub had emitted a discreet 'phwoar' when he had introduced her to the smoky atmosphere some four months previously.

She came from Manchester, or Liverpool, or Leeds. One of those places anyway. A graduate trainee at the Ministry, she had been placed for six months in the outlying office in the suburbs where he held a low-profile, menial post. They had met in the shabby kitchen area, with its refrigerator full of grey-green mould and the stench of curdled milk, and its lime-encrusted no longer stainless steel sink. She had been searching for a mug that was at least not so filthy as to pose a health risk, and he had offered her his spare one, together with a gleaming teaspoon, which he had fetched from his desk. She was a looker, so he had turned on the charm, framing himself as an oasis of humanity — and cleanliness — in this desert of anonymity.

87

He had explained to her how the hierarchy worked. He was an underling, a clerical officer buried under a pile of management and paper, and not so very different from a Dickensian quill-wielding clerk. She, on the other hand, was an executive officer, of the graduate cadre no less, one marked for potential greatness, or as much greatness as the Department of Education and Science could muster.

And so it had progressed. Lunch was followed by dinner, and visits to the cinema. His age — he was some twenty-three years older — seemed not to matter to her. If anything, it seemed to be an advantage. She found people of her own age so immature, she said. Eventually they had found themselves in bed together. This was very satisfactory. Maureen was youthful, exuberant evidence that the world was at last emerging from the guilt of war, untainted and uncon-strained by loss, guilt and deprivation.

He had quickly learned that she thought of herself as a radical. Horrified by the church-organ-playing yachtsman Heath, despairing of grimy Kagan Gannex Wilson, she was a vociferous member of an obscure Trotskyist political organization. This did not dismay Roy; she could be a card-carrying member of the provisional wing of the Tufty road safety club as long as she emitted those gratifying little yelps in her nakedness every so often. Her earnest do-gooding political commitment rather amused him, though he took care to hide his mirth. He had on occasion to pay lip service to her feminism, but it did not particularly affect their life together. He took care not to talk about current affairs, lest his less egalitarian view of the world became evident.

They had come gradually to the idea of living together. The decision had been at least partly practical. Neither of them was exactly flush, with their meagre Civil Service salaries, and they were spending more time together. He found himself navigating towards a calculation that he might hitch his fate to hers. While they did not work in the same office in the building, he knew well that Maureen was both gifted and highly regarded. When she returned to head office she would be going somewhere. Her radicalism was if anything an asset here in this outpost, but she might later need to tone it down somewhat. He could advise her on that: she seemed to see in his bluff practicality a kind of wisdom.

Cohabitation was a significant point along this continuum. It gave him the chance to assess at leisure whether a life with Maureen was a long-term option for him. He had never lived with anyone before, as an adult. He did not count his time in the post-war military. He was unaccustomed to the trivial and important compromises and found himself frustrated not to be able to lead his life without let or hindrance. Whether the sex and the promise of financial security were sufficient compensations was an open question. But still they drifted on and the direction of the current was clear to both of them.

The available time to make his choices was finite. Maureen was some distance from primly conventional, but there remained for her some imperatives and living together unmarried was only slowly becoming regarded as normal. She might, just, be content for them to be together on a more permanent basis without getting wed; but she would require him at some stage to achieve an at least low-friction relationship with her parents, with whom she remained close. Roy had, so far, been able to avoid the dreaded train journey to the dark frozen North, with its Neanderthal miners, its pints of mild, its fat women wearing headscarves as they washed the doorsteps of their dreary little houses, its horrible bleak towns and the even bleaker moors. He was not eager to meet Maureen's family. He understood that her father and mother knew of his existence, doubted that they knew his age and was almost certain that they did not know that Roy and Maureen shared a home and a bed.

His main conclusion about this new life was that it was boring. He no longer had the liberty to come home in the evening, sit before the television in his vest with a bottle or two of Bass, eating fish and chips from the paper. He could not easily spend his wages at the betting shop, or absent himself at the Arsenal for most of a Saturday before returning home and flopping drunk on the bed. He had had to hide his stash of smutty magazines carefully. He could not bring women home from the local.

There was some respite. Maureen had meetings at least twice a week and Roy could escape to the pub and Kenny and his mates. But the ale there now had the taste of tame mediocrity and increasingly he would find himself in the West End looking for trouble, even on those nights when Maureen did not have her earnest, world-changing conclaves.

2

He was coming to a definitive view on this version of domestic bliss. It did not take long for it to crystallize into a single vision. The equivocations became rapidly smaller and finally vanished. He saw a way out of the doldrums of his awful office job. Unlike Maureen, he could draw no gratification from being a tiny part of the decision-making machine that would determine the — educational, at least — lives of the younger generation of this country. Such grandiose notions left him cold; in his lowly job he couldn't influence anything even if he wanted to. Which emphatically he did not. What nonsense, he would harrumph to himself while indulging her youthful conceits. She would learn, but not quickly enough for him.

He was looking for a business opportunity and rapidly found it, in what he had become accustomed to think of as his playground. Soho remained a grubby, dark, dangerous place, an underworld set yards away from the glitz of Regent Street. Graft and gangsters ruled here still, offering titillation to one section of the population, outrage to another, and suffering to those who interfered. The sad pros whose shelf life had expired and who had been kicked out of their sordid nests by their erstwhile pimps bore witness, mainlining on heroin as they tried to pick up on the streets — a couple of quid for a fuck in a doorway.

It had been in the alleyway between two clubs that, at two in the morning, he had come across Martin White, lying in his own vomit and incapable of response. He had known White as a front-of-house man in one of the clubs. His toffish manner had, it seemed, offended one of the gangland clientele and Martin had found himself out of favour, homeless and on the drink. However, Roy could see for him an important role in his plans. He had flung him three quid, told him to get a room for the night in one of the numberless flea-ridden flophouses in the vicinity and to be at a certain coffee bar at four that afternoon.

It was at that meeting that Roy engaged Martin with a deliberate intensity.

'This is our time,' he told him. 'Things are changing in clubland, the sex trade is becoming respectable. We need to ride the wave.'

Martin hesitated. Roy fixed him with that determined, blue-eyed gaze. 'Do you want in or not? There are a thousand others like you I could drag out of the gutter if you prefer. It's just your lucky day. You can fuck off back to your alleyway if you want.'

Not true. Roy wanted Martin for that oleaginous charm, that dashing profile, at least once he had been cleaned up a little, and for those connections which Roy lacked. They smoked and drank their milky coffees from glass cups and resolved to change their world.

'I know of a little shop that's going under on Berwick Street,' Roy said. 'I think I might be able to lay my hands on the money for the lease.'

'I've got some mates in Brussels with contacts in the right places.' said Martin. 'They may be able to source some stuff from Sweden and Denmark, very explicit. Mags and films. We wouldn't have to go through the usual middlemen. I can also get hold of wacky baccy. And pills.'

They decided they would launch the new shop aggressively and unapologetically, taking sex out of the back streets and making it a mainstream product. As a sideline, they could deal discreetly in narcotics, to appeal to their younger, more affluent clientele. The path was already reasonably well worn by those flamboyant men with flared trousers and thick moustaches who had made their nightspots planets in the nocturnal constellation.

'But the market's wide open,' said Roy. 'It's ripe. This is our moment.'

3

September crept into October and fog settled over London. Roy took a couple of days sick from the office and, with the benefit of his little private nest egg, held in a long-term deposit account at Lyons Bank, lobbied his bank manager for a loan to start up a new business.

'Soho,' said Mr Price dubiously. 'Not exactly the most salubrious of districts.'

Mr Price wore a bank manager's spectacles over his thin nose. Below it he had grown a bank manager's moustache.

'Exactly,' replied Roy, eagerness written on his face. 'But it's on the up. All the more reason to get in before prices go sky high.'

'Hmm. I'm not sure the bank would wish to become involved in an area or a business that runs the risk of being viewed as disreputable.'

'Oh no, not at all,' said Roy, tut-tutting. 'Oh no. I wouldn't want that either. I'm trying to establish an entirely above-board business here. I'd hope the bank would understand.'

'Quite,' said Mr Price, lips pursed sceptically. 'Tell me more about this business.'

Roy had resolved to be perhaps a little liberal with the truth. No need to frighten the horses.

'What I'm trying to do is to create something,' he said. 'To turn a small, grotty shop into a business with roots in the community. And of course to make some money at the same time.'

Mr Price appraised him. 'And what exactly do you intend to sell in these premises?'

Roy's glare turned quickly to a smile. 'A number of things. We'll be selling books, we'll be screening avant-garde films, we'll be providing a venue to drink coffee and discuss current affairs.'

'So, a kind of modernistic bookshop, then?' It seemed an effort to spit the words out, and Mr Price frowned.

'If you like to think of it that way, yes. The area is steeped in a long literary tradition, as you

94

know. And in among all the tat and sex there are still a number of people of that ilk. Intellectuals, with money to spend. And of course the shop would draw people from all over the metropolis. It's ideally located, centrally, close to the Underground.'

'And the premises?'

'A bit run-down. The current occupant is nearing retirement. He's happy to hand the place over to me. I've managed to get a good deal on the lease, but time's short. It doesn't need much to tart the place up and make it look presentable. My business partner has good contacts with suppliers and is currently in talks with them. We're most optimistic.'

'I'm sure you are,' said Mr Price. 'You will be aware that this is not precisely a propitious time for new businesses. Consequently banks will approach any new investment with extreme caution.'

'Oh yes,' replied Roy, 'and quite right too.'

'If I may say so, Mr Courtnay, you do not exactly seem to me to be the kind of person who would see his future in catering to the needs of . . . a bohemian clientele?'

'If you mean, do I associate with a bunch of long-haired, self-obsessed hippies, the answer is most certainly no. But I'm happy to take their money. That's the beauty of it. You see these things they laughably call businesses, these cooperatives, these well-meaning women with their self-knitted tie-dyed umbrellas, and you don't know whether to laugh or cry. But I can make a business work.'

'I see. Personally, I wouldn't entertain the notion for a moment. The issue is not so much you as a potential borrower, or your business acumen' — he affords Roy a thin smile — 'as your target audience. Wholly unreliable, in my view, as well as, I must say, morally question-able.'

'Quite so,' said Roy with a smile. 'But — '

'However,' continued Mr Price, holding up a hand to stop him, 'I am prepared to put this up to head office. I dare say views there may be rather more progressive than my own. I wish you every good fortune.'

4

At work he played surreptitiously with scissors, glue, a typewriter and an old letter from his bank, producing a collage that would pass muster when run through the new Xerox machine in the corner of the typing pool, which was guarded assiduously by the head of the clerical staff. He waited until the lunch break, when, with sweating fingers, he made his copy. The first effort was reasonable, and he ran off two more just to be safe. Back at his desk, his attempt at Mr Price's signature was rather too shaky for his liking and he was glad to have a second copy.

It was a regrettable but necessary subterfuge. The wheels of Lyons Bank ground exceeding slow. He was confident of receiving the loan but needed to sign the lease straight away. There was no way of covering the gap other than by producing a letter confirming sufficient funds in his account and signing a cheque that, he hoped, would not be cashed immediately. Further cheques would need to follow for utilities and the modest fit-out of the premises. Cheques would not be necessary to buy stock: in this business hard cash was what it would take before Martin's continental suppliers released goods to them. Roy had ideas about where to find the liquid assets to effect the necessary deals.

He left the office at four, claiming illness. He reckoned he'd need the next day off as well. But he required this job only for a short while longer. Soon he would be released from the long grey linoleum corridors and liberated into the bright lights of the real world.

5

It was high time for one of their periodic arguments. She could start a fight in an empty room, he always thought. Well, so be it; it was convenient right now. In fact it was necessary. It would not take much to escalate it to the proportions of full nuclear war.

What was it to be this time? The state of the bathroom? His lazy habits? Martin popping round all the time and staring at her tits? From the perspective of now, he could not fathom how they had come together or why they remained together. She was so much younger than him for a start, which was evident to anyone who came across them. Younger not simply in years. Maureen was naive and almost infinitely enthusiastic. If he had ever possessed those qualities they had been knocked out of him a long time before. Life-affirming was beyond him: he didn't see the point.

Maybe she'd been drawn to the force of his being. Maybe she'd needed a father figure, having come down from the primitive North to the Big Smoke. Maybe she just found him sexually irresistible. Any or all of these could apply. He didn't care. It had palled and outlived its usefulness. In fact his advantage was flowing in an entirely different direction now. At one time there had been, for him, available sex with an attractive younger woman, someone to cook his meals and look after his home (not that she was particularly good at either), and the potential material benefits of a high earner in the household. But when they had opened the joint building society account he had not reckoned on her being so gobby and strident. He had put up with the sound of her voice with infinite patience.

Well, not for much longer. Now it was all about the process of extricating himself to his best advantage.

It was work, when it came. They were sitting in the lounge after their evening meal, the sound of the television turned up loud to drown the noise of the young couple in the neighbouring flat, with their Stones or Bowie or whatever it was. Roy suspected they must be junkies, they looked so gaunt and white, with straggling identical hair, pale smiles and eye sockets darkened to blue-black with the fatigue of listening to rock music at all hours of the night.

The building in which they lived had been hastily partitioned in the 1960s. With its peeling, faded woodwork, its botched pointing and the vandalism of its improvised division into flats, it was now barely recognizable as a once comfortable merchant's house of the nineteenth century.

They occupied one third of the ground floor. Below them, in the highly undesirable basement flat, with its dark and dank corners, lived the quiet, pious West Indian immigrant couple who, he supposed, kept themselves neat enough, he with his job on the buses and she the school cleaner. Across the hallway lived the little junkies, touchingly naive and young, destined for their early graves, while above them was the rake-thin embittered old man, with his flat cap and collarless shirt and a visage where the razor each day missed a large swathe of its duty, reportedly a widower, who glowered whenever they met in the communal areas. Roy had no idea who, if anyone, occupied the remaining two flats. It was noisy and cold in this place, it was dismal and hopeless. He knew there was a better life to be had.

She walked to the television and switched it off. The thumping beat and the tuneless shrieking could be heard through the wall.

'You don't really care about anything, do you?' she said. Her voice when she hectored him took on a shrill harshness that crashed around his ears. 'Least of all your career.'

'Depends what you mean,' he replied. 'I do my job.'

'That's all it is, though, isn't it? A job.'

'That's all any job is. A job. You do your work and they give you your money. End of story.'

'Don't you ever think we're doing something more important than that?'

He shrugged before saying with deliberation, 'It's important for me. It pays our bloody bills. Keeps the wolf from the door.'

'Do you ever commit to anything?'

'Commit? What exactly does that mean? And anyway, why should I? Beyond an honest day's wage for an honest day's work?'

'Because we can change the world, if we want.'

He looked at her with an expression of astonishment.

'Change things? And why would I want to do that? Assuming, for the moment, that such a stupid idea held any water. The world is what the world is. We just get on with it, getting whatever we can from it.'

'You don't care about anything, do you?' she repeated.

'That's for others. I get my orders and carry them out. I get paid. Or if I don't do what I'm told I get fired. Simple as that.'

There was a loud thud from the flat above. Possibly a suitcase had been dropped, or a body had hit the floor.

'I'm just interested in getting on with things. Not theorizing. Not changing the world.' He hurled this last out with a bitter, thin line of spittle that hung like gossamer on his chin. He wiped it off with his sleeve.

She was silent, at a loss. It was as if she suddenly lacked the power, or the will, to contend with this.

'I don't know what to say.'

'Well, don't say anything, then,' he riposted immediately, but with intent.

'Shall we just stop this conversation now?' she said.

Despite its sharpness, he knew that for her this amounted to a proposal for a truce, however uneasy. Early, he thought: normally they arrived here much later, exhausted and impotently frustrated each with the other. Perhaps the edge to his voice had alerted some subliminal instinct in her. But he was not about to let go. Oh no.

'I've had about enough of this bleeding-heart nonsense,' he said. 'I'd like to teach the world to sing. In perfect harmony. Well, buy a bloody Coke, then, and shut your trap.'

She was visibly alarmed. This was not how the game was played. These were not the rules.

'Well, you know what you can do, then,' she said quietly.

'Yes,' he said decisively.

Her eyes narrowed slightly and he was certain he could sense her flinch.

He was not proud of it. It had happened when he was at a vulnerable point, when he had returned from the pub on a particularly dark and windy night. She had gone on and on, about something he could not now recall. So he had belted her, quick and hard, about the temple. A short, sharp shock. It had not been sufficient to knock her from her feet or inflict greater damage, but no doubt she was dazed. Her head had lolled elastically on her neck for a moment. It had had the desired effect: the momentary look of animus had turned to fear and then, gratifyingly, to compliance. It had been spontaneous and unplanned, but he had learned from its efficacy.

He had felt no shame. In the circumstances the act, while not precisely desirable or elegant, had been defensible; even necessary, he now thought. He looked at her and saw that glint again in her eyes.

'Why don't you go and spend a few days with your mum?' he said, and it was less a placatory question than a quiet command.

As she looked at him her resentful fear melted into resignation.

'Yes, I might,' she said, and he continued to look at her steadily.

6

Busy busy busy. Time to get weaving. Taking his belongings and removing all trace of himself, he had moved swiftly out of the flat, having learned enough to last a lifetime about playing house. He cleared the building society account, placing some of the money into his own account but retaining most as ready cash. They had opened that account together, at Maureen's insistence, to save for a mortgage. So much for her being unconventional and against the system. So much, now, for happy families. He had enjoyed ripping up the passbook.

He resigned from the Ministry by means of a curt letter painfully scratched out with blotchy biro on grubby Basildon Bond. To hell with the notice period, he had thought; to hell with the final month's salary. Let them find me, let them sue.

The shop was now his home. It was squalid but liveable: there was neither hot water nor heating and he had to sleep in the tiny windowless back room on a threadbare old couch that bore grisly stains and exuded an unpleasant aroma. But he had known much, much worse in his lifetime. The bank loan had been declined, so there was a potential cash flow crisis. But for the moment he could juggle, using the money from the building society account and citing the bank's ineptitude to the landlords. The sale of the first consignments would see them right. The important thing was that he once again felt alive, no longer an emasculated zombie wage slave. He chuckled: Maureen would habitually speak of the dignity of labour. There was no dignity, he thought: labour was subjugation, and all subjugation was humiliation.

Martin had been on the blower with his associates. It was worth the cost, frantically slotting ten-pence pieces to feed the insatiable appetite of the telephone around the corner. The first consignment was to be expected in days, although details had yet to be finalized. Meanwhile they had set to redecorating the dingy little shop, covering the window first with newspaper. They had ripped out the ancient carpet, painted the dark walls that reeked of tobacco with white emulsion and slapped gloss paint over the dented old counter. For their stock, Martin's contacts in Belgium, the Netherlands and Scandinavia were vital. Roy provided the business know-how and the backbone.

He was just thinking of climbing uncomfortably from the sofa and brewing a cup of tea for himself when an impatient rap came on the front door of the shop. He threw off the frayed grey blanket and, taking his time, dragged on his shoes, ran his fingers through his hair, tucked his shirt inside his trousers and shuffled towards the noise, which had not abated. A short, snappily dressed young man stood on the other side of the glass door. He looked impatiently at Roy, who looked him up and down, taking in his chalk-stripe suit with wide lapels and flared trousers, his Chelsea boots, his wispy moustache, his Brylcreemed hair and his cocky expression. He knew his type: on the make and in a hurry. No doubt there was some angle here and Roy would have to hear him out: some special offer on some tame porn or knock-off booze, or suchlike. Well, he would listen politely.

'Mr Mannion, is it?' asked the young man brightly. Roy had taken the precaution of using the name for this piece of business.

'Who's asking?' said Roy brusquely.

'Name of Smith. John Smith. No, that really is my name.' The young man laughed to denote the

104

practised joke. 'Like a millstone I carry around with me, that name. No one believes me. But here I am. Large as life. John Smith. Care to see my driving licence?'

Roy looked uninterested. It could well be a hooky one anyway.

'Why should I? What do you want?'

'You're new on this plot, aren't you? My associates and me knew Archie well. Good old boy. One of the best. Old school. Knew his civic duty, played a part. No, Mr M. I thought I'd just come by and welcome you to the area on behalf of the local businesses. I may have seen you around before in fact. You may have noticed me.'

'Can't say I have. Where's your shop?'

'Oh, my business is all over the place. I don't have a fixed base. Me and my associates are in the business of providing services for our customers. And we sincerely hope you'll shortly be one too.'

He grinned broadly. Roy did not. He was bored. He was having none of this schoolboy shakedown.

'What kind of services?'

John Smith's good humour did not leave him. He smiled again and said, 'Mr M. You're a businessman. I'd have thought you'd have some kind of idea.'

'Maybe I have. Maybe I haven't. Enlighten me.'

'All kinds of things. We're entrepreneurs. We can help with supplies, food, drink, literature, that kind of thing. I hear you're opening a bookshop here.'

'You seem well informed. Where did you get that from?'

Mr Smith ignored his question. 'Staff, even. We've got a good stock of, ahem, very presentable employees. If that's what you're interested in. We have good relations with the local filth too. Can make some introductions for you if you like, to ease your path. Pretty much anything.'

'Thank you. But I think we're well catered for,' said Roy gruffly.

'One of our most popular lines is security. We look after a lot of the businesses in the area. Not nice if you're starting up a new business in a new area to fall foul to burglaries or what have you. We can make sure that doesn't happen.'

'Not interested. Thank you.'

'Whereas if you don't get sorted with the right kind of insurance all kinds of things can happen. Or my associates may be interested in a joint venture. A merger, shall we say? Or even in taking over your business for the right price if it has any prospects.'

'Just clear off out of it, will you, sonny? Or I'll give you a clip round your ear for your pains.'

The boy continued to grin. 'No need to be like that, now, Mr M. We don't want to get off on the wrong foot, do we? Don't want no little misunderstandings. You'll probably need some help along the way. Some goodwill, shall we say?'

'I don't need scumbags like you and your little pals shaking me down.'

'My word,' said Smith. 'You do have a temper on you, don't you, Mr M? A word to the wise,

106

this is not good for customer relations, or for community spirit. We all like to get on. We don't like nothing to rock the boat. Bad for business. Especially for the one doing the rocking. Can I suggest you give it some consideration? I'll come around tomorrow so that we can talk brass tacks.'

'You can bugger off and if you come round here again I'll kick your arse for you.'

'We obviously haven't hit it off. Maybe if one of my associates dropped by?'

'I'll kick his spotty arse for him too. Now just piss off and don't come back.'

'You may be making a big mistake.'

'What? You going to call by with a few of your pals, are you? I don't think so. Do I look like I'm quaking in my boots?'

'Not a good move, Mr M,' said John Smith, wagging his finger.

7

'Trouble,' said Martin a few days later. 'Big trouble.' He was out of breath when he entered the shop.

'Calm down, Martin,' said Roy. 'Now tell your Uncle Roy all about it.'

'Did someone calling himself John Smith come by the other day?'

'What if he did? I can handle him.'

'It's not him you have to worry about. It's who he represents. He's only the softening-up act.'

'It's just an amateur protection racket. All we

need to do is stand up to them.'

'You don't understand. They go back years. They own most of the properties, or if not have the landlords' balls in the vice. They'll let people go about their business so long as they don't shit on their doorstep and pay their dues.'

'Storm in a teacup. Teething problems. We'll be all right.'

'No. I don't think so. They've had me in and given me a good talking-to. The big men, not your John Smith. They don't like you. Not much we can do about it.'

'All right,' said Roy slowly. 'How much?'

'It's beyond that.'

'So what? A pitched battle along Wardour Street? They wouldn't want that, would they?'

'No, they wouldn't.'

'What's the deal?'

'They'll compromise. They don't want the bother.'

'That's good. So. What. Is. The. Deal. Martin?'

'We clear out today and leave the keys on the counter. As in piss off out of London.'

'Or else?'

'They didn't specify. There's more.'

'There always is.'

'They know about our consignment. I'm assuming they know from the far end. They've tipped off the Old Bill about when and where. The consignment's been seized at Folkestone.'

'And we're to take their word for that?'

'They told me exactly how it was coming in. My contact down the dock says it's buzzing with cops and Customs down there. Smith's bosses will give us thirty minutes — I pleaded with them — and then there'll be another phone call that goes in to tell them where it was headed. Then the Flying Squad will be on us. Just a little hurry-up, they said.'

Roy considered momentarily, then spoke. 'Right, let's go.'

In silence they gathered together Roy's belongings in a grip. With a damp cloth he wiped all the surfaces that he imagined he might have touched. He removed the keys from his key ring and placed them on the counter.

They slammed the door behind them as they left and walked swiftly to the Tube station, their collars turned up.

'What now?' said Roy when they had finally settled in a pub at Ealing Broadway.

'I have some ideas. Whatever got into your head, Roy?'

'I've never been pushed around by anyone. Least of all a little lowlife like that.'

'That little lowlife is the nephew of one of the big boys. Very highly regarded. That's us finished here.'

'So what next?'

'Pastures new,' said Martin with a smile, draining his pint glass.

8

Roy disliked intensely being wrong when Martin, idiot Martin, was right. But he was: a precautionary and careful pass along Berwick

Street confirmed a burnt-out shop front in the place of his hopes and dreams. Unless it was an elaborate ruse of Martin's by some obscure means to wrest Roy's savings from his grasp, the next move of which he would shortly witness, it was simply true. No, no, Martin did not have the wit for the grand scheme. Oh no.

He had returned to the Paddington hotel room and waited. The room, under the eaves, was cheap as well as nasty, but he did not want to spend more than he needed of his funds before his life began again in earnest. He was bored. The room had no television and he returned from his excursion to Soho with his copy of the *Sun*, which he read from cover to cover. He slept for a while in the afternoon.

It was even worse being dependent on Martin. For the moment, Martin was in the lead, sorting out their travel arrangements and obtaining passports from a contact he knew in the East End. Roy had no option but to trust him: he had removed all his cash from his bank accounts but dared not set out on his own to put things right. He was bereft of ideas, devoid of contacts. With his light manner at their meetings each evening, Martin unwittingly piled more indignity on to Roy. At some stage in their joint career, Martin would pay for this.

★   ★   ★

Tonight, allegedly, they would be on the move. For the photographs to be used in their new forged passports that Roy judged prudent just in

110

case the police should arrest them as they attempted to leave the country, they had each had their shoulder-length locks cut to a short-back-and-sides and shaved off their moustaches. Martin had been dispatched to the East End to have the passports made up. We shall see, thought Roy, we shall see whether young Mr White turns up.

But he duly did, and Roy felt a hatred that was undampened by its irrationality. Martin had reduced him to this: impotence and dependence on a generally harmless and usually useful fool. He disguised his contempt, as effectively as Martin concealed his new-found superiority, in cheerful solicitousness.

It was a big night, not just for them. Crowds milled around central London, many heading for Wembley and the big match that would see England qualify for the World Cup in Germany the following year. To give him his due, Martin had thought it through. While the Metropolitan Police strained to effect crowd control in London and residual lazy coppers watched Brian Clough drone his ITV punditry on control room televisions, they would be going against the flow.

Once they had negotiated the Tube and the teeming concourse at Victoria, things became easier. They found an empty carriage on the boat train and the worst to contend with was the waiting, as British Rail vainly resumed its daily struggle to get a train away on time. People straggled into the compartment, a blinking German student with evidently not a clue obliviously knocking him on the knee with his sharp-edged rucksack, two ugly Italian girls chatting volubly, three smiling and loud Dutch boys. Soon there was the full complement of eight and Roy contained his seething anger only by feigning to doze. This was not travelling in style. This was not what he had imagined for himself.

Eventually the train pulled out only forty-five minutes behind schedule. It screeched to a jarring halt outside Dover station, shaking him from the deep slumber he had fallen into, and waited almost twenty minutes before, apparently without reason, jerking forward again.

They waited until their young companions had disgorged from the train before picking up their bags, shrugging their coats on to their shoulders and heading through the passage towards the ferry and passport control. Roy checked mentally that he had his currency well hidden in the bottom of his grip. The sense that if he were to be detained and his belongings searched it would all be up was, in a strange but familiar way, calming. He had travelled this path before. The only factors in play at this moment were his demeanour and fortune, good or bad.

Martin and Roy separated and he hung at the back of a cluster of young people, evidently on a trip of some kind, of excited English secondary school children. He looked at their shabby guardians and loosened his tie, mussed his hair and adopted a world-weary expression. His new passport indicated, after all, that he was a teacher. It was over in a moment once he had waited for all twenty-six children and the adults to pass and ensured that he followed them immediately. The official looked at him, bored, scrutinized his passport fleetingly and handed it back. Simple as that, and he felt an inner glow.

As he boarded the vessel by the glare of the dock lights a blaring radio carried by one of the seamen announced that England had drawn against Poland and would not after all be at the 1974 World Cup. England, my England, he thought, as he glanced back at Dover. Good to get you off my back for a while.

They were well into their third celebratory pint at the bar when Roy raised the subject of their plans for the future. The ferry lurched and swayed on the rough seas and empty glasses slid on neighbouring tables. They were almost the only people in the half-lit space. Martin looked wan and extinguished his cigarette, but Roy's stomach was stronger.

'What next, Martin?' he asked.

'Hadn't given it a thought,' slurred Martin. 'The main priority was clearing out before the rozzers found us.'

'Quite right,' said Roy calmly, and waited a beat. 'But we do need a plan.' He smiled encouragingly.

'Thought we'd find some cheap hotel in Paris and take it from there.'

Roy sighed, almost but not quite imperceptibly. He said, 'All right. That'll do for starters. But then?'

Martin looked blank.

'You've got some contacts in Brussels?' said Roy, prompting with a cocked eyebrow.

'Yes.'

'Who deal in various commodities?'

'Yes, but if you — '

'Yes?'

'You'd need money for starters.'

'I reckon I could lay my hands on some cash. Seems a pity to waste these lovely new passports.'

'If you're thinking of going back to England . . .'

'I didn't say that. But if your pals need some help getting stuff down from Scandinavia or over from North Africa, who better than a couple of upstanding British businessmen to help them? I'm sure we could turn our hands to that. Don't you agree? As long as the price is right. And, as time goes on, set ourselves up properly in the import-export business.'

'Cut them out, you mean? They won't like that.'

'You're getting ahead of yourself, Martin. That's not what I said. Let's just make ourselves useful in the first place and see where that takes us, shall we? Or have you got a better idea?'

'No.'

'Well then. You just set up the meetings and I'll worry about the money. How does that sound? All right with you, is it?'

'I suppose so.'

'Good,' said Roy soothingly. 'Excellent. I'll drink to that.' He allowed himself a little inward grin. He had reasserted a healthy measure of control.

7

Domestic Bliss

1

They are spared Roy's presence this weekend. Distracted and muttering, ill-tempered after a bad night's sleep, he has taken himself off to his own place, to sort his affairs out. So he says. He plans to place most of his belongings in storage and to sell up. It is his last chance to make a modest profit, he claims, given the state of the property market.

'That's why I'm consulting Vincent,' he had said over breakfast. 'You have to look after yourself. I've seen a lot in my lifetime. You don't get to our age without having a history, do you?'

It is not a question and she has heard this refrain before, despite his reluctance to talk about his past and his occasional contradictory insistence that he has led a humdrum life. He could at least make the effort to be consistent. Evidently he sees her as the gullible type.

He barrels on regardless. 'Maybe I've seen more than you. I'm glad you've led a sheltered life, truly I am. You wouldn't have wanted to see some of the things I have. But then again I've learned about preserving the important things in life. You have to look after all you've worked to secure. Your assets, your interests, your family.

You'll want to leave a future for Michael, and Stephen and Emma, when you, I mean . . . Let's face it, we both have to be realistic. We're well into that age when at any moment . . . '

She smiles meekly at him, as if he were reading the weather forecast from his newspaper.

'I mean, if at any stage you'd like a word with Vincent . . . '

But for now he is gone to settle whatever affairs are to be settled, and she has some breathing space.

Stephen is with her. His offer to drive Roy to his home was brusquely declined.

'Piece of cake. Wouldn't mind a lift to the station, but then change at Reading, cab from Paddington and Bob's your uncle. I probably won't be back until tomorrow. Lots to sort out.'

The air is easier without him, which is not in the least surprising. There seems to be a sustained exhalation as they potter in the kitchen and there is almost a relaxed elegance in their counterpoint movements around the house. He grinds coffee beans at the counter as she washes parsley. As she turns to cut the herbs, he moves with perfect timing to the cupboard to locate the cafetière. He pours the boiling water from the kettle as she reaches for the biscuit tin. They complete this wordless choreography by walking together into the lounge and settling by the pile of Saturday broadsheets, she in her upright chair, he sprawling somewhat on the sofa.

The herbs are drying on kitchen paper for the omelette she will cook for their lunch in an hour or so. Then they may go out for a short drive into the countryside before he deals with his emails and a few other pressing IT matters at the kitchen table. She may have a nap in her chair or perhaps simply listen to Bach with her eyes closed. They have talked of ordering in an Indian meal in the evening. Roy cannot abide spicy food, so this will be a treat.

2

Vincent opens his mouth but does not speak. He seems to be working his way up to something. Eventually he says, 'Why are you doing this, Roy? You can do without the bother. You must be well enough off. You can't need the money.'

Well, a little disclosure will do no harm, at this stage in his life. It will be good to explain, if only to Vincent, his only legatee so to speak in this world.

'I can always do with more,' he replies. 'You can never have too much cash. Besides, it's what I do. I do it because I can, because I'm good at it. And these people. These stupid complacent people. They don't know what it is like to suffer. They sit at the centre of their own lives, warm and cosy. They need shaking up.'

He could have added, it's a weakness, a compulsion. The painstaking construction of the lie and its intricate underpinnings: they make the adrenalin flow. In a previous life he was taught not to show joy at getting away with the big lie, and to avoid the urge to embroider to within an inch of believability just for the thrill of mocking

117

the mark. One big lie is all you ever need, he knows through experience, and to feel the joy solely internally is gratifying enough. It's necessary not to ignore the endgame; but that's not where the sense of accomplishment lies for Roy. It's in the execution, the act of deception. But Vincent wouldn't understand. He's a singularly joyless person.

'They're nice enough people,' he continues quickly, 'of their sort. Privileged, smug, small-minded. You'll get to meet them. You'll probably like her. I do.'

'And yet it doesn't stop you?' says Vincent.

'Why should it? It's an important lesson for her. Albeit at a rather advanced age. I like her, but I only know her because she presented herself. From the get-go. In my time I've had to . . . deal with . . . plenty of people who've been pleasant enough.'

It is not imperative, though, to do this; he could scrape by on what he has left, though it has dwindled alarmingly over the past few years. But this is where he derives his satisfaction and while he likes her he also sneers at her. And as for her dreadful family, good grief.

They return to the business at hand, after the rather embarrassing partial opening-up. No, on reflection disclosure is not a good thing, thinks Roy. It doesn't salve the soul. It invites questions, not least from oneself, and upsets the certainty at which one has arrived. At his age he can do without such perturbations.

Vincent will be called in when Roy has been able to persuade Betty that she needs his advice.

118

This will take some tenacity, though he has started along the way. He runs through who else Betty may wish to have there: with luck the callow Stephen, with slightly less luck her son, Michael. Both should, ultimately, be manageable. Roy takes some care in prescribing how Vincent should present himself, his demeanour and even the clothes he should wear. Vincent is not offended; he knows well Roy's attention to detail and that, generally, he is right.

They run through the basic script. It can only be an outline since they will need to extemporize considerably, not least to deal with queries that Betty may have. Roy reinforces the key messages and the boundaries beyond which they must not stray. There are some tricky areas that have to be gone over more than once, mainly concerning how to manoeuvre Betty into entering into it all jointly with Roy. Vincent and Roy could manage separate accounts, but this would involve more technical wizardry than they would prefer and expose the whole venture to greater risk than normally acceptable.

Finally, they tackle the information technology issues. The accounts are already set up and Roy has tested online access discreetly on the slim tablet computer that he keeps concealed in his bedroom at Betty's. Roy explains that when it comes to the moment, for the sake of dramatic verisimilitude, he wants them both to transfer funds to a joint account in their names in an obscure off-shore financial institution. Vincent feels that this may be problematic but realizes that Roy, as ever, wants to do things with a flourish. He emphasizes just how important it is for Roy to shift the funds on from there at the earliest opportunity. The endgame will then be on them and he will need to have made his next plans in advance, ready to deploy immediately.

They may well not have a further opportunity to confer at length before the wheels are in motion. After that their chances to talk may be snatched and unreliable, so it is important that both are entirely clear on the collective vision and contingencies should events take an unexpected turn. With Betty, Roy will want to maintain the appearance of complete transparency and not to arouse even minimal doubt. This is well-trodden territory for the two of them, with far tougher adversaries, and they shake hands before Roy heads for the return train. It will not be a problem. Oh no.

3

'I think,' he says, 'I owe you an apology.'

'Oh?' says Betty. 'Why's that?'

'I've been thinking. While I've been away. You've told me all about your life and your family and I've been a little . . . '

'Reticent?'

'To put it mildly. Unlike you, there's been little of interest. But you see, I can't say I feel any pride in my life. And I don't care for opening up, or whatever they call it. I was brought up to mind my own business. But I owe it to you to tell you rather more about me than I have. If, that is, we're about to take the next step.'

'Meaning?'

'If, as you suggested, I'm to sell up and to move in with you permanently.'

'I rather thought you'd already moved in. And I didn't know it was my suggestion,' she added pertly.

'Yes, well. Selling my little flat will formalize it. As well as giving us the funds to secure a wonderful future together.'

'Indeed.'

'I want you to be clear on one thing. I've never told you any lies. I've simply been, well . . . '

'Economical with the truth?'

He scowls and says emphatically, 'Oh no. I don't like that expression. Perhaps I've not been as forthcoming as I might have been.'

'I was joking, Roy. Only teasing you.'

'Oh. Yes. Well. At any rate, this is me. It's a short and humdrum story. There's nothing to alarm you. A good cure for insomnia. To begin with, I come originally from Dorset. I have to tell you that I was something of the black sheep of my family. My father was a country rector there, like his father. As the eldest son, I was expected to follow in their footsteps. I was put up for a private education and slated to study theology at Cambridge. But then the war intervened. And besides, I was — I am indeed — something of an adventurer. I signed up as soon as I was able but sadly never got to serve on the front line in the push. It was a mixture of the training requirements, the chaos of the times and the fact that the war was in fact entering its final phase and fizzling out. Those who had fought the hard yards were generally permitted to apply the coup de grace. We youngsters were held in reserve. It's always been a regret of mine. I was in what they laughably call military intelligence. But I suppose I served my country as best I could. I was part of a small group sent to Europe to investigate incidents and try to locate fleeing war criminals. We had some success. It taught me a lot about life, though there are some experiences I'd not want to wish on anyone else.'

'For example?'

'Oh,' he says, discomfited. 'Things I don't speak of to anyone.'

'Even me?'

'Especially you, my dear. Things of which you should not know. Things that changed me as a man and made me what I am today.'

He regards her sadly, and she fancies she might see tears form in the watery corners of his eyes. But then again, she may be mistaken.

'I moved on. I didn't leave the army immediately, though I could have returned to my studies and faded nicely into a rural curacy. I did have my chance to serve on the front line, in Korea. By then I was a captain, promoted through the ranks. Those were tough times too. They have bitter winters there. I'd all but lost contact with my family. My perspectives on life were rather different from my parents'. Less timid, I have to say. But I regret bitterly not having made the effort. I've never found the courage to pick up the threads.'

'You could do so now,' she says. 'I could help you.'

He shakes his head vehemently.

'No. All gone now. They're all dead now, no doubt. There are the later generations, I suppose, but the last thing they will need is some distant long-forgotten relation landing on their doorstep.'

'I'm not sure . . .'

'No,' he says decisively. 'No. Anyway, I left the army in 1953 and was at a bit of a loose end for a while. I had a variety of jobs. Before I knew it I was pushing thirty and it was time to do something with my life. I was living in London then but decided I should be out in the sticks. I moved to East Anglia, near Norwich, and that was where I met Mary. She was an uncomplicated girl, from a modest background, with simple needs. I'd long lost any desire for status or position. I was more interested in starting a family and striking out on my own. So with a small plot of land I began a market garden. I taught myself everything. I'd read avidly into the early hours and then spend the next day putting my learning into practice. And shortly we had Robert. It would have been the most joyous day of my life had the birth not been so difficult. From then on, there was little to report. I was building my business up and to be frank I spent most of my time on that. It does me no favours to say so, but I neglected Mary and Robert as the business became more successful. Until, that is, she fell ill. It was a terrible few years, as she slowly became worse and worse. And then she was gone. I've never felt so low in my life. That would have been the early 70s. Robert was about fifteen. We grew apart — it must have been at least partly the grief we couldn't express to one another — and eventually, when he was about nineteen, he left suddenly. That almost did me in, I can tell you.'

He pauses.

'What did you do then?' she asks gently.

'I sold up. I told myself I needed a new start. Moved back to London. Got into property. And investment. It was the beginning of the boom years. That was a mistake. City folk. I got mixed up with the wrong crowd. I was getting drunk every night and my so-called partners were fleecing me left, right and centre. I was almost ruined. Eventually I saw sense and in 1985 took what I had left and returned to Norfolk. I managed to buy a small nursery there from a chap I used to know who was retiring, and that kept me going until I retired myself. In fact it did quite well and I could live in some modest comfort. And that's the whole story, more or less. Until you came along.'

'And Robert?'

'He travelled the world and we had no contact until 1995. Then out of the blue I had a letter from him from Australia. I don't know how he found me again. Probably the internet. I've still not seen him since we parted and we're in touch only infrequently. He never comes to England.'

'Would you like to see him?'

'Not really,' says Roy. 'We have so little in common. And I'm afraid I'm unduly rigid when it comes to my moral standards. I don't approve of his lifestyle and I doubt I could reconcile myself to it. Best just to leave it as it is. Anyway, there you have it. I felt it only fair as we enter this new phase in our lives . . . '

'The last movement, possibly,' she says with a smile.

'Yes. I felt you needed to know about me. I'm afraid my experiences have made me rather taciturn. There's little I can do about that. I've simply learned not to trust people — not you, that goes without saying. I don't like talking about myself, and that won't change. But if you have any questions . . . '

'No,' she says absently.

8

March 1963
Flooding

1

A hard, hard frost. Like the whole of the last three months or so. So cold it became difficult to think. Especially on a Sunday morning when you'd been dragged from your pit at no notice, from that snug fastness into this. He shivered as he thought of it and yearned for his bed again.

Fog. Bitter blank freezing fog wafting across the Fens. There was no wind. Snow remained thick on the ground, the snow of weeks past, accumulated like memory. The roads had been cleared several times but were coated in black ice yet again.

He leaned against the driver's door of the lorry, his fingers numb and shaking as he commanded them to light his cigarette. He was on his own, waiting for Bob. Mr Cole had long ago left, taking the lorry driver with him. This was something that required the deft ministrations of Bob, and Mr Cole had not had the patience to wait. 'You'll be all right, won't you, Roy?' he'd said. 'I'd better get the driver back to town. Took the poor bugger an hour to get to Old Ma Forsyth's and the phone.' The poor bugger would probably be hunkering down by

126

Mrs Cole's stove and drinking her tea. More than could be said for Roy at present.

It had taken them forty-five minutes to locate the vehicle down the old King's Lynn road, a solitary spot which on a day like today would hardly ever be passed. When he had broken down the driver had simply struck out on foot for the nearest sign of habitation without noting his location. The fog was almost impenetrable and Mr Cole had inched the van along the road from Essenham village, the driver sitting uncomfortably in the back and giving vague instructions. He had little idea where the lorry was.

Eventually they had found it, straddling the main road. The driver claimed he'd hit a patch of ice, braked and slid to an uncontrolled halt, stalling the engine in the process. He had been unable to restart it. Undoubtedly something as simple as a flooded carb; but Mr Cole insisted that Roy wait for Bob. Presumably he could charge more that way.

Bloody Norfolk, thought Roy. For the past five years he had been a glorified odd job man in the village. The market garden in the summer he enjoyed, but that was entirely seasonal. Mr Brown was far too much of a mean sort to keep him on for the full year. So when October came he was forced to search around for whatever was available. More often than not Cole's Garage was the only port of call. Still, it kept him in beer and fags more or less. It was far from fulfilling a destiny, though. It was scratching a living.

A shudder ran up his spine and back down.

Where was Bob, effortlessly cheerful Bob, fifteen years younger than he, with optimism to burn and a wedding in the offing? Bob, the qualified mechanic, who did have prospects, especially when Old King Cole decided eventually to sell up and retire. Cole had a soft spot for Bob. Roy he always regarded with curious suspicion, as if he had committed some infraction that Cole could not call precisely to mind. In fact Roy had been on his best behaviour since washing up here.

He tried again to light his cigarette and this time succeeded. He sucked greedily at the paper tube and heard the crackle that was little more than a rustle as it burned. He took the cigarette out of his mouth and observed it critically for a moment, teasing a stray fleck of tobacco from the unburning end with a numb finger and thumb. The cigarette gave him at least the apparition of additional warmth.

Silence. That was the main thing about these parts at the best of times. Stranded here in the middle of nowhere in a winter fog was a world separated. A world of forlorn silence and isolation. It was as if he had died and his soul had been untethered. Not that he had many ties, but now he felt unmoored entirely. He found this energizing rather than concerning: no safety nets but no constraints.

2

In essence Bob was a good lad. He had grown up in his remote village and had never left it.

Bob had his sweetheart, Sheila. She too had grown up here. Bob would tell him regularly that they'd been destined for each other from their first day at the infants' school in the village. Their families, amused, had conspired in this myth and so it had turned out. They were engaged to be married in the summer and Sheila was busy filling her bottom drawer.

Bob had energy and enthusiasm and could, to his credit, envisage a world beyond. This was a trait Roy encouraged, generally in their sessions at the pub. Invariably Roy would have to escort Bob back to his parents' house and knock on the door with a wry smile and eyebrows raised, much to the chagrin of Bob's father.

Speed and horses were Bob's passions. He was small, wiry and athletic, like his father, and had once had aspirations to become a jockey. His father had forbidden it because twenty-five years earlier he himself had been a promising stable boy at a prestigious training stable near Newmarket, but had broken his leg badly in a fall. It had taken years to rebuild his life and he didn't want Bob to go through the same anguish. But Bob still hankered and went to the races at Newmarket and Doncaster as often as he could afford it.

He sped around his little world on his Triumph motorcycle, for which he had spent some years saving and which he kept in pristine condition. This too was to be a casualty of married life, potentially traded in for an Austin A35 or perhaps an Anglia in a year or so. But in the meantime he accelerated along the straight fenland roads, sweeping the flat monochrome before him in a rush of air and roar of motor.

3

Was that the sound of a distant motorcycle Roy could hear on the still air? No, it was a trick of the disorientating fog, or of his expectation.

He climbed into the cab again, hoping for a hint of greater warmth, and slammed the door with a tinny clang.

Five years. At times it seemed a lifetime in the stifling fenland gloom, all damp and turned in on itself.

He observed his calloused hands, toughened by manual labour. Physically, he was more than up to it, but that wasn't the point. It just wasn't supposed to be like this. Roy wasn't meant to be one of life's also-rans, doing the hard work that sustained the successful in their positions. Things must change, soon.

He could hear only the sandpaper scrape of his hand across his jaw as he felt his face. He had had just a matter of minutes at five in the morning to pull on his trousers, his boots and his shirt and tie before finding the thickest sweater he could wear under his jacket and overcoat. He would have been grateful for a slurp of hot, sweet tea to run through his body. He exhaled experimentally and watched as the vapour from his breath drifted in a cloud to the windscreen of the vehicle before beginning to dissolve into condensation. For want of anything better to do,

130

he delved around the interior of the cab, reading the invoices collated neatly on the clipboard, perusing an old copy of the *Daily Sketch* and finding a paper bag half full of pear drops in the glove compartment. There was a grubby grey army blanket crumpled untidily under the passenger seat. He picked up the crank handle that lay in the passenger footwell but he told himself again to wait for Bob and his box of tricks.

4

It was relatively easy to take the rise out of Bob. Make reference to his country bumpkin demeanour and existence, light blue touch paper and retire, to laugh sardonically at his expense.

There was, though, a sort of purpose in the ribbing. Bob wanted, and needed, to see more of life before entering the open prison of marriage. He listened enthralled as Roy told him of his exploits in immediate post-war central Europe, arraigning Nazis at the end of a pistol, or of his later journeys around the world with Lord Stanbrook, arriving back at Raffles Hotel just in time to catch a Singapore sunrise. Most of this was approximated, at least, but it seemed somehow to fire something inside Bob that resembled an imagination.

In truth he despised them all, Bob included, who, though he liked him, was simply the most palatable of these heavy-footed dullards. This period of respite had been tolerable if surprising when it had come, but five years: oh dear. Now was the time to return somewhere near the hub of things.

So he bided his time and entertained himself by stoking Bob's ambition and wanderlust, and annoying Bob's father, who had lectured Roy on more than one occasion about his fancy ideas. Roy had duly ignored him, not exactly grinning in his face. Not exactly.

Tweaking Mr Mannion's tail was, however, barely sport; and rather beneath his aspirations. He wanted to return to the world of dinner jackets and hunting tweeds, of whispered conversations over a cigar and a port, where things were fixed and cogs oiled, of glamorous, haughty women eager to assuage their boredom and contempt for their husbands through sex.

Under his tutelage, Bob had shown genuine signs of becoming restive that extended beyond barroom chat. He had argued with his father, indicating that he rather fancied trying his chances in the Smoke. He had gone to the barber's in King's Lynn, where he had acquired a reasonably spectacular quiff that he tended with painstaking care. He had taken to wearing a leather jacket. He dashed around on his Triumph, the stainless-steel parts of the engine block and chrome exhausts shined to a bright finish.

5

Finally, there was the distant buzz of a motor-cycle.

He strained to hear, then was certain. The noise was becoming louder.

Soon Bob would have his hands among the oily innards of the vehicle, a cheerful surgeon jabbering away nineteen to the dozen, grinning as he worked, his Woodbine between his lips. Eventually he would remove his oily fingers, wipe them on a rag and proceed with a flourish to fire her up.

By now the noise was recognizable as Bob's motorcycle, no longer an angry little buzz but a guttural grating roar as the throttle was opened. Roy went to the long snout of the truck and opened the bonnet. He would drive the truck back to the garage and Bob would follow on behind. It would be a bit early for a pint, but perhaps Mrs Langley, Roy's landlady, would knock up a fry-up for them. Like most women, she had a soft spot for cheeky young Bob.

He'd be freezing on that thing. This must be one of the first times this year that Bob had been out on it. When on earth would warmth return to this country?

The sound of the approaching motorcycle grew louder still. The shattering of the silence was welcome to him; things began to move.

And then the world stopped again.

Still attending to the bonnet of the vehicle, Roy had a sudden sense of imminence. He would later put this down to an unconscious reckoning that the sound of the motorcycle was too loud and close, but he had no time to reason this out.

The motorcycle motor screamed. Somewhere

on the other side of the truck and unseen by Roy, it revved helplessly as traction was lost. There was a loud thud, and Roy felt the lorry shake briefly as an impact occurred on the opposite side. It quickly settled again. He could hear the sound of metal clawing at the tarmac and even as he was aware of sparks underneath the lorry he watched the motorcycle, an angry writhing beast, slither into view from beneath it and skate some yards down the road before stalling.

The oppressive silence returned. Roy still had his hand on the bonnet, holding it open. There was no sign of Bob.

It took some presence of mind for Roy to let go of the bonnet. It crashed down and the echoes rippled into the mist. He stood for a moment, helpless, before coughing, simply to make noise, to hear its hollowness, as if to confirm his own existence.

An odd, detached foreboding spread through him which did not quite amount to dread. Experimentally, he croaked, 'Bob?', then found his voice and shouted more loudly. No response. It took him a moment more to get his leg muscles to respond and begin the long journey to the other side of the truck.

Bob had been impaled on the cross-member that jutted out from the cast-iron chassis of the flatbed lorry. He had seemingly met it square in his midriff and he was suspended from it as if in mid-air, the tips of his toes touching the ground, in a sitting position, his arms extended as if he were still riding.

It must have been a freak occurrence. He wondered how fast Bob had been travelling: a reckless sixty, seventy, ninety miles an hour? Stupid boy. What flow of blood had ensued had ceased, spattering the ice-covered road with an almost symmetrical circular pattern. The scar of the motorcycle's further trajectory could be seen under the truck.

6

He had no sense of cold now. All he felt was numbness, physical and mental. Total silence had returned. The fog hung heavy and white.

He ordered his brain to work. His first conclusion was an odd one. This dreadful sequence of events should trigger an automatic and corresponding reaction. He should, of course, do what he could for Bob, but was there any point fretting around his mortal remains? Possibly he should vomit at the terrible sight in front of him. He should begin grieving for his friend in whatever fashion was suitable. Perhaps not keening, but something more fitting than simply raising a glass at the pub that evening. He should make his way as quickly as possible to the authorities, so they could do whatever was appropriate. Well, maybe, in a moment.

But none of these things came to pass. He regarded Bob with dispassion, and a sigh formed that he was able to suppress. A bit inconvenient, this. Or possibly not.

Shortly Bob had passed from being a friend to

a conundrum in the abstract, a series of practical challenges that comprised an intriguing package of threat and opportunity. What did he need to do at the scene to effect decency just in case some passer-by should happen on this, though the chances were admittedly tiny? How would he get to the nearest police station? What would he say to Bob's parents?

Or.

It did not take long for the binary choice to form in Roy's mind. Stick or twist? As ever, his instant choice was to twist. He understood, both rationally and intuitively, that the next few days and weeks would require a certain deftness of touch. He needed also to develop ways to explain it all, so far as they were feasible, against the event that the practicalities mounted and defeated him. He applied cold logic, telling himself that it was in such circumstances that he performed best. He would act calmly, suppressing all anxiety, and take one rational step after another. Speed would be critical.

Roy surveyed the scene, walking a few yards in each direction down the two intersecting roads. It was potentially doable, if risky.

He returned to the vehicle and looked again at what remained of Bob Mannion. Shocking. Oh dear, oh dear. The next tasks were going to be unpleasant in the extreme, but there was no shirking them. He collected the blanket from the cab. No doubt the driver would miss it and scratch his head, but needs must.

Bob's torso remained adhered to the chassis. It looked now as if he was leaning, drunk, against the side of the truck for support. Roy laid the blanket out flat, eased it under Bob's feet and positioned it with care. He took a good grip of Bob under the arms and, after a deep breath, pulled him backwards. In life Bob would have been a featherweight, so the practical elements of this posed fewer issues than the conceptual. Eventually Bob came free with a sucking squish and Roy laid him on the blanket, taking care not to look too closely. The blanket had just enough play for Roy to use the corner to wipe away the girder end of the chassis on which Bob had been impaled. He then set about the grisly business of emptying Bob's pockets without getting any of that mess over himself. He could not entirely avoid catching sight of Bob's face: he looked contented, almost angelic. He would have been pleased that his quiff remained, immobile. At least Roy could reason he seemed at peace and could not have suffered.

That part of the job, at least, was over. Good Lord, it had begun to rain. This was the last thing Roy required. The background score to his efforts was no longer that deathly quiet but the patter of rain on ice. Water began to run down his neck. He shivered.

Parallel to the larger of the roads was a large drainage channel, one of the network of waterways that had been constructed at various points since the seventeenth century to take water away from these lands and make them agriculturally viable. This channel would feed into the Middle Level Main Drain, no doubt, and eventually into the Great Ouse river before it flowed into the North Sea. The channel was old, badly if at all maintained and overgrown, clogged, it seemed, with weeds and reeds. Evidently it had been ignored for many years. Beggars could not be choosers, though. He was not wagering on Bob's body ever reaching the sea.

Stepping carefully down the steep banks of the ditch with a crunch of the iced grasses at each tentative pace, he finally reached the water's edge. The surface was solid. Roy estimated that at this, its narrowest point, the ditch was about two yards across. It would have to do. Holding on to a thin branch of a tree that grew at forty-five degrees from the bank, he brought the heel of his boot down experimentally on the frozen surface. He met resistance. He tried once more, with greater force, and broke through. A gush of cold brackish liquid covered his ankle as he slipped slightly. He steadied himself and pulled his foot out of the water. Fetching the crank handle from the lorry, he set about enlarging the aperture, in which he intended Bob's body to reside. It was makeshift, he knew, but there was nothing else for it.

With both hands, Roy dragged the blanket to the edge of the ditch and positioned it carefully, before pulling on one side. Bob's body toppled down the bank, rolled and with a plop fell into the water.

The surface settled and the body rose slightly, floating but sitting low in the water. Roy could see clearly Bob's back, pierced by the square hole, his hands and his feet. He scrambled down the bank. There was nothing he could use to weight the body down. It was something he should have considered before he placed it in the water. He did what he could, nudging the body into the side of the channel less visible from the road and covering it with icy fronds of undergrowth that he managed to tease away from the bank.

The effect was not professional but just, just might suffice. The body would probably only be found in a determined search, which was unlikely provided he managed things appropriately in the next hours and days. Anyway, the die was cast and he should not fret. He had done his best. He tried to blow warmth and life back into his frozen hands as he walked back to the lorry. The moment of the next decision was upon him.

He decided he must dispose of the motorcycle. He could not risk attempting to start it again and ride it back to the village. No one could see him, on a motorbike or otherwise, and imagine he was Bob Mannion. If, however, he could get the truck motor started, he should have the time to implement the plan that he was already sketching out in his mind. If not he would have to trudge those miles back to the nearest house and then improvise.

He walked over to the motorcycle and inhaled the heady strong smell of petrol. Righting the machine, he tried to kick-start it, without success. There was only one thing for it. The channel where he had deposited Bob's body was far too narrow to accommodate the motorcycle with any semblance of disguise. He walked along the road to which the channel ran parallel, searching for a point at which it broadened. About half a mile away, at the next intersection of roads, the channel fed into a wider, perpendicular body of water, which had already begun trickling.

Roy was conscious of precious time slipping through the hourglass, never to be recovered, and of his potentially exposed position in the next phase. He paused, and spoke to himself in the silence, his breath wreathing away into the mist. Panic never does any good. Risk is life. Just function.

He returned to collect the motorcycle. Leaning his weight against the handlebars, he pushed. His boots slipped on the ice and he bent further and heaved, achieving first a tiny movement, then greater momentum. Shortly the truck disappeared from view behind him as if it had never existed and none of it had happened. Except that he held the evidence to the contrary in his hands. He pushed on, his shoulders and thighs aching with the effort, deliberately mindless until he had reached the point he had set himself. He was punctilious in not stopping short of the mark even though it was arbitrary. A yard or two wouldn't have made any difference. But it would have made a difference in his mind.

It was raining harder and he was becoming wetter. The channel here was much wider and deeper. The water was beginning to flow again, bit by bit. The thaw seemed to be setting in, and quickly.

Roy wheeled the motorcycle to the edge of the

bank and pushed it with a heave. It clattered down the steep bank and hit the water at speed. The front wheel dug in and the motorcycle somersaulted. Most of the frame disappeared from view, but both wheels protruded from the water.

He sighed. There was nothing else for it. Angrily, he pulled off his boots, socks and trousers and scrambled down to the edge of the water. It was shockingly cold, though he had to wade in only a couple of paces in order to reach the motorcycle. The water came up just above his knees. He pushed hard and shortly the motorcycle keeled over on to its side, invisible now. It was the best he could hope for.

Clambering up to the roadside and carrying his clothes and boots, he ran and slithered on the ice back to the truck as quickly as he could. Using those parts of the blanket that were not already dirtied and dampened by the spillage of Bob's body matter, he wiped himself off as best he could. He put on all of his clothes and his boots and sat on the step of the cab briefly, shuddering violently. But this was survival and he had to move.

He located the truck's crank handle and placed it in position after checking that the gearbox was in neutral. He turned the handle twice to prime the engine before climbing into the cab. The vehicle had a choke control, which he pulled to halfway. He knew this was guesswork, and he knew equally that this beast might well rebel, fling the handle in the opposite direction and break his arm as he tried to crank it. His only other option was that long walk in cold, wet clothes.

This was the moment. Despite the cold he took off his overcoat and cap to permit the best possible attack and bent in position carefully before grabbing the handle and turning it with as much force as he could muster. Nothing. He tried a second time. Again nothing. The third time he tried, the vehicle seemed to rock slightly as if something might have happened, though Roy was unsure what. At his fourth attempt the engine spluttered, coughed, fell and then spluttered again. Roy leapt back and jumped into the cab. He jabbed the accelerator with his foot and throaty, hesitant life came to the motor. Keeping his foot on the throttle, he eased the choke control in. The throatiness disappeared gradually and the petrol engine whined. At length he decided he could safely remove his foot from the accelerator. The engine idled safely enough. He felt joy. The plan was still on.

He tossed the filthy blanket in the ditch where Bob's body lay and retrieved the crank handle before climbing back into the cab, depressing the clutch and clunking the gearstick into first. He applied a little throttle and gently, ever so softly under his heavy boots, released the clutch. The wheels began to spin at first but then found traction. The truck moved forward and, gingerly, he turned it so that it faced down the road towards town. The manoeuvre was not straight-forward on these narrow roads. It was difficult, given the cold that numbed his body and his state of high alert, to summon the necessary deftness of touch on throttle and clutch. He succeeded, however, and then, edging forward and eventually reaching a moderate speed, he drove to Essenham.

Yes, flooding. That was all it had been. Bloody flooding.

7

Mr Cole and the driver were drinking tea in the garage.

'Got her going, then?' said Mr Cole in that facile rustic drawl. 'Bob, was it?'

'Bob never turned up. I fiddled under the bonnet and got her started on me own.'

'Where's Bob, then?'

'Search me,' said Roy. 'I waited ages. Then gave up. You sure someone went to his place?'

'Course I bloody am. Me bloody wife went over there. Mrs Mannion said she'd get him up.'

'I reckon he'll still be in bed. Anyway, all's well.'

'You look bloody freezing. You're shivering. And wet.'

'Yes, well. It has been a bit cold in case you hadn't noticed. And it's been raining for the past hour or so.'

'The thaw's started, then?'

'Maybe. Anyhow, I'm going home to warm up and get a bath.'

The driver grunted without gratitude as Roy handed over the keys. He felt some anticipatory pleasure at the man's confusion and displeasure

143

when eventually he discovered that his blanket had disappeared.

He did not go directly home. If challenged, he would have said that he had gone to check whether Bob was still in bed. As usual the Mannions' back door was unlocked. He opened it and called cautiously, 'Anybody home?'

There was no reply. The Mannions, staunch attenders, would be at church. He had reckoned on this and, looking at the kitchen clock, calculated he might have twenty minutes. The warm fug of the kitchen was enticing and the aroma of roasting beef beguiling, but after a further precautionary shout and having warmed his hands briefly on the Aga, Roy was on his way upstairs.

It was as if Bob had just risen. The covers were pulled across the bed untidily, crumpled sheets and a pillow crushed in the corner against the wall evidence of a disturbed night's sleep, and the pink candlewick bedspread had been tossed to the floor. It felt cold, yet his smell remained, that distinctive aftershave he wore each day, to Mr Cole's amusement, among that indefinable mixture of male sweat and pheromones. Clothes were scattered around and on the glass-covered top of the incongruously feminine dressing table were a pile of old newspapers and some loose change. Bob Mannion had not been a tidy person.

Roy pulled a battered suitcase down from the top of the wardrobe, conscious that these might be the most perilous moments of all. He loaded the case with a selection of Bob's clothes, chosen at random. At the back of the wardrobe he found an old shoebox. Inside were a number of letters, which he scanned without interest. Most, which he discarded, were from Sheila. He stuffed what letters there were from the bank into his jacket pocket, together with the chequebook he found in the box. In his pocket he already had Bob's house key and wallet containing four pounds and his driving licence.

Now, the difficult part. He searched among Bob's belongings for a scrap of paper and eventually found a small pad of Basildon Bond. He knew Bob's handwriting well, from the invoices and receipts that he had written out very deliberately and with evident concentration at the garage. Thankfully, Bob was not a proficient writer. Roy would have described him as semi-literate at best. Rather than attempting copperplate, Bob had always written in laborious capital letters, which were relatively easy to mimic. Roy kept the message short:

SORRY. GONE TO WORK AT MR HURSTS STABELS. COUDNT TELL YOU OR SHEILA. PLEASE LET HER NO. I HAVE TO DO THIS. DONT FOLLOW ME. SORRY AGIAN. YOUR SON ROBERT MANNION

That would do. Roy knew of no Hurst's stables, but that didn't matter. It would make the job of investigation impossible if, as he surely would, Mr Mannion elected to try to find his son.

145

Roy tidied the bed, put the remaining clothes in a single pile on the floor and placed Bob's key on the note, which he left on the dressing table.

It was time, once he had secreted the suitcase at the garage, for that bath and some sleep.

8

The thaw was upon them and temperatures rose to the low sixties. It was a bizarre feeling, having survived that winter and emerged into a life once more.

Roy did not return to the remote location where he had left Bob's body. Nevertheless he fretted. The thaw had led to a swelling of the rivers and waterways. He feared each day that Bob's body might float away in the flood and drift downstream, washing up somewhere. He awaited the knock on the door. He had no story for this eventuality but thought that a repeated assertion of total ignorance might just see him home. If the police interviewed him it would be tempting to paint in some detail that might lead them to conclude that Bob had been waylaid by person or persons unknown — some hint at strange voices in the area where he had been waiting patiently by the lorry, for instance — but he knew this would be unwise.

As he had anticipated, Mr Mannion quizzed him on Bob's state of mind before his disappearance.

'Did you think Bob was behaving funny?'

'No, there was nothing unusual, though it was

odd he didn't turn up Sunday morning. He's usually pretty reliable.'

'Did he talk to you about wanting to be a stable boy?'

'Yes, I know all about him and horses. He did talk about it a lot, to tell the truth, but I didn't take an interest.'

'Did he ever talk about going to work for some Hurst?'

'Hurst? Nah, can't remember. Doesn't ring a bell. He talked about Cheltenham, though. Thought it was the usual pie in the sky, if I'm honest. In one ear and out the other.'

'Was he having second thoughts about getting married?'

'Yes, now you mention it, he did say he felt marriage was a bit like a noose around his neck. Have you thought of going to the police?'

★　★　★

He knew he must sit tight, ticking over the minutes and the hours and the days and the weeks. After three weeks, he took a few days off and, saying that he had to visit an aunt in Weston-super-Mare, took the long train journey to London and from there to Cheltenham. He found a boarding house, where he was on his most charming behaviour and took a room for two nights, paying in advance. Over breakfast he told the landlady that he was from London and considering taking up an executive post with the local council.

'Would you object to receiving mail for me

until I move up permanently?'

'No, Mr Mannion, not at all,' she had said.

'There's no need to forward anything. I'll be back regularly to pick stuff up. There'll be nothing urgent.'

He opened a new account at Lyons Bank in Cheltenham in the name of Robert Mannion, giving his newly acquired address. He showed the clerk Bob's driving licence and chequebook as evidence of identity, together with the letters and statements he had gathered from Bob's room. At Martins Bank, just down the same street, using the name Mannion again, he said that he was moving permanently to Cheltenham to work with horses, and requested that his account be transferred to the local branch.

Back in Essenham, there was still no word of Bob Mannion's whereabouts. When he saw Roy in the pub that weekend, Mr Mannion told him conspiratorially that his wife wept every evening. Mr Mannion was spending much more time in the pub now than he ever had.

'At least we got a postcard this morning. From Cheltenham. It's a relief. At least he's alive.'

'I should still contact the police if I were you,' said Roy.

'No. He obviously doesn't want to be here. The agony his mother's been through, though.'

Nearly four months after Bob's death Roy was ready to make his move. Summer had arrived, days that seemed almost never-ending. The skies across the Fens were unimaginably large and the high, long clouds that dashed through did not threaten rain. He gave his notice to Mr Cole in a low-key fashion and said he was going to try his luck in the Smoke, paid his landlady, packed his belongings in a small suitcase, newly purchased from Parke's department store in King's Lynn, and took the evening train to Liverpool Street.

Having found lodgings in south London, he paid a brief final visit to Cheltenham as Robert Mannion, to transfer his remaining funds from Bob's Martins Bank account to the new Lyons Bank account. He left instructions to transfer that account and its funds to its Clapham branch. He relayed the bad news to his prospective landlady with an expression of deep regret that the post, after all, had sadly fallen through.

Now he was able to start afresh.

9

Men and Women

1

Bob Mannion. How odd that he should come to mind. Roy cannot recall any particular sense of sadness. It was all utility, the requirement for immediate response and action. Even today he is impressed by his ability to corral his thoughts and proceed logically. And that winter. The coldest for over two hundred years. No one had thought it would ever come to an end. For Bob it hadn't.

Roy now feels, if not sorrow, a kind of regret at Bob's death, mindful at the same time that in dying Bob had delivered him a route out of his plight, stranded on the Fens, left behind by the floods. Having moved back to London, he had become submerged in the metropolis, after a short time cautiously able to dip into the bank account he had opened in the name Robert Mannion with Bob's money, even occasionally to be Mr R. Mannion, indeed Roy Mannion, when it served his needs.

Over the years the natural accretion of identity had occurred, that circular evidencing and self-referencing that came to prove beyond doubt that he was Mannion. The availability of an alternative persona, backed by official documents, has been more than useful. At times the challenge had been to maintain the flickering self that was Roy Courtnay. It is possible, though unlikely, that shortly he may need again to take the wraps off Mannion and give him one last lap of the circuit. Depending, that is, on how things go with Betty and how assiduous and litigious her family choose to become.

Regrets? He's had a few, especially when he and Vincent had had to do over Martin, Bernie, Dave and Bryn. Especially Martin, the poor sod. But not really. Live by the sword et cetera, et cetera.

But Bob Mannion. Really. What has triggered that thought? The strange chemistry of the brain.

To his surprise, he is crying. His reflection in the mirror confirms this. He sees his long, tired face, those eyes once fierce and now merely mournful, and the streaks of tears running down sagging cheeks. He places his razor carefully on the basin and grips its sides with both hands to steady himself as he sobs.

Bob was like all those others left behind, he tells himself. Once in the past they might as well be dead. Thinking about them: to him, it's a waste of time and energy. For him, they are dead anyway.

Maureen, he knows, is in the public eye. Formerly a junior minister in the Department for Education, she now pronounces from on high in the House of Lords, a vociferous and rather irritating supporter of the deprived and sundry minorities. Easy from such a privileged vantage point. Perhaps he should have backed that particular horse for a little longer. It had, though, just been a fork in the road. For him she too is as dead as Bob, and has been since that day he walked out of their dingy Clapham flat.

Those sisters, all those years ago. They had needed a lesson too. And received one. The elder ones had laughed at his gaucheness. The younger one had humiliated him. They had all learned.

Lord Stanbrook's son, Rupert, whom he once dandled on his knee, is now the ailing fifth earl, with the scandal-beset feckless playboy son. Rupert's own father, Charles, is long departed.

He hasn't kept tabs on them. He's picked bits up in the media and the rest he's just invented. It doesn't matter. Dead. All dead. To him, leastways. And none to be grieved, save perhaps Bob. Bob was a good lad, like Vincent is but in a different way, impressionable in the right way, malleable. And who could argue that Bob, in his death, had not been extraordinarily helpful?

'Fuck!' he shouts loudly. There is yet fire in his belly. 'Fuck.'

What is he doing? Rambling away like some muttering old pensioner. Get a grip, man. At least now he knows when he's drifting. The time may come when he doesn't even realize it. Better dead than gaga. But he knows he isn't. He doesn't forget. He remembers everything. Dementia isn't his problem; fixity of purpose is. Losing the will to strive is what he fears.

'Fuck,' he says again, more quietly as he regards the face in the mirror with a cold dispassion. He does not particularly like what he sees.

'Roy?' calls Betty from downstairs.

'Yes?' he replies.

'I heard you shouting. Is everything all right? Are you OK?'

'I'm fine, my dear,' he replies evenly. 'I thought I'd cut myself shaving. Not so nimble as I once was. But it's all right. Sorry. 'Scuse my French.'

2

He has begun recently to call her 'my dear' more often. Too often, really. At first it was occasional and hesitant; now it is close to automatic, especially when he chooses to be patronizing. Which is not infrequently.

She is not sure whether this is a considered process of establishing himself yet more prominently in her life, or whether it is entirely unconscious. Need she fear a proposal? The thought of his attempting to go down on one knee is almost enough for her to dial 999.

Finally, she supposes it is harmless and quite sweet in its way, if sweet were ever a term one might use in connection with him. And she remains glad that he is still here.

They have had their sandwich lunch and she has lit the gas fire. They sit together in the living room, she with her book and he with his hands in his lap, bored and irritable.

'What do you really think of women?' she asks, for want of something better to say.

* * *

Roy's heart sinks. Not one of those interminable discussions that come from nowhere, head in no direction that he can distinguish and seem calculated to humiliate him. He'd had enough of that to last a lifetime from Maureen. But better not turn this into an argument.

Men and women, he thinks. Two completely different species.

'What do you mean, my dear?' he asks civilly, but glaring.

It appears she is not going to be put off. 'I suppose our generation's accustomed to a different relationship between the sexes.'

Give me strength, he thinks. But he retains his composure.

'Oh, I don't know,' he says, treating the question as though it were reasonable enough. 'I'm not an expert on these things.'

'You don't have to be an expert, surely?'

'Well, no. I didn't mean that. I've known a few women in my life.' He hopes the arch smile might do the trick.

'Yes?' says Betty.

'And. And, well, I've always found that I get on with women. See eye to eye with them. Lots of men don't, you know. I like women. Especially you.'

'I understand that. But in general? The differences between men and women?'

He thinks: they do like to talk, don't they?

'Well, I could ask the same question of you. What do you think of men?'

154

'Fair enough. I find men these days more insecure than they were. There are plenty who seem utterly secure in themselves. Rather more secure than they should be, in reality. But . . . '

He looks and listens.

' . . . overall men seem less . . . solid . . . than they were. And more full of spite. I suppose it's only natural. As we've become 'liberated'. Though I can't say I feel especially liberated,' she continues. 'Before, our roles were clearly defined. But two wars have seen all of that change.'

History, he thinks. More history. She's bloody lecturing me. Good God. But he beams polite attention at her.

'I suppose it's only to be expected that men should feel unsettled and threatened. Not that women seem to be the winners, particularly.'

'Hmm,' he says.

'One sees more extremes. Lack of confidence, but also aggression. Expressions of insecurity, both of them.'

'I suppose so,' he says. 'I've never lacked confidence.'

'No, but that's you, isn't it? You were taught to be in charge. Simply because you're a male. You were conditioned not to think of things any differently.'

Saved a lot of bloody time too, he thinks.

She continues. 'What I'm saying is that men no longer quite know what they're supposed to be.'

'Weak, a lot of them. We're pretty straightforward when it comes down to it. No complications, no hidden emotions. Don't think I'm against

155

women's rights. But men who are unsure of their quote unquote identity are drama queens. I just think we are who we are and getting on with things is all we can do. Thinking too much can get you into all kinds of grief.'

And talking.

'So, women. What are we like?'

'Where do I begin?' he says, smiling. 'Marvellous. Wonderful. Confusing. Frustrating. Illogical.'

She says nothing. He knows he is striking the wrong note but cannot find the right one.

'What I mean is,' he ventures, 'I'm all for a bit of mystery between men and women. If I had it all worked out I'd be a much unhappier man.'

'I thought you did have it all worked out,' she says, smiling.

Good. We may be making our way back to terra firma.

'Oh no,' he says. 'Certainly not. Everyone has to have an answer for everything these days. Not me. If we just lived a little, did what we were good at, toned down the thinking, we might all be a bit better off.'

'So a lack of knowledge is a good thing?'

'Oh no. Of course not. But . . . '

'You still haven't answered my question. About women. About me.'

He ventures another sheepish grin.

'Betty, I've nothing but respect for you. You've achieved so much in your life. You leave me standing.'

It is an unstoppable, pointless juggernaut. Roy is not concerned about the sense of what he says;

it simply fills the gaps. He hardly stops to consider whether his statements are comprehensible, let alone cogent, still less whether he actually believes this garbage. It's all just part of the game, he thinks: men and women.

He bestows on her a look of undiluted venom veiled by a beneficent smile. She is too stupid to see it, he thinks.

★   ★   ★

He doesn't realize I can see it, she thinks. She enjoys making him squirm, in a way. He cannot, or will not, marshal an argument. He is right that he is less intelligent than she is, so there is an element of cruelty in her tweaking him like this. It is good, though, to see him floundering, mildly discomposed and losing control. He is just babbling. It is a small vengeance, perhaps taken unwisely. She supposes she will later need to make it up to him, by saying the thing he wants to hear.

3

He is in the lavatory, in some difficulty. The stomach cramps have arrived again with no notice and he has had to rush upstairs, speedily dropping his trousers and underpants and settling on to the thing with a momentary sigh of relief that there had been no preliminary mishap before the onslaught. A painful and troubling series of detonations rock the core of his body

157

with shots of kerosene fire, followed swiftly by a noxious cascade of liquid during which his entire being seems to be sluicing into the bowl. He is alarmed by the explosive force of the action. He bends forward, his every muscle tensed in a vain effort to gain mastery. The smell, sulphur and rotting innards, is unspeakable; he is close to gagging.

He sits there and lets it happen. He has no choice. It is involuntary — it seems almost as if a valve has blown and he is being rid of badness — yet it is also effortful. His organs and reflexes are no longer his to govern. This is happening to him in the most intimate fashion, yet he has no say in how he responds. He is afraid, both of the moment and of a near future of which this may be a waymarker. It is the loss of control that he fears most, not the pain, not the indignity. He whimpers quietly.

When he is, finally, null and void, he is exhausted. He remains seated awhile to steady himself, trembling and wheezing, anxious, unduly hot, mind racing. Having cleaned himself as best he can and holding his trousers up by a shaky hand, his braces dangling and his shirt tail untucked, he shuffles slowly through to his bedroom, using his free hand to support himself against the wall. Eventually he flops on to the bed and there is an audible twang from the springs. Exhausted still, his sphincter burning sore, he stares at the ceiling and forces himself to think.

Betty has proved something of a disappointment in a way. So gullible and ripe for the taking. No challenge. It's all been too easy, with no adrenalin burn. Well, no matter. Diversion and entertainment were only secondary reasons for this whole enterprise. More importantly she is, to use the phrase in vogue these days, minted. The letters from her fund manager that he reads at his leisure when he goes through her bedroom while she is out tell him that. And if her complacency and gullibility mean less challenge in the game, it may be no bad thing. If this adventure has shown him one thing it is that you become less agile in every way as you age. Once this one is over that will be it for him. A sad thought, but there you are.

She calls from downstairs, 'Are you all right, Roy?'

'I'm OK,' he replies weakly.

She comes upstairs and enters the bedroom. 'Oh dear,' she says, seeing him spreadeagled in unkempt disarray on top of the counterpane. He is flushed and agitated. 'You don't look too well.'

'I'm fine,' he says with a small confiding smile. 'Just taken agin something I've eaten. I'm all right really.'

She sits on the edge of the bed. 'Are you sure?' she asks, her brow furrowed in a particularly attractive way. If only he had known her in her youth. And his.

'I'm quite all right, thank you, my dear,' he says, kindly smile still intact. He pats her hand.

'I've been thinking, Roy . . . '

'Yes?'

'Perhaps I could benefit from reviewing my investments. But I don't know where to begin.'

He is at once alert and with difficulty props himself up on one elbow.

'Surely you have someone who handles your portfolio?'

'Well, yes, this company . . . '

'Company? Ah.'

'What is it, Roy?'

'I'll wager they take a large commission each year for doing very little. I suppose they write to you every so often. Do you know anyone there by name? Have you ever spoken to anyone there?'

'Well, no. The funds were invested so long ago and I wouldn't know who to ask for. They seem all right from the letters.'

'I'm sure they are. In their own way. But . . . '

'They lack, I suppose, well, the personal touch.'

'Hmm.'

He waits. She must say it, not he.

'I was wondering . . . '

'Yes?' Not too quick.

'You mentioned you knew someone . . . '

'Vincent, you mean?'

'Yes. Your friend.'

'Oh, Vincent's not so much a friend as a professional. Though I'd trust him with my life.'

'Do you think he'd be prepared to talk to me about my investments?'

'Oh yes. I'm sure he would. On a non-commitment basis of course. If I put a word in I've no doubt he'd be happy to speak with you.'

Easy. Much easier than he had imagined. The pain in his stomach seems to have dissipated a little.

10

August 1957
Never Had It So Good

1

They would have to make a rapid and discreet departure. This meant the sprinkling of thousands of francs among those who would facilitate it: first and foremost the hotel manager and down the hierarchy through the head concierge, the desk clerk, all the way to the lift boy. He formed neat piles on the desk as he calculated the exchange rate.

They had completed the packing, admittedly rather haphazardly and frantically, and Roy rang down to the front desk. When he was put through to the manager he said quietly, 'We're ready.'

'I am not sure,' came the reply, 'whether I should contact the police after all. I have the reputation of the hotel to consider.'

He did not have time to count to ten, so he counted to three.

'That's what I'm thinking about too, Claude,' he said, his voice laden with sympathy and regret. 'It's the very reason we need to manage this together.'

'But if the police later discovered that I have assisted the escape of a felon . . . '

161

'Lord Stanbrook is not a felon,' said Roy with irritated emphasis. 'I've explained it to you. It was a misunderstanding. A situation that got out of hand. I'm trying to handle this with delicacy.'

'Hmm. But it is I who am left to deal with the consequences if the police begin to ask difficult questions.'

'There are no consequences for you. There are no difficult questions. You simply say you've no idea where the noble lord is.'

'That is easy for you to say. But it is I who am taking the risk with the name of this hotel. On my own.'

'Not at all, not at all. Oh no. We're both attempting to preserve the reputation of the George V. What could be worse than the arrest of a member of the British aristocracy in its halls? What would your clientele think? I see your point, though. I'm asking a lot of you. You've a lot to take on trust. On reflection, I think the consideration I mentioned may be a little too modest.'

With this, the conversation was easy to complete. Roy counted out a few more notes on to the largest pile on the desk. His employer was sitting in the bedroom on the edge of the bed. Through the open door Roy could see he had his head in his hands.

He walked through and touched him gently on the shoulder.

'All right, Charles. We're just about ready to go. Five minutes?'

'Problems?' asked Stanbrook.

'Not really. The manager wanted more, that's

162

all. Par for the course. There'll be no problems.'

He gave the manservant careful instructions. He must wait two hours before travelling to Orly in the car that had been ordered. He must take His Lordship's luggage with him.

The manservant remained in the room. Roy led Stanbrook down the corridor to the waiting lift. They each carried a suitcase, for show. The manager was inside with the attendant.

'You are leaving very early,' said the manager, addressing Roy.

Stanbrook stood at the back of the lift, looking dazedly into the mirror.

'I want to complete the formalities at Orly well before time. I'd like to avoid any misunderstandings.'

The lift took them to the sub-basement and the shabby underpinnings beneath the shiny carapace. The shattering of glamorous illusions did not matter in the circumstances. The manager led them through long corridors lit by bare light bulbs strung along the centre of the roughly plastered ceiling.

Roy took a brief, anxious glance from side to side outside the trade entrance before ushering Charles quickly into the car. He did not trust the manager.

There were a couple of moments to take stock once the driver had clanked the vehicle into gear and pulled away, the transmission whining like a reluctant child.

Thank goodness last night he'd seen what was happening before it really got out of hand and been able to drag Charles away. Thank goodness they'd told everyone they were staying at the Crillon.

Thank goodness he'd had the foresight to pack Charles's civvy passport. He checked again that it was safely in his inside pocket, together with his own. He had his small attaché case on his lap with the rest of their documents and the all-important cash. Charles seemed to be holding up. He was looking distantly through the side window of the car, but at least the tearfulness had dried up.

They sped towards Orly and sunlight skidded off the windows. Through the corroded transmission tunnel of the old Citroën Roy could see the tarmacadam flash by beneath their feet.

Now was the moment. In his passable French Roy told the driver that they had changed their minds and required a different destination. He waved a wad of notes in the old man's face and directed him to drive to Calais, telling him that if he arrived there in time for the three o'clock sailing the fare would be doubled. Absurd: that amount of money would have been sufficient to buy the old crate outright, and a tankful of petrol into the bargain. The driver grunted with a sour expression that Roy took to be acquiescence. For good measure, he reminded the driver that he knew these streets and would detect immediately if he took an unusual route. Pure bluff, of course. The driver grunted once more. A sidelong glare was all it took to elicit an acceptable if not enthusiastic apology from the driver.

Roy turned to look in the back. Charles had

fallen asleep, lost and vulnerable. The poor sod must be exhausted. Roy, however, needed to remain alert as the car raced through the northern French countryside, the smell of hot leather and male sweat rising. He looked impatiently left and right at the unremitting flatness as they made their way up the *route nationale*. Three hundred kilometres or thereabouts. The driver would have to go some if he was to make it.

At Calais they alighted at the port. The driver had earned his bonus and sped away. Roy smelt salt and thought of England, and safety. They smoked a cigarette by the harbour wall while Roy watched for unusual activity that might suggest their imminent detention. Satisfied, he strolled to the office, engaged his winning smile and bought a pair of foot passenger tickets from the pretty girl there. Foot passengers who turned up at the port without tickets would, he guessed, be relatively rare. They would be noticed, but this was a risk that had to be taken. It should not matter given the genial mien he deployed.

They delayed until the final moment before running for the boat, sprinting through concrete concourses and submitting briefly to a passport check. Roy half feared an officious check here, just to spite perfidious Albion, but all that was required was more charm, a ready smile and the use of rather more fluent French than had been deployed with the railway official to compliment France's wonderful capital city, its efficient rail network and its friendly natives.

It was not until they had disembarked at

Dover that Charles Stanbrook uttered his first words since leaving the George V.

'Where's the bloody car, then?' he asked.

'I couldn't ring ahead from the hotel. That manager would have been listening to every word.'

'So how do we get back?'

'The train, like everyone else. Ticket office is over there.'

'Fuck,' said Charles, before melting back into a sullen silence. He allowed Roy to guide him by the elbow.

At Victoria they took a cab to the London residence. As they crossed the threshold Roy made the usual transition from directing Charles, his unruly charge, to being Lord Stanbrook's faithful employee.

2

He liked this job. He had fallen on his feet almost ten years before when the post came up. Opened up invitingly in front of him, more like.

After the incident back in '46 he'd been put on light duties for some time. He hadn't been sent back to his home unit, which in any case was in the process of being disbanded. They hadn't really known what to do with him. First he flew a desk in an office in Brussels, working on what would later be known as the Treaty of Brussels. A very small cog in a very large machine, and floundering in the sea of words. Not his thing at all. Oh no. Then he was shipped off to Vienna to deal with transport dockets for the British occupying force.

It was there that he had met Major Stanbrook of the Intelligence Corps. They took to each other instantly and Stanbrook had finagled Roy on to his staff. When Stanbrook decided to take up his place in the Lords, he asked Roy to become an unofficial aide. Roy had jumped at the chance.

In the days after coming back from France Lord Stanbrook regained his characteristic ebullience. Almost immediately, Roy set off once more for Paris to iron out the unfortunate misunderstandings that had occurred. Claude at the George V was more obliging, no longer faced with the imminent end of his career. Claude had successfully managed matters with the police, deploying an expression of wounded ignorance, and gave Roy the name of the inspector who was dealing with the case.

At the police station Roy received a polite welcome. Monsieur l'Inspecteur was intrigued to learn what had actually occurred. It shook him to discover that the truth was somewhat different from what he had heard from various of the club staff and the alleged victim himself. Roy explained the unfortunate circumstances of the skirmish and subsequent accident that had led to the man's two broken arms and insisted that any allegations regarding His Lordship were both groundless and maliciously motivated. The man himself had since admitted that he had misunderstood Lord Stanbrook's intentions towards the young woman he had been accompanying. The inspector shook his head with a weary knowledge of the world.

'My employer is a wealthy man,' said Roy, 'a pillar of British society, a government minister and, I have to say, of unimpeachable integrity. He will not fail to go to law if these scurrilous and baseless accusations are pursued.' He gave the inspector the business card of the expensive lawyers in rue de l'Échelle whom he had already engaged on the matter. Then he suggested that he buy the inspector a coffee, or indeed something stronger.

They stood at the bar, smoking the American cigarettes Roy had thought to pack before leaving London, each with a café express and a small glass of marc. Roy drained his glass and the detective followed suit. Roy signalled for refills.

'The difficulty is,' he said, 'that there are just so many people looking for an angle. Any angle. It seems there's been something of a moral collapse since the war in which our nations fought so valiantly side by side. Honesty is no longer valued; it's all about what you can get away with.'

The inspector nodded. He was not expected to speak.

'Lord Stanbrook is — well, he wouldn't want to be described as a war hero — a courageous man who continues to serve his country. It would be most unfortunate if his reputation was dragged down by some scoundrel. I'm sure it's not something your country would want either.'

He paused. He did not know whether he had

spoken enough and they could quickly conclude their business. He had a train to catch. Both knew implicitly that the conversation was a formality. The deal had been done when the police officer accepted the offer of a drink. As ever, though, the lie had to be maintained. For a little longer, evidently.

'I'm certain that no officer of the Paris police would wish to be complicit in allowing extortion to take place. Least of all you, Jacques. May I call you Jacques?'

The other man inclined his head slightly. Roy detected the hint of a smile.

'In that case I'm reassured. My work is done. I've no need to protest my employer's innocence any further. I have complete confidence in your judgement. But should anything unexpected happen, you know how to contact me.'

With that, he put his hat on, placed a large-denomination bill on the zinc for the barman, shook hands with the police officer and walked out of the cafe, leaving behind, placed below the evening newspaper he had bought on the way in, a rather plump envelope. He made his train with ten minutes to spare.

3

The rules when they were at the London residence or the country house were different from when they were, as Lord Stanbrook put it, on the razzle.

Informality was out of the question. Roy's

169

employer was His Lordship rather than Charles and appropriate deference was de rigueur. Nor would Roy have wanted it any differently. It was less complicated. There were moments of awkwardness, particularly when Stanbrook required Roy's presence at dinner with guests at Burnsford, but these occasions were relatively infrequent. The guests concerned would generally be aware of the reasons for Roy's presence and his standing with his employer. There was, for Roy, little more than a need for care with words and actions, part of his professional repertoire. He found it relatively easy to circulate among these people.

This was one of those more relaxed weekends. No political guests. They were to gather for an informal dinner on the Friday, the guests arriving according to the time they had been able to escape the rigours of London. Burnsford House was located in the anonymous Midlands, south of Birmingham and east of the twee Tudor affectations of Stratford, but well away from the grimy industrial cities of the East Midlands. Unprepossessing Northampton was the nearest town, but visitors by train were more generally collected at Daventry.

Having delivered a rather irritable viscount and his wife to the house, shown them to their room and left them to unpack, Roy sat smoking in the study, undisturbed. The party this week-end would be small. They would be ten at table tonight: Lord Stanbrook and his long-suffering wife; their daughter Francesca; Viscount Wexford and his wife, Margaret; Joachim von Hessenthal, a German count of Stanbrook's long acquaintance; Oliver Wright, the Foreign Secretary's private secretary; Roy himself; and Sir Thomas and his wife, Sylvia. Sylvia. He sighed quietly.

Roy was there to make up the party, as Lady Stanbrook did not like to dine with odd numbers at her table. This at least was the fiction. To be sure, if one of the guests failed to materialize he would drop out. But his presence at the table had little to do with the numbers.

They would dress for dinner only on the Saturday. He had some time, therefore. Wexford and his wife were already here, von Hessenthal was being conveyed by his own driver, and Roy would avoid at all costs being present to greet the Bankses. This left Mr Wright. Roy checked his watch and saw that he had a few minutes to savour his cigarette and cup of tea before setting off for the station in the Humber.

'I understand you'll be joining us for dinner,' said Wright as the windscreen wipers marked time on their journey back to the house.

'That's right, sir,' replied Roy. 'Informal dinner tonight. Formal tomorrow.'

'Righty-ho.'

Oliver Wright was a pensive young man, angular and gaunt to the point of apparent malnutrition. In government circles he was known as a policy genius and quite the eligible young man going places. Wright sat beside Roy in the front of the car, his bony white hands turning restlessly in his lap as if he was made nervous by Roy's deft handling of the vehicle at speed through the puddles and around country

171

corners. He frowned.

'Where exactly do you fit in in the house?' he asked. 'I mean, if it's not too presumptuous a question.'

'Not at all, sir,' said Roy. 'My role is as Lord Stanbrook's aide on business matters. A factotum, you might say.'

'You run the estate for him?'

'Oh no, sir. I've very little to do with the estate itself. Beyond me, all that stuff. Lord Stanbrook has diverse business interests. I manage his portfolio inasmuch as I ensure that all necessary matters are attended to and nothing is forgotten. I accompany him on business trips.'

'A fixer, you mean.'

'If you care to put it that way, sir. Though doubtless Lord Stanbrook might express it slightly differently.'

'Quite. Have you met this von Hessenthal chap?'

'No, I haven't. I understand Lord Stanbrook knows him from before the war. Both were army officers of course and knew each other professionally in the 1930s. I doubt whether the Graf von Hessenthal would regard it as a happy coincidence, though, that Lord Stanbrook was the major to whom the general surrendered his weapon in 1945.'

'And who else will be there?'

'Lord Stanbrook's daughter Francesca, as well as Lord Wexford and Sir Thomas Banks and their wives. I believe you know Sir Thomas?'

Wright looked at Roy as if significance attached to the question. Roy kept his eyes on the road and accelerated into the corner, just enough for the vehicle to slide on the road surface and alarm Wright yet remain fully under Roy's control.

'Yes,' said Wright. 'We've come across each other on government business.'

'That reminds me. His Lordship asked me to emphasize that this is an informal weekend. Relaxed. Emphatically not a duty weekend. He wants everyone to feel completely at ease. No discussion of politics or other matters of government. No, um, standing on ceremony.'

'Got it,' said Wright.

Roy fancied that he might have smiled for the first time during this journey.

4

Sylvia looked across the table at him with what she judged to be suitably disguised desire. Her judgement on discretion and subterfuge, born of experience, was infallible.

He was beautiful, simply beautiful. It was the only way she could describe him. Tall, effortless, languid, yet muscular and athletic, with foppish blond locks that periodically he swept away contemptuously from his brow. And those eyes: blue yet with depth and apparent scornful omniscience, and frightening. From his looks he might have been an Oxford blue, captain of the England rugby fifteen, or a captain in the Commandos. But he would never be confused with one of her class: apart from his slightly unplaceable accent, he possessed a greater steeliness. He excited her and scared her in equal measure.

The beard. It was not a sobriquet she sought but one that vile Gertrude had flung at her. It was a word, in this sense, that Gertrude had evidently picked up on her recent trip to New York. To Sylvia's knowledge the vulgar term had not yet reached British society. This had not prevented Gertrude from using it during one of their private teas.

Sylvia's marriage had not so much been arranged as arrived at. The delicate problem had been the subject of much discussion, in hushed tones and in opaque terms, between the parents before her mother commented that Tommy Banks would be a good catch. Sylvia had acquiesced in the fashion expected of her and from there it had fallen into place on a predictably smooth path, seemingly without her involvement. But Sylvia had known precisely the kind of marriage into which she was entering.

★   ★   ★

Roy glanced discreetly at Sylvia. She seemed to be staring at him, but possibly this was his own self-consciousness at work. This was a tacit agreement that suited all parties moderately well. And moderately well was the English way. He doubted whether the supercilious German count would be remotely aware of the delicate balances in play.

She was indeed strikingly attractive, with the

174

poise of her breeding and upbringing, her thin oval face, large eyes and pert nose framed by a fashionable chignon that exposed to best advantage that delicious neck, whose surfaces he would shower with kisses. She was full-bosomed and slim, almost thin.

Sylvia had confided her fantasy of remaining married while shaping a future life with him, maintaining a filigree approximation of respectability. He knew it was nonsense: she would in the end adhere to her social norms and anyway he could see in her the sclerotic old crow she would later become. For as long as it lasted they would restrict themselves to their furtive liaisons at weekends such as this, during the week at the town house she shared with Sir Thomas, and on various snatched occasions at discreet hotels in the Home Counties. This suited him rather better than the complications of what he might call a relationship.

After dinner the men took their port and cigars in the library. The count droned on about his estates in Sachsen-Anhalt in the eastern part of Germany.

'Germany is so uncivilized,' he announced. 'The rabble has taken over. In the east they have created their socialist state. Their state! It is the Bolsheviks who run it in reality. It is an experiment that will fail. It is even worse in the west, with their economic miracle. Completely unsuitable people are becoming prosperous at the expense of the old values. In their own way these people are as unacceptable as those who came before.'

'Do you have difficulty getting to your land in the east?' asked Wright.

'Not at present, no,' said von Hessenthal. 'I have a reasonable relationship with the authorities there, despite their dogma. I have to ensure that I make appropriate contributions and cultivate agreeable relations with the local Party men, but it works. I cannot guarantee it forever, however. The border is continually developed and I hear rumours every so often that the authorities are seeking to regularize the position of my properties. Regularize is the expression they use. Steal would be mine. Fortunately, I have sufficient funds and land away from their grasp.'

'You live mainly in London?' asked Wright pleasantly.

'That's right. I have land also in Bavaria. But Germany today is so cheap. Unpleasant. East or west, it makes little difference.' He shuddered for dramatic effect, then said, 'I do not wish to be impolite, Charles, but may I ask a question?'

'Of course,' said Stanbrook.

'It seems that you have invited one of your staff to dinner.'

'Courtnay? Well . . . '

'I have to say it makes me rather uncomfortable to be discussing my affairs in such circumstances,' he said, looking directly at Roy with a distaste that he did not attempt to hide.

It's not me you should be worrying about, thought Roy. It's the likes of Oliver Wright, itching to get their claws into you. But he smiled back benignly.

176

'Well,' said Stanbrook, 'Courtnay is in a different position from most of my people. I — '

'No, sir,' interrupted Roy. 'Please. I was about to turn in anyway. Goodnight, gentlemen.'

He stood from the leather armchair, stubbed out his cigar and, still smiling broadly, left the room. In his peripheral vision, he noted the count's eyes following his leisurely progress with undisguised animus.

In truth he was unaffected by von Hessenthal's comments. He was better off out of these conversations stilted by politesse and the utter tedium of the inevitable game of billiards. He went to his room and prepared himself for Sylvia.

She was waiting for him. He was rough with her, as was her preference, pinning her weak arms as he pounded relentlessly into her softness with little regard for her well-being. There would be time for tender embraces later in the night, though no place for love. She shrieked exultantly and soon it was over.

Sir Thomas and Oliver Wright would be in the next bedroom shortly. At four Roy would be turfed out to return to his own bed and the same would happen to Wright. The doors to the interconnecting bathroom would be unlocked and by the time the breakfast trays were brought up marital bliss would have been reinstated. No one in the house would be fooled, save perhaps the obnoxious German and his man, but it would satisfy the niceties.

As she whispered to him, lying in his arms, he did not listen, looking with blind eyes to the

177

ceiling. I despise these people, he was thinking. I despise you.

5

The next morning he thought better of mingling with the party and took his breakfast in the kitchen with von Hessenthal's bespectacled manservant. He discovered that Ernst Maier had only recently been appointed to the count's staff. Breakfast dragged as Roy had to listen to the boring little man in his badly cut suit while he told his life story in good English spoken in an appalling accent.

Hoping to shake Maier off, Roy announced he was going to take a walk in the gardens. Maier said he would accompany him.

'Things are changing in Germany,' said the little man, 'as they will all over the world. The West has capitalism today but in the future we'll all be together under a socialist government.'

'Quite the speech for the servant of a count,' said Roy.

'I wouldn't describe myself as a servant. And I doubt the count would either. I'm more an executive assistant. The count knows the necessary compromises. At home he never refers to himself as the count. He's plain Hessenthal, Comrade Hessenthal on occasions. He refers here to his 'estates' as if they still exist. In fact they're being developed into cooperative farms as we speak. He's desperately trying to secure some kind of compensation. My job is to awaken him to the realities. And to keep him from the grasp of such as your clever Mr Wright. I'm trying to do this gently. I'm not heartless. Some of my comrades call me soft.'

Maier stopped and turned to Roy.

'We all have to predict the future and make the necessary provisions,' said Maier. 'Arrive at accommodations. I'm sure you've had to do that.'

A most peculiar little man. Roy began walking again. He said, 'No doubt this moment in history creates the need for some odd arrangements. Strange bedfellows. I can understand that the count — or Comrade Hessenthal — has needed to make adjustments.'

'Indeed. And he must make more. We all must.'

For a while they walked in silence through the rose garden, Maier paying no attention to Lady Stanbrook's treasured collection. They found themselves some distance from the house, strolling through the small copse close to the boundary of the estate.

'As, no doubt, must you.'

It took Roy a moment to understand that Maier was continuing the conversation where he had discontinued it.

'Well, as you all say, we must all cope with changing circumstances. I'm a pretty adaptable chap. I get on all right.' He smiled modestly.

'Yes. I can see that,' said Maier, as if in doubt. 'But you may need to be able to adapt again in the future.'

'To a new socialist state? I hardly think so. I

179

doubt many in England would share your world view.'

'I'm sure not. We could debate that at some other time. But there could be more pressing reasons for you to consider your position.'

Roy continued to humour him. 'Like what? I don't understand.'

'Perhaps I can explain.'

Coming out into a meadow as they circled back to the house, they sat on the trunk of a felled tree. Maier took out a packet of Russian cigarettes and offered Roy one. He declined. Shrugging his shoulders, Maier lit his own noxious-smelling tube and wiped his brow with the grubby sleeve of his jacket. The sun bore down on them relentlessly but neither man removed his jacket.

'After the war you were something of a fearless pursuer of concentration camp employees.'

'Where did you hear that?' said Roy, alert but disguising the fact with a long and lazy stretch of the arms.

'Isn't it true, then? I was informed that this is what you did.'

'I did get involved in some of the clear-up work after the war. It was completely routine. In fact very trivial.'

'You're too modest. Heady days, weren't they? Confusion, destruction and chaos, yet we were constructing something from the horror. I can testify to that. I was conscripted to the German army in 1940 but captured in the retreat from Stalingrad in '42. It was the finest thing that happened to me. I was able to prove my loyalty to socialism. I volunteered to help destroy the Nazis.'

'Very noble,' said Roy.

'Not particularly. It was survival. To survive, we do what we have to do. Don't we?'

No answer was required or expected.

Maier continued. 'Things happened in all the chaos. Things we didn't want to happen. But somehow we coped with them. Though you weren't involved in the conflict, I believe you know a little of this.'

'How so?'

'In your endeavours to track down Nazis. I believe that there was a tragic incident where one of your comrades lost his life.'

Roy was silent.

'A sad event,' said Maier. 'But one through which you came. And I'm glad to see you're settled now.'

'How do you know this?' Roy regretted the question as it left his lips.

'Our authorities maintain archives, of course. I have some contacts in the right places. They took the trouble to search out the particular records, which give a vivid account of the incident. It was prepared by our Russian comrades. I was fortunate to gain access to it. But this sun, it's fierce. Shall we go to the house and have a drink of water? Perhaps we'll talk further later.'

He stood and waved his hand in front of his face in a futile attempt to move the still, dank air.

Back at the house, Maier seemed somehow to vanish without Roy registering it. He must speak again to the wiry little man but he must not

181

chase him. He could not afford to be the supplicant.

After lunch Lady Stanbrook sent for him at Sylvia's prompting. He was required to play tennis, whatever the count's feelings. First, there was a singles competition for the men. Von Hessenthal sat out, claiming a leg wound he had sustained during the war, and watched with an acerbic expression while sipping lemonade. Roy dealt with Sir Thomas, probably twenty years his senior, in short fashion before Oliver Wright somehow contrived to lose to short, stout Lord Stanbrook, who beamed as he wiped sweat from his bright red forehead.

The ladies declined to play their own singles, so the men moved immediately to the final. Becoming bored and with the thought of Maier nagging at him, Roy dispatched his employer in even more abrupt fashion than was normal. After the six-love pasting, Lord Stanbrook was gracious if slightly bemused. When they played, Roy normally gave no quarter — nor did Stanbrook expect him to — but this had been brutal. Roy's mind was elsewhere and he excused himself, leaving the remaining men and the ladies to organize their mixed-doubles pairs. Sylvia looked disappointed.

Maier was sitting at a table on the terrace in his shirtsleeves, reading a book. Roy sat next to him. Good Lord, it was hot, and it was good now to sit in the shade.

Maier said, 'Did you win?'

'Yes. What you were saying earlier.'

'Yes?'

182

'What are you driving at?'

Maier closed his book and placed it carefully on the table.

'I'm glad we may talk frankly. I mentioned that we all have to secure our futures. There may be a way in which you can help yourself in this regard.'

'How?'

'By performing a service for our country.'

'Our country? What do you mean, our country?'

'I meant my country and Hessenthal's, of course. What else? What I'm suggesting is in all of our interests. I presume I can skip the preamble about understanding between nations. You have access to information that would be of value to my comrades and me. To assist us would assure your future position in the scheme of things. And we will pay you. Very well. Even a socialist state can pay well. From each according to his ability, to each according to his need. And I can see your need may be very great indeed.' He smirked.

'Absolutely not. I'm going to report this to Lord Stanbrook.'

'Feel free. But I believe you won't. You'll think first. You'll consider the consequences, and the benefits you'd be forgoing. This is good. There's time for you to do this.'

'I don't need time,' said Roy quietly. 'I'm a loyal British citizen. I want nothing to do with this, or with you.'

'Of course. A good speech. That's your right. It's a natural immediate response. But give it some thought. We'll see each other again no doubt.' Smiling, Maier stood and bowed almost imperceptibly, in an oddly military manner. 'Until then.'

6

It was the following Tuesday, sooner than he had imagined, that Roy's path again crossed that of Ernst Maier.

He had returned to town with Lord Stanbrook the previous day. Walking through St James's Park, he spotted them, leaning casually against the railings, looking at him and smiling. They raised their hats and he attempted to pretend he had not noticed them. In his peripheral vision he saw them move quickly, as if to intercept him at the next junction of paths. He turned around and marched back the way he had come, to return to the club.

They caught up with him, slightly out of breath, still smiling. Maier wore the same cheap shiny suit that hung from his shoulders. Roy recognized the other man, though he had not seen him in over ten years. Then, in Berlin, he had been one of the Russian liaison officers, a captain, Roy recalled. Karovsky.

Roy had little choice but to stop.

'Did you forget something?' asked Maier.

'Sorry?' said Roy.

'I asked whether you'd forgotten something. You turned around as if something had just occurred to you.'

184

His companion grinned at him, as if he had just told a priceless joke.

'No. I mean . . . Why are you following me?'

'We're not.' Maier affected an expression of wounded innocence. 'Yuri and I were taking the air in your beautiful park. You happened to pass by. You do remember Yuri Ivanovich, don't you?'

The other man spoke before Roy had a chance to respond. 'Captain Courtnay, is it not?' He paused and gave a bright, tinkling laugh. Something was greatly amusing him. 'We were both in Berlin at the same time. Don't you recall?'

Roy adopted a pleasant expression. 'Why yes, of course. Different context. No uniform.' He extended his hand and Karovsky shook it warmly. 'Do you live in London now?'

'No, just visiting,' said Karovsky. 'I often think back to those days after the war. We were all caught up in history, were we not?'

His English had improved. Or perhaps it had always been this good. Roy could recall a truculent officer who had insisted on laborious translations by his interpreter.

'I suppose so,' said Roy. 'Heady days. Though I didn't think of them like that then. Things happened so quickly. What brings you to London?'

'Oh, this and that,' said Karovsky vaguely, smiling. 'I often think of your German interpreter and what happened to him. Dreadful story. What was his name?'

'Yes. Hans Taub. Dreadful.'

'Have I ever told you about it, Ernst?' said

185

Karovsky, turning to Maier. Maier nodded but Karovsky clearly needed to stick to his script. 'An awful affair. Our friend here and his colleague were going to arrest some minor Nazi. In our zone. I sent a team to support them but it all went wrong. Poor . . . Hans, you say? Hans ended up dead in the firefight that erupted. We all saw our share of deaths in the war. But the war was over. Tragic. Just some crazy fascist.' He shook his head and looked directly at Roy. 'You've changed, Captain Courtnay,' he said. 'I'm not sure exactly how, but you've changed. I believe Ernst had a quiet chat with you at the weekend. You were unconvinced. I trust you've not told anyone else about it?'

Roy said nothing.

'I thought not. Then perhaps we can discuss the idea further. We can offer you whatever assurances you require . . . '

'I'm not interested,' said Roy. 'I've told you once.' He began to walk away.

Karovsky spoke more loudly. 'We can offer you all the necessary reassurances about your safety, and I think you understand what I mean. Whereas if you choose not to speak to us those assurances are, what do you say, off the table.'

Roy turned and walked up to Karovsky, red in the face, clenching his fists by his side. 'Did you hear me? I don't need your reassurances. I shall be reporting this to the police.'

A smartly dressed woman in a red dress looked at them and hurried on. Karovsky's face as he rolled back on to his heels retained its equable smile but Roy could see unease in his eyes.

'Come now,' said Maier, the peacemaker. He put his hand on Roy's arm. Roy looked at it for a moment before Maier pulled it away. They must know that Roy could swat them like flies if he wished.

Karovsky had regained some of his composure. 'Be reasonable, please, Captain Courtnay. We're in the centre of civilization, in St James's Park. I'm a senior Russian diplomat and it would be unfortunate if the police had to deal with an assault by a member of Lord Stanbrook's staff on one such as me. Unfortunate for you, I mean. All kinds of misunderstandings could arise.'

Roy calmed, realizing his arms were half raised, ready to grab the Russian by the lapels.

'That's better,' said Karovsky. 'All I want to do is to chat. I have some pictures from Berlin that you might like to look at. Why don't we meet for dinner one evening this week? Then we can sort it all out over a glass of wine and a good feed. I can assure you it is very much in your interest, Captain Courtnay.'

'I'm not interested, I keep telling you.'

'I heard you. But I must insist that if you're looking to what's best for you, you should come along. Listen, rather than detaining you here, I have a table booked at Galbraith's fish restaurant tomorrow evening. You do especially like fish, don't you? Or was that your friend Hans? I can't remember. I always got you confused. It was all so long ago and memory fades. The table's booked for seven. I'll see you there.'

In unison, the two men began walking briskly towards the nearest exit, turning their heads to smile at each other as if sharing a joke. Roy stood for a moment before striding off in the opposite direction. He had completely forgotten where he had been going. He turned and headed back towards the club.

7

He did not go to Galbraith's. He heard no more from Maier or Karovsky. The sky did not fall in. Not immediately, that is.

Two days after the confrontation, Roy was reading the newspaper in the breakfast room of the London residence when he saw the figure of David Millward, Lord Stanbrook's political private secretary, silhouetted in the door frame as he moved past. Millward returned and reappeared at the door. He leaned against the frame and fingered it thoughtfully.

'Morning, Roy,' he said.

'Morning, David. How goes it?'

The two of them had little to do with each other but enjoyed the amicable relationship of passing acquaintances. Roy had no interest in politics and David seemed generally appreciative of the man who kept their principal's nose clean away from the hurly-burly of government.

Millward beamed. 'Never better. Just dropped by to pick up some papers for the boss. Debate on arms procurement this afternoon.'

'Oh yes?' said Roy and returned his attention to the newspaper.

'Actually,' said Millward with unaccustomed diffidence, 'I wondered whether you might have time for a quick chat.'

'What about?'

'Oh, this and that.'

Roy folded his newspaper and laid it neatly on the table.

'Perhaps better in the boss's study,' said Millward. 'You know . . . '

They walked together up the flight of stairs.

'Terrific weather we've been having.'

'Yes,' said Roy.

'A touch too hot in London, though. One craves the countryside on days like this.'

'Indeed. We're off to Burnsford at the weekend.'

'Oh really?' Millward seemed slightly put out.

They took their seats in the study, Roy spreading his large frame on the leather chesterfield and Millward sitting primly in one of the club chairs.

'Well then,' said Millward, 'this is somewhat awkward.'

'Yes?' said Roy, blinking very slowly.

'The boss has been contacted by those people who are paid to do these things. Those people in the shadows. You know . . . '

'I'm not sure I do.'

'The spooks.'

'Ah.'

'Well, it appears they've been following around some Russian character who's visiting London.

And the other day they spotted him with one of his East German associates talking to you. In St James's Park, to be precise.'

'Really?'

'Yes. The German fellow is some kind of member of staff of Count von Hessenthal. He was at Burnsford last weekend.'

'Indeed. Ernst Maier.'

'Exactly. Care to tell me what the chat was all about?'

'Not really. I didn't take to Maier. Then he and his pal bumped into me in the park.'

'It seems you had an altercation.'

'Yes. I knew the Russian from my military service, in Berlin. He wanted to resume the relationship. I didn't want to. That's all there was to it.'

'I see. Quite straightforward, as you describe it. But I'm afraid it's not that simple. The thing is, the spooks seem to think that you may have been asked to provide certain services.'

'Services? What services?'

'Come on, Roy. It's not difficult to imagine, is it? You occupy a, shall we say, delicate position. They'd no doubt see great value in suborning you.'

'Well, they didn't suborn me. I terminated the conversation. Your spies should be able to tell you that.'

'I'm glad to hear it,' said Millward soothingly. 'Very glad. But, you see, they do rather insist on speaking to you.'

Fear ran through Roy's veins. 'I think I'd prefer . . . '

'I'm sure we all would. The boss doesn't want those beggars crawling through his affairs either. But they are insistent. It's all rather . . . '

'Awkward. I know. You said.'

'There is an alternative way, though. The boss has managed to negotiate a possible different solution.'

'Which entails?'

Millward leaned forward.

'Well, Roy, it's not ideal. But His Lordship has managed to agree with these people that they will take it no further provided you terminate your employment with him and withdraw with appropriate, um, discretion.' He smiled minutely with the gratification of having lighted on an apposite word.

'I'd rather stay on and take my chances,' said Roy gruffly.

'Well . . . ' The word was long and drawn out, and repeated. 'Well, I'm afraid we don't see that as an option. And nor do those people. This may be a bit of a blow, but I'm afraid that we've reached a bit of an impasse so far as your future employment with Lord Stanbrook is concerned.'

'You're sacking me?'

'I think Lord Stanbrook prefers to think of it as letting you go. With considerable regret, of course. He believes it's the only possible way, in everyone's interests, not least your own. He doesn't want to put you through all that, if at the end of it you may be compelled to resign anyway. And of course he himself must remain unimpeachable. I'm afraid he can have no proximity to anything that whiffs of espionage.

I'm sure you can see the logic. So sorry, but that's that.'

'Can I at least speak to him to state my case?'

'Afraid not. He's in the House at present and there is this Bill to nurse through.' Millward adopted an apologetic expression.

'And should I decide to brazen it out?'

'You've every right to do whatever you choose, of course. I was simply trying to offer a solution that might be more, um, elegant, and in your interests too. You're completely at liberty to ignore my advice. I can't predict the consequences.'

'Would Lord Stanbrook keep me on?'

Millward smiled briefly. 'I think we're beyond that point. I'm rather afraid you have to accept that your employ with His Lordship is at an end. I think that in the court of public opinion a dismissal in these particular circumstances would seem perfectly justified, given your contact with these individuals. But I very much hope it won't come to that.'

Roy thought, his face impassive.

'Of course,' said Millward, 'His Lordship would be suitably generous in view of your sterling efforts for him. He has seen fit to set work in train to secure you alternative employment. One of his father's former gardeners runs a small nursery in a delightful little Norfolk village. I've been so bold as to arrange that you could start there next Monday.'

'I don't have a clue about gardening.'

'The position's more one of general duties. It won't be onerous and the wages will be more than sufficient. And there's one other thing.'

'Yes?'

'Lord Stanbrook is extremely grateful for all your hard work. He's authorized me to offer you appropriate financial compensation in lieu of notice and in recognition of your loyalty. I've made out a cheque. The job offer and the remuneration are, so to speak, a package. They go together.'

With his spindly fingers, he deftly drew out a piece of paper from his inside pocket, placing it on the low table in front of the couch. Without touching it, Roy leaned forward and looked at it, expressionless.

'And how long would I have? When would I need to clear out?'

Millward smiled, without triumph. 'There's only so long that we can hold the dogs off. I think from all perspectives it would be preferable if you can have left before Lord Stanbrook returns this evening. I've taken the liberty of purchasing a ticket from Liverpool Street for this afternoon.' He took the piece of card from his pocket. 'We will of course have your trunk sent on to your lodging address, which is on this piece of paper, as are the details of Mr Brown's nursery. He will expect to see you next Monday.' He placed a neatly typed note, together with the ticket, on the table beside the cheque.

Roy looked at him with undisguised hostility, which the other man either did not see or chose to ignore.

'Good,' said Millward with a smile. 'I think that's settled, then.' He proffered his hand, but

Roy looked away at that moment. 'Well, I must be on my way to the House. Good of you to be so reasonable, Roy. If you could please leave your keys with Mr Percival. I'll let him know.'

He stood and left.

Bloody bastards, thought Roy. Every single one of them. Bloody bastards. But he picked up the cheque, the ticket and the note and went to his room to pack.

11

Money Matters

1

Vincent arrives with his solicitous expression, all furrowed brow and concern. His M&S suit exudes neither opulence nor poverty.

'I won't insult your intelligence, Mrs McLeish,' he says, after the preliminaries and by way of introduction to his script.

'Betty.'

He looks at her for a moment, perplexed.

'Thank you, Betty. I see you were an academic. You'd be surprised how much my job consists of spelling things out to clients in words of one syllable that would seem to be self-evident to you and me. Clients like Mr Courtnay excepted, of course. So I don't intend to insult your intelligence. Please stop me and ask if you have any questions, though. And you too, sir.'

Vincent looks shyly across the table at them.

'Stephen,' says Betty. 'First names, please. That way we'll all feel far more comfortable. And perhaps you would be better off treating me like the most unintelligent client you've ever come across. I'm a total ignoramus in financial matters.' She simpers cheerfully.

'Well then. This is the point at which in my normal consultations I read you a description of my role as an independent financial adviser and tell you my responsibilities under the law to the Financial Services Authority. Then I give you a form and ask you to sign it. But I understand from Mr Courtnay that you would prefer to forgo all of that.'

Roy has been studiously looking at his hands. He looks up now but says nothing.

'That's right. Roy said he trusts you. I don't see the bureaucratic mumbo-jumbo adds any value.'

'OK. But if you'd like to go through the due process now is the moment to say.' He pauses and no one speaks. 'In one sense this is good timing.'

'Why?' asks Stephen.

'Because certain of the investment options I've recommended are . . . unconventional. They fall outside the scope of the normal UK regulations, which have yet to catch up with market developments. And they're beyond the jurisdiction of the FSA.'

'Because they're illegal?'

'No, sir — sorry, Stephen. Absolutely not. I wouldn't deal in unethical or unlawful products. The position is this: I have access to unorthodox international streams of investment and financial instruments that are, if you like, leading edge. The industry has yet to catch up. That's why the prospective returns are higher than you might normally expect.'

'What kinds of returns?'

'It's difficult to be precise, Betty. Obviously the value of investments can fluctuate. But with the spread of investments I'm proposing, tied up for a five-year minimum period, I'd estimate an annual return of 15 per cent at the most pessimistic prediction, which would see your capital over the five-year period appreciating by around 100 per cent. Much more likely is a return of 25 to 30 per cent per annum, and your investment in those circumstances would appreciate almost fourfold.'

'But there is risk?' asks Betty.

'There's risk in everything,' says Roy. 'Even in crossing the road.'

Vincent looks at him for a moment. 'There is risk, yes, within certain tolerances. Clearly I can't look into a crystal ball, but I can assure you these investments are at the risk-averse end of the scale. This is a prudent way of saving. Would you like to know more?'

'Yes, please.'

'You'll have heard of the fast-growing economies of developing nations. You may have heard the acronym BRIC?'

'No.'

'The BRIC economies are Brazil, Russia, India and China. I'm not suggesting investing there. Brazil has suffered in the recession. The Chinese government is attempting to hold down growth to reduce indebtedness. Russia is beset by corruption and political issues. Their bubbles haven't burst, far from it. You could make decent returns still. But nothing like what could once be achieved, and the risk profile has ratcheted up. So I wouldn't recommend them. I'm turning more and more to other countries.'

'Such as?'

'Turkey, Malaysia and Indonesia. Nigeria possibly. These are economies on the up. Largely down to three things: population growth, an aspirational younger generation and enlightened economic policies in government. Now, investments in these countries aren't for the novice. There are issues with each — corruption, for example. I've found the need to deal with a great degree of caution and discretion. I've recommended a spread of investments to Mr Courtnay across all of these countries. I've recommended putting less into Nigeria quite specifically because of issues of corruption and fraud. You'll be aware of the various crude scams done by letter or email?'

'Yes.'

'Good. Then let me assure you again that I proceed with great caution. One thing I do have to point out is the need for confidentiality. The products and investments I'm about to describe aren't generally available. The institutions with which I'm working are publicity-shy. None of this is unethical. What we're doing when it comes down to it is assisting the growth of underdeveloped nations. But it's a matter regarded by those countries as private. I can't stress this enough.'

He pauses and leans back to let them assimilate what he has said.

'Now,' he continues eventually, 'I've had a preliminary look at the table of assets that you kindly filled out. I genuinely believe your assets could do better for you than your current portfolio. And I think there are things I could well offer you.'

Betty smiles. 'Well, that's good news.'

'Yes. I'll need to go through all of your finances with you with a fine-tooth comb, however. I hope you won't find that too intrusive.'

'I'm sure not, Vincent.'

'One final thing.'

'Yes?'

'Something for you to think about. And Mr Courtnay too. There is a way in which we can reduce the overheads and streamline the whole investment. If you and Mr Courtnay were to build up a joint portfolio we could limit introduction charges, transaction fees and administrative costs. They can mount up.'

'I see,' says Betty.

'As I say, something to consider. It doesn't change the advice I give you. It's simply another thing to think about when making your final decision. You can choose to invest separately or together. Entirely up to you. Now, if I could run through this long list of questions with you. Please interrupt if anything is unclear.'

2

'I'm not really sure,' says Stephen.

'Nor am I,' said Betty.

'You've not had a lot of involvement in money matters,' says Roy. 'It's natural you feel a little uneasy.'

Vincent has gone. They are looking at the sheaves of projections and brochures he has left with them.

'It's all a bit bewildering,' says Betty.

'Hmm,' says Stephen.

'You trust Vincent, Roy?' asks Betty.

'With my life, Betty. As far as I'd trust anyone. I'm not stupid, you know.'

'No, you're not.'

'It's terribly difficult, I know. But I've never known Vincent's judgement to be wrong. He's prudent. He spreads investments between safe options and speculative ones. Perhaps the returns don't end up as spectacular as some, but at least you're not staking all your money at the roulette wheel.'

'That's what it feels like,' interjects Stephen.

Roy passes him a sidelong glare but his voice carries a different tone. 'Of course you're right. Of course that's exactly how it will seem. But this is highly scientific, you know. Vincent has explained to me all about his algorithms and his computer programs. He knows what he's doing.'

'Isn't that what the bankers said before the crash?'

Roy sighs. 'I think you'll find that Vincent and his clients came out of the crash rather well. Vincent's not a herd animal. He does the legwork and comes up with his own conclusions.'

'So he doesn't follow orthodox wisdom? That in itself sounds risky to me.'

'Perhaps you'd just better give your grand-mother the space to make up her own mind.'

'No,' says Betty. 'I want to hear Stephen's

opinion. In fact if I go ahead I'd like Stephen to be fully involved. I'd like him to read all the prospectuses and other literature. I'd like him to apply his young mind to things that my old one might miss.'

'Of course, Betty. I didn't mean to — '

'No, of course not. It doesn't matter. But Stephen needs to be involved. What's your feeling, dear?'

'I feel uneasy. No doubt Vincent's very good at what he does and Roy's right to have faith in him. But you're comfortably enough off without this, aren't you?'

'I suppose so. A little more wouldn't go amiss. And I would like to be able to leave something more substantial to you, your sister and your parents, and to a couple of good causes.'

'I'm sure we wouldn't want it. We're not interested in your money. It's only money, after all.'

'Only money. Pah.' It seems to spurt involuntarily from Roy. 'There speaks someone who's never been short.'

'Quite,' says Betty. 'I understand your reservations, Stephen, but I'm minded to go ahead. I'll sleep on it. But unless I change my mind overnight I think I'd like you to set things in motion with Vincent. Go through the literature, read the forms for me and make sure I'm signing the right things, please.'

She stands and crosses the kitchen to fill the kettle and switch it on.

'Cup of tea?' she says brightly.

Roy casts Stephen a sly smirk. Stephen looks back equably.

It is quiet at last in the house. Stephen has left them and Betty has prepared a light sandwich supper. It is rare that either of them can manage a full meal these days.

'Stephen's quite right, you know,' says Roy. 'Concerned for your best interests. You must be proud to have a grandson who cares so much.'

She pours the tea. 'Yes. But I've made up my mind.'

'I thought you needed to think about it overnight.'

'That was really for Stephen's benefit. What Vincent said makes absolute sense.'

'Good. I wouldn't want you churning it over in your mind through the night. We'll need to discuss what Vincent was saying about a joint pot.'

'It does seem to make sense, doesn't it?'

'Oh yes. I think so.'

'I just need to be absolutely certain it's the right thing.'

'Of course. There was something else I wanted to talk about with you.'

'Yes?'

'It's timely, I think, as we embark on this joint venture. I thought we might wish to cement our relationship further.'

'What do you mean?' she asks quickly.

'I'm not about to propose marriage, if that's what you're afraid of,' he says with a smile. 'I reckon we're both a bit long in the tooth for that kind of business. No, I was thinking we might take a leaf out of these youngsters' book and be a bit wild.'

'In what way?'

'I was wondering whether we might think about sharing the big bedroom. After all, when you're in sight of the finishing post it's nice to feel a little human warmth. I certainly miss that, of a night. The sound of another's breathing, even if you can't sleep yourself. It's somehow soothing. It makes you feel all's right with the world.'

She looks alarmed.

'Oh no, not that,' he continues. 'Goodness me. Certainly not that. That was over a long time ago, for me. No lead left in that particular pencil. Pardon me for my crudeness. I was just thinking, sometimes I feel lonely. You must too. We can do each other a favour and comfort each other. A nice cuddle in bed every so often is all I was thinking.'

'Well,' she begins, 'it's a lovely idea. But we did agree when you first moved in that our relationship would be for companionship, not romance.'

'Granted. But we've moved on from there. My feelings have moved on. Yours haven't?'

'It's not that, Roy. It's certainly not that. It's just that . . . Alasdair.'

'I know you were very much attached to him.'

'Yes. I'm sorry. I still feel an absurd bond of fidelity.'

'It's not absurd at all, Betty. It's admirable.'

'I just couldn't, Roy. It'd feel like a betrayal of sorts.'

'You don't need to explain. I understand. It's perfectly all right, of course.'

She smiles gratefully. 'And anyway, I doubt that you or anyone else could put up with my snoring.'

'I simply can't believe that you snore, Betty. You of all people.'

'You'd better believe it. I snore for England. Have done for years. It started in my fifties.'

'Well then. It seems I've had a lucky escape. Friends?'

They grin at each other.

'Yes, of course. Roy?'

'Yes?'

'You never say the word love, do you?'

'Does anyone? In real life? Of our generation, at least? Men, anyway?'

'I don't know. But you certainly don't use it. Not about the past. Not about us.'

'Would you like me to? Would that make you happier? Because I can certainly have a go if you'd like. I'd feel awkward, but I can give it a bash. Because your happiness is of paramount importance to me. I've grown very attached to you. Would you like me to speak of love?'

She smiles. 'No, that's not what I meant. It just occurred to me. I wouldn't like to force you to come up with something against your conscience. And it is after all the English way, isn't it? Not to speak of such things. We talk of fondness and attachment, because it's safe.'

'Well, I suppose so. But if you'd like me to tell you I love you, Betty, I'd most certainly do so.'

'I'm sure you would, Roy. Thank you, but no.

It really wasn't what I meant.'

He is relieved. The fact of the offer to share a life beyond companionship, however bogus, may just have sealed the deal. Even better that she declined. He would now not have to contemplate all that, at least not for the moment.

12

May 1946
The Centre of Things

1

Berlin. Everything revolved around this city. Their six months in Vienna had been fun, if that was the right word, but no one there really wanted a full-scale search for the petty functionaries of the Nazi camps any more. The momentum was for speedy reconciliation and reconstruction, or as speedy as anything could be when dealing with the Russians. The Western powers were now reasonably confident the Russians would pull back eastwards, keeping Prague and Budapest in their ambit. Awkward characters like Roy Courtnay and his interpreter, Hans Taub, their tenacity stoking dispute, were no longer required.

They had been assigned to Hanover, in the British occupied zone of Germany, a relative backwater. They operated from a small office opposite the main railway station. Hanover, like much of the rest of the country, had been brought to rubble and to its knees. Provincial and quiet, however, and they were allowed to go about their business with little interference from above, levering assistance from other military units by sheer force of character. Captain

Courtnay was persuasive and the British soldier of almost every rank was generally up for sport now the war was over and the clear-up had begun, especially if it involved hunting down the bad guys.

Courtnay's superiors had little interest in his activities. They had bigger fish to fry and post-war military careers to cultivate. He reported nominally to a major but kept himself away from HQ as much as possible. He had a staff of five: his secretary, three NCO clerks and his German interpreter, Taub. Hans Taub and he were jokingly known as the Gruesome Twosome, after the cartoon film that had come out the previous year. They'd hit it off the moment Taub had been sent from London.

They were physically alike: tall, blond and imposing. Taub possessed certainty. He had not had the benefits of a rural upbringing and the conditioning of a minor public school education, designed to insinuate an inchoate feeling of inferiority. He was not an Englishman by birth, swimming in compromise, awkwardness and embarrassment. Perhaps not all Englishmen were like Roy — or indeed all Germans like Taub — but Roy found Hans's lack of diffidence liberating. Taub, the son of a liberal journalist who had fled Germany and later committed suicide and a mother who had been executed in 1939, was brimful of certainty when he might have been burdened by grief and doubt.

Roy discovered in himself something hidden yet always present, a confidence that at times surged in his physicality, his enthusiasms and his judgements. He could now begin to give it expression. Hans's simple attitudes made his petty repressions seem self-indulgently and unnecessarily complex.

Generally the two of them would go out to do the interviews. If arrests were in the offing, a call to the military police would serve up a team of beefy, maleficent-looking men to help with the dirty work.

He was doing scarcely more than going through the motions. The work didn't challenge him; nor did it result in a particularly greater good that he could discern. Most of it could be done within the zone. The majority of the camp underlings had not travelled far. They could be picked up, like rabbits stationary in the headlights, in the towns and villages around Celle. Their compatriots were generally more than happy to give them up. The people who really mattered had either already been detained or were long gone. De-Nazification had become mere process, and a process in which few believed. It was a means of returning to normal, whatever that meant after these years of chaos and suffering. It amounted to something of a production line: identify, locate, arrest, process, charge, prosecute, de-Nazify, jail or release.

Occasionally they had to venture into the American or French zones to undertake inquiries, but not beyond the dividing line of the Harz Mountains to the Russian zone. Dealing with the Red Army was simply too much trouble for the return. By design or accident, they were shambolic and uncooperative.

Roy and Hans worked hard and played hard, immersing themselves at night in the hedonistic, morally questionable life of a city in chaos, escaping the sorrows and the grief. Not that there was much of 1946 Hanover to paint red.

But Berlin. This was a first. Their search for Klaus Müller, a former administrator at Bergen-Belsen, had brought them here. Müller, a Berliner, had moved to Celle when he married in '37 and now evidently thought his home city was a safer place to lie low. Rather than passing the inquiry to the British authorities in Berlin, Roy had persuaded his bored boss to authorize him and Taub to travel there. Roy hoped it might be a chance to find a route back to a function that he could plausibly describe to himself as important. He was interested not in advancement, but in doing some measure of good. Soon enough he would find himself back in Oxford, no doubt to pick up his ecclesiastical studies again before taking a curacy in Dorset, close to the family home. Or would he? This war had changed him, like so many millions of others.

He could not say it had brutalized him. His faith remained intact. His instincts remained passive and pacifist, though he had been required consistently to display the opposite behaviours. Moving through Holland in 1944, he had led from the front, placing himself in the same danger as his men, and they had respected him for it. He had always insisted on compassion for the German soldiers they winkled out in pockets of resistance from ruined buildings, even when minutes earlier they had been killing and

209

wounding his own men. But what the war had taught him was the capacity for brutal malice of one human being towards another, and this was something almost regardless of uniform, rank or social class.

He felt this when he typed his short poems, which with every attempt took on a more worldly, cynical edge. His NCOs ribbed him as he hammered at the keys at every lunch break. '*War and Peace*,' they joked. But he loved the little portable that he carried with him. It conferred an odd sense of security and certainty that his spidery scrawl could not, even in the letters home that he could not bear to write by hand, something else that amused his staff no end.

When he typed those regular-as-clockwork weekly letters he found less and less to say. There was less and less of him to connect with them. He was not sure whether he could aspire to a life of obscure rural service; or whether it could now match his visions.

2

The house they sought was in Marsiliusstrasse, near the Jannowitzbrücke station and the River Spree. It lay just inside the Russian sector. They had considered making a quick covert incursion to lift their man, but that would have meant also crossing the American sector and the Americans had said they could not afford yet another rupture of already poor relations for such a small gain. They decided to chance their arm at the Allied Control Council in Schöneberg, in the south of the American sector, where the occupying forces administered issues that crossed the physical boundaries between them.

They had spent two days in the broad halls, powerless, smoking and waiting while the bureaucrats discussed and mediated their request. There was no solid precedent to fall back on: at first the Russians wanted Müller for themselves, then acknowledged that, since the crimes had all been committed in what was now the British zone and the British held all the evidence, they might have to cede to them. The British, as politely as they could, indicated that they would not be prepared to serve up the results of their findings, or their witnesses, to a Russian judicial process. The Russians questioned whether a judicial process was strictly necessary. The British and the Americans reeled back theatrically. Then the Russians decided after all that Herr Müller was small beer.

It had been that much simpler back in Vienna, though not without its arm-wrestles. At least if one was persistent enough there was the chance that reason might prevail in the end. And you could tell the Soviets didn't really have their hearts in it. But Berlin was important to them. While they might be prepared to let Vienna drift back to its complacent stolidity, the price, tacitly at least, was Berlin. So every battle here was to the death, and rational thinking played little part.

Finally, a compromise was reached. The Russians would accede to an arrest by the British but would not allow a British armed support team in their sector. Barnes, the major allotted to their case, had warned them of this likelihood and the associated dangers.

'Language is the least of it. The Russkies'll be sloppy. There's no discipline in their ranks and they detest officers and foreigners. They won't look after you or your interpreter.'

Roy shrugged. 'I appreciate your concern, sir, but it's a routine lift. We've done it dozens of times.'

Nor was he concerned that the Russians would not permit them to wear uniform or to carry arms. 'There's no reason to believe Müller will be armed and I want this as low-key as possible. We'll snaffle him before he knows anything. I don't want a squad of troops bursting into the place.'

'On your own head be it, then,' said Barnes sniffily, before signing the necessary papers and washing his hands of the operation.

So here they were, sitting in the gloomy office just off Alexanderplatz, waiting for Karovsky, the irritable Red Army captain, to authorize their plan. Karovsky smoked one of his foul-smelling Russian *papirosi* cigarettes, having curtly refused Roy's offer of American. He leaned back in his seat and again scanned the order from the Control Council, as though he thought its contents might change on a third reading.

'British Military Intelligence,' he read in a cracked accent, and laughed. He signalled to his interpreter, who shambled over from his desk. Through him, he said, smiling, 'I like you people. The strangest people, but I like you. We are your enemies. You once had an empire. You like to pretend you're still important. We liberated Berlin and now you wish to come on to my streets to undertake one of your trivial arrests.'

'Hardly trivial,' said Roy equably. 'The man we're trying to arrest was an administrator at Bergen-Belsen.'

After the time lapse imposed by the translation, Karovsky waved Roy's statement away. 'Germany's full of war criminals, minor and major. Perhaps all Germans who are in denial about their nation's crimes are criminals. I don't know. Why should I choose to help you?' He spread his hands wide in a gesture of ignorant supplication.

'Because you have in front of you a direct order from the Control Council, perhaps?'

Karovsky grinned. 'You've recently been in Vienna?' He had clearly done his homework, despite his apparent casualness. 'Yes, I've heard things are marvellous there. Order is being restored quickly so that the Austrians can get back to their blissful ignorance, their waltzes and their *Sachertorte*. Relations between the Powers are marvellous.' He laughed scornfully. 'But Berlin is a different place. Vienna, we don't really care any more. But don't imagine you have a free rein in Berlin. As to the Control Council, it comes out daily with its absurd demands and decrees. I ignore them as I see fit. With the full support of my senior officers. So whether you may conduct your petty operation is up to me.

213

Not this piece of paper.'

He pushed the order across the desk, waited for the translation, then grinned. Roy looked at Hans briefly.

'Well, if that's your final word . . . '

'I didn't say no. But if you do proceed it will be on my terms. None of your British uniforms. And I will wish to interview the prisoner myself. Just to double-check that you English aren't trying to deceive us. Again.'

'All right,' said Roy. 'As long as I'm present. Perhaps if you'll allow us simply to do a recce of the address today, we can discuss the op tomorrow. We don't need your help. We'll just have a look at the address from the outside.'

'You think you don't need our help. But I insist. You can take three men with you. They'll keep out of sight. You're not carrying weapons, I take it?'

'No. Would you care to search us?' said Roy lightly in response to the other's sceptical look. A calculated risk: a body search of an English officer would cause a hullabaloo at the Control Council, and both men knew it.

'Thank you. No.'

3

They were grateful for the unseasonable cool, which provided the pretext for their greatcoats with their capacious pockets containing contraband for smoothing the path and an illicit weapon in case things did not go to plan. Their

214

suits were ridiculous. They had been provided by the Russians, looted no doubt from some low-end tailor's shop. Courtnay and Taub had travelled from Hanover by train in uniform, carrying only their coats, wash kits and a change of underwear. The suits were several sizes too small, forcing a rolling gait on them so tight were they around the thighs, and the jacket buttons strained to hold. They looked like clowns. Roy had the sense that this was an indignity forced on them by Karovsky for his own amusement. He, with the seniority of rank, had at least been able to bag the blue serge. Hans's grey chalk-stripe was a good four inches too short in the leg, showing his boots to bad effect. He looked simply absurd, though in this devastated city the comic was largely absent or unnoticed. They were at least grateful that they had been able to find hats that fitted more or less. And they could now pose as civilian police.

They stood by the cathedral, almost in ruins, its cupola a mere skeleton, and looked over the Spree, in which debris floated and a filthy grey scum scudded to the banks. They walked down Unter den Linden, past mounds of rubble that were being diligently cleared by German workers wearing close to rags. Russian troops stood chatting and smoking. Huge hammer and sickle flags flew triumphantly from the ruins of the imposing buildings that lined the once great avenue. There was no sign of the linden trees.

Taub looked distraught. 'This was my city,' he said. 'Look what these people have done to it. You could stroll down this street before all this.

Mind you, as long as I can remember it's always been in some kind of crisis. Socialists and fascists. Marches and speeches. Street fights and sabotage. Prosperity and collapse. Poverty and wealth. Always clashes. Perhaps it was just my family.'

'Your father involved you in his politics?'

'Not really. They were both politically engaged.' The last word was spoken with bitter emphasis. 'But my father took me everywhere with him. Politics. This is what you get.'

'Perhaps it'll be a more peaceful place in the future.'

'You don't believe that. The Russians and your Western powers will fight over this city and my country forever.'

Such vehemence was not the norm for Hans Taub.

'We have a job to do,' Roy reminded him.

'Yes,' said Taub, brightening, 'and I've got plans for this evening. We might go back to that club . . . '

It was all one could do in the circumstances. Block out the horror with frantic enjoyment and little regard for the consequences.

They had almost reached the Brandenburg Gate, where a huge portrait of Uncle Joe Stalin, covering most of the pillared structure, smiled down on them. They turned into Wilhelmstrasse and made their way to Voss Strasse, just to look at the small conical tower and modest doorway that marked where the final days of that horror had played out. It was here that the bodies, allegedly, had been burned. The area was

216

guarded by twitchy Russian soldiers, who approached them brusquely and began shoving Hans. Roy quickly produced papers from his pocket and the situation calmed somewhat. They walked swiftly back to Alexanderplatz for their rendezvous with their escort and discussed their tactics.

'Unless we're very lucky the troops they give us will be hopeless,' said Roy. 'More danger to us than help. We'll try to ditch them as soon as possible. Or at least get them into the background. Can you work on them?'

'Assuming one of them speaks a bit of German or English,' said Hans.

'Good. Now we know that this Müller character is out during the daytime.'

'So his wife said. She receives letters from him each week and that's what he says. The Russians know nothing about him?'

'The Russians have no record of him, or of his landlord. The Russians have no records at all. Or so they say. Let's just scout round the property and take it from there.'

4

As Roy had predicted, the Russian soldiers allocated to them were surly and taciturn. Hans managed, barely, to communicate with the corporal and together the five men, a shambolic crew, trudged towards the address.

Hans fished in his coat for cigarettes and gave the privates one pack each and the corporal two, before leaving them at the corner of Blumen-strasse to joke and curse the English.

The small apartment building looked no more shabby than the others in the street. This was not saying very much.

Klaus Müller had prevailed on an old school friend, Franz König, to lend him a room. König was a waiter and worked mainly during the evenings. Müller had found a job under an assumed name at the Buildings Department of the Russian authorities. They knew all this from Müller's wife, who had proved very cooperative when faced with the prospect of being prosecuted for assisting the flight of a criminal.

They walked past the building, but this told them nothing. The front door hung off its hinges and they decided to go inside. The apartment they were looking for was on the first floor. There was a stench of rotting food, or worse, as they climbed the stairs. Before the war this might have been quite a grand address. The stairs were wide and ornately balustraded. Now, however, it was shabby and showed the signs of looting when the Russians, less than a year before, had swept through the area like a plague. Apartment doors were smashed in and unrepaired. Every step kicked up clouds of dust.

Eventually they found a door with a piece of paper roughly pinned to it. Scrawled capital letters declared curtly that this was the apartment of König.

Roy looked at Hans, who raised his eyebrows.

'In for a penny, in for a pound,' whispered Roy.

They knew the drill. Initially Hans would do all the talking, to convey the impression that they were the German police. This would generally gain them access and put the subject at a kind of ease. They had obtained Berlin police papers that would pass muster. Then at an appropriate point they would announce themselves more fully.

At Roy's nod, Hans knocked loudly. There was silence, then a scrabbling inside. Shortly the head of a middle-aged man with a receding hairline appeared around the door, edged open cautiously.

'Herr König?' asked Hans politely.

The man stared at him for a moment, wide-eyed. 'Yes,' he said eventually, slowly, having picked the question over. 'How may I help?'

'Simply a routine inquiry,' said Hans with a smile, flashing his police documentation. 'We're sorry to bother you.'

The man looked at Roy, who raised his hat slightly by way of greeting. He regretted it the moment he had done so. He and Hans had been through this before. I can't explain, Hans had said, but a German would never do it like that. You're declaring you're English as clearly as if you said: how do you do? Just nod briefly, if you have to do anything. But reflex had kicked in again. König didn't seem to register it.

'May we come in, please, Herr König?' asked Hans.

'Of course,' said the little man hurriedly. 'Sorry. What was I thinking?' He opened the door and they entered a shabby dwelling. The wide hallway gave on to what had once been a grand drawing room but which had been ransacked. Plaster cornices hung perilously from the ceiling. Boards were missing from a floor that lacked carpet or rugs. The furniture was gathered at one end of the room: two sofas and a random collection of dining chairs. Everything was coated in a thick layer of dust.

König was unshaven and collarless in his shirtsleeves. His eyes carried the bleariness of a night's drinking. From the smell of stale sweat, he had evidently not bathed for some time. He looked at them beseechingly, as if lost.

'It's about a guest of yours,' said Hans.

'A guest?' asked König.

'That's correct. Klaus Müller?'

'Ah. Klaus. An old school friend. He's just staying here a couple of nights or so. I'm afraid he's not here at the moment.'

'No. So we understand. He's at work?'

'I'm not sure where he works,' said König.

'No, you wouldn't be,' said Hans thoughtfully. 'But it doesn't matter. Klaus isn't due to return shortly?'

'How should I know? I'm not his mother. But no. I don't think so.'

'It's not important. It was you we wanted to speak to anyway.' Hans took out a notebook. 'Can we just begin with one or two questions about yourself? You work as a waiter?'

'That's right. Zum Goldenen Bären in Karl-Liebknecht Strasse.'

'And you have a clean criminal record?'

220

'You should know that.'

'We do. But, please.'

'Yes, a clean criminal record.'

'No involvement with National Socialism? No work for the Party? No official work for the National Socialist regime?'

'Absolutely not. Those scum — '

'Indeed,' said Hans sharply. 'It seems no one ever supported them. It's a wonder they ever came to power.'

There was a pause.

'Coffee, gentlemen?' said König. 'I'm afraid all I can get hold of is ersatz.'

Hans softened slightly. 'I may be able to help.' He took from his pocket a small paper packet of real coffee and proffered it to König, who lifted it to his nose and inhaled the aroma with evident pleasure. 'I may be able to find some more in my pockets. Depending on how things go.'

Roy nodded at him, prompting.

'And while you're making the coffee maybe we could have a look in Herr Müller's room.'

'Certainly. This way.'

They were led into a darkened fusty room. Roy clicked the light switch. There was no power. He drew back the heavy curtains and sunlight poured through filthy panes. Motes of dust hung in the air like pauses in time. The bed was unmade, the crumpled sheets filthy grey. A small suitcase lay open at its foot.

'Well then,' said Hans, and the little man went to the kitchen with his small bag of coffee.

It was hot in the room. Roy and Hans took off their greatcoats, piling them on a chair, and surveyed the task ahead. There was little to look at here. The wardrobes had been looted. A quick glance through the suitcase, under the mattress and under the bed itself. The sound of a pan clattering came from the kitchen.

'Keep our friend company,' said Roy, 'and carry on pumping him. This won't take long. We'll come back tomorrow with our pals.'

Hans left the room and Roy began his desultory search. No weapons, as they had assumed. There would be nothing material here. No clues. There was, after all, no mystery. Grab your man and go back to base. Back to Hanover in a couple of days, once Müller was processed. A depressing thought. Where had Taub got to with that man König?

He heard a plate smash and stood up, stiff and alert. Moving swiftly and as noiselessly as possible, he pulled the service Webley from his coat pocket as he left the room. He edged down the corridor and could see the light in the kitchen shining through the open door. Drawing closer, he looked through the door jamb. He was met by a pair of eyes gazing directly at him, wild and afraid.

'Come in, English,' said the little man. 'Careful. Always careful.'

Roy could see Taub kneeling in front of the man, facing the door. The man was sitting on a chair and had grasped Taub around the neck, the edge of a kitchen knife pressing against the skin of his throat.

'Careful,' said the man. He then spoke in German, which Hans translated breathlessly.

'He says you must come into the room immediately or he'll slit my throat.'

Slowly, Roy worked his way around the door and into the kitchen. He held the revolver before him pointing in the direction of the chair. There was no possibility of a shot. He might well kill Taub or miss altogether.

'Ah,' said Roy as casually as he could. 'I see. Herr Müller, I presume.'

The little man did not reply. He whispered and Hans continued to translate. 'He says to put the gun down on the floor.'

'All right. I'm going to do this very slowly. We don't want any little accidents, do we now?'

He bent at the knees and placed the weapon carefully on the rutted kitchen floor.

'The safety catch is on,' he said, and Taub translated.

Müller spoke again in his feverish whisper. His eyes, wide and darting, betrayed near panic. This is tricky, thought Roy.

'He says to slide it over here. And then leave the room.'

'Righty-ho.'

He stared into Taub's eyes. Taub returned the look and his message of acknowledgement was clear.

'All right, then. I'm going to slide the weapon with the bottom of my foot. Gently does it.'

Taub translated and Roy placed his large boot on the top of the Webley, pushing it forward with an amount of force he estimated not quite sufficient to carry it to Müller. The three men watched intently as the hunk of destructive metal

223

skittered its progress across the floor. It came to rest about halfway between Roy and the other two men.

'Ah,' he said, 'not worked out too well. Would you like me to shift it a bit closer?' he addressed his question to Müller, and observed him as Taub translated.

'No,' was the angry reply. 'Just go.'

Roy turned and walked out, peering back through the door jamb. Müller was evidently working out his next options, none of which was without risk. To reach down for the gun while keeping Taub under control with the knife at his neck could prove difficult. To try to leave the apartment without the gun appeared to present even greater dangers. To attempt to kill Taub with the knife before reaching for the gun would have uncertain consequences.

The universe narrowed to this next sequence of events. Their three lives hinged on these moments. To Roy, it seemed as if time had slowed and all activity had focused on an inviolable centre: here and now.

Müller had made his choice. Roy watched as he prepared himself for his next move, taking a deep breath. He was, it seemed, a careful man. This was the cue for Roy to tense his own muscles.

Müller shoved Hans forwards and made a leap for the gun. Roy judged this a bad move, and rounded the door swiftly, diving towards the same small area of floor. Hans, recovering, attempted to trip and barge Müller. He stumbled and they found themselves, the three of them, on a trajectory to the prize. Müller flailed blindly with the knife as he moved, to keep the other men away. But each would be prepared to take a few slashes to the body to survive this.

They came together, each wild and panicking as he scrabbled almost comically for his existence. Roy felt he would undoubtedly win this battle, with his training and his experience, but the little bureaucrat was nimbler and stronger than he had counted on. Hans became the likely loser, but perhaps Roy could save them both. The absurd thought occurred to him that whatever happened there would be the most almighty administrative and political difficulty afterwards.

They wrestled desperately. Blood spattered as the knife connected with flesh. A loud bang brought a sudden split second of silence and stillness. Then the revolver boomed again. A longer silence, before Müller ran from the room.

★ ★ ★

He sat, bleeding profusely from a wound in his upper arm. Blood seeped through the grey fabric of the suit, darkening it like ink on a blotter. He would live, unlike his unfortunate comrade. The shots had been fired from beneath his jaw as he struggled with Müller, the weapon close between them against their chests. They had taken clean half his face off, leaving an angry mess of red flesh, cords and blood, garish muscle and white bone. Grey brain matter had spilled negligently on to the floor. An eyeball stared madly, freed of its socket but connected to the optic chiasm by the fragile membranous wet skein of the optic nerve.

He collected his breath. He felt cold. He did not, yet, feel pain. Perhaps he was dying after all. But no, he would not die. He looked again at the mess that had been the face. He crawled over to the body and checked the carotid artery for a pulse. There was none, so far as he could establish in his own weak state. Absurd, he thought, just going through the motions. He reached under the shirt for a name tag. There was none. It must, like his own, have been left with their uniforms at the Berlin barracks.

He left the gun on the floor and stood, uncertain on his feet. He vomited profusely on the floor. It did not purge him. The image of the face would not leave him. He staggered along the narrow corridor of the apartment, in part to seek warmth, in part just to get away from there. Finding the bed, he pulled on the greatcoat and sat again, shivering uncontrollably. He heard the sound of boots clattering on the stairs before he passed out.

5

He was taken to a Russian military hospital and swiftly transferred to the British sector. He later learned that this was on the orders of Karovsky, who did not want the complications of explaining the incident to his superiors. In the

226

British hospital they cut the suit from his body. He noticed irrelevantly in the haze of pain that its right arm was now black with blood that obliterated the pale stripes of the cheap suit. They tended to the incision that had cut neatly into both the deltoid and the biceps muscles. He was told that his injuries were serious but not life-threatening. The sharpness of the knife had done him a favour. In time the chances were that he would regain full mobility in his right arm, but there would be a lengthy period of convalescence.

A captain from the military police came to interview him two days later.

'Courtnay,' he said pleasantly, 'I'm Craig. I need to interview you about this little incident. Bad luck all round, if you ask me.'

'Yes?' he said blankly.

'There are added complications when dealing across the sectors. So as neat and tidy as possible, eh?'

He nodded.

'What I propose is that I take you through what happened and you confirm whether or not my version is accurate. That all right with you?'

'Fine.'

'Wonderful.'

Craig described, step by step, the events of two days previously. He read out the order issued by the Control Council. He ran through the conversation with Karovsky and his offer of support. He confirmed that three Red Army soldiers had been deputed to assist them.

'Those boys will get a roasting for going

AWOL. In our internal report at least. Not that we'd think of sharing our criticisms with the Russians. Things are quite difficult enough as it is. Now, time is pressing so can we move to the critical part, please?'

Craig consulted a report he held in his hand, prepared, he said, by the Russian military police. The British had been given access to neither the scene nor the Russian investigators.

'Now, they list the weapons found at the apartment. I've pieced most of it together, but do correct me if I'm wrong about the sequence of events. This Müller chappie sees you outside and invites you into the house. You assume he's the owner. König, I believe. Quite naturally. You weren't to know. You go into the apartment and he goes into the kitchen. You chaps follow him. He pulls a carving knife from a drawer and threatens you both. You attempt to dispossess him but he manages to slash you. You're out of action. The knife clatters away somewhere and your colleague Hans goes in search of it. But our Mr Müller makes a dash for his bag and lo and behold pulls out a pistol. Your interpreter, brave man that he was, though perhaps foolish, grapples with him and the blighter shoots him, drops the gun and runs off. Does that sound about right?'

'Almost. It's just the gun — '

'Yes, the gun. We've looked into that. Service-issue Webley. Our records show it was issued in 1942 to a private in the Yorkshire Regiment. Reported lost in Bielefeld in April 1945, probably stolen during the final push. Or at least that's what our records show now, and that's what we're telling the Russkies. All right with that, are we?'

'Yes,' he said weakly.

'Well, that's all tickety-boo, then. Sorry about your pal. Rather it were a Kraut interpreter than a British officer, though, eh?'

6

He attended the funeral, this dry ritual the only testament to the death aside from the desultory investigation. Their unit had been broken up and the others sent back to Aldershot. He liked to think they would have attended if it had been possible. Evidently the major had better things to do. The padre had not researched any of the records, so it was a short service. It seemed that in death Hans Taub was an embarrassment all round.

He had asked whether he would be sent back to England. If he particularly requested it, it might be organized, they said. There was a convalescent facility near Bad Oeynhausen, the headquarters of the British Army of the Rhine. No, don't worry, he'd said: HQ BAOR would be fine. He'd be back to full fitness before too long.

At the convalescent centre he was reunited with his belongings. In the battered suitcase he found some chocolate saved for a rainy day. This was some rainy day. He ate three bars in quick succession, then had to rush to the heads to throw up.

There was confusion over his medical records. They had been lost in transit at some point in the war. He was chided by the physician appointed to his case for having left his dog tag with his uniform, but later a medical orderly told him it had the wrong blood group anyway. 'Happens all the time,' said the orderly cheerfully. The days passed in a familiar routine that bred in him contempt. In the mornings he had physiotherapy to attempt to bring life back to his arm. By and by, it began to work. Lunch was at twelve sharp. In the afternoons, if the weather was fine, those patients who were mobile would generally be encouraged to go for a health-giving stroll. If it was raining there was a library of dog-eared books. In the evenings there were organized indoor games: bridge or quoits or, worse still, charades. He avoided them assiduously.

He had no visitors. He received a letter from one of his staff, who wrote from Aldershot. He did not reply. His senior officers had better things to do than to visit and be connected with an invalid, a failure.

Periodically he saw an army psychologist. They, whoever they might be, must be concerned about his withdrawn behaviour. Or perhaps it was a routine peacetime frippery.

'Bound to have trauma,' said Parsons. 'Natural feeling, old boy. Thing is, not to let it get on top of you.'

'It doesn't,' he said quickly.

Parsons regarded him, considering, it seemed, what next to say.

'Must have been a bit grim. That close up.'

'It was.'

'Want to tell me about it?'

'Not really.'

'Close, were you? You and this interpreter?'

'Not particularly. We worked together.'

'Socialize together?'

'Just the normal amount.'

'Good man, was he?'

'He was all right, yes.'

'I see. Must have been distressing for you.'

'How would you feel if someone you'd been working with had his face shot off in front of you?'

Parsons seemed to give the question fair consideration. 'Dreams? Nightmares?'

'No.'

'Chose not to go back to Blighty, I see?'

'I want to return to duty as soon as possible.'

'Right. That's the spirit.'

Several of their conversations followed this well-worn path and left Parsons with a furrowed brow as he wrote his notes at the end of their sessions. He would leave the office, pull the door quietly behind him and return to his book. He presumed that at some stage Parsons would give him the all clear.

It was not normal for him to prevaricate over anything, but he put off for as long as possible the letter addressed to the Rev. and Mrs J. M. P. Courtnay at the Vicarage. One long July evening, as twilight began to fall and martins fluttered outside the window against the darkening blue, he sat down at the typewriter and composed a reply to the several anxious letters he had received. His arm allowed some movement now in the fingers of his right hand and this was good exercise.

'Dear Mother and Father,' he began. 'I am sorry I have not been able to write until now. Thankfully my arm is healing and I am better able to produce this most difficult letter.'

He considered what he should write next, deciding finally that he should keep it brief. The accident, as he called it, had changed his life irrevocably. Perhaps it simply typified the change in him since military service. He would not be returning shortly to England, either to his place at Oxford or to the family home. He saw a completely different future for himself. For the time being he planned to remain in some capacity with the military, though front-line activity was out of the question. He would then see where fate took him. He thought a clean break was the best solution all round, so he would not be writing to them again. He would not reply to any letters they sent him. He assured them that he was perfectly well, both physically and mentally, and that this full and final decision was made perfectly rationally. He regretted the upset this must cause them and thanked them for his loving upbringing.

He signed the letter with a jagged, painful 'Roy' and placed the paper once again into the machine to add a postscript apologizing for his inability to write by hand.

He had had enough of this place now and

lobbied for a posting. After three weeks he was sent to the office in Brussels that was beginning the work of codifying the Allied Forces' operating status in Europe following the war.

13

Holding On

1

He emerges from a fitful sleep into the bright light of the ward. Around him he can hear the sound of businesslike bustling, but it is not to do with him.

He can recall vividly the moment the revolver skidded to a halt on the floor and that split second when all three men saw that they had arrived at a turning point. He can recall his heart leaping in fear-fuelled exultation as he made for the weapon. He can recall the two other men doing the same, and the silence of an age before the coming-together. He can remember little else. In his mind there is a blur of action, the flash of the blade, pain in his arm and then the absence of pain, blood spattering, the crunch of bodies colliding and the report of the Webley, astonishingly loud at such close quarters. It booms now, in his head. But then what? He is not even sure who he is.

He opens his eyes. The activity in the ward concerns a patient across the way whose bedlinen is being changed. Nothing too drastic and thankfully no one looks towards his bed. He closes his eyes again to think. He hopes he will shortly be released from here and resume real life. The office in Hanover has always seemed so humdrum; now it is enticing. Marjorie, the office dragon, and Derek, Bert and Ernie, the three clerks. He has managed to get hold of some real coffee from the American PX. They will love that. But then it begins seeping back. Things will not return to normal, though he does not quite know why.

Still, as soon as this wound heals he will be out of here. He shifts position and pain jags through him. The odd thing is that it seems to be in his side rather than his arm. Even to think is an effort and he feels tired.

The next thing he knows, there is a gentle voice flowing over him. 'Wake up, Roy,' it says. He wants to say: I am awake, don't you realize? I just want to keep my eyes closed. I just want everything to stop moving, existing. But the voice is sweet, as is the waft of verbena perfume, and he cannot resist opening his eyes.

There she is. How can that be? Sweet little . . . No. Impossible, he realizes as the thought swirls in his brain.

Gradually he is able to focus. No. How could he be so stupid? It's that old woman. The one he lives with. What's her name? Such a simple thing, a name. At least it should be. He's always prided himself on his memory for names. Almost within grasp. Betty.

And with the name fragments come drifting back, weightless. That little mews cottage by the Green. Vincent. Oh yes. Vincent. The drugs they give you. That must be it. A bit off-colour, that's all. He takes her hand and holds on for dear life.

A doctor comes into view, carrying a clip-board.

'Well then, Mr Courtnay,' he says.

Yes! Courtnay. Captain Roy Courtnay if you please. Present and correct.

And then it begins to float into place. The world turns slowly. Planets coincide gently. His memory docks again inaudibly and there is clarity. Just a little turn, he thinks.

'You've had a nasty fall, Mr Courtnay. A couple of cracked ribs. They'll be quite painful.'

Why is he telling him this? Why is he speaking so loudly? He doesn't need telling his ribs hurt. But he is mute, staring up at the man-child who is attending him. Long tousled hair, T-shirt under his white coat. Hasn't shaved. Complete mess.

'You'll be right as rain in a few days. I said right as rain, Mr Courtnay.'

The doctor smiles encouragingly. Roy thinks: have I turned into some imbecile overnight? He coughs but still does not speak.

'And after that perhaps we need to discuss options.'

He notices he is still holding Betty's hand and his grip is becoming tighter. He looks up at her but she is looking at the doctor.

'Perhaps we might have a word after your visit, Mrs Courtnay.'

'I'm not Mrs Courtnay,' says Betty with a shy smile. 'I'm just a friend.'

'I'm so sorry,' says the young man. 'Please forgive me. I just assumed.'

You might almost believe in his sincerity. It seems Betty does.

The doctor wanders off in his trainers, his hands in the pockets of his coat.

'How are you feeling?' asks Betty.

Did she not hear the doctor? I feel terrible. I'm in pain. But he smiles, and says, 'I'm all right. Just a bit of a turn.'

'Maybe you've been overdoing things.'

'How?'

'All the financial stuff. Vincent.'

'Oh no,' he says decisively. 'Just a bit peaky. Must be some kind of virus. Back on my feet in no time.'

'I'm worried. You mustn't rush things.'

'Don't you worry about me,' he says. 'Be back home in two shakes.' He looks up at her.

'It gave me a fright,' she says.

'No doubt. Must have been a bit of a crash.'

'The ambulance crew were excellent. They were there in minutes and took charge.'

'Good. Listen. Could you get in touch with Vincent? I'm sure he'd like to know and, depending on how long I'm laid up, he might want to drop in on me.'

'All right. Do I have his number?'

'I think your Stephen does. If not it'll be on the papers he gave you.'

'All right.'

'Betty?'

'Yes, Roy?'

'Don't let them put me in a home. Please.'

'What are you talking about, Roy? Who's said anything about a home?'

'It's just a funny turn. I'll be fine. Don't let them put me in one of those places.'

'Don't be silly,' she says, smiling. 'You'll be back home before you know it.'

2

'The doctor wanted a word afterwards,' Betty tells Stephen. 'He suggested we should consider 'other options' when he's discharged.'

'Such as?' asks Stephen.

'Isn't the euphemism obvious? Some desperate institution with a Happy Valley cover name. He wants social services to do an assessment of care needs. You won't be surprised to learn that he doesn't want a bit of it. He can see the slippery slope.'

'You should consider it seriously. What's the diagnosis, anyway?'

'A couple of cracked ribs. Painful, but he'll recover. They put the fall down to high blood pressure. Anxiety may have brought it on. He has a heart condition that's kept under control by medication. They've upped the tablets.'

'Anxiety?'

'Yes. Presumably all the stress with Vincent and the money.'

'We've done nothing to heighten his stress levels. It's all going remarkably smoothly. Whatever he is, he's not a panicker.'

'I know. But he is very old, you have to remember. Like me. And he'll be more frail than he looks.'

'We should think about the home option.'

'I heard you the first time. They did some cognitive tests on him too. For signs of dementia. He's been disorientated since the fall. The tests aren't fully conclusive. They need to do more, but it could be that onset is occurring. If confirmed, given his age they'd anticipate full development being quite swift.'

'How swift?'

'Months, probably. Maybe a year or two. Possibly weeks.'

'Doesn't that settle it? You can't possibly take on that burden. He has to go into a suitable home. Then disengage.'

'If it is dementia the early stages shouldn't be too problematic,' she says in a matter-of-fact tone. 'There'll be long periods of lucidity. As time goes on the confusion will increase. The doctors will monitor it and there's always the option of a nursing home later.'

'But why? Just let it all go.'

'Perhaps I'm selfish, but I can't. I can't let go. Not just yet. I'm holding on. Not losing my nerve. We have only a few weeks more of this, you know, once he's out. Would you believe, just before he had his accident, he asked me to share the large bedroom with him?'

'What did you say?' says Stephen quietly.

'What do you think? I laughed it off. Perhaps we should consider getting a double room together in some awful Sunset Pastures place.'

Stephen evidently does not share her amusement.

'We spoke of love,' she says. 'Or at least I did.'

'Love?'

'Yes. It slipped out, rather. It was something to say. I simply said love didn't seem to be part of his vocabulary.'

'Slightly injudicious, don't you think? Talking to him about love?'

'You sound like Gerald.'

'Sorry. It just seems a bit risky. To be fair to him for one moment, it's hardly a question many men in their eighties are equipped to answer.'

'No. He was a bit at sea. Anyway, I don't really care about the risk. This whole adventure is one big risk. And it is rather amusing to see him so uneasy. With all his certainty. A bit cruel, perhaps, considering what's just happened. But that's as maybe. The subject was soon closed.'

She pours the tea.

'I'm just so . . . '

'Yes?'

'Concerned for you, I suppose.'

'It's all right. I have things perfectly under control.'

'I know, but I just worry. It's a huge thing to take on. And him being so close, physically. I worry it might end badly.'

'I'm immensely grateful for your concern, Stephen. And it makes a huge difference to know that you're there — watching my back, isn't that the expression? But I can cope with him. Really I can.'

'I just admire you so much and it makes me sick to think he might be able to hurt you.'

'Oh, Stephen. He can't hurt me. I'm pretty tough. And though I may have experienced a few things in my time I'm not sure I particularly deserve your adulation. I'm just a perfectly ordinary person.'

'You're not.'

'Yes I am,' she insists, and they are silent.

'But thank you,' she says eventually. 'You've been such a help, and a good friend too if I may say so. You've really made it possible for me to do all this. With your help I can manage him.'

3

'I didn't know what to bring,' mumbles Vincent. 'Grapes, I thought, or something . . . '

'I bloody hate grapes,' says Roy.

'I didn't know that.'

'Half-bottle of Bell's would be nice. To pop under my pillow.'

'Anyway, I brought these.' Vincent gives Roy a brown paper bag containing a box of cheap chocolates, which he accepts wordlessly and places on the side table.

'I wanted to make sure we were still on track,' says Roy.

'You are kidding, aren't you? I thought you'd want it all on hold. Until things were clearer.'

'By which you mean if I get out of this place in a box or not.'

Vincent stares at him and does not deny his thinking.

'Nah,' says Roy. 'Take a bit more than a little fall to put me out of action. Bruised and battered, maybe, but not beaten. Down but not out. Be back home before you know it. Full speed ahead as far as I'm concerned.'

'You sure? I mean . . .'

'What? You having cold feet or something, Vincent? Betty fluttered her eyelashes or something? You a little bit besotted?'

'No, nothing like that,' says Vincent irascibly. 'If you must know, I'm looking out for you.'

'Thank you kindly. But no need to do that. I've coped well enough over the years.'

'This is madness, Roy. It's suicide, or close to it, you doing her over. You've got yourself neatly set up there. She looks after you and surely that's what you need now, not more money.'

Roy laughs. 'You are having seconds, aren't you? Not like you. Think I'm going to pop my clogs in the middle of all this and leave a mess for you to clear up? More for you, I'd have thought. Betty's not one for reneging on deals. You'd have my stake money in your back pocket too. You'd be quids in and all you'd need to do is to fade neatly into the background.'

'No, it's not that, Roy. This is crazy. Why are you doing this?'

'I've told you before. It's what I do.'

'Not good enough, Roy. You'll destroy her and you'll destroy yourself.'

'It'll have to be,' says Roy sharply. 'I don't have to explain myself to you. You get paid well enough to keep your trap shut and do what I want. Or is that it? You think this is our last gig together and you can shake me down for some more? What is it you want? Sixty per cent? Seventy?'

Vincent shakes his head. 'No, it's not that. I just don't think you should be doing this.'

'So does that mean you're out? Because if so you could have had the decency to tell me earlier. You leave me in a right mess, I can tell you.'

'No, Roy. I'm in, still. If it's what you definitely want. I was just saying you have time to pull out if you want. No hard feelings. No payment necessary for what I've done so far. I'd be happier to let it go.'

Roy relaxes in his bed and adopts a calmer tone. 'No, we're hanging on with this one. To the bitter end. Look, Vincent. This is my life. Dodging and weaving. This is me. We both know that it's you too. I know what makes you tick, Vincent. No, when it comes to it I'll die in the saddle, talking some greedy mark into doing something stupid. Maybe this one, maybe the next. Now, can we get on with it?'

14

December 1938
A Faraway Country

1

Snow had already arrived in Berlin, driven by the chill wind across the steppes. Konrad Taub and his son marched through the streets in the teeth of the blizzard, unable to converse, simply covering the ground with grim resolve.

Taub rang the bell and pulled off his gloves, banging them against the brickwork to shake away the residue of snow. Hans imitated him and looked up at the grey sky, thick flakes floating down, then caught on the wind and hurled violently. It resembled chaos.

A servant opened the door and admitted them without speaking. Carefully, they removed their coats and stamped their feet on the doormat, which was as large as the rug in the main room of their small apartment. Traces of snow and wet dribbled on to the mat. Hans shivered as the warmth made him realize how cold it had been outside.

They knew their way and the servant departed with a nod, carrying their coats. Away from the turmoil of the wind and the snow and the dark busyness of the city, it was quiet here, with a beguiling calm. All that could be heard was a distant murmur somewhere deep in the house, the preparations for the Christmas ball in the evening to which neither Hans nor his parents had been invited. The meeting with Schröder would be short.

They climbed the stairs and walked to Schröder's study.

'Ah, welcome,' he said. 'How are you, Konrad? And Hans? It's cold outside. A coffee? Maybe a schnapps?'

'A small glass, perhaps,' said Taub.

Schröder found a bottle and glasses in a cupboard. 'It's chaos round here. The party this evening. Magda is frantic. She thrives on it. I'm sorry we didn't invite you. I thought it best.' He said it in a matter-of-fact voice.

'No. I understand. I doubt it would be our kind of occasion.'

'Nor mine,' said Schröder with a smile. 'But it's expected of me. Not, you understand, that we invite any of those awful Nazis. But our relationship is, I think, best kept low-key. For both our sakes. Renate is well?'

'Yes. As busy as ever.'

'So, young Hans. How old are you now?'

'Fourteen, sir.'

'I wonder whether you might wish to join us in a glass of schnapps, Hans. If your father would permit it.'

'No, sir. I don't think so, sir.'

'Please, Hans, if you would like to,' said his father.

'No, Father. I don't think I'd like the taste.'

'A sensible young man,' said Schröder with a

smile. 'It's good to avoid the demon drink as long as possible. I'll order something from the kitchen for you. What would you like? I'm sure there must be some chocolate cake somewhere in the house.'

'It's all right, sir. I'm not hungry or thirsty.'

The two men sat with their drinks on leather sofas that faced each other in front of the blazing hearth. Hans remained standing, his cap in his hand, his shoes continuing to drip melt into the carpet.

'Well then, Konrad. What's the latest?'

Hans was fascinated by this room. The walls were lined in rich, dark mahogany bookcases, floor to ceiling, and each shelf was full of books. There was a small ladder that matched the bookcases so that the top volumes could be reached. A large, heavy desk, the size of his bed, faced inwards from the window. Its surface was covered almost entirely with papers, arranged carefully in neat piles, each, he imagined, covering a different aspect of Herr Schröder's business empire. Despite his curiosity and boldness, he would not have had the temerity to look at the papers even given the chance. The room was lit in sections, a large lamp illuminating the desk's surface, discreet lighting in the bookcases to aid navigation there and two heavy iron floor lamps behind each of the sofas to supplement the fierce bright light of the fire. This was the sort of room he wanted as his refuge.

The two men, keen to discuss their business, had evidently forgotten his presence.

'War is definite,' Schröder was saying.

'That's what everyone thinks,' replied his father.

'No. What I mean is that I know that it's their firm intention to have war once their preparations are complete.'

'How do you know?'

'Ravenstein. We supply to him. He's not exactly a sympathizer, but then again he's not exactly out of sympathy. He's a personal friend of Speer. He's been asked to increase production for the next six months with the express purpose of being ready for conflict part-way through next year. Hitler will find some pretext to precipitate it. Probably Danzig. You may tell your confidential contacts.'

'And as for the diplomatic effort? Britain's appeasement?'

'Ravenstein says it suits Hitler. He thinks Chamberlain is a convenient fool. He may buy Britain a few months, but he's also giving us more time to sharpen our tools. Hitler won't let Chamberlain affect his plans. The British are a busted flush. The point is, though, Konrad, what can we do? We can expect atrocities against Jews to increase. Ravenstein says plans to develop the concentration camp programme are well in hand. And they're considering mass forced emigration of Jews to the east. With militarization as well, we're on an unstoppable path to hell. Now's the time for you and your associates to act.'

'The question remains the same as ever, Albert. Precisely how? We have no military

247

structures, we have no money, no weapons, no expertise. We'd be slaughtered. I'm a journalist. I'm not a political figure, let alone a leader. I have no idea what to do. It's too late to sow unrest in the factories. They're too full of patriotic fervour.'

'Your friends outside the country?'

'I'm a liberal, Albert. And I have my contacts. But Britain and her allies? They will contemplate and consider and be reasonable until it's too late altogether for reason. It's too late already, but they don't know it. They simply think that the Sudetenland is a distant country. They'll think the same of Poland or Czechoslovakia. Or France and the Netherlands if it comes to it. They think of us all as far away, so long as we don't interfere in their interests. And by the time we do interfere, it'll be too late.'

'Then we must do what we can.'

'I agree. What do you have in mind?'

'The Jews will suffer most in the next few years. They'll be victimized, even more than today. I shudder to think what will happen. It would be the same for us if we were Jewish. Just an accident of birth or religion.'

'So?'

'So we need to establish a means of saving them from us,' said Schröder. 'A means of enabling them to escape, as many as can. I'm prepared to find money. Large amounts of it. But you will have to work on the practical details, with your friends outside the country.'

Konrad paused, and looked over to Hans.

'Hans,' he said, 'I'm sorry. We forgot you were

248

there. We've been boring you with our political talk. Please, you're excused.'

'Hans,' said Schröder, 'why don't you go and find the girls? I'm sure they're around the house somewhere.' Schröder stood, and Hans felt him watching his progress down the corridor before he closed the door of the study.

He padded along the corridor, jumping experimentally to feel his feet sink into the plush pile carpet with a deadened impact. Despite the distant noise of servants scurrying and furniture being moved and cutlery and crockery being laid on tables, up here it was quiet. He opened one door and then another, but there was no one. He looked in the formal drawing room and then in the cosy little snug on the opposite side of the wide corridor. Outside, it was snowing heavily.

Eventually he heard excited voices behind a bedroom door. He opened it slowly. There they were, the three elder sisters.

Charlotte giggled with delight. 'Oh, it's little Hansi. Come in, come in.'

Once, he had been glad to be their little Hansi. Anything that brought him access to their fragrant presence had been bearable. Now he resented being called little. He was taller than any of them and much more powerful. The sense that they were making fun of him made things worse.

Nonetheless he went in. Charlotte was the middle of the three, aged eighteen, and the most skittish in Hans's view. She was also the one he found prettiest, the one he wanted most to kiss. Her lips were red, ripe and full. But any of the three would have done. Hannelore was the eldest, marginally more serious than the other two. She had already started working in her father's factory. Anneliese was simply too young for him, though three years his senior. She was just so immature.

None of these girls had ambition or intellect. They were all frivolous and he was not familiar with frivolity. His own father and mother were serious and thoughtful, and encouraged him to be so too. In this family Lili, the youngest sister, would be the studious one.

'We're trying on our dresses for the party tonight, Hansi,' said Anneliese with fake coyness. 'Would you like to see them?'

'Er, yes,' he said, blushing. 'I suppose so.'

They laughed. 'Oh, dear Hansi,' said Charlotte, 'are you coming to the ball tonight? Will you be our prince?'

'Er, no. I'm not coming.'

'Stop teasing, Charlotte,' said Hannelore. 'Are you here with your father, Hansi?'

'Yes.'

'I do hope Daddy will stop work soon,' said Anneliese. 'He needs to get ready too.'

The room smelt of cleanness and soap, and of them. He was embarrassed almost to the point of squirming, yet he was glad to be here. The brightness of it all was dazzling. He longed to reach out and touch one of them. Even better if one of them touched him.

'Aren't you warm, Hansi?' said Charlotte. 'Isn't it warm in here, Anneliese?'

'Yes,' answered her sister. 'It's so exciting.'

'Are you hoping your lieutenant will be here tonight, Hannelore?'

'Well, he's accepted the invitation.'

Her two sisters giggled in unison.

'I hope he brings some of his friends,' said Anneliese.

They chattered as if he were not there. He did not mind. He wished he could be invisible but remain there always. To watch. This was Charlotte's room. He wished he could watch her as she prepared for this evening and be there on her return to see her remove her make-up carefully in front of the mirror, before shaking her dark hair and removing her dress. He wanted to see her remove her underwear and to see her plump breasts freed from their bounds, to watch her step out of her knickers and to savour the sight and the smell and the taste and feel of what lay beneath.

He felt an aching, yearning hardness and dared not move for fear they would notice. They laughed and shouted, moving around him as he sat primly on the edge of the bed.

'Sorry,' he said when he found himself looking into Hannelore's inquiring eyes. 'What did you say?'

'Hansi's daydreaming again,' she said, laughing. 'I said, would you like to see us in our gowns?'

'Er, yes,' he replied.

'Well then. You'll have to stand outside for a few minutes while we get ready. Off with you. Out.'

She marched him outside the door, where he

waited obediently. He did not dare a glance through the keyhole but stood, stiff and still.

Eventually the door opened again and Anneliese peered around it.

'Fashion show,' she announced, and opened the door wide.

He went in and each of the girls sashayed in front of him in turn, grinning, posing, blowing kisses towards him. He was bedazzled but expressionless, gulping inwardly on the seat at the dressing table that they had turned to face the room. Anneliese touched him gently on the leg and he looked intently at the spot where her hand had brushed him. He was beginning to feel heady with the fragrance of perfume and girl. Hannelore tousled his hair and he grinned inanely. The girls danced together and Anneliese reached for him. He stood and she pulled him towards her. He knew to place his hand gently at her waist, but no more. She took him with her as if tied by gossamer, moving gracefully. He clumped gamely in tow.

Hannelore laughed and clapped her hands. 'I hope Daddy will let us drink some of his champagne,' she said.

Hans giggled for no reason.

Charlotte threw herself back on the bed, sighing. Her wide dress flew up. He could see her lace petticoats. He did not divert his eyes. For a moment, just a second, he saw her drawers.

Without realizing it, he had stopped dancing. He pulled Anneliese close to him, still looking at Charlotte. Anneliese resisted but he was a strong boy. He was aware of her thigh against his hardness and it felt good.

'Don't,' she said loudly. 'Hans, no. You'll crease my dress.'

He released her and she moved quickly away from him. There was silence in the room. All three girls looked at him. The full import of the exchange was clear to everyone.

Eventually it was Hannelore who spoke, with forced cheerfulness. 'We really must get ready for tonight, Hans. Your father will be waiting for you now, surely?'

He detected scorn in her expectant look. Bitches. Without speaking, he left the room and slammed the door behind him.

Furious, he pounded the corridors, kicking his feet out before him. A maid who passed him suggested he might come down to the kitchen for a hot chocolate with whipped cream. He glared at her. He hated this house.

Lili was in a window seat, her feet folded neatly under her, reading a book. She called him back after he had passed the room.

'Hans! Hans! Have you seen the snow?'

He groaned inwardly. He'd had enough of the others. Now he had to deal with this child. He could, feasibly, walk on, carried by his blackness, but something drew him back.

'Yes, I've seen it.'

She stood and came to the door.

'Isn't it wonderful? I'm going to ask Mama if I may play outside later.'

'You have your party tonight. And it'll be dark soon.'

'I'm not allowed to go to the party. I'm to go to bed early. But I shall watch from the stairs, whatever they say. Maybe I'll play in the snow tomorrow. Would you come and play, Hans?'

Lili was by far the youngest of the sisters. His parents had joked that she must be the Schröders' afterthought. He did not know what was amusing about being an afterthought. She was ten years old, a baby.

The difficulty was that Lili adored him, though not in the same way as the elder daughters. For them he was a kind of pet, a puppy. Lili looked up to him; he was her hero. It was embarrassing, but not entirely unwelcome. Sometimes he would enjoy her rapt attention; on other occasions, like now, it filled him with impatient contempt.

'No,' he said, 'I have more important things to do.'

'That's a shame.'

'I don't actually play children's games any more.'

She looked up at him sadly, her brown eyes scanning him curiously. He relished the effect of his cruelty and willed his own eyes to transmit cold indifference.

Once he had tolerated her. Once she had not been so irritating. Once he too had been a child. He had even sat patiently while she carefully cut a lock of his blond hair for a locket she had received as a birthday gift from an aunt. Rather too much hair in fact. She had held it aloft, examining it delightedly in the sunlight before kissing it and placing it in the locket. He had chuckled to himself, he remembered. He would not do that now.

He touched her arm with his hand and felt her cold skin.

'Let's play something now,' he said.

'All right,' she replied.

He ushered her into her room and closed the door behind them. The snow was falling heavily outside and grey was turning into dusk. They could barely see each other.

He stood before her and with his hands on the outside of her arms lined her up to face him directly. He looked down at her.

'Have you ever kissed like them?'

'Like who?'

'Them. Like grown-ups.'

'Do they kiss differently?'

'Yes. Would you like to try?'

'With you?'

'Yes. Of course.'

'Well yes, I suppose.'

He reached down to the little girl and pulled her towards him, holding her close to his body. He could smell her and feel her warmth against his chest. He stroked her arm before placing his left arm around the small of her back, his other arm over her shoulder. It was awkward, this manoeuvre that looked so natural in the movies, but eventually they were where he wanted them to be. Her midriff was against his stiff penis, which also pressed against his own belly. She could not fail to notice it; he wanted her to.

He bent to place his mouth against hers. Her eyes were wide open, startled. He liked the fear.

She will be a pretty little thing one day, he thought. Their lips touched in a moment where he imagined he must become a different human being altogether. Later he would discover otherwise.

He pressed his mouth hard against her softness, moving insistently to urge her lips apart. They did not open, and Lili's mouth muscles tightened. He thrust his tongue into her mouth, against her teeth, and eventually forced his way through. Uncertainly she submitted, opening herself reluctantly to him. Excitedly, he explored with his tongue. This was the first time he had done anything like this.

Eventually he gasped. She looked at him, fearful, out of breath, and made to move away. But he still held her arms.

'Did you like that?' he said eagerly.

'Well . . . ' she said doubtfully.

'Shall we do it again?'

'I don't know. If you like.'

He reached down again. This time it came more naturally. He savoured the wet of her saliva on his tongue as it ranged again inside, as if he were discovering something new and fundamental about another. Even if it was only Lili. Gradually he freed his right hand and shucked up her skirt. She pulled away but he had her firmly gripped by his other hand. His tongue continued to probe while he found the elastic of her knickers, and insinuated his fingers underneath, feeling the marble-smooth skin of her thighs. She squirmed but he pulled her hair with a sharp jerk that made her compliant. To his annoyance she was whimpering. He found the fleshy notch that he was seeking and ran his index finger up and down it before locating his real objective. Roughly, he thrust his finger into the soft gap and she flinched. The second time he rammed two fingers, meeting resistance from her pubic bone, and she yelped in pain. He released her and she collapsed on the floor.

He had had enough. Lili had served her purpose. She was weeping silently and holding her belly. He sniffed his fingers curiously. 'Filthy bitch,' he muttered. 'You dare say anything to anyone.'

Was that it? It had not been enjoyable. He walked the corridor angrily towards the study. Maybe he should have done the whole thing. Perhaps that was it. Maybe there was just nothing at the end of it all. Maybe that was the trick they played on you. All that excitement and then this. Nothing. Bitches. Thinking they could humiliate him.

He paused at the door. The two men were still talking. He put his ear to the door.

'Sometimes I wish I too were a Jew,' Schröder was saying.

'You don't really mean that,' Konrad Taub replied.

'Actually I do. I could at least hold my head high alongside my friends who are being victimized. As it is, our nation is being divided, into the persecutors and the persecuted. Those who choose not to become involved fall into the first category. We need people like you, Konrad.'

'And you too, Albert.'

'But I do not oppose publicly. You do. You put yourself in the way of danger for the sake of your fellow men. That is a particular sort of bravery.'

'Or foolishness. And I'm quite careful. I sense my limits when I'm writing.'

'You go right up to them. You and Renate are courageous people. You'll be remembered in history.'

'Perhaps for struggling pathetically against the inevitable,' said Konrad. 'With words. Laughable. Now, you're sure you're happy with me passing on the information you've given me?'

'You'll pass it on anyway. And yes, of course I'm happy. Anything that impresses on them the seriousness of the situation. And of course I will do more. Whatever is required.'

'We need to consider networks. We need to think about what damage can be done to the war effort.'

'Whatever's necessary. It's too late now for half-measures.'

'You're a brave man, Albert, whatever you say.'

He turned his spite on them. These self-congratulating, self-deluding fools, with their politics. His own father. Pathetic. Disgusting. Thinking they could change the shape of things. Whatever their fantasies, the real world was arranged rather differently. He knocked on the door, opening it hesitantly.

'Father . . . '

'Heavens, is that the time?' said Konrad. 'We must be getting home. I have another meeting this evening.'

'And I must get ready for the party,' said

Schröder. 'Goodnight, Konrad. Goodnight, Hans.'

2

The snow had stopped by the next morning, though it remained bitterly cold. There was a layer of ice on the inside of the bathroom window when he rose at six and went through the ritual of his morning wash as swiftly as he could.

His mother was already in the kitchen, standing by the small range. She poured him coffee and he wrapped his hands around the steaming bowl. She took a bobbing egg from the pan and placed it on his plate, along with two slices of rye bread and a generous portion of butter. He accepted them without thanks.

'Where's Father?' he asked.

'He's left already. He has a meeting.'

He ate in silence as she watched him.

'What?' he said.

'Nothing. You're growing up quickly, that's all. You're not a little boy any more.'

He grunted and asked whether there was any cheese. He was always hungry these days.

'How are things at school, Hans? Are the boys still on about your father?'

'No, not really. They got bored with it.' This was a half-truth. He had discovered strategies to reduce the abuse.

'We're on the right side, you know.'

'I know. You've explained it enough.'

'But if it gets too difficult at school you must tell us. We need to talk about it. I may have to go and see Herr Professor Wolff about it.'

'No need,' he responded gruffly, and thought with grim humour of them speaking to his headmaster. What good did they think their seeing Wolff would do? Konrad Taub, the pinko journalist regarded with suspicion speaking with rumoured deputy Gauleiter candidate Hermann Wolff? Did they see some meeting of minds here? He had his own means of sorting out the situation which did not require their interference.

'It's all right. There's no problem. My marks are all right, aren't they?'

He knew they were. His parents were both intellectuals, that term bandied about these days in disgust. At least it would mean that the basic equipment for achievement was there. What he did with it depended on him. He certainly would not be wasting his potential in the same way as his parents on lost causes of one kind or another.

'I may be out when you get back, Hans,' his mother said. 'I have a meeting in Neukölln. I'll leave the key with Frau Schärner next door.'

'All right,' he grunted, not interested.

He walked to school through dark streets. The glint of dawn had yet to appear. The snow's soft fluffiness had gone. Now it was frozen and compacted underfoot. The thoroughfares had been cleared efficiently but the pavements and walkways remained covered. At least this meant there was no black ice. The hardened snow was treacherous enough, but navigable. Vapour billowed from his nose, and he heard himself inhale and exhale as he made his steady progress. The Jewish grocers at the corner of Wilhelmstrasse had again been burned overnight. Embers glowed and a group of callow Brownshirts not much older than he was joshed with each other and kicked at the smouldering remains to keep warm. Their voices echoed in the muffled white cityscape.

Inside the school he felt instantly warm. The pipes and radiators clicked and ticked as he made his way to the secretary's office. Most boys would have been turned away sternly: not Hans Taub. She told him to return at the end of school, at one fifteen.

The morning dragged. Latin was followed inevitably by mathematics, and then chemistry and German. Hans excelled in all of these subjects, the primary reason why he remained popular with his teachers in spite of his dubious parents. He gained a measure of respect too from his fellow pupils by helping them with their work.

At the end of school his classmates rushed out. Someone's uncle had been told by someone who had a brother in the Gestapo that the Jewish jeweller at the top of Blumenstrasse was about to be arrested and that the Brownshirts would be in charge of looting and ransacking. There was sport to be had, and just possibly the odd watch to be acquired.

Hans remained in the building and sat waiting in the outer office for admission to the principal's study. He was reminded of a

261

conversation the previous week with Herr Professor Wolff in the same room.

'I can understand why you are eager to join the Hitler Youth,' Wolff had said, 'but we need to consider the effects. I am sure you do not want to cause a rift with your parents. In any case, I think there may be better ways for you to serve the Reich. I am sure the Führer would prefer you to assist in different ways. There will be time for glory in the future.'

He had made his choices accordingly and now had a proposal to make. It was perilous but it was the only way out of the mess created by his idiot parents.

'Come in, Hans,' said Wolff, a studious university professor and senior Party member who had been parachuted into his post after the dismissal of his unreliable predecessor three years before. Another man stood in the room, altogether less bookish and more practical.

'May I introduce Herr Weber of the Gestapo.'

Weber seemed Hans's sort of person. Upright, muscular and vigorous, he was younger than Hans might have expected. He shook hands with a firm grip and looked into Hans's eyes. Hans felt Weber might have been looking into his soul.

'Now then,' said Weber. 'I understand you wish to do your country a service. Discreetly, I mean. You'll be pleased to know I have experience in such matters. Involving discretion, that is. Now, will you tell me what you wish to say?'

Direct and to the point. This was what Hans wanted.

'Yes, sir,' he said, faltering at first, but then gaining confidence. 'I have something to offer you and I'd like something in return.'

Weber smiled. 'A bargain. Yes, we can manage that, within reason. It has to be right for both of us, however. How can I help you?'

'My parents are foolish, sir. We both know that. I can't help but love them. I know what they're doing is likely to lead them to prison but there's nothing I can do to dissuade them.'

'Have you talked to them?'

'No, it's not worth beginning to.'

'That's probably just as well. The less they know of your feelings, the better.'

'That's what I thought. But I'd like to save them from themselves.'

'Admirable. Go on.'

'I have information I think you'd want. But I want to protect my parents as well.'

Weber smiled again, that smile that said every problem had its solution. 'I understand. A dilemma. Let's see whether we can sort it out. What's the information?'

'I thought, sir, we might agree first on what should happen once I've told you.'

'Well, that depends, really. What did you have in mind?'

'I'd like my parents to leave the country. I'd prefer to stay, but I'd have to go with them. They wouldn't leave without me.'

'I see. The information would have to be very important for us to permit this. And while we might be prepared to see your parents leave — the greater the number of disloyal irritants outside the Fatherland the better, in one sense — actually to cause them to leave without making it obvious why would seem a problem. Deporting them wouldn't be a good example to set. Whereas if they simply fled . . . Do you see?'

'Yes. I've thought of that,' said Hans.

'Oh, good. Very good.' Weber smiled again.

'And on the first question, yes, I think my information would be important enough.'

'Hmm. We shall see. If I were to say yes in principle you'd have to trust me first with this information. I'd give you my word, but obviously if I genuinely believed what you told me was merely trivial, there'd be no deal. Does that sound fair enough? Do you trust me?'

'Yes, sir.'

'Good man. Then we can move forward. Deal?'

'Yes, sir. Could I have it in writing?'

Weber laughed. 'Deals like this aren't usually subject to contract. But yes, I'd be prepared to put my signature to something if it made you happier. For your own safety, however, I'd need to retain the document.'

'That's all right, sir. I trust you.'

'All right, then. Fire away, Hans Taub.'

'I overheard Albert Schröder and my father talking in Herr Schröder's study.'

'This is the factory owner Schröder?'

'Yes, sir. They were discussing the government and saying that war's inevitable.'

'Yes?'

'Herr Schröder said it was terrible. He and my father discussed what could be done about the situation. He offered money to help Jews leave the country. He wanted to help opposition to the Führer. Later they discussed damaging the war effort in Herr Schröder's factories.'

'Sabotage, you mean?'

'Yes, sir. Herr Schröder told my father he was willing for his factories to be damaged if it harmed the German war effort. He asked my father to pass this information outside the country.'

'Anything else, Hans?'

Hans sensed that what he had said might not be sufficient. 'Yes, sir. Herr Schröder told my father he's a Jew. He has Jewish blood.'

'I see,' said Weber, who had been noting this down. 'This could be important. Or possibly not. I simply don't know. Can you remember exactly what was said, and by whom?'

'Yes, sir, and it's all true.'

'I don't doubt it. But I do need to think about it.'

'Our deal, sir?' said Hans tentatively.

'You've no need to worry. I'll keep my side of the bargain. The question is whether we can do anything with this. That's what'll make it important or unimportant. Would you be prepared to sign a statement?'

'Yes, sir.'

'Good man. You said you had ideas about how to make your father go overseas?'

'Yes, sir. It involves Herr Professor Wolff.'

'I see. Tell me more.'

Later, Hans was asked to leave, with an agreement to talk again the next day in the principal's office.

★ ★ ★

'Do you believe him, Wolff?' asked Weber. 'Might he have got this wrong?'

'He's a very intelligent boy. Yes, I believe him. But we have something of an ethical problem.'

'Yes?'

'The boy is a minor. It is one thing denouncing your parents for insulting the Führer when he comes on the radio. This is quite different. The consequences could be significant.'

'I'm aware of that. But the difficulties may be surmountable.'

'Do you have any corroboration for what he says?'

'That's something I'll have to check. Frankly I doubt it. They may have talked out of turn in front of little Hansi, but Taub and Schröder are generally cautious individuals. Of course we know of Taub's visits to the house, but beyond that . . . '

'You would not wish to see whether the boy can obtain further information about Schröder and his father?'

'I doubt he'd be able to. What he said would be sufficient to condemn both of them anyway, if we could prove it in a court of law. Also, the time when we have room for manoeuvre for arrangements like this may be limited. By this time next year . . . '

'This is the unsupported testimony of a fourteen-year-old.'

'I suppose so. If you put it like that. But it's compelling and I suspect even more so when we

266

get the detail down on paper. His age doesn't damage his credibility. What he said is entirely believable. And there's this. There's a great deal of doubt about the Schröders. They have bohemian connections. They make no effort to espouse the right ideals. To be candid, my colleagues could welcome a concrete reason to edge Albert Schröder out of the picture. His business is a good one and can make a contribution to the war effort. The wrong man's in charge, though. Schröder is regarded as unreliable. With good reason, it seems. And it'd be good to have Taub senior out of our hair. There may be the possibility of a little latitude.'

'What do you mean, latitude?'

'It may be more convenient to gloss over the fact of Hans's age, for instance.'

'But when it comes to examination in court . . . '

'Oh, there's no question Hans would actually appear as a witness. The state protects those who are public-minded enough to offer confidential information. The presiding judge of the People's Court will simply read the statement and hear my testimony.'

'You would be prepared to omit relevant facts?'

'Of course not. I simply don't believe the boy's age is particularly germane. More pertinent is his reliability, and we seem to have established that. There are plenty of adults whose reports would be far less detailed and accurate. And if you and I have the choice of protecting the Reich or allowing known criminals to go scot free on questionable procedural grounds, then we surely have to err on the side of justice. I'll think about it overnight. Please have the boy available tomorrow.'

3

The next morning Hans was called from his first lesson by Herr Professor Wolff and taken in a car to an anonymous office block he did not recognize near the Ku'damm. It was exciting and at the same time unnerving. He might easily be incarcerated in this grim place. The Mercedes parked underneath the building and he was escorted in the lift to an empty office on the fourth floor.

The office was panelled in walnut and had deep blue carpets. Around a long polished conference table were twelve leather-upholstered chairs. Hans walked around the table and counted them twice. One long wall was dominated by a huge swastika flag. He felt a frisson of pride.

Weber entered quickly with two other men. He was wearing a black uniform so smart that Hans immediately coveted one. Weber said, '*Heil, Hitler*,' and saluted. Hans did not know whether this was a trick or a test. He responded with an outstretched arm and a bold '*Heil, Hitler*.' This was so much better a feeling than when he had practised it in his bedroom, or saluted in class. This was for real, and he felt just slightly taller. The three men smiled, a little patronizingly he felt.

Weber was businesslike. 'Now then, Herr Taub.'

It took Hans a moment to realize that Weber was referring to him. He sat on one side of the table with the other two men and invited Hans to sit on the other.

'May I introduce two colleagues from the legal department, Herr Engel and Herr Ziegler? As you've made a number of serious allegations we are required to ensure complete accuracy in taking your statement. We must at all costs avoid a miscarriage of justice. Legal counsel are present to confirm that this statement has been taken in accordance with the law of the Reich and is admissible in possible future legal proceedings.'

Legal proceedings. Hans had, he supposed, understood that this was an inevitable consequence of the information he had given to Weber the previous day. But to hear it said out loud made it all the more concrete. The kernel of a qualm germinated in his stomach but was easily quelled. That bastard Schröder was after all planning to betray the Fatherland. And so what if the family would be humiliated and ruined? They deserved all they got.

'Do you understand?' asked Weber.

'Yes, sir,' said Hans.

Patiently and kindly, they took him through what he had told Weber the previous day. Hans had an excellent memory and was able to recall more or less word for word what he had said. He stuck closely to the same script, venturing the odd extra detail but avoiding wholesale additions even when invited to provide more information by Weber or his two lawyers. The three men each had a copy of what seemed to be an identical document in front of them, which they checked carefully at each stage.

Engel pressed him on the circumstances of his hearing what his father and Schröder had said.

'For the first part I was in the room,' he said. 'They simply forgot I was there. Herr Schröder was so keen to begin the discussion. I went away then and returned later. That's when I listened outside the door.'

'You would say that you heard the conversation clearly?'

'Yes, sir.'

'And there were no other persons in the room? You could recognize the two speakers quite clearly?'

'Yes, sir.'

Engel pursed his thin lips. 'So you are quoting the direct words of these two individuals?'

'Yes.'

'I want to ask you about your father's response to what Herr Schröder had to say,' said Ziegler, the friendlier of the two. 'Your father is a socialist, I understand.'

'He calls himself a liberal, sir. I don't know a lot about politics, but I think that means he is on the left?'

'Indeed.' Ziegler smiled at him. 'Now, would you say your father was happy with what Herr Schröder proposed?'

Weber looked sideways at Ziegler and cast a

warning glance in Hans's direction.

'No, not happy, sir. Not really. Of course I couldn't see their faces.'

'If I may interrupt for a moment, Herr Doktor Ziegler,' said Weber. 'I've noted Hans's impression that his father seemed shocked at the boldness of Herr Schröder's statements. I believe you said, Hans, if I've written it down correctly, that 'whatever my father's personal views he would not be disloyal to his country at a time of national crisis'. Do I have that correct?'

'Yes, sir.'

'I ask,' persisted Ziegler, 'because it appears that for some reason Herr Schröder had the impression that your father would be passing his information on to third parties. Do you have any idea why that might be the case?'

'None at all, sir.'

'Very well.' Ziegler smiled again, and their business was all but done.

Weber gathered together the three copies of the document they had been perusing and neatened the edges. It seemed to Hans a rather feminine gesture.

'This is a statement I had prepared for your signature, Hans. Read it carefully. It is a legal document. Then, if you're happy, please sign each copy.'

Hans took a moment or two to pretend to read the document. In truth the adrenalin burst had robbed him of the ability to concentrate. Casually, he signed the three copies.

'Well then,' said Weber, addressing Engel and Ziegler, 'you gentlemen may wish to begin the

271

process. I need to discuss some practical details with Herr Taub.'

The two lawyers filed from the room.

'Three days,' said Weber. 'That's all I can guarantee you. There's a chance the process of drawing up warrants may take longer if I drag my heels but three days is the maximum on which you can count. You'll need to be gone by then. After that it'll be as if our agreement never existed. In the meantime, if your parents are arrested for reasons outside the bounds of our agreement, the same applies. Do you understand?'

'Yes, sir.'

'I've spoken with Herr Professor Wolff. Later today he will do as we discussed.'

'Thank you, sir.'

'And your parents will need exit visas. They'll have to obtain them through Herr Professor Wolff. I'll brief him what to say. I can do nothing about foreign entry visas. I'm assuming your father has contacts abroad who can supply whatever is required . . . '

'I suppose so, sir.'

Weber's mood lightened somewhat. 'Then all that remains is our written contract.' He took a single sheet from his pocket and looked at it for a moment before handing it to Hans to sign. Hans did so without reading it.

Weber said, 'London, that's where you think your father will head?'

'Yes, sir.'

'You'd be prepared to serve the Reich while there?'

'Of course.'

'There's always a requirement to keep tabs on annoying little communities of dissenters abroad. You may well be contacted by one of our fellows.'

'Yes, sir.'

'I'd like to make one thing clear. I view your father as a traitor. I'm allowing him to go because you and I have a bargain. I'm a man of my word. If it were up to me I would personally wring your father's neck. But there it is. We have our deal. You've been a very brave and a very clever little German, and you've served your country. It will be noted. Goodbye and good luck.'

In the car on the way back to his school Hans replayed the conversation and savoured each drop of sarcasm in Weber's words. Well, fuck you too, he thought, and smiled.

4

His father was working on an article when the rap on the door came that evening. Hans went quickly to the window and glanced down to the street. He could see no cars but now fully expected Weber to have reneged on the deal. His father scrabbled at the table, struggling in his panic to pick up the papers that lay before him and seemed to stick to the surface. Renate opened the door to the main bedroom, where Konrad thrust everything under the bed. Hans was sure both his parents knew this was a futile action, a gesture and no more.

Hans watched his father compose himself and go to the door.

'Ah, Herr Professor Wolff,' he said, surprised.

'Herr Taub.'

'Do come in.'

Wolff entered, stamping his shoes clear of wet snow on the doormat and handing his overcoat to Hans's mother. He peered around the small apartment, his curiosity evident even as he attempted to conceal it. Hans did not know what Herr Professor Wolff might expect of the lair of two liberal intellectuals. A mire of squalor and filth denoting their depravity, a coterie of revolutionaries trading polemics, a cache of weapons and explosives? What he would have seen was a perfectly normal apartment consisting of a bathroom, two small bedrooms and a larger single living area comprising lounge, dining area and small kitchen, clean and tidy, perhaps a little worn and old, as the Taubs had not prospered since Hitler became Chancellor.

It was peculiar to see his headmaster here. Wolff seemed a fastidious man, entirely at home in the familiar environs of his study, where he could find security in his carefully arranged books and the neatly aligned pen and pencils on the blotter on his desk. Here, he appeared nervous, his eyes flicking to and fro and his fingers moving swiftly, interlocking then parting, twirling and bending, to no obvious purpose.

'Is it about school?' asked Hans's father. 'Is Hans in trouble?'

'Pardon?' said Wolff, an expression of perplexity coming to his face. He was not cut out for

274

this, thought Hans. But his unease might serve a purpose. 'Ah, no, nothing like that at all.'

Konrad and Renate Taub waited for a moment.

'Then?' asked Konrad.

'Ah yes. If it were convenient, it would be helpful, I think, to have a private word.' Wolff glanced at Hans.

'Without Hans?' asked Renate.

'Indeed.'

'We do not keep secrets from our son,' said Konrad. 'Whatever you have to say you may say in front of him.'

'I rather think . . . '

'It's all right, Father,' said Hans. 'I'll read in my room.'

He went to his tiny bedroom, which overlooked the snow-covered courtyard, and left his book unopened on his bed. He listened at the door. Wolff was attempting to speak quietly but he was so accustomed to making bombastic pronouncements that it took little effort to hear what he was saying. Hans's parents' responses were more difficult to discern.

'Herr Taub,' said Wolff, 'we can agree on one thing at least, namely that we disagree wildly on almost every topic. I find your views anathema and I am sure you regard mine with equal distaste. But I do acknowledge that, however misguided, you believe in your country. I am here, therefore, on an errand of mercy. I see in your son the makings of a fine young man. But I fear that owing to your views your son's future will be destroyed.'

Konrad Taub replied inaudibly.

'No no no,' said Wolff. 'I am not here to proselytize or try to convince you of the error of your ways. Things are much too far along the road for that. I am here for a specific and very practical purpose. And you should know that this is at considerable personal risk. You need to understand that we live in a very different world today from even five years ago.'

There was silence. Hans strained to hear whether his parents spoke. But it seemed that this pause was for dramatic effect, before Wolff continued to declaim.

'Whatever our differences, I am here to tell you that you are in severe and immediate personal danger. As you know, I am heavily involved in Party matters. I have it on the highest authority that a warrant has been issued for your arrest.'

Hans could well imagine his parents' shocked expressions.

'The reasons will be as clear to you as they are to me. I have been informed discreetly. The consequences are obvious. You will be tried for sedition, with a predictable outcome. Hans's future will be uncertain. If he is fortunate he will be fostered or adopted. But I rather doubt that will happen. After all, he will be the son of two traitors.'

Wolff spoke without emotion. 'There can be no mistake. No doubt at all,' he was now saying dismissively, as if talking to a particularly stupid pupil. 'I am certain of my facts. The nation at such times of crisis needs to know precisely who its enemies are.'

As he heard the bitter tone of his father muttering, Hans could imagine. Wolff looking directly at him with contempt through his rimless spectacles.

'I am not here to debate with you, Herr Taub. I have come here because I wish to save your innocent son from ruin. I am here to give you some facts. What you do with them is for you to decide. You can denounce me if you wish, and we will both end up before the courts. That is a risk that I have calculated.'

Wolff cleared his throat noisily before continuing. 'Of course you can choose to be a hero. You can be a martyr to whatever cause it is that you support. What I find heartless is that you seem content to sacrifice your son. I suppose that is your prerogative and what I should expect from someone like you.'

Konrad Taub spoke again and while Hans could not hear his words his tone was angry.

'No, I cannot intervene with regard to Hans. Officially I do not know. Once the arrests have been effected he will be taken somewhere — I do not know where — and it will be impossible for me to do anything.'

Hans could hear Renate interrupt, her voice almost shrill, but still could not distinguish individual words.

Wolff continued, speaking through her. 'You have an obvious choice to make, it seems to me, and you do not have much time. I also feel I may have made this visit in vain. I hope not.'

Heavy footsteps crossed the room and then came back. Hans assumed they were those of his father. Someone dragged a chair back noisily and sat heavily on it. He heard the soothing tones of his mother's voice.

'Ah yes,' said Wolff, as if he had forgotten something important. 'It would of course be difficult for you under normal circumstances to leave the country. But I have contacts and may be able to obtain exit visas. It will be for you to acquire an entry visa wherever you go, if you see sense. I would be prepared to do you this one last service, but only for the sake of Hans. I will be at the school by six thirty in the morning. You may wish to consider your next steps overnight and if you want my assistance please see me there. Bring your papers. After that I will be prepared to help you no more.'

There followed a brief final exchange before Wolff said loudly and in apparent anger, 'I hope you will understand the potential difficulties I am prepared to risk. For the sake of your son. Goodnight.'

Hans heard the door slam. He went quickly to his bed and picked up his book. But his door did not open until several minutes later.

His father knocked before coming in. He said quietly, 'Hans, your mother and I have something to discuss with you.'

5

Two evenings later at Frankfurt station, Hans and his father were awaiting the departure of the overnight train to Paris. Konrad Taub was

278

dressed soberly. His firebrand beard had been shaved off and his hair trimmed. He murmured occasionally to his son in his best approximation of a reassuring tone.

They had taken the train from Berlin the previous morning, leaving Renate to neaten the remnants of their existence there. Konrad and Renate Taub were dutiful and orderly, and viewed it as their civic responsibility to manage their affairs sensibly.

On the evening of Wolff's visit and after they had decided they must leave Germany the three of them had sat at the kitchen table and compiled a list. Konrad would see Wolff first thing the next morning to ask for the exit visas. He would go from there to the British Embassy, where he knew someone who, he was sure, could arrange for visas for France and England. Neither he nor Renate expressed concerns that Wolff's offers might be a ruse to incriminate them. In a sense, Hans found their instinctive trust almost touching. But inside him the seed of doubt about Weber's good faith in this transaction was growing.

After Konrad had obtained the visas, he and Renate would go to the bank and withdraw as much cash as possible. The rest they would arrange to be transferred to the account of Renate's sister. They would need to buy train tickets. They would pack carefully, and there would be letters to write to family and friends. It was obvious that not everything could be achieved in a single day, so they agreed that Renate should remain in Berlin for an extra day to work through the other items on the list, ranging from settling their account at the grocer's to informing her friends at the welfare centre where she worked that she and her husband were taking a break in Bavaria for a few days.

Hans had argued that she should drop everything and simply leave with them if they took seriously what Herr Professor Wolff had said. Knowing they did not fully appreciate their situation, he challenged their logic, but in vain. 'It's me they're interested in, Hans,' his father said. 'Your mother's not in danger. We can't leave just like that. We need to get everything in order.' Hans felt desperate and irritated at the same time but had known that to insist further would be both pointless and potentially perilous to him.

The plan had been for Renate to join them on the train, but clearly this would not happen. The large clock on the platform had just ticked past eleven p.m. Steam rose in grimy clouds to the cathedral-like arches and the glass roof of the grand terminal station as the engine gathered its strength. Hisses and the sound of the announcement of the train's imminent departure broke the night silence. There was no movement on the platform, monochrome in the artificial light. It seemed that the passengers had boarded and everything was now reduced to waiting. Four minutes to go. They climbed aboard and slammed the door behind them.

'She'll catch us up later,' whispered Konrad. 'We'll see her in Paris.'

There were several emptier compartments on

the train but Konrad insisted on taking the last two available seats in this one, to silent glares. Their travelling companions were, it seemed, businessmen but not particularly successful ones, travelling second class with no sleeping arrangements. There was a solitary woman, blonde, pretty and in her thirties, thought Hans, who pouted defiantly at the men, daring them to look at her or talk to her, and signalling consequences if they did.

The train moved with a jolt and edged slowly through the suburbs to the invisible black countryside, where it thundered through the winter night. They were on their way to England, that faraway country, distant if not in geography then in philosophy. The swaying motion, the regular beat of the engine and the clack of the rails were comforting and after the rush of excitement Hans felt utterly exhausted and found sleep.

He awoke suddenly. The train was silent and still and the compartment dark. His father leaned on his shoulder, his head lolling. Carefully, Hans nudged him so that his head rocked to the window of the corridor with a small thud. Konrad did not wake. There was the sound of heavy breathing in the compartment and the foul smell of eight bodies emitting their unguarded odours, leavened by the sweet lavender of the woman's scent. No one else was awake, it seemed.

His eyes were coming to terms with the light. He glanced out of the window. He could see lamps but no station signs. Opposite his father sat the woman, pressed into her corner seat, avoiding contact with the thin moustached stranger next to her. She too was asleep, her mouth open, and her skirt had ridden up. Hans could see clearly the suspenders that held her sheer stockings up, and a morsel of thrilling porcelain flesh. He stared, then something made him look up. She was looking into his eyes and smiled maliciously. She opened her legs further and Hans could see more white leg and the light sheen of her underwear, soft silk and peach-coloured in his mind, though he could not in fact make out the detail. The woman closed her eyes with a smile and, it seemed to Hans, leaned back further, turning her legs minutely towards him. Perhaps he imagined this; but the sight of her skin and that fabric was real enough.

He tried to concentrate on the pleasurable sensation this generated in his groin. For a while his arousal sustained wakefulness, but eventually sleep flooded him once more as the train resumed its journey.

Hans woke again later. Everyone else in the compartment was already moving, dishevelled but preparing to leave the train. Ties were straightened, hair was combed, hats were clamped on heads and fingers screwed sleep out of eyes. The woman calmly applied her lipstick, glancing at him without expression. The beam of a spotlight pierced the darkness in the compartment.

'What time is it?' asked Hans more loudly than he had intended.

'Three forty,' his father replied. 'We're at

Aachen. We have to disembark for passport checks.'

The train conductor walked down the corridor, rapping each compartment window as he passed.

'Everyone out,' he shouted. 'Quickly.'

The occupants of the compartment stood awkwardly, apologizing, jockeying politely for space. Hans's father reached for his suitcase.

'No need to take that,' said one of the men. 'This is just papers. They're not interested in contraband. Just people. You'll be back soon enough.'

Konrad nodded and left the case on the rack.

They filed out of the compartment and off the train, the blonde woman going first, and joined the orderly queue that snaked into the customs hall. It was bitterly cold as they exited the carriage and not much warmer on the station concourse. As he crossed the platform Hans looked down the length of the train. They were detaching the German locomotive and on the neighbouring platform its French replacement snorted steam as if waiting impatiently.

Once they were inside he could smell her perfume drifting sweetly towards him. He looked down her elegant back and saw the straight black seams of her stockings, and thought again of that shiny, softly creased fabric and what it concealed. She smoked a cigarette in an ivory holder and he inhaled its aroma greedily, wanting everything of her.

His father was nervous, feeling inside his pockets for his papers. The woman turned and said, 'It's such an inconvenience, isn't it, getting off the train and back on again? They only introduced these measures recently.' She flashed a patronizing smile and inhaled on her cigarette.

'Yes,' replied Konrad, flustered. 'You travel to Paris often?'

'Oh yes. I'm a fashion designer. I work with several studios. And you?'

'Journalist. Preparing an article on Monsieur Cocteau. My first trip to Paris for several years.'

'And is this your personal assistant?'

'Ah no. This is my son, Hans. I thought it was time he saw Paris.'

'I see,' she said, turning to him. 'A young man of his age. So much to see in Paris.'

Hans looked directly at her and held her eyes for a moment. He thought he noticed a conspiratorial grin on her face that he found delicious but at that instant the queue began to move.

Hans looked sideways. She was smirking at him, not apparently making fun of him but amused at his excitement. He longed to reach out to touch her, to feel the flesh under her skirt, or on her arm, just to know that she existed and that he did too. But the queue was speeding up and she had to regain her place.

Four trestle tables were set up, two on each side of the passengers as they processed through the dimly lit hall. It was easy to work out the routine. At each table were two men in field-grey uniforms with SS flashes on the lapels. One sat and asked questions, while the other stood and looked sceptically at the subject, as if with the intention to intimidate. In the shadows at the side of the hall stood four further men, overseeing everything.

Each person was called forward and processed moderately quickly. It seemed that people were selected almost at random for deeper questioning. Even that appeared desultory. But for most people the ordeal consisted solely of a close examination of their papers and a cursory, uninterested few questions.

They were getting closer. Konrad watched intently as the guards went about their business, as if he could divine some answer to the problem of negotiating the next few minutes safely. Hans whispered to him to stop behaving so nervously.

The woman in front of them was called. As she stepped confidently forward she half turned to Hans and his father and smiled again. His father, distracted, did not see her.

Hans watched as she strode to the table. She was doing this with panache, he thought. She smiled brightly at the two men in turn and placed her papers neatly and decisively before them. They reciprocated with thin bureaucratic smiles. She joked, but Hans could not hear what was said. It was possible, he thought, that she was alerting them to his father's agitation.

The seated man laughed and glanced at his partner, who picked up one of the documents on the table, while the other leafed through her passport. Hans attempted to feign a casual lack of interest as he focused intently on what was happening.

Hans and his father were now at the head of

the queue but were not, for the moment, called forward. All activity at the other tables had ceased and the only person being processed was the blonde woman, apparently oblivious to the stillness, speaking animatedly with the officials and smiling broadly. Of course. She was a marker. That was why she had spoken to them. She was there to pick them out.

Alternatively, thought Hans, she would be back on the train shortly and would ask herself what had become of that good-looking but highly strung journalist and his handsome son. He wondered what would happen to their luggage: whether some minor functionary would be deputed to the train to find the bags of the traitors and take them back for examination. He glanced around, expecting at any moment the grip of a gloved hand on his arm.

He saw one of the officials make a discreet hand signal, unnoticed, it seemed, by the woman, and three of the men in the shadows began to move. This, then, was it. Hans braced himself. But it was not his arm that was grasped. The men moved towards their colleagues at the table. In a well-practised motion they took hold of the woman under her arms and ushered her swiftly and efficiently towards a door at the back of the hall. She said nothing: it must have been the sheer shock, Hans thought. The commotion, such as it was, was over in a matter of seconds. The man seated at the desk made a neat pile of her papers, stood and walked through the door with his colleague.

'Mein Herr! Bitte schön.'

Hans and his father heard the irritated tone of the man's voice shouting at them and started in unison. They were being called forward to one of the tables. The examination was brief and peremptory. There was a railway timetable to be adhered to. There was a delay to be made up. The officials were down a quarter of their strength.

In less than two minutes they were walking back to the train in silence.

15

Signed, Sealed and Delivered

1

It was, he thinks as he tries with difficulty to guide the link through the first buttonhole of his right cuff, the first time he fully realized the potential of intrigue and surreptitious interventions. Until then he had not understood that convenient secret arrangements could be arrived at between individuals just as between hostile states. He had come with this little enterprise to comprehend the power and facility he held to nudge the planets into a constellation that coincided with his interests.

Weber had been relatively easy to play; Wolff, despite his intellect and academic achievement, was no more than a fool. There had been lessons to learn, however. He had left himself far too much at the mercy of Weber's honesty in completing his side of the deal. There should have been checks and balances to make sure he delivered on his commitments. He had emerged wiser.

And of course his mother. Most unfortunate. At this distance it is the only formulation that feels appropriate. Perhaps devoid of the emotion that he should have lavished on the woman who had given him life, but honest nonetheless. In truth he had been an inconvenience to her, shrugged absently out of her womb in the middle of her theorizing and agitating. She had tried to educate him politically at an early age, without success. Konrad had been the more romantic and traditional of the two. He had held the reluctant Renate to him while she looked impatient; and he had cared for little Hansi most of the time.

He is back on his feet now and relatively well. It was a close shave in the hospital and he had fully expected to be consigned to some institution. If their roles had been reversed he would have shunted Betty off before you could say Jack Robinson. Full marks to her, though. Even in recovery his hands shake and he continues to fail to tease the pointed end of the cufflink through the eyelet that seems smaller today than it has ever been. He is becoming irritated.

He sighs: oh, what he has lived through, certainly in comparison with the likes of Betty. His father had later discovered that Renate was arrested the day after they left Germany. Weber had adhered strictly to the letter of their agreement. The rest was predictable: the show trial, the reports in the *Völkischer Beobachter* and the conviction. Perhaps less obvious was the hardening of attitudes inside Germany in the period between her arrest and her sentencing. In May 1939 she was executed by firing squad at the Spandau barracks. What more was there to be said, or thought? It had been unfortunate, but precipitated by his parents' wilful stupidity. Now he has little trace memory of his mother.

He pulls off the shirt in frustration and throws it on to the bed. By good planning he has another crisply ironed shirt on a hanger in the wardrobe, this one with buttons instead of the pesky double cuffs. He stands for a moment in front of the mirror in his vest. Oh dear. The sagging dugs. The grey flesh of his biceps hanging like flags from his arms. The redness of his face. The milk-yellow of his irises. The corn-like texture of the white hair. It is happening.

They had been taken to Scotland to a country house, where, while his father was debriefed by Birch, the former second secretary at the British Embassy in Berlin and now a middle-ranking functionary in British intelligence, he was looked after by a kindly housekeeper. Eventually Birch had worked out what to do with them and he was sent to boarding school in Herefordshire for the beginning of the spring term. His father went to London to write propaganda at the BBC and to swim in the sea of German political and intellectual émigrés, looking among them for Nazi spies. In the school holidays Hans stayed with his father in his small Putney flat.

Albert Schröder's arrest and trial also attracted press attention. It was announced that he had been found guilty and executed. Word came through the émigré networks that his family had been taken into protective custody, a well-understood euphemism. The next events would have followed with cold inevitability. No one spoke again of the Schröders, the favoured family with all the advantages who had somehow fallen foul of the regime.

He brings himself up again and puffs out his chest. He ties his tie carefully and brushes his hair. It may be near but he is still here, full of life and power. It is almost time to take the stage.

Following the outbreak of war Konrad Taub was classed as a category C German, posing no security risk, and he remained in his job. In 1940 the situation changed dramatically as Germany approached the English coast and the Blitz began. All German nationals were interned and Taub was no exception. Birch managed to ensure that Hans remained at his school, and worked to overcome the bureaucracy and have Konrad released into his custody. Too slowly, however: Konrad committed suicide in October 1940, in despair and grief, it is to be presumed. The funeral was a difficult affair, attended by sundry émigrés and the solitary figure of Birch, who tried to avoid talking to the other mourners. It was with Birch that he exchanged those awkward condolences — it seemed that Birch was more affected than he, who thought that his father's suicide was a sign of weakness — and it was Birch who continued to pay the bills at his school and later found him gainful employment as an interpreter. He had then taken care to distance himself from the gaunt, sad old bachelor with his drooping moustache.

The life he has led, he reflects as he makes his last preparations, splashing a little cologne over his cheeks. He is ready, spruce and alert, to face the moment.

2

'Sunday best, Roy?' says Stephen, a smart-alec grin on his face.

'Come now, Stephen,' says Betty. 'Best behaviour. We ancient people always dress up when something important's happening. Can't you see I've made an effort too?'

She is too indulgent towards the boy. 'Some of us have certain standards,' he says caustically. He notices that Stephen is in his customary jeans and T-shirt, hair all over the place.

'What time is Vincent due?' asks Betty.

'Should be here shortly,' replies Stephen.

While Betty checks that the table is ready, with milk jug, sugar bowl and teacups, and that the tin is full of those expensive foil-wrapped biscuits, he stands, a little unsteady on his feet, and glares into Stephen's eyes. This takes the smile off his face.

The doorbell rings and Stephen lets Vincent in.

They seat themselves at the table, the two investors on one side and Vincent and Stephen on the other, to commence their momentous piece of business.

Vincent takes out a series of papers. He really is good at this theatre. The documents are professionally produced and have the right language. Vincent walks them solemnly through the forms, carefully pointing out clauses and subclauses that may or may not be relevant and explaining the legalese for Betty's and, ostensibly, Roy's benefit. They nod their heads periodically, though Roy is certain that Betty has not followed matters at all. She is precisely where Roy and Vincent need her to be.

Stephen is a little more of a problem. Ineffectual he may be, but Vincent has told him that the young man is bright and observant. He has followed the paperwork carefully and checked the financial institutions. At one stage Roy and Vincent had considered creating a dummy account in a non-existent tax-haven bank so that Betty could happily deposit through a third party and Roy could avoid the inconvenience of stake money — much less than Betty was being asked to stump up but a not insignificant sum nevertheless. Owing to Stephen's attentions they had judged this too risky. Vincent regarded the traditional old go-to, the ubiquitous rubber cheque, as implausible in these connected times. There was nothing for it, then, but to shell out. Against Roy's instincts, but needs must.

'All right, then,' says Vincent. 'Are we ready to sign the forms?'

He holds out his ballpoint pen. Roy shuns it, reaching into his inner pocket for his expensive fountain pen.

'A touch of style, I think, is required,' he says.

'Yes,' says Betty, a broad smile on her face. 'We must do things in style. We need to become accustomed to it.'

They each have their sheaf of papers to sign. Betty waits while he works his way through his, his hand shaking, his signature unsteady and spidery. He hands Betty his pen when he has finished and she signs with her neat hand. It is then

Stephen's turn, to sign as witness to the proceedings, and Vincent pores over the documents one more time to check that there are no errors.

'Good,' he says finally. 'Shall we effect the transfers?'

Vincent removes his laptop from his briefcase and switches it on. Stephen fetches Betty's laptop.

'Have you both set up the transfers with your banks?' asks Vincent.

'Yes,' they both reply.

'Then all there is to do is to confirm them. They will take place instantaneously.'

'Shall I go first?' says Roy, smiling. He knows that it will reinforce the genuine nature of the transaction if he puts his money in before her. 'You know how to do it, Vincent?'

'Of course. You'll have to put in your passwords, but I'll tell you which buttons to press.'

'Hopeless, I am,' he says. 'You can't teach an old dog.'

Watched closely by Stephen, Vincent navigates to the home page of Roy's bank. He carries his laptop to the other side of the table. Betty, Stephen and Vincent avert their eyes while Roy logs in and allows Vincent to navigate to the page they are looking for. Roy watches, grinning — he hopes sufficiently inanely — as Vincent says, 'Right then, Roy. All you have to do is to go through this little menu.'

'Menu?' he says. 'Ridiculous word.'

'All right. Now. 'Do you wish to make this transaction?' If you do, put the cursor in the 'yes' box and click.'

He obeys dutifully, moving the cursor with the

mouse painfully slowly and, he hopes, with evident lack of expertise.

'Now. 'Do you wish to confirm this payment?' Click 'yes' again. Or of course 'no' if you have any last-minute concerns. This is the point of no return.'

Quickly, he clicks on 'yes'.

'All done,' says Vincent, returning to his seat. 'Now, Betty, would you like to do the same? Meanwhile, I'll log on to the Hayes and Paulsen site.'

'Hayes and Paulsen?' asks Betty.

'The British Virgin Islands bank,' says Stephen patiently.

'Of course. My memory.'

She beckons Stephen over. Careful, thinks Roy. Mustn't show too much interest. No chance of that. Years of experience.

Betty points and clicks intently as she gains access to her own bank account, with Stephen guiding her over her shoulder, and eventually she has finished. She looks up expectantly.

'Remember to log off,' says Stephen.

'Oh yes,' she says in her ditziest voice. 'Silly me.'

'All right, then,' says Vincent, standing again and placing his laptop on the table between Betty and Roy. 'I'll log on to Hayes and Paulsen now.' He plays with a little keypad, the size of a calculator, he has produced from his pocket. Betty looks at him quizzically but he ignores her.

'Now then. You can see here the current balance at Hayes and Paulsen.' He clicks another link. 'And here is the list of transfers into the account. You can see that both of your transfers are there.'

'Oh, thank goodness for that,' says Betty.

Roy observes her wryly.

'You can both log into the account,' says Vincent. 'All I have to do is to take you through how to set up your logins.'

He takes two envelopes from his briefcase and hands one to each of them. They contain a set of instructions and a keypad, which, he says, is central to the process. Roy has been taken through this several times already but acts suitably dumb as Vincent runs through it again, prompting him to think up and remember passwords as he creates his online access.

'I don't know why we're doing this, Vincent,' he says when they have finished. 'I can't use a computer for toffee and I'll never remember all that. I don't even own a computer.'

'It's important that you and Betty, as my clients, have twenty-four-hour access to the account. You need to be able to check the balance whenever you wish. Call it form if you wish, but it's important.'

Too right it's important. But he simply looks at Betty and shrugs. 'What did I say, Betty? He's a stickler. A real stickler.'

Betty too is taken through the process, slightly bewildered it appears to him.

'Well then,' says Vincent. 'We're all set up. With these little devices you can log into the account at any time. You have full access, but please don't make any withdrawals without speaking to me because at any stage I may be moving money around on your behalf to make investments. I also have access as your broker. You can see how much remains in the joint account and every so often money will come back into it. I will provide you with periodic profit and loss statements so that you know exactly how your investments are doing.'

'Profit and loss?' says Stephen.

'A figure of speech. Loss will not come into it, provided my judgements are correct. But I've explained the risk factors in depth.'

Betty sighs. 'Phew. I'm glad that's all over. It's given me a bit of a headache. Time to celebrate, I think.'

'Oh yes,' says Roy.

Betty fetches glasses from the cabinet and chilled champagne from the fridge. She asks Stephen to uncork the champagne and pours four glasses.

'Don't mind if I do,' says Roy.

'Not for me, thank you,' says Vincent. 'I'm driving.'

They toast each other and drink happily, while Vincent places the signed forms in clear plastic folders, puts his laptop into its protective case and slots his pens into their designated places in his briefcase. Finally, he offers a terse but civil goodbye.

3

They are alone. Stephen has departed after only one glass, leaving Roy and Betty to empty the bottle. Roy has had the majority of the champagne and in truth feels rather tipsy. He cannot hold his drink as he once could. It was a useful facility but it does not matter any more. Not with Betty.

'Well now. The first day of the rest of our lives.'

'Yes,' says Betty. 'Vincent will look after our money, won't he?'

'As if it was his own, my dear. He'll do us proud.'

'And we can expect some returns within six months?'

'Indeed. Let's start booking those cruises now.' He smiles, quietly exultant.

'It's such a shame that you have to go up to London so soon. We should be together this weekend. Couldn't you invite Robert here instead?'

'Well no, not really. He's only over here for a day or so. He's off to a kitchen convention in Belgium. He's just stopping off in London overnight. Besides, he'll be on his way by now.'

'I'd like to meet him.'

'All in good time, I'm sure,' says Roy. 'We might even go over to Sydney to see him now we're fixed for money.'

'I'd like that very much. I suppose you've seen much more of the world than me.'

'I've lived a bit. I've had my excitements. Alarms and excursions. Capers and scrapes. I've had a rich and full life.' His head floats gently from the drink and he understands vaguely he must be cautious.

'I'm sure,' she says. 'But you said you'd led a

pretty humdrum life.'

'Oh, one doesn't like to be too boastful. I've witnessed things you could barely imagine.' He smiles and thinks: how true. She hasn't a clue. 'But anyway, I'd better pack my bag. Are you sure Stephen's happy to take me to the station tomorrow?'

'Quite sure.' She smiles back at him.

16

Lili Schröder

1

Though she did not fully understand it at the time, Lili Schröder's life ended and a quite different one began with the assault in the Tiergarten villa.

In Hans she had seen spite in all its purity for the first time. Before, she had sensed something of hatred in the way young men shouted with creased, enraged faces on the streets and jostled frightened old men with beards. But her parents had ushered her into fashionable coffee houses or luxurious cars or the KaDeWe department store as she craned her neck. Until that winter twilight with Hans, these were aspects of behaviour and character of which she was only distantly aware. She knew the world contained unpleasantness and that she was insulated from it, but that was all. She did not imagine her privileges and protections could fall away.

She lay in pain as jagged pulses rippled through her body, accompanied by a dull but enveloping ache. She did not know whether the pain was as severe as she imagined, or whether shame and horror magnified it. She wondered if it would pass, conceiving it as at least possible that she might die in the next hours or days. Of course she would tell no one, not even her mother, not because Hans had instructed her but because she felt such guilt. She had brought filth and disgrace on herself and somehow it would be infectious if she told others.

Eventually the pain subsided a little. The sense of dirt did not, however. She rushed to the bathroom, so that she would be ready in time for the simple meal before the evening's festivities. She washed herself as best she could at the basin, splashing water carelessly over the thick yellow carpet and her white dress, then washed again, and again. She rubbed soap on her underpants, trying to rid them of the specks of blood, disposing of them eventually in the washing basket. In her bedroom, she checked that she was not still bleeding before putting on fresh underwear, placing one of her handkerchiefs carefully inside in case she later did. None of this made her feel cleaner, or safer.

The meal was a subdued affair, not as it should have been before such a glittering evening and not as it usually was. Only her mother seemed as bright as ever. Her elder sisters appeared distracted and whispered to one another in a manner that suggested concern. She knew Daddy was not fond of these grand balls but went along with them for the sake of 'the girls', as he called them all, and for social convention. From where she usually watched at the top of the stairs, he did a good job of hosting despite his natural diffidence and seriousness. This evening, though, he looked absently at the snow falling outside.

'Are you worrying, my darling, that people will not turn up in this weather?' asked Magda. The girls usually loved it when their mother called their father darling.

'Pardon?' he said. 'What did you say? Sorry. Yes. I wonder how many will cry off.'

'I doubt any will. Snow isn't going to put too many Berliners off.'

'I suppose you're right.' He rallied and smiled. 'Still, no harm in hoping, eh?'

'Albert, you love these occasions as much as I do. You know that.'

'I very much doubt that, my dear.'

'You'll get into the swing of it once people arrive.'

'I'm sure you're right,' he said doubtfully, and turned to the window again.

'Lili, you may watch the girls dress and then you must go to your room. You may read until eight o'clock and then you will turn your lights out.'

'Yes, Mama,' said Lili.

'It's a very strange atmosphere this evening,' said Magda, with a gayness that seemed forced. 'Normally you three would be chattering away and I would be interrupting to remind you of your duties. And Lili, you'd be asking question after question. No one seems to be excited.'

'Oh, but we are, Mama,' said Hannelore with apparent enthusiasm. 'Of course we are. It will be wonderful. I'm so looking forward to it.'

Lili followed her elder sisters to Charlotte's bedroom, which was designated as the dressing and make-up room for the party. Each of them bathed in the tub next door before returning to begin the task of dressing. First, there was a layer of underwear to be put on, then hair to be shaped and set with lacquer. Gowns were hoisted and lowered with exquisite care so as not to disturb the elaborate coiffures. Bracelets, necklaces and earrings were fastened and checked in the mirror. Finally, sitting in front of the dressing table, they each experimented with make-up from the extensive compendium of items that Hannelore owned. There was less giggling and excitement than normal. At one point Lili heard Anneliese say with some earnestness, 'Hansi . . .', but she was stopped mid-sentence by a glance towards Lili. Then their mother came to hurry them along and they were gone. She sat on the bed among the untidy, still-warm mess of clothes, lonely, distraught that she could not confide in her sisters.

The music struck up downstairs and guests began to arrive. Lili waited several minutes before taking up her usual position on the landing, overlooking the entrance hall. A cold breeze came up the stairs each time the large front door was opened by one of the staff. Smart young men in military uniforms, the friends of her parents, her sisters' giggling girlfriends and the obligatory social guests were announced by Bauer, at his self-important loudest, and shook hands with her parents and sisters.

Lili found she was no longer interested in the spectacle and went quietly to her room. As she undressed she found the locket containing Hans's golden hair. She pulled it from her neck, went to her bed and thrust it in the gap between the wooden floor and the skirting board in which she had stored secret notes, mainly the childish love letters to Hans that she had never sent. She never wanted to see the locket again.

2

It passed, as the shadow of a cloud passes. Guests may have commented the next day that the Schröders had seemed rather less delightful than in previous years, that Albert may have appeared preoccupied and fractious and the girls a little aloof. Later, a context would be found.

The family awoke the next morning feeling that they should have put more into the previous evening's festivities. Magda had drunk rather too much champagne, through nervousness and an indistinct feeling of unease at her husband's and daughters' distraction, and was beset by an insistent headache. Albert went early to his office and worried at the accounts while thinking about when he should see Taub again. Hannelore took her seat at her desk in the same building an hour or so later as the day brightened and her mood with it. Charlotte and Anneliese had a late breakfast and went shopping for Christmas presents. The pain in Lili's body had passed and she could not quite believe that it had happened as she recalled it. She sat in her window seat and read, distracted and unhappy.

★ ★ ★

It was three mornings later that the SS came calling, at five a.m. Lili did not hear the commotion at first but came out to the landing to see her father, head bowed, being led down the grand staircase in handcuffs by two officers in smart uniforms. He did not turn to look at her, or at her three sisters, also standing outside their rooms in their dressing gowns. Magda waited by the door to watch the little procession into the white landscape. She was not permitted to say goodbye to her husband.

They were fortunate that they were a sufficiently prominent family to attract the attentions of the SS proper rather than a group of grubby SA Brownshirts. They enjoyed the services not of mere thugs but of sophisticated thugs. The officers understood that the Schröders were well connected and adhered to procedure with an insinuating politeness.

The girls were permitted to dress in private and eat a rushed breakfast with their mother.

'The authorities will see that this is a mistake,' she said, and Lili was not sure whether she was speaking to the four daughters, the SS men or their servants, who stood and watched, not permitted to prepare the meal. Or, quite possibly, to herself. At any rate, she sounded desperate. 'It's a simple case of mistaken identity.'

The SS captain in charge said with courtesy, 'Let's hope so. In the meantime it is my duty to take you into protective custody. For your own safety. We cannot predict what citizens may do when they hear of your husband's arrest. Sadly all too many people are taking the law into their own hands. You will be conveyed to a detention centre. I am told it is comfortable enough. But of course not as luxurious as your beautiful house.' He permitted himself a smile. 'Would that be a Dürer I happened to see in your husband's study? Magnificent. I once studied the history of art. Now, if you are ready? One small bag each, please. And you have nothing to be afraid of. If what you say is true, you will be back in this house before you know it. We must trust to the Reich's system of justice.'

A van took them to an anonymous building on the outskirts of the city. During the journey they were silent, not daring to share confidences, not able to offer one another false reassurances. The van drove through two sets of gates. Their reception was brisk but civil. Their belongings were logged individually in a large stiff-backed book before being taken for storage. In a small room they were each given a rough grey serge uniform and told to change. There was even a child's outfit for Lili. A female guard watched them and placed their own clothes into a large brown paper bag. Back at the reception desk Magda was told to sign the book that listed their belongings. They were shown to a white-walled, cold room just large enough to accommodate five thin beds. There was no bedlinen, only a dirty blanket folded at the foot of each bed.

Their mother muttered repeatedly, 'It's a mistake. We'll be home shortly.'

Eventually Charlotte interrupted her. 'Don't

say that, Mama. We all know what's going to happen.'

Her mother stared at her.

'No, Charlotte,' said Hannelore gently. 'We don't know. Mama may be right. And Lili . . . '

Hannelore looked at her and smiled, soothing her with her eyes. But Charlotte had no regard. 'We've seen the families. We've forgotten them. No one's ever come back. It would take a miracle.'

'Well, let's believe in that miracle,' said Anneliese.

They fell silent again.

3

The publicly appointed defence lawyer met Magda and the girls in a small, shabby office at the detention facility. Lili did not remember hearing his name. Though a kindly looking man in an old-fashioned wing collar, he sat on the only chair and spread his papers on the rickety table, leaving Magda to stand before him like a supplicant. Lili tried to pay careful attention but could not stop herself watching the trees swaying in the wind outside.

The man told Magda that the family lawyer was sadly unavailable to represent them. In any case it was doubtful that sufficient funds remained to pay for him. Their assets had been confiscated pending judgement. He had been appointed by the court in their interests and would do his very best for them. He smiled comfortingly before continuing.

'Your husband's case will be heard in two weeks' time,' he said, 'and then your position will be clearer. But there are separate considerations, not least your husband's Jewish heritage.'

'But my husband isn't Jewish.'

'Of course. That may be so. But it appears that the state may contest that assertion. There is an allegation that one or more of his grandparents may have been Jewish. Researches are now taking place. Given that your husband's maternal grandparents grew up in Pomerania, however, this may prove problematic. We're reliant on the Polish authorities.' He looked at her with a little smile of helplessness. 'Whether or not one or both of his maternal grandparents was Jewish is of course critical to a judgement as to your husband being a non-Aryan of the first or second degree.'

Lili was having difficulty following the logic.

'But neither of his mother's parents were Jewish,' said Magda. 'They were Germans, from Danzig, with German passports. That should be simple enough to check.'

'Do you know for certain?'

'Well, no. It never seemed important.'

'Indeed,' said the lawyer cheerfully. 'Check they will. Diligently. Naturally they cannot simply accept a citizen's word. And given the, er, questions regarding your husband's integrity and therefore the family's, they will also be checking carefully your own ancestry.'

'Of course,' said Magda. 'I understand.'

'Should it be discovered that relevant facts

have been concealed from the authorities by you or your husband, there will be an impact. But the greatest consequences will flow from your husband's trial.'

'I'm sure Albert would never be disloyal to Germany. He's not interested in politics.'

'Naturally you would say that. But you can't expect the state to take it on trust. Especially in the circumstances.'

Magda stared at the man. Lili's attention drifted. All she wanted to do was to return home and lie in her soft feather bed. It had begun to snow again and she watched the flakes driven by the wind. It was cold, always cold here, and the boredom and the dirt and the despair accumulated in their squalid little room.

Finally, the funny little man with the wing collar was saying goodbye.

'I'm sure it will all work out for the best,' he said, as Anneliese wept. 'We'll meet again shortly to consider what we should do next.'

Her mother had not yet cried; not even in the deep of night when she could not sleep had Lili seen tears on her mother's face. Hannelore embraced Anneliese as she shook. Charlotte stared on blankly. Lili felt sad but was not quite sure why. Possibly because of the distress of her sisters and her mother's clouded face.

4

She did not see the lawyer with the wing collar again.

If only they had known these days would be so precious. They had certainly not seemed so at the time. They were confined to their room apart from their short excursions into the winter cold to walk around the bleak courtyard. She did not know whether they were kept there or chose to remain. Every so often, a meagre meal would be delivered, usually cold, by a woman with an unsmiling face. Each time Lili wanted to use the stinking lavatory facilities along the corridor her mother went with her. The corridors were deserted, though Lili could hear the distant sounds of children chattering somewhere else in the building. They did not sound happy but she might have been projecting her own feelings on to them. She knew something was seriously wrong but could not bring herself to believe that her father had done anything sufficiently bad to visit this upon them.

It could only have been a short number of uneventful weeks but Lili later recalled them more vividly than the following years.

She would wake first and try to gain extra warmth by twisting the rough blanket around her more closely. She would lie quietly and watch her mother sleeping on the bed opposite hers. The beds were close enough together for her to touch her mother but she never dared do so for fear of waking her. Magda was near to exhaustion anyway. But sometimes Lili would stretch her neck and reach her face towards her mother's so that she could feel her breath on her cheeks and sense the life in her. When it was bitter cold, Magda would invite Lili into her narrow bed, and they would put one blanket on top of the other and Magda would wrap her arms around her and squeeze her and bury her face in Lili's dirty hair, and Lili would snuggle back so that every part of the back of her body was touching her mother's. But the bed was too small and Lili too restless at night. She insisted unless it was just too unbearable that she was warm enough in her own bed. Because she knew her mother needed sleep.

They would all rise together and she would watch as her mother and sisters summoned the facial expressions that would say to one another: it's all right, it could be worse, soon it will be over. None of them believed it but it was a means of navigating the day. One of the sisters might be able to find a corner of bread and some water for breakfast and then they would talk, avoiding stories of the life they had once led and instead looking forward to the lives they would later enjoy. Lili had decided she would become a teacher and that she would never marry and that she would move to a small village in Bavaria where she would live in a cottage.

'A gingerbread cottage?' Charlotte had said, laughing.

'Why, yes,' Lili had replied. 'How did you know?'

Every so often the talking would stop, for a reason Lili could not divine. Anneliese would turn her back on her sisters and whimper. Hannelore would comfort her. Charlotte would stare into the middle distance and Magda, grey lines framing her eyes, would sigh.

In the afternoon, perhaps after a bowl of thin soup, they would be allowed out to walk around the building. They walked in a yard bordered on one side by a blank windowless wall and on the other three by uncultivated scrubland. They were somewhere outside the city, yet it did not seem to Lili as if they were in the country. Tall fences topped by three long coils of barbed wire marked the boundary.

During the evening they talked again, always in undertones as if they might disturb someone, or quietly played the childish games they had made up. They never spoke of Albert Schröder, and something inside Lili told her not to ask Magda about her father. At a certain point, never predictable, the light would cut out abruptly and it was time to try to find sleep.

5

They heard nothing about the proceedings against their father. Their life consisted of waiting, for invisible processes to be completed and decisions to be taken. That much seemed to be tacit between her mother and the people who oversaw their detention, ordinary people for the most part, with haunted and harried looks on their faces. Or possibly this was a complexion Lili later placed on them.

The next phase was managed with characteristic precision by the authorities, and a little finesse. Magda was called to the facility manager's office on the floor below to discuss certain legal matters. She followed the burly supervisor obediently, head down; she had already been conditioned in the way of things.

'We'll practise some French when I get back,' she said. They had taken to lessons together, with no books and relying on Magda's and the other girls' own knowledge. It was a way of passing the time.

A few minutes later the supervisor returned. She said brightly, 'Showers. They've fixed the boiler at last. You girls will be the first to use them. Your mother will have a chance when she gets back.'

She handed over thin, stiff towels, the colour washed out, threads hanging from them, but laundered at least, leaving one on the bed for Magda. The girls filed along the long linoleum corridor and into a suite of rooms they had never seen before, better maintained than the rest of the accommodation.

'New clothes as well,' said the supervisor. 'And a medical checkup. I'll leave you to get ready for the showers. They're just through there. Leave your dirty clothes in a pile in the corner.'

They undressed and looked at the new underwear, trousers and tunics that lay on the benches. Hannelore folded and stacked the clothes they had taken off and, carrying their towels, they walked through.

It was a communal shower, with more than enough space for them all to stand together. Charlotte found the tap and they watched as the powerful flow became warmer. Eventually it was steaming hot and they walked under the healing waters. Lili realized that no one had spoken since their mother had left their room but now they were giggling and whispering.

It felt like a rebirth, the warm water cascading down on them. There was even soap. Grey runnels of grime drained down the sluices below their feet. Finally, the supervisor called from the adjacent room, 'Time's up.'

Buoyed, they dried themselves by the benches and pulled on the clean clothes. Charlotte made a neat pile of the towels.

The supervisor carried a clipboard. 'Medicals now,' she said, 'and then please, straight back to your room.' She opened the connecting door to another room, in which, Lili could see, a bespectacled woman in a white coat stood waiting.

'Schröder, Hannelore,' announced the supervisor, and Hannelore walked with her into the room.

'Until later,' she said, smiling.

The supervisor closed the door firmly behind her. The remaining three girls were excited.

'It must have been sorted out. Perhaps that's what Mama is talking about with the manager,' said Anneliese.

'We'll soon be home,' said Lili.

'I'm going to put on my best clothes and dance in the ballroom,' said Charlotte, 'on my own.'

It was only a few minutes before the door opened again. Hannelore did not come back.

'She's back in your room,' said the supervisor, smiling in reassurance. 'Now, Schröder, Charlotte.'

Charlotte walked into the room, giving a little wave as she went. A small patch of darkness crossed Lili's consciousness but it was soon gone as Anneliese took up the commentary on what she planned to do when they arrived home. After a short time she too was gone.

Left on her own, Lili began to think. Their mother had told the other girls that if they were ever separated one of them should always stay with her. But there was no need to worry. They were on their way home. Or at worst, they had had showers and would be back together in the room in a few minutes.

It seemed only seconds before the door opened again.

'Schröder, Elisabeth,' the supervisor said.

'But it's not been long enough,' said Lili.

'Of course it has. You must have been daydreaming, my girl. Now come along.'

Lili stood up.

6

Even as she stepped through the door she sensed what was happening. There was no particular pretence. She had no idea what subterfuge had taken Hannelore, Charlotte and Anneliese from here. By the time Lili was called forward, there was no need. As a child, she was manageable.

She followed the supervisor meekly along the corridor, down the stairs, through the metal rear door of the building and on to the waiting transport. At the age of ten, she had already begun to know the trade-offs and the parameters of her new existence. Together with her intelligence and alertness, this knowledge would be crucial to her survival. She did not struggle or resist.

Years later she spent a semester as a visiting professor at one of the Ivy League colleges and made the mistake of agreeing to stand in for an absent colleague to deliver one undergraduate lecture of a series on the Holocaust. Clearly the administrators had not known of her own life, simply that she was an expert on twentieth-century European history and politics. Her experiences were not among the few details about herself she had chosen to share, so the college staff were not to be blamed.

During questions, a pretty young female student in the third row, who had been gratifyingly attentive throughout the lecture, said of those who had been through the camps, 'Gee, so brave. That pain, that suffering.'

This met with murmurs of approbation, but one young man who had spent the whole hour fidgeting and scribbling intently on his pad raised his pencil.

'I don't know,' he said in a whining drawl that she found irritating, 'these people weren't brave. They had no choice. They were just in that situation. And,' he said, waving the pencil more vigorously, 'they didn't resist. Why was that?'

She could not recall her reply but could vaguely remember the ruckus in the lecture room. Strangely enough, though, she agreed with him in a way. She was no hero. It was simply survival, and she would have betrayed any of her fellow captives for an extra crust of bread each week. She would have welcomed any of the guards between her legs if it would have staved off death. There was nothing noble about her life in the camps.

After the war, once she was safe, she would periodically try to recall those years. But, especially in the comfort of their farmhouse in the Scottish Borders, memory failed. The reconciliation between the Lili who had undergone all of that and the present Elisabeth was impossible. The cord between them was broken. It had been a different person, in a different world. The parties in the Tiergarten villa and those dull hours waiting in the detention centre with her sisters and her mother were far more vivid in her memory. As was the image of Hans Taub as he rammed his fingers inside her, bold, blond and blue-eyed; vicious and demonic.

The filth and the pain and the fear and the despair in the camps were unimaginable to her afterwards. Not only could she not recall events, she could not summon up inside herself the odour of her feelings. As she sought adequate description, the words themselves brought distance and an antiseptic, anaesthetizing effect. Whatever the documentary evidence, including the number tattooed on her forearm, it was impossible to believe that this body, these hands and this mind had burrowed through all this and emerged. She did not suffer from nightmares and reasoned that she was unable to equate what had happened with the person she now was. No doubt a professional psychologist would say otherwise. She must be in denial, with suppressed memories that at some point would return to harm her. But she had no appetite to revisit the past. She had survived and that was sufficient.

She did so by becoming as insignificant as she could. She later discovered that a clerical error had consigned her to the concentration camp when she should have been fostered. This at least was what the record reflected; it could just as easily have been the result of some undefined personal animus towards a traitor's family on the part of an anonymous, powerful official.

At first, emerging from the cattle truck in her rough uniform and edging uneasily into the sunlight, she had been adopted by a kindly elderly Jewish couple. She was quickly regarded as their grandchild and became embedded in the community of the camp. She could not later remember what they looked like or their names. There was a vague recollection of the woman's warm embrace and the man's smile, unconnected with any facial features. At some point they became separated. Whether they were removed or died on work detail, she could not remember or never knew. Like so many others, they ceased to exist, and she was simply carried on the sea of squalor, thrown here and there by the waves, just trying to be a speck in the centre of it all.

She too was moved, not selected individually but simply as part of a tranche of livestock herded on to a train and transported elsewhere.

She did not know where she came from or her destination. It happened three times. Each camp had its own unique properties and topography to which she had to habituate herself; each was uniform in its destruction of the soul. Away from the dull gaze of the guards, personality still existed, to be sure, but it was being systematically crushed. Her existence became a continuum of work, hunger and a desperate effort to avoid sickness and disease.

She could recall well, however, the days leading up to their liberation. Suddenly — it seemed to her suddenly — there was a buzz in the camp. The guards had in previous months worked them even harder and food had become still shorter in supply. The numbers of people daily taken from work details and sent to the looming grey building with the four chimneys increased. And then things slowed down and the guards seemed to adopt a kind of grimacing lassitude.

Their numbers gradually dwindled until in the middle of one night the camp was alive with the sound of starting motors and businesslike shouts. The inmates watched as the commandant and final guards drove off into the dark forest that surrounded the barbed wire.

Still they did nothing but wait. There was no food but no one broke into the kitchen compound or the barracks that the guards had inhabited. They were accustomed to days without food.

It was three days before the first British jeep drove by, its occupants seemingly so stunned that they simply sat in their seats, then drove away quickly. Later that day salvation, or as close to it as can be achieved in this world, came to them. Elisabeth would later remember the waiting more than the days after the British opened the gates.

She was fortunate enough to have contracted typhus. When they were liberated, the British brought bread and cheese and meat, plundered from the nearest town. They knew no better, and nor did the prisoners as they gorged on the rich food. Several died as their digestive systems failed to cope with the abundant proteins and fats that now filled their bellies. Elisabeth, on the other hand, had no appetite.

It was not, for her at least, a joyous time. She could remember a deep depression falling on her during the time she spent in the military hospital. This was release, then; but she was so numbed that she could not feel happy. Nor could she feel sad. The weight of events and the inhumanity she had witnessed crushed her.

It was several months before she discovered, at first tentatively and then with more certainty, the fates of her parents and sisters. Albert Schröder had been found guilty of treason. Magda was convicted as his accomplice. Both were executed. This much was on record. What had happened to her sisters was never firmly established. The records were not clear on events immediately after the detention centre and subsequent traces were fragmentary. She knew beyond doubt that at some stage they had perished in the camps, a fact established by omission. They were not among the survivors whose identities were carefully logged by the Allies.

Elisabeth had retained only slight hope that they might still be alive. When she discovered the likelihood was negligible she found it impossible to grieve. To all intents and purposes they had died the moment she was parted from them and their corpses had been added to the towering pile she had witnessed. She did not feel shame at her coldness. She felt the coldness.

In May 1946 she left the displaced persons camp near Hanover, boarded a train that took her to Ostend and then took a boat across the Channel. She was being sent to England and as she boarded the vessel in a warm spring breeze she felt excitement, and no guilt.

7

Elisabeth Schröder was of an awkward age, no longer a child but not yet an adult. She was placed in the care of John Barber, a don who had recently arrived back at Pembroke College in Oxford after his war service, and his wife, Eleanor. In flowing white nightdresses and dressing gowns, her long grey hair hanging loose and free, Eleanor haunted the corridors of the large Jacobean house day and night like a thin silver wraith. She was a kindly woman, but shortly after Elisabeth had joined the Barbers Eleanor was diagnosed with ovarian cancer. It was clear that death was upon her. Elisabeth felt no embarrassment at its presence and the Barbers were gently candid. This did not prevent John Barber from pacing the rooms of the house in soft despair, as if somewhere he could find the solution to all this, an expression of puzzlement and distraction on his plump, florid face. He tried to do his crying in private, though more than once Elisabeth found him in the library or the boot room, lost, weeping as he stared through the mullioned windows.

John and Eleanor Barber were childless, unaccustomed to the presence of young people in their home. This suited Elisabeth, who did not want to be treated as anything other than a stranger. The draughty old house was large enough for the three of them to pass a day without meeting one another. As she recovered her sense of self, this was what Elisabeth needed.

The intention had been that the Barbers should familiarize her with life in England. She had not a word of English, so the placement with an academic who specialized in the German Romantic novel would be advantageous. The middle-aged couple would teach her, care for her and help build her confidence.

In the event it was she who cared for them as they stared at the vortex of what was to come and took their first tentative steps into it. Eleanor's condition became rapidly worse. It did not minutely trouble Elisabeth to tend for her, spending nights soothing her as she writhed in pain, fetching and carrying, and calmly clearing the mess of her foul bodily excretions as she descended further into the hell of her final months. Nor did what was to come concern Elisabeth. She knew death intimately, and it was not to be scorned or feared. It simply was.

At the same time she learned again how to be a human being. She rediscovered compassion. When Eleanor Barber died at the end of the long winter of 1947 Elisabeth was more affected than she had imagined she would be. The thousands of deaths of which she was directly aware during the war, the hundreds she had witnessed at close quarters: these had not evoked similar feelings. For this she was annoyed with herself, but in the midst of his own grief John Barber said gently that at least she could once again feel.

It was in 1950 that she thought about university. She wanted initially to apply for a place at Oxford so that she could continue to live in the house with John Barber, but he blocked the idea. One afternoon he made a pot of tea and sat with her in the drawing room, unembarrassed but hesitant.

'My dear, I'm afraid I must insist you study elsewhere. The idea of you studying here at Oxford is simply out of the question. You need to discover a life beyond this house, a life of your own, and you cannot be tied to me. And for my part, if you do remain it is almost inevitable that I shall form an attachment to you that borders on inappropriate.'

She laughed and said, 'John, don't be so silly.'

'No. I may be fat and fifty-three years old, but sadly I do continue to have such feelings.'

'But John, you're such a lovely man.'

'I think if you knew me better you might revise that opinion. It is certainly one I do not share. I wish it were otherwise.'

'I'll be so upset if you send me away.'

'As no doubt shall I. But I'm sure it's the best thing for you. To discover a wider life. To see new horizons. Become truly independent. And it will be better for me. We'll see each other between terms. If, that is, it's what you want.'

'You know it will be.'

She hid her offended feelings, perversely pleased at the sensation that affirmed humanity, and acquiesced. It was her idea to change her name to Barber by deed poll, but she knew it pleased John.

'In practical terms it may make things easier,' he said. 'The wounds from the war are still raw and even at our most prestigious academic institutions misunderstandings occur. Besides, the administrators would no doubt mangle the name Schröder. You could of course call yourself something even more commonplace, such as Smith.'

'No,' she said. 'Barber will do nicely.'

Elisabeth Barber went up to Cambridge University in September 1951, studying history. She knew that she owed her place in part to a beneficial view of her own history by the authorities and to a degree to John Barber's contacts. But equally she knew that she was highly intelligent, that she had swept through the previous years avidly consuming every piece of learning before her, and that academia would play a vital part in her future life.

8

It was when she graduated that she understood for the first time that she had become an adult. She had spent the previous three years studying seriously, as young women needed to do if they were to stand a chance against their male counterparts. She knew she needed to be much more accomplished than her nearest male competitor to succeed.

John Barber attended the ceremony and bought her a mediocre lunch at the University Arms.

'And what are your plans now?' he asked over dessert.

'I really don't know,' she replied, defeated by this innocuous and obvious question. 'I hadn't thought. Relax for a while and then find something to do, I suppose.'

'The Civil Service might be a good bet. They're always on the lookout for bright young things. Or I suppose there's commerce. You'd be a very sought-after commodity, on the strength of your degree alone. And when they meet you, they're sure to be bowled over. But I suppose I'm biased.'

'Am I a complete idiot, John? I mean, I haven't given it the first thought. Not even for a moment.'

'Well, there's no rush.'

'I could become a teacher,' she said. 'Yes, that might suit me very well. Or . . . '

'Yes?'

'Do you think I have it in me to be an

academic of some sort? You know, one of the provincial red-bricks. Nowhere as grand as here. Might I just be able to make a go of it?'

A broad smile came to his face. 'There's no need for false modesty. Of course it would be a possibility. More than a possibility. I'd have you down as a dead cert. Would you like me to have a word? I do have contacts around the place, not just in Oxford.'

She looked at him quickly. 'No. Please no. This is something I want to do under my own steam. I have to find my own way. You do understand, don't you?'

'Of course I do,' he said, and smiled again.

She realized then that she had found herself, or sufficient of herself to live without consulting others or asking their permission. Opportunities shimmered before her, tempered only by her own modesty. She was not certain what she would do, but it would be entirely she who determined it.

As things worked out, it was as easy as John had predicted. She had already arranged an appointment with her tutor to thank her for her help. Over tea she asked tentatively, 'I wondered whether you might consider supporting me in an application for further study?'

'I was rather hoping you might ask me that,' said the tutor, leaning back on the battered leather couch. 'Of course. I'd be delighted.'

'Do you know what the process is?'

'Process?' she said. 'Oh, no doubt there will be the odd form to fill out. There may be an interview at some stage during the summer. But

I rather think the important parts of the . . . process have been completed.' She looked at Elisabeth and gave a smile before continuing. 'Of course we've informally discussed potential candidates for postgraduate places in the Senior Common Room, and your name comes up with regularity. You may take it as read that you'll be accepted. And you can be fairly sure a scholarship will also be forthcoming.'

9

Cambridge became her town, rather than simply the venue for her education, as she came to inhabit her adult life. She made the rooms she had been allocated comfortable and began to buy cheap but tasteful works of art in the market. She worked less frenetically and anxiously and in her spare time learned to cook. She regretted not having had the opportunity to study a musical instrument, remembering Charlotte, at eighteen an accomplished flautist with prospects of a place at a conservatoire in a European capital. For Elisabeth, it was now far too late to acquire a level of expertise that would satisfy her. Instead she consumed classical music avidly and attended all the concerts she could.

Every inch of the quiet, benign town was hers. She explored its alleyways and parks, now shunning the college life in which she had previously been immersed. She enjoyed exchanging gossip with those she met on the communal stairways but little else of the fervid intellectualism of the place. She made friends but preferred to meet them in pubs in the surrounding villages, reached by bicycle. She continued to discover what she consisted of and what made her happy and unhappy. Eight years earlier, the concept of happy or unhappy would have been alien to her.

She was not a conventional student. She kept herself apart from her fellow postgraduates and was to be seen only rarely in the Middle Combination Room of her college. She studied how her few female peers dressed and chose differently. She began for the first time to say what she thought, rather than what she thought she ought to think, as she built her thesis on the economic circumstances underlying the First World War. Her new supervisor, once an iconoclast but by now a fully paid-up, sweaty, sherry-drinking old fart, viewed her as a dangerous quantity, which she took as a compliment. It may have had something to do with the fumbling pass he had made at her that she rejected, leaving him no scope to fall back on ambiguity or misunderstanding.

There were, depressingly, other men too. The experience of meeting them was dispiriting because, like her supervisor, they seemed interested only in what she symbolized: an attractive young woman and the promise of sex. Any attempt at intellectual intercourse with her was superficial and patronizing, designed to nudge her towards the other kind. And they knew so little, so very little, of this world. She rebuffed them steadfastly until she met Alasdair McLeish, a graduate law student, a diffident Scot with dark Celtic good looks.

What followed was as straightforward, low-key and sensible as they were. Friendship was followed by a formal courtship and finally by an awkward visit by Alasdair to Oxford to see John Barber. The awkwardness was largely Barber's: he felt he had no locus in the matter of Elisabeth's choices. Things eased when Alasdair explained that this was a formality and a courtesy. If Barber had reacted adversely he and Elisabeth would have married in any case. But Alasdair McLeish liked to do things by the book.

Elisabeth then became a fellow of the college and her life seemed to be on a straight track to distant retirement. It was she, rather than the demands of her future husband's career, who changed that course, applying for a lectureship at Edinburgh. She was successful and while Alasdair completed his studies at Cambridge she moved to Edinburgh to set out just how she would pursue her research.

★   ★   ★

Elisabeth McLeish would not have described herself as a particularly contemplative person. The demands of an academic career, together with the upbringing of her children, would have been sufficient to distract her from introspection had she been that way inclined naturally. Which in fact she wasn't.

It was not until 1997 that everything stopped

329

again and she was delivered back to the spiritual emptiness of 1945. Keenly aware though she was of her self-indulgence, she felt that all that had been built in her life during the intervening years had been destroyed.

She was smiling when this thought struck her. The occasion was Alasdair's funeral, as they waited to enter the church, when her grand-daughter blurted out the question. Blurting was rather Amanda's way.

'Weren't you ever fed up with each other?' she asked, as if it were a requirement of every human relationship. 'Didn't you ever just want to do your own thing?'

With someone she loved less, Elisabeth might have employed a rather more stern tone. But the query prompted that distant, reflective smile that would be seen on her face in years to come, her eyes following her mind to a distant place. In some part of her she could not stop herself again being pleasantly surprised by Amanda's lovely sing-song Scottish lilt.

'Well, I did rather do my own thing,' she said. 'Alasdair wouldn't have wanted me not to. But my thing was all about stability and continuity. And friendship. I'm afraid we were rather boring. But back then individuality wasn't really regarded as a virtue, least of all in a place like Edinburgh. There aren't any skeletons in our closet. We must have been rather a disappointment to you all.'

'No, no,' said Amanda. 'We looked up to you so much. I wish I could live my life so simply.'

'It's a complex world, my dear. Perhaps the

50s were some kind of respite, or a delusion. My early years weren't exactly simple.'

'I know. I didn't mean. It's just.'

'It's all right. I've no lessons to offer. Maybe because I'd had such a tumultuous life I yearned for something more steady and solid. I'm sure millions of others did after the war. It doesn't make it right. But I do feel for you young people, trying to make sense of everything. There, listen to me. So very patronizing. I'm sorry. What was it John Lennon said? Whatever gets you through the night. I'm sure he was right.'

She was aware that, while her words might appear deliberately spoken and to make sense, the centre of her consciousness was elsewhere. This was not such a challenging facility for one who had been accustomed professionally to operating on several levels, mentally constructing a thesis during a boring departmental meeting or internally testing an idea during a tutorial. But it was not something she generally deployed with her family.

It was, she supposed, excusable given the circumstances that she should be thinking of her dead husband, her parents, her sisters and herself.

Alasdair's death had been far from unanticipated. Diagnosed with prostate cancer some four years previously, he had immediately retired and begun planning the period of between two months and five years he was told to anticipate. World cruises, sports cars, bucket lists and mawkish farewell parties were not on his agenda: a simple, gentle wind-down with his family was what he sought. He hadn't done so badly on the prognosis, he'd said the week before, when the immediacy of death was so obvious. For her part, Elisabeth had deluded herself that she could cope with this, riding her grief with her customary fortitude. She was, after all, accustomed to loss.

In fact her life imploded. That detached smile, the fixed display of control, would remain and she would continue carefully to regulate outward displays of emotion. In private only would there be tears. She would discipline herself not to lose control of her practical life — the few pieces of research that continued under her supervision following her retirement, maintenance of the house and grounds in immaculate condition, diligent attention to her good causes.

She foresaw all this as she sat without expression in her pew, the service occurring around her somewhere far away. Grief was to be expected, she knew, though its self-absorption must be curbed. Her loss was a bottomless well into which she found herself calling continuously, with no echoing response. This much was routine, she told herself. Was it more than that? She could no more answer that question than attempt the pointless comparison of her grief with another's. It would have been unnatural not to have felt his absence keenly, that man who had been remarkable precisely because he had seemed so unexceptional to others. Competent, but diffident and lacking in charisma, would have been the faint praise. Not to her, nor to her children and grandchildren.

Somehow she must reconstruct. Guilt flooded together with the pain at her selfishness. Even now she found it impossible to mourn for her parents and her sisters, whose lives had been unarguably more tragic and their deaths immeasurably more horrific. Impossible to visualize them in life, she thought as the obsequies played out. Impossible to imagine them as warm, physical beings, with thoughts and emotions and character, or to think of their deaths. Let alone to weep.

★ ★ ★

Some three years later she resolved to discover what had happened, back then. She had never before sought any answer to the conundrum that was her past, never subscribed to theories that she needed, for true contentment, to winkle out the truth. She had never looked for that dreadful American thing, closure — being perfectly content for it all to be there, packed in the recesses, never to be aired again — and certainly not for revenge.

But now she wanted to know. She was not sure what precisely she was seeking: knowledge, the truth, retribution, repayment of some obscure debt. She engaged Gerald Glover, once a postdoctoral researcher under her supervision, now a professor at a university in the north of England, to undertake research on her behalf in his spare time. She could have done the work herself but wanted, for reasons that at the time were uncertain, a demonstrably independent and objective job done of it. Gerald did the work during university vacations, under terms of strict confidentiality, engaging a series of research students, the last of whom was Stephen Davies.

When she had been Gerald's academic supervisor in the 1980s, he had fallen under her unwitting spell. He was more than willing to undertake the research and interviewed her in her vast granite Borders house. She talked for more than three hours for the tape, detailing her life until her marriage.

'What are you looking for, then?' asked Gerald gruffly.

'I'm not really sure, if that's not too unsatisfactory an answer.'

'Of course it is. It's completely unsatisfactory.'

'Well then. Answers.'

'Come on, Elisabeth. That's no good. Too vague. You'll have to do better than that. You've run enough research projects. You know the adage. They're only as good as the specification at the beginning.'

'I do believe that's your adage, Gerald. Not especially memorable or inspiring, is it?'

'All right,' he said, shaking his head in frustration. 'But it's perfectly true. You don't want me thinking you've turned into a batty old woman. What are these questions you want answers to?'

'Isn't that obvious, from the account of my life you've just heard?'

He waited a couple of beats as if summoning his patience. 'It may be, it may not. What's the single question to which you're seeking the answer?'

'Well, I suppose how my father and mother ended up being prosecuted, and how we came to be sent to the camps.'

He fidgeted. 'Meaning?'

'Meaning who told those lies. And why.'

'Progress at last. Hallelujah. The who will be difficult enough. The why may turn out to be impossible. You do realize, don't you, that the authorities may simply have taken against your father? By your account, he didn't exactly go out of his way to curry favour with them. It's entirely possible they may simply have lighted on a malicious comment from a business rival.'

'Possible, Gerald, but unlikely, I'd say. You know as well as I do that at that stage the authorities were maintaining at least the appearance of due process. There will have been a report somewhere or other.'

'Quite possibly in the Russians' hands. Or destroyed. I don't fancy our chances.'

'Ever the optimist. That's what I love about you, Gerald.' She beamed at him and could see that despite himself he was won over. 'There'll be a trace somewhere, Gerald. You know there will.'

Indeed there was. It had taken a good eight years, but there was a trace. Then Gerald and his assistants pulled at the end of the string, and it all began to unravel.

One winter's evening Gerald and Stephen had sat with her in the drawing room in front of a log fire. Gerald asked Stephen to present their findings. For Christ's sake, no PowerPoint, she knew he'd have said to the bashful, rather pretty young man with long eyelashes behind his spectacles. No bloody visuals at all. Just talk. And don't make it too obviously scripted. She likes the sense of a conversation.

Numerous names were discussed. A disgruntled middle-manager in Albert Schröder's main factory who had been overlooked for promotion. A servant whom Magda had dismissed for pilfering. The owner of a competitor business who knew Hermann Goering personally. A writer who had been ridiculed at one of Magda's salons for views that verged on the fascist. In the end they succeeded in narrowing it down to one compelling candidate.

Hans Taub.

10

They have gathered in the empty lounge of the mews cottage. It looks even smaller to Elisabeth with the furniture removed. Elisabeth sits on one of the two kitchen chairs that remain. Gerald takes the other, while Stephen stands.

'He's gone, then,' says Gerald.

'I rather think so. Don't you?'

Gerald looks at her, that mixture of astonishment and distaste on his face so familiar from when she was his supervisor. She has never been able to work out whether he is so bad at hiding his feelings or whether this is an artifice, deliberately constructed to conceal what is really going on in that rather egg-shaped bald head.

'Um, I took him to the station two hours ago,' says Stephen. 'Saw him on to his train. It left on time.'

'Well, that's the last we'll see of him, I suppose,' says Gerald.

'Hmm,' says Elisabeth non-committally. 'I suppose we'd better get a move-on. My own train is . . . When is it, Stephen?'

'About fifty minutes. We have plenty of time.'

'The practical arrangements. Please may we run through them again?'

'The let runs out on the house at the end of the month,' says Gerald. 'But we'll deliver the keys back this afternoon, once you're safely on the train. As you can see, the men have taken the furniture to the charity shop. Cleaners will be in on Monday. And that's an end to it.'

'What if, you know, what if he comes back?' asks Stephen.

'I shall leave him a note. I've already written it.'

'What does it say?' says Gerald.

'None of your beeswax, young man,' she replies. 'It more or less covers everything.'

'My guess is he won't come back. He'll cut his losses.'

'I'm not so sure,' says Elisabeth thoughtfully. 'If not, I'll post him a copy. If he's still traceable.'

'Either way he's going to be a very disappointed little boy. All the transactions have taken place, haven't they, Stephen?'

'Yes. The account was drained down this morning. Vincent was kind enough to do the necessary. And yes, we have checked. It's all safely back in Elisabeth's account, including Roy's stake. Or rather Hans's. Where only she can access it. I've got all the documentation. And his keypad to log on. Do you . . . ' He looks at her questioningly.

'Yes. I'll take them,' she says. 'His things?'

'I bundled them up and threw them in that old suitcase he left here,' says Stephen. 'I was going to take them to the charity shop. Or failing that to the council tip.'

'All right.'

'Stroke of luck, Vincent coming onside like that,' says Gerald.

'Well, given his background . . . ' says Stephen. 'It would have been manageable otherwise. But tricky.'

'Not luck at all. Stephen accomplished that part of it extremely cleverly,' says Elisabeth. 'Hidden talents.'

She smiles at him. He glances at her shyly and smiles back.

'Makes a change from the day job,' says Gerald. 'I'd never seen a career for myself in confidence tricks.'

'No,' she says. 'It's not something I'd care to repeat myself.'

'Still. All over now, eh?'

'Hmm,' she says. 'Time to go, I think.'

17

Change of Plan

1

At last her journey is over and she is back home. It feels peaceful on the platform, beneath a grey-blue sky, the air fresher than she recalls, with the tang of the countryside. Her things have been sent on; all she carries is her handbag. Andrew had suggested a car to take her the whole way, but it was not the extravagance that deterred her. It would have tired her unduly, cramped in the same space, prising herself out at motorway service stations with the customary charm of cut-throat British plastic commercialism. Besides, she likes the train. Though the old civilities have faded, even on the railway, it is a way to travel, rather than simply to go. She has negotiated the hordes in London, at Paddington skipping swiftly, or as swiftly as a sprightly octogenarian can, into a taxi, then out into the pell-mell of King's Cross and straight into the first-class lounge, where a kindly porter fetched her at the appointed time to guide her to her seat. No chance of meeting him by chance: he would be wherever he would be, totting up his putative gains and certainly not meeting his imaginary kitchen-designing son. She must accustom herself to not calling him Roy.

And here is Andrew now, grinning broadly, with the bearing of his grandfather and the same bashful innocence. He fair sprints up the platform and gathers her carefully in his arms.

'Gran!' he says. She cannot stop the tears. That Scottish brogue as strong and steady as ever. 'It's great to see you again.'

'And you too, Andrew. How is everyone?'

'Sound as a pound. Looking forward to seeing you. We thought you'd maybe like a quiet night at home. Maybe Dad and Auntie Laura will drop by, but we've plans for a meal tomorrow night. I'm so pleased to see you. I take it everything went well. How was the journey?'

'It was fine, thank you. It's good to breathe the air again. The thing is . . . '

2

'Bugger!'

'Bugger!' he says again, but it makes him feel no better.

He is standing in his vest and underpants by his bed in the hotel suite. The indulgence is by way of a small, solitary celebration. Vincent, as he knew he would, has declined to join him. So here he is, on his own. He can afford such extravagances every so often, even more so with Betty's little nest egg nicely tucked away. Which brings him back to the point. Bugger: he thinks it this time, as uttering the word has had no effect.

The contents of the small overnight bag he took with him from the mews house are laid out on the bed. Back there he has left some old clothing in his room, mainly for verisimilitude in case she strays inside. After all, this is supposed to be a brief weekend away to see his son. She does not know that the son does not exist and that she will never see him again.

He does not wonder about Betty. Now it is over and done with she has ceased to be. There is no point speculating how long it will be before she discovers he is not returning and that she has no money left. Some thought will need to be given to whether she or that nerdy young grandson will attempt to track him or Vincent down. Indeed, they may contact the police. Good luck to them. He will have to consider whether the name Mannion should be resurrected. No need to decide just yet. Now is the time to bask in it.

That bloody keypad: if only he could lay his hands on it. Vincent told him it would be prudent to transfer the money into his own account at the earliest opportunity and this is that opportunity.

He looks again and scratches his head. Two sets of underwear and two shirts. A washbag that has been emptied on to the bed. One razor, one tube of shaving cream, his shaving brush, one can of antiperspirant, one tube of toothpaste, one tube of haemorrhoid cream. Better not mix those two up, he chuckles to himself, and returns to the task. The small tablet computer is there that all the time he has had secreted in the lining of that crappy old suitcase together with its charger, so that he could email Vincent, keep track of things and monitor his bank balance. But he needs the keypad as well. He feels inside the washbag and checks that the damned thing has not become snagged up in his neatly folded shirts. Systematically he searches each pocket of his overnight bag. It is completely empty. He goes to his jacket, on its hanger in the wardrobe, and takes it out. His wallet, some small change, his mobile phone, his handkerchief and a half-consumed pack of extra strong mints have already been removed and placed neatly on the bedside table. He feels around each of the pockets again. Empty. Likewise his trousers.

Bugger.

He is all too prone to these lapses now. Once an error like this might have proved terminal. Many of his schemes had involved precision and exquisite timing. At least with this one he has a little latitude. Just as well this is the last of these little enterprises. For the moment, at least. He allows himself a small smile. It must still be in the suitcase, where he had stored it alongside the tablet. He can distinctly picture slipping it into the overnight bag, though. Sent to try us, these little mysteries. Strange thing, the mind. Plays tricks.

Ah well. It may be irritating but is just an inconvenience. What do they say? Don't sweat the small stuff. He takes a sip of his Scotch and picks up his mobile phone. Vincent can sort it. He can do the transfer.

He can't get a signal. He marches around the suite looking intently at the display, but to no

342

avail. Wearily, he pulls on shirt and trousers, ties his shoelaces and takes the lift down to the ground floor. He will not pay the extortionate rates they charge in these hotels.

In the lobby there is still no signal. He steps out on to Park Lane. Hyde Park looks magnificent in the summer evening sunshine and he inhales the end-of-day smell of the city, heated tarmac, diesel fumes and a whiff of fresh-cut grass from the park. Still no reception. Peculiar.

Back in his suite he has little option but to reach for the telephone on the desk. He dials Vincent's number but there is no reply. He is prompted to leave a voicemail but for the moment declines to do so. He switches on the tablet and, following the instructions on the card on the desk, he fires up the internet. Eventually he finds Hayes and Paulsen Private Bank. He goes to the online banking page, but without the keypad he cannot log in. He finds the customer service number, in the British Virgin Islands. This is going to cost an arm and a leg.

He dials the number and a bright mid-Atlantic voice answers.

'Hi, you're through to Hayes and Paulsen Private Bank and this is Shayla speaking. With whom am I speaking, please?'

'My name's Roy Courtnay.'

'Well, hi, Roy. How may I help you today?'

'I'm a customer of yours. I'm trying to transfer some money from my account. I haven't got my keypad thingy with me. The thing that you put the codes in.'

'Your H&PPad?' she prompts.

'That's right.'

'All righty. Let's see what we can do here.'

'Is there any way I can log in here without my H&PPad?'

'We-ell, not really. Where are you located, Roy?'

'London.'

'OK. London, England?'

'That's right.'

'And you've lost your H&PPad.'

'Not exactly. I forgot to bring it with me. I've left it at home. I'm staying in a hotel.'

'All righty. We can courier another out to you. I just need to ask you a couple of security questions and then I can cancel the old H&PPad and issue you a new one. We can courier it to you right away. First I need to take your details and the account details too.'

He gives her both, and she emits a small squeal of pleasure when she finds him on her computer. He exists.

'OK, then, Roy. All we need to do now is to cancel the old one and get the new one on its way.'

'How long will it take to get to me?'

'It should reach you in a couple days, Roy.'

'That's no good. I need to do the transaction now. Today or tomorrow. Is there any way I can do this over the phone?'

'Of course, Roy. Just so long as you've set up the telephone banking facility and the transaction in advance.'

'I haven't.'

'I see.' It is apparent that Shayla has run out of ideas. 'We-ell, you see, Roy, we do go the extra mile to protect our clients' security. So if you haven't set everything up, I'm sorry . . . '

'A branch, then? You have a London office?'

'We do. But it's a trading office, not a branch. And I see from your records that yours is an online account, Roy.'

'I'm going to have to go home, aren't I?'

'It looks that way, Roy. Unless someone can bring the H&PPad to you. I'm sorry for your inconvenience, but I really don't see any other way. Do you live far from London?'

'About ninety minutes.'

'I guess it could be worse. Is there anything else I can help you with today, Roy?'

'No.'

'Well, thank you kindly for calling Hayes and Paulsen Private Bank.'

He puts the receiver down, furious. He tries Vincent once more but there is still no answer. He leaves a message.

There is nothing else for it. He'll have to return there. He needs to think. Son missed flight. Delayed two days. It'll have to do. He'll go back first thing tomorrow.

He rings the number at the house. The answering machine clicks in. Betty must be out drinking tea again. Or having a nap. Impatiently, he says, 'Pick up, Betty,' but she does not. He leaves a message telling her that his son has been delayed and he needs to pick up a couple of things. He will return the next morning. It is thin but needs must. She'll never suss.

3

The key scratches on the lock. They look at each other for a moment as if to confirm what they have agreed. Andrew picks up the two tea mugs and goes into the kitchen, leaving the door ajar.

It has been a tiring day and night. They paused only briefly at her home, so that she could collect some clothes and apologize to her children for her change of mind. They climbed into Andrew's big car and he drove down the A1 at some miles above the speed limit. On the way he booked hotel rooms and she spoke briefly with Stephen, who retrieved the key of the house from the letting agents.

They arrived at the hotel at ten in the evening. Stephen met them in the lobby. 'Didn't reckon on seeing you quite so soon,' he said.

'It just didn't feel right,' she replied.

'There's no guarantee he'll come back.'

'There are few if any guarantees in this world. But I think he won't be able to stop himself. The thought of all that money dangling there will torture him. And of course he won't be able to contact Vincent. He'll risk it just this once, with some cock-and-bull story.'

'But won't he be suspicious at the disappearance of the keypad?'

'I shouldn't think so. He'll simply think he's left it here by accident. He's becoming forgetful. It won't have occurred to him that you might have pinched it when you fetched his bag. On one level he's suspicious, on another he's so utterly credulous.'

She was exhausted, her limbs ached and her head was throbbing. The next morning she suspected she might have been slightly irritable with Stephen. She slept well, however, and woke refreshed.

And now the key is slotted hesitantly into the lock.

★ ★ ★

'Well then,' she says when he enters. 'I got your message.'

He stands in the middle of the room and looks around as if stunned. It is a few moments before he says, 'Good Lord, what's happened here?'

He sees Andrew in the kitchen and glares balefully at him. Andrew regards him mildly in return but says nothing.

'Who's he?' he asks, placing his overnight bag on the floor.

'Robert was delayed?' she says.

'Yes. His flight was cancelled. He flies in tomorrow morning. I'll meet him then.' He speaks the words almost in an absent chant.

'Yes, yes,' she says. 'Of course you will.'

'I'll book into some hotel . . . But what's happened, Betty? What on earth is going on?' He stares at her.

'I was rather hoping the penny might have dropped,' she replies calmly. 'Or maybe it has. Whatever, as these young people say. It makes little difference. We'll get there in the end.'

'What are you talking about, Betty? And who's

he?' He jerks his head in the direction of the kitchen.

'Oh, that's Andrew. Are you all right, dear?'

'Yes. Fine,' calls Andrew.

'Andrew's here just in case.'

'In case of what?'

'How is Robert, by the way? He must be annoyed to have been delayed.'

'He's all right. He phoned from Sydney airport.'

'Did he really? To your mobile? That must have been expensive.'

'Yes. Well, he had to. Otherwise I wouldn't have known.'

'Strange,' she says with a tone of inattention, yet still looking him in the eye. 'Hasn't your mobile phone been cut off?'

'How do you know? Has a letter come?'

She says nothing.

'Well, he may have left a message at reception in the hotel,' he says. 'I get a bit forgetful these days.'

'Yes, you do, don't you? I rather thought you were meeting him at the airport.'

'Oh yes. Change of plan,' he says with greater confidence.

'Change of plan all round, it would seem.'

'What do you mean?'

'Isn't it sinking in? Just a little? It's very disappointing. I always thought you were on the ball. Shall we sit?'

She sits on one of the chairs and he takes the other. He looks around the bare room again and says, 'What is this, Betty? What's going on?'

'I'll take it slowly, shall I?' She looks at him with an expression of concern, as if his well-being is paramount. She holds up an envelope. 'I'd written you a note. But I thought it wasn't really adequate. Or fair, come to that. So I decided it was best to do this face to face. Besides, there's been a change of plan on my side too. I'm so glad you decided to come back.'

'What makes you think I wasn't coming back? After I'd met Robert.'

She sighs and waits briefly.

'Never mind. Let's persevere, shall we? Now, where exactly to begin? At the beginning or the end?'

'I never did pretend to understand you, Betty. But you've really got me this time. What's happened? Talk to me, Betty.'

She simply smiles at him.

'Don't worry about it. We can sort it out. When I get back from London. Meanwhile, I must get on. I just have to pick up a couple of things from upstairs. Then we'll order a taxi and I'll check you in at one of those motorway lodges for a couple of nights. When I'm back we can sort it all out. Been in worse scrapes than this in my life, I can tell you.' He grins reassuringly.

'I'm sure,' she says.

'So I'll just pop upstairs and then we'll be off.'

She reaches into her handbag as slowly he levers himself up. 'Would it be this that you forgot?' She holds out the Hayes and Paulsen keypad and he is still, looking at it.

'Now are things beginning to take shape?'

He sits back down again, heavily. His

349

expression is unchanged.

'My career's taught me the benefit of careful research. I've an inkling you tend to do a once-over-lightly and then leave it at that. It's all there, you know. My work and my life, more or less. Available to all-comers, or at least most of it, if you'd cared to look at it in depth. Gerald couldn't credit it. But I knew you. I knew your arrogance. I recognized you as soon as I met you in that awful pub. The photographs were helpful. But when I met you in the flesh, it was so clear. Even I thought it was a bit risky at that point. We all did. But we didn't account for your obliviousness. Your single-minded pursuit of the mark. It had been some years, I suppose. And I was somewhat at an advantage. But still.'

She smiles sweetly.

'What are you trying to tell me? That you've been trying to con me? If so — '

'I think on reflection we'll start somewhere near the beginning. With a little boy — rather a large boy actually. Hans Taub.'

He looks up quickly. There is the minutest pause of less than a half-beat before he says, 'I've no idea what you're talking about.'

'Hmm. I was expecting you to say that. But you are Hans, aren't you?' She looks at him questioningly.

'No, of course not. Come on, Betty. I'm Roy. You know that. I'm not any, what was it, Hans?'

'So you don't know of a Hans Taub?'

'I never said that. As it happens a German I worked with straight after the war was called Hans. He was my translator. Taub was his second

350

name, I think. When I was stationed in Hanover. He met a tragic end, though.'

She is nodding. 'Yes. Killed in the line of duty by a fugitive, I believe.'

He looks astonished. 'That's right. I was with him at the time.'

'You were, weren't you? So very much so. It was a strange affair, wasn't it? You and he were so alike, all the contemporaneous statements say. We've been able to track down a couple of the old staff from the Hanover office. They're almost as old as we are now. They talk fondly of the Gruesome Twosome. And what I love about official records is that they're so, well, official. One delights in seeing the emotion behind the officialese. The British account is patently designed simply to placate the Russians and put the whole incident behind them. It's so transparent. I'd have loved to see the Russian report, to compare and contrast. But of course that would be impossible. We had to make do with second-best, which was good enough. The old East German records. We only began looking in 2001 and it had all been lying there for more than ten years since the Wall came down. At first it didn't occur to us to look there. I use 'us' in the liberal sense of course. I really mean Gerald and his helpmates. He's the researcher whose services I paid for. Stephen's boss. He pretended to be my son, Michael. But no doubt we'll come to that later. Am I taking this too quickly for you, Hans?'

He looks at her and glares.

'Where was I? Oh yes. One of Gerald's people

was doing a research project on the Stasi and thought she'd just have a quick look. By quick look, I of course mean a matter of weeks going through the 1950s records. We academics love that sort of thing — you know, needles in haystacks. And there it was. A joint approach by the East German espionage agency and the Soviets to the aide of a junior defence minister in 1957. Unsuccessful, it seems, and the aide disappears from view. To a casual observer it'd mean very little. Just one of those Cold War pranks. But to us . . . '

'What does this have to do with me?' he asks with a note of petulance.

'Everything, of course. The approach was made to a certain Roy Courtnay. And Courtnay is such an uncommon name. There were several things that were important in that report. One of them was a reference to that incident in 1946 where Hans Taub was allegedly killed. In the little dossier was a summary of the Russian officer's report from the time. He was under the distinct impression the survivor was Hans Taub. But he let it pass.'

'We only met Karovsky for an afternoon. He was very unhelpful.'

'Yes. Karovsky was the name. You've a good memory for names. He was convinced enough that it was Hans Taub to track the man down later in London and to attempt to blackmail him. Shall we move on?'

'Do what you want.' He shrugs his shoulders.

'Am I boring you? The other interesting thing was that Hans Taub was apparently instrumental in denouncing a wealthy family to the Gestapo in 1938. The Schröders. The parents were executed and the children sent to the camps. Taub's father fled Germany with his son. His mother wasn't so fortunate. So the East Germans were keen to talk to Taub. Or is it Courtnay? Which shall we settle on?'

He looks up at her, wary. 'Please yourself. It's all Greek to me. He was a nasty piece of work, then, this Taub. I didn't know any of this when he was working for me.'

'Yes. He was only fourteen in 1938. Which raises a point of what I suppose you'd call academic interest.'

'Yes?'

'At what age can we take true responsibility for our actions? The legal age of responsibility in this country is ten. Do you think you had responsibility for your actions when you were fourteen, Hans?'

He grunts.

'Personally, I think Hans was well in charge of his own thoughts and actions. He was disgusted with the Schröders, he was disgusted with his liberal parents, but most of all he was disgusted with himself. So he flailed out. He even had a written contract with the Gestapo. Karovsky was going to confront him with it in 1957. I think Hans knew full well what he was doing to Albert and Magda Schröder, and to Hannelore, Charlotte, Anneliese and Lili.'

'This is nonsense. I'm Roy Courtnay. I grew up in Dorset. I went to war. I've lived a life. So what?'

'Indeed you have. We've been through it all. The convalescence, Lord Stanbrook — his personal archive, to which Gerald gained access, gave us a lot of detail — London and all those adventures afterwards. You were quite elusive, but then Gerald is very good at his job. As were his assistants.'

'This is nonsense. Where's your proof for any of this?'

'Proof? Well, Gerald's done a pretty thorough job. History generally isn't about proof. It's about the truth, or as close to it as we can get.'

'There's nothing, is there? What's this got to do with you anyway?' He is red in the face.

Andrew starts moving towards the living room, but Betty says, 'It's all right. Hans isn't going to do anything rash. Are you, Hans?'

'My name is not Hans,' he says through gritted teeth.

'No. I thought you wouldn't be satisfied,' she continues blithely, as if he has not spoken. 'I anticipated you might require something more compelling than mere historical commentary. Do you remember our trip to Berlin?'

'Yes,' he replies dully.

'Wonderful, wasn't it? The sunset over the Spree. The Berliner Philharmoniker in full flow. I did think we needed some time to ourselves, though. You seemed somewhat jaded and bored.'

He allows her to continue.

'I thought I'd go back to those lovely villas near the Tiergarten. In fact I knocked on one of the doors. No, I'm teasing you now. I'd made the arrangements weeks before. The owners were delightful. They were only too happy to let me have a look around. I hope you're keeping up, Hans.'

He is sullenly silent.

'There was a specific purpose. We weren't there just to see the house in which the Schröders lived. We trooped up to the first floor. There was Albert's study, newly done out and very high-tech. None of that horrid dark wood any more. Rather oppressive, I always used to think. A bit intimidating. We looked in one of the bedrooms. They've all been carpeted now, with a rather plush pile in a tasteful shade of beige. I'm afraid we had to prevail on them to pull up a small corner. They didn't mind at all, since it was for a good cause. You don't know what I'm talking about, do you, my dear?'

'I don't have a clue.'

'Bear with me, please. When we pulled back the carpet it was still there.'

'What,' he says with forced patience, 'was there?'

'The gap between the skirting board and the floor, of course. And even more surprisingly after all these years, so was the locket. We could see it with the help of a torch but we couldn't reach it. The owner of the house managed to winkle it out with a screwdriver. I will get to the point, I promise. In fact I'm there, almost. We managed to retrieve the letters and the locket. But of course it was the locket that was of greatest importance.'

'Oh, really.'

'The letters were the ramblings of a silly little

355

girl. But the locket contained your hair.'

'My hair? What do you mean, my hair?'

'Don't you remember? It was in my room. I persuaded you to let me have a lock. You had obviously had second thoughts, though, and you were glowering madly. A bit like you are now. But I pressed on regardless and pretended I hadn't noticed. Gay as a spring lamb. You got very angry when I cut off rather more than you bargained for. I laughed. But of course you remember. Happy days.'

She beams at him and sighs.

'Of course one applies one's intellect to such situations. And technology too. Recovering the locket wasn't simply a matter of nostalgia. There was rather more to it. It was a matter of proof. Gerald's a rather fussy man and, like you, wanted everything to be conclusive. And DNA testing's a marvel. You left us plenty of samples in the house while you lived here and it was simply a matter of sending them off to a lab together with the hair from the locket and waiting for the results. I rather think you've caught up with me now, more or less.'

4

'It was a long time ago, Betty,' he says wearily. 'What should I call you? Betty or Lili?'

'Elisabeth is my given name. I prefer it spelled and pronounced the German way. One of my idiosyncrasies.'

'But . . .'

'They're just diminutives of the same name. Tut-tut. Keep up. Still, here we are. Yes, it's been a long time. I'm not quite sure what that's meant to signify. The distance of time doesn't seem to me to erase the facts.'

'Why I'm in the skin of Roy Courtnay is complicated.'

'Actually, to be precise, you're not in the skin of Roy Courtnay,' she interrupts. 'Rather the reverse.'

'I stand corrected. So exact. Originally it was a series of misunderstandings. Roy died a horrible death and I was badly injured. I was unconscious and the Russians were in a rush to get us back to the British sector. They confused the two of us and it snowballed from there. It got out of control.'

She looks at him sceptically.

'I took advantage, I'll freely admit. But I had little choice. I was only a translator. I had no guarantee of employment. I'd have had no military pension.'

'Your English must have been good, even back then. It was quite a chance you were taking.'

'I'd spent four years in England, three of them at school. I'm good at languages. You know me. I'll chance my arm at anything. It was a calculated risk.'

'You didn't even think of Roy's family.'

'Well, no. You forget, Lili, those were tough times . . . '

'I don't forget, Hans.'

'No. Of course not. You know all too well. You know what it is to have to survive. That's all I was doing. Surviving. And nothing was going to bring Captain Courtnay back. Lili, I'm so glad you came through. I always hoped you would.'

She regards him steadily. 'I really would prefer you to call me Elisabeth. Or should I call you Hansi?'

He looks down at his clasped hands. 'It was an insane time. The world went mad for a few years. But your family's incarceration had little to do with me. The Gestapo pressured me. They put words into my mouth.'

'That's not quite what the record indicates. The East Germans had pretty comprehensive records.'

'They tricked me, Elisabeth. You have to believe that.'

'Do I really?' she asks. 'And what do I have to believe about what you did to me?'

'When?'

'When you assaulted me.'

'Assaulted you?'

'Shall I be more specific? In my bedroom the night of the Christmas party. When your father was talking with mine. When you probed me with your brutish fingers. When you showed me how inhumane human beings can be. Perhaps I should have been grateful for the insight into inhumanity. It came in handy.'

'I don't recall any of it. You're imagining — '

'What? That it happened? That it was you?'

She speaks evenly and he listens without comment. He raises his eyelids for a flash of a contemptuous look towards her, but he cannot sustain her gaze.

'It's funny. The most vivid memory is of you sniffing your fingers afterwards. You seemed so casually disappointed by the whole thing.'

He draws a breath. 'What is it you want, then?'

'You wish to cut to the chase. There's always a deal to be cut. So let's get to the nub of it and work out the details.'

'Well then?' He raises the courage to look at her. 'What do you want?'

'It's a very good question. But let me ask you: did you ever imagine the consequences of what you did?'

'Not fully. I suppose I understood your parents would be in some kind of trouble.'

'Hmm. Why did you do it, then? Had I so disappointed you by not responding to you in the way you desired?'

'I don't know,' he says. 'Your sisters were unpleasant to me. I was upset. My father was such a fool. I was angry with him. My parents were idiots. I saw them being imprisoned and dragging me down with them. This was a way of solving that problem, temporarily at least.'

'And solving the problem of the happy, prosperous Schröders too.'

'I don't know.' He shrugs his shoulders, the sullen fourteen-year-old again.

'What made you make those allegations? Just petty spite?'

'Our fathers were talking about sabotaging the war effort.'

'And our so-called Jewish heritage?'

'I thought it was more or less what the Gestapo man wanted to hear. It was a means of

359

getting where I needed to be.'

'It was a lie. We weren't a Jewish family.'

He looks at her and says, 'I didn't know whether or not there was Jewish blood in your family. I suppose I shouldn't have done it. It was just . . . necessary. He insisted I say it.'

'That's not the point. Whether or not we were Jewish. I'd be happy to be thought of as Jewish, even though I'm not. I'm proud to be associated with that suffering. I feel proud of this.' Since moving to Britain she has been careful to wear long-sleeved clothes, and especially so since living in the same house as him, but now she pulls up her sleeve and thrusts her forearm towards him, showing the number with the triangle. He is expressionless. 'The point is that your saying anything at all was wrong. It made no difference whether or not we were Jews. Whatever excuses you may prepare about your immaturity, you were responsible for what you said.'

He looks at her as if he cannot comprehend what she has said. 'It wouldn't have made any difference if I'd said nothing.'

'But you didn't say nothing.'

'Your father and my father were conspiring against the state. I told no lies about that.'

'They were conspiring against evil. You chose to conspire with it.'

'I was fourteen years old, for God's sake. How was I to calculate all these things?'

Just for a few moments neither of them speaks. It seems that Elisabeth is spent. But she finds her voice again.

'I'm curious. You don't feel guilt?'

'About what?'

'Any of it. Me, my family. Your parents. Roy Courtnay. Bob Mannion.'

'Guilt. That's a very difficult emotion. No.'

'No. You don't, do you?'

'It was . . . '

'Expedient?'

'That's rather harsh. It was what I had to do. I had no options. Or I thought I didn't. I had to do it to survive. You know all about that.'

'And afterwards?'

'Afterwards. Then it was in the past. It couldn't be undone. I hadn't made any of it happen. I had just . . . I had just . . . '

'Yes?'

'Taken the opportunities that presented themselves. That's not so terrible, is it?'

'And now?'

'I'm an old man. What's done is done. I can't put things right. What point would there have been in torturing myself with guilt?'

'I didn't realize that to feel guilt was an elective decision.'

'What is it you want from me? Money? I don't understand.'

She is calmer now, calibrating her voice to a lower pitch and speaking with deliberation. 'I know. You fail to understand a great deal. You fail to understand that I may not want anything at all from you. That there may be no bargain to be struck. There may be no price to pay. I've had a change of plan too. Let me tell you something.'

He looks at her but does not speak.

'When my husband died, I was lost. I've no way of judging whether I was more desolate than any other widow who's just lost her husband, but in my mind I went straight back to the end of the war. You might imagine that liberation was a happy moment, but it gave me a sense of my fragility and impermanence. An empty vista of fear. When Alasdair died I had the same fear. I had to discover meaning. I wasn't about to find it in religion — I think we can both agree on that. So it had to be something else. Finally I thought I'd found it. The search for the truth, and a reckoning of sorts.'

'Which is why we're here,' he says quietly.

'Yes. Quite comical in a way,' she says, 'two ancient turkeys, their necks creased and wobbling, jabbering away about things that are all but forgotten. The lessons at least. Scratching for meaning. It rather underlines our irrelevance, wouldn't you say?'

His eyes flare. 'I suppose so.'

'Where were we? Yes, what do I want? It rather evolved, I should say, as we began to make headway. First of all I simply wanted to know, then we discovered more or less the truth of that. We knew it had been you, Hans, and no one else. The challenge then was to follow your trail. You're an elusive man.'

He musters a wry smile and says, 'Story of my life.'

'Indeed,' she says sardonically. 'It wasn't so difficult. I won't take you through it all. But I think we managed to cover most of your escapades and scrapes. Do you have any mock modesty to display now?'

He shakes his head.

'I thought not. Our little search obtained a life of its own as it gathered momentum. Gerald in particular was like a dog with a bone. He can be a vindictive man. Most surprising for such a mild person. Not one to cross. And finally there you were, clear as day. Roy Courtnay. Vincent was most helpful filling in the details we'd missed.'

'Vincent?' he says in surprise.

'Yes. Our private detective chappy tracked him down quite easily once we'd met him. We wondered whether it was worth trying to have a quiet word with him. Certainly, once we'd established his antecedents. Did you know his grandfather was a Jewish émigré from Poland just before the Second World War? Probably not. Stephen did an excellent job of chatting him up and he was more than happy to oblige. It's been a bit of a redemption for him. He filled in several of the gaps.'

Hans slumps but looks defiantly at her.

'We'd found you and we were stuck as mere historians. So we employed our private detective, a nice young man from Chingford. He managed to root out all kinds of stuff. Quite remarkable. You hardly left your flat, but you were heavily involved in internet dating. You can see the direction in which we're heading. There was a big, how shall we put it, throughput. Our chap diligently located many of the prospective partners you'd met and later discarded, and interviewed them. Did you know you once got through five in a single month? I'm actually quite

363

surprised there's such a large supply line of lonely old women.'

Roy grimaces as Elisabeth continues cheerily.

'You'll be familiar with the picture that emerged. Most ladies you rejected after the first meeting. The ones you met for a second time were of interest. You wanted to advance the relationship very rapidly and were fascinated by their financial positions. Nicely dressed up as due diligence before you committed yourself. Each time it seemed that either the lady didn't meet your criteria or she somehow felt uneasy about you. That was the basis of the plan we formulated. I was keen to come into direct contact with you again, but at that point lacked that total certainty, despite all the evidence, that you were Hans Taub. So the solution was quite simple.'

'Meet me through internet dating.'

'Exactly. Quite neat, don't you agree? We mapped out a basic plan. I rented this little cottage on a long-term lease and moved in, ready to see how it went. And I think hook, line and sinker is the right expression, don't you? Gerald later came up with the idea of playing what I think is known as the three-card trick. I would allow you seemingly to fleece me when all the time that was what was happening to you. We had all the equipment. Stephen is a whizz on the IT, though we did leave some things to chance. The beauty of it was that I didn't actually need your money, so we could just abandon the idea if it all became too difficult. But we were rather good, weren't we?'

He does not respond to her eager look.

'Gerald played my son, Michael, in the little piece of theatre that we thought necessary for credibility. His wife was his real wife, his daughter was one of the earlier researchers who returned for a guest appearance and Stephen of course was Stephen. Who's clearly not my grandson at all. Didn't we all do splendidly? Stephen in particular? We all breathed a sigh of relief when you turned down the invitation for us to spend Christmas with them. I knew you would. And of course I didn't get the tests done.'

'Tests?'

'I'm rather all over the place, aren't I?' she says gaily. 'The DNA tests. I didn't go to the house, though it was lovely to picture myself doing so. It was a nice story, wasn't it? You'd have been proud of it. I didn't get the locket. I doubt it's still there. Even if it were, could we have tested the hair? Would that have proved anything? Gerald's very keen on all this technology. Thought it the only way to find incontrovertible proof. But we know better, don't we? I told him not to be so literal and that we'd find a way somehow. And we have, haven't we?'

'And your point?'

'Point?'

'Where are we going with this? Apart from demonstrating how stupid I am? Am I to understand that you've taken all my money?'

'Ah yes. The money. That really is the important thing for you, isn't it? Or is it the sense of victory versus defeat? It doesn't really matter. To take your money was the plan. It satisfied Gerald's rather atavistic revenge instincts. Stephen seemed rather keen on the notion too, particularly once he'd met you. But really it was my decision. I thought that this might be the way to put you behind me. And we all rather enjoyed the journey.'

He stares at her.

'Don't look so scared. Change of plan, remember? It'd been nagging for some time, but it was only on the way home yesterday that I really thought better of it. I decided it wasn't right. I didn't want to be like you. The note too. Not good form. I rather owed it to you to say what I had to say directly to you.'

'Owed it to yourself, you mean.'

'How so?'

'So you could get the satisfaction of seeing me squirm.'

'Hans, you do judge everyone as if they think the same way as you. I was dreading this conversation in fact. Besides, you don't exactly strike me as the squirming type. I simply thought it was fairer to see you once more.'

He looks at her and laughs caustically. To her, he is that bitter, contemptuous fourteen-year-old boy again, standing over her. Momentarily, she teeters and swoons, then regains her balance.

'So far as your money goes, you may have it back. I've prepared a cheque.'

She reaches into her handbag and produces a piece of paper, which she proffers to him. With trembling hand, he reaches out and snatches it from her. He makes to tear the cheque.

'No,' she says briskly, and he stops, having made only a nick in the paper. 'Think before you make a grand theatrical gesture in a fit of pique. You always were so impetuous and moody. I won't trouble myself to write out another cheque if you change your mind.'

His arms are still outstretched, holding the cheque between his fingers. He gives himself time to think as his arms shake with infirmity. Finally he lowers them and places the cheque neatly in his wallet, glaring steadily at her all the while. Those eyes, she thinks. But everything passes, in time.

5

They are eating the sandwiches that Andrew had been sent to buy. Elisabeth had whispered to him to be quick. She hadn't felt afraid exactly, more uneasy. She watches Hans, his attention fully on his food and the cardboard beaker of coffee he has before him.

'So,' she says. 'That's it, I suppose.'

He seems calmer now, placid even, possibly resigned to it all. The physical fear she felt while Andrew was out of the house now seems faintly ridiculous. She hopes she did not betray her feelings. It would have been a kind of victory for him.

'It's beyond me,' he says, shaking his head. 'Your little stunt, I can't pretend it's not all been rather upsetting. And unnecessary. Why couldn't you have simply spoken to me?'

'I'd have thought you of all people might understand that. Once things were under way it was rather exciting. I didn't think I had it in me. But of course it all comes naturally to you.'

'Hmm. Touché, I suppose. It's rather late in one's life to learn one's lesson, but I think I may have.'

'Really? That would be something of a surprise.'

His expression turns to hurt. 'That's a bit below the belt.'

'Below the belt. Interesting choice of words.'

'I've made mistakes, I'll admit. Some with consequences I never intended. I'm no saint . . . '

'No.'

'But I hope it's all behind me.'

'Wonderful,' she says, 'but somehow implausible.'

'Lying's part of me, I suppose,' he admits meekly. 'It's who I am. I wish I was clever and could claim some psychological reason for it. It's been like that for as long as I can remember. Ever since the Gestapo man, at least. But I'm right, aren't I? Lying is how we lead our lives. It's the way we get on in the world. Whether you're selling second-hand cars, whether you're the prime minister, whether you're a climate change scientist. It's just how things are. The truth is secondary.'

He looks at her and smiles, gently beseeching.

'Hmm,' she says. 'I don't think so, Hans. I don't mean to be rude. Or perhaps I do. Do you really think we can talk about the way of the world? That we can sweep it all under the carpet by your telling me that dishonesty is just the way we lead our lives? That with one bound you can be free?'

'Elisabeth, that's very ungenerous.'

'Yes. But accurate, I think.'

He looks away.

'Hans,' she says, 'this isn't an act of vengeance, or even justice. You know what your life has amounted to. It must be disappointing.'

'So says you.'

'Yes. So say I. And a little self-exculpatory hustle won't help you in my eyes.'

'Who are you to judge me?'

'I think I'm pretty well placed.'

'Have you finished?'

'For the moment.'

'I'm not interested in what you think. I'm not looking for your forgiveness.'

'That's more like it. I'm sure you're not. I doubt forgiveness enters your thinking. Or understanding. But fear of the approaching infinity does, I'm sure. You feel it as much as I do. The difference is that you've nothing to take heart from.'

'And you have? With your irrelevant scribblings?'

She smiles. 'It's tempting to think you're being deliberately obtuse. But you're not, are you? You really can't see.'

'See what?'

'That goodness does exist, however much we seek to deny it, just as much as its counterpart. Oh, never mind.'

She sighs.

He grunts and says impatiently, 'What is it you want from me?'

'Want? Nothing really. I'm not seeking contrition from you. Not with all that rage burning inside you. I've no desire to be reconciled with you. I don't even want you to comprehend. I just want to look you in the eye, feel your intimidation and emerge untainted. Surviving you, that was the point of it.'

She smiles at him with a warmth of feeling that surprises even her. It is not hostility, it is not victory. It is something resembling contentment. To be able to smile at this moment is in some strange way liberating.

'I wish you no ill,' she says. 'I really don't. For some time I have borne this malice towards you, but it's gone. I'm beyond you. So I think we will leave it at that. Andrew?'

6

A few seconds after they have left the house and he has held the car door for her, Andrew pats his jacket pockets, a little too theatrically for Hans's taste. He sees him talking to her through the open door before coming back to the house.

He knocks on the door. It is not the knock of a confident individual.

Hans takes a while to answer, then looks him up and down for the first time. He had not given him much attention earlier.

This Andrew does not seem as if he could have any connection with her. Broad, verging on pudginess, with tousled black hair, a tanned almost Latin complexion that is Plasticine in texture, he smiles bashfully as he stands obediently for this appraisal. Appearances can be deceptive — very much so — but he seems to be totally the unreflective type. No presence. Unlike Elisabeth, to give her her due. But on further consideration, a little like she had once seemed to him: complacent and single-faceted. Oh yes, they can be very devious, people. Physically, though, very unalike: Andrew with his large ungainliness, as if his enthusiasm might inadvertently crush something he loves; Elisabeth, petite and slim, of small features and large eyes. He somewhat obvious and ugly and happily shy; she direct and challenging and teasing and, Hans now finds, beautiful. Elisabeth: he must remember to call her that.

'Sorry,' says Andrew, breaking the silence between them. 'I seem to have forgotten my phone.'

'Oh,' grunts Hans.

'And my grandmother asked me to remind you that the lease runs out on this place on Monday. The agents will be in then. But of course there's no furniture anyway . . . ' He speaks with that smooth Scottish brogue. 'May I come in?' he asks, his smile intact but becoming less confident. 'I think it must be in the kitchen.'

'What?' says Hans. 'Oh, do what you want.'

He stands to one side, but only partly, so that Andrew has to sidle past him uncomfortably. He fixes the younger man with a piercing look and

371

Andrew averts his eyes, bustling through to the kitchen.

'Here it is,' calls Andrew from the kitchen, and comes back through. His expression changes to hostility. 'It was in my pocket all along. But we both knew that, didn't we?'

Hans holds the door handle still, ready to usher this nonentity out of his life for good, but Andrew pushes the door carefully to.

'Let's not do this here, eh?' he says, moving into the living room and turning to signal that Hans has not complied quickly enough.

Hans follows meekly enough, but regards him with no attempt to disguise his contempt.

'What?' he says.

'We'd all heard about you, of course,' says Andrew. 'My grandmother never kept it a secret from us. She told us about you. But it never seemed real. It seemed impossible that a boy could have done all this harm to her family. To my family. That's why it's good to meet you.'

'Yes?' Hans is bored with this.

'Yes. Meeting you, what seemed so surreal is now so natural. It all falls into place. She's right: you are evil.'

'Have you finished?'

Andrew's seriousness breaks into a smile. 'People know me as a nice guy. I work for an agricultural insurance company. I don't have a high-powered job, I'm not ambitious. I work hard, get on with my clients, and that does me. I suppose others would think of me as an amiable small-town plodder. Which is fine by me. But appearances aren't everything.'

'Really?' Hans rolls his eyes. 'Interesting, I'm sure.'

'But we're both more interested in you, really, aren't we? No one really knows what makes you tick, do they? Least of all you. At a guess I'd say you hate yourself more than anyone else. My gran said as much.'

'How Freudian. Or is it Jungian?'

'I don't know. What I do know is that you're a very unhappy man. A sad old bastard. Really, you deserve to be put out of your misery.'

Hans recoils in alarm, his eyes wide.

'Not that I'm about to do anything like that,' says Andrew softly. 'I'm known as a gentle giant, after all. Just like my grandaddy. But I do think it'd somehow be right for you to live the rest of your life in worry.' He pauses. 'Money's really important to you, isn't it? Or what it symbolizes?'

'How perceptive. Your grandmother will be getting rather impatient. I can imagine how deferential to her you must all be. If you're trying to unsettle me, I'm sorry to disappoint. Bigger people have tried to do that. And failed.'

'I'm sure that's true. No. I'm a gentle guy, Mr Taub. But I do have this rather unkind streak. Generally I like to keep it well hidden. But . . . '

He takes a step forward and prods Hans in the chest. Hans starts, and feels his back touch the wall and his knees begin to crumple beneath him.

'Cheque,' says Andrew.

'What?' says Hans.

'Cheque. The one my gran gave you.'

'Oh.' He fumbles in his pocket and pulls out his wallet.

'Thanks.'

Andrew holds the cheque up, examines it, tears it into several pieces and lets them fall on to the carpet.

'My gran's a very moral person, you see,' he says, 'and very forgiving. I'm more vindictive. I guess it's the male psyche, partly. Freud or Jung, I couldn't give a toss. I'll not be fretting whether you've learned from your experiences. But I will take satisfaction from knowing that you've suffered, if only materially. It's primitive, it's uncomplicated, sure. But that's just me. Mind how you go, now.'

He turns and leaves the house.

18

A Turn for the Worse

1

I . . .

Just a little turn is all. Right as rain. Back on my feet. Just a turn for the worse. Mind your own. You. Yes, you. Come on if you think you're hard enough. Me scared? Are you having a laugh?

'M-M-M-M-M — ' he stammers. 'Maureen!' he eventually bawls with elongated vowels.

Their names churn through his head involuntarily, with no let-up. He cannot make them stop.

Maureen. Dave. Charlotte. Bob. Martin. Charlie. Bryn. Renate. Magda. Marlene. Anneliese. Konrad. Hannelore. Roy. They're all here. Plus more. Price. Craig. Taub. Courtnay. Smith. Others too he can't place just at the moment.

They're all watching him.

'Sylvia.' A plaintive whisper, with ice in his fearful heart.

They lie in perfumed sheets in her large bed. Sweat cools on his torso. It is as if he has been in a rain shower. His hair is drenched. He watches as a salty drop runs from his shoulder, blackening the silk. He has held it off. Soon he will be required to hammer away again. Hammer and tongues. This is how she wants it, with her cruel eye. And what she wants, she gets. Regardless of his exhaustion. Next door Sir Tommy is getting his too, from that milksop from the Ministry. A neat arrangement. Wheels within wheels, oiling the wheels. The springs in the two beds creak in rhythmic unison, a weird symphonic syncopation. Filthy bastard, Sir Tommy. The whole lot of them, bastards. Plotting his downfall. All in it together. Charlie Stanbrook, Albert Schröder, Old King Cole, Bryn, Bernie, Mr Smith, old Mr Precise fucking Price of the good old Lyons Bank. And the rest of them. Not a propitious time. But a most propitious time to rip that weaselly wispy moustache off your quivering lip. Teach you a lesson, all of you. Herr Weber, Renate Taub and her pipsqueak hubby. Think you can fool me, you got another think coming. Just leave me be.

He's still sweating as he mounts her again. She grimaces with joy as Weber pins him with that smile again. Well, are the Schröders Jews or not, boy? Yes, sir. Speak up, boy. You don't sound sure. Yes. Sir. That's better. And how do you know for certain? Schröder told my father, sir. And you're prepared to testify to that? What, sir? In court? No, to the world. Like this, sir, with no clothes on? Well, of course. Not got much choice, have you? Rock and a hard place. And you was in the khazi how long? How long was it, Bernie? Thirty-three minutes precisely, Bryn. Well, there you go. You was in the khazi thirty-three minutes precisely, was you? So how come you wasn't there when we checked the stalls? We wants to know, don't we, boys?

BANG! Dear old Roy, his life hanging by a thread. No, he was always one for exactness. His eyeball hanging by a thread, to be precise. He wants to reach out and pluck it off, to tidy it up. Go on, says Bob. Do it. And he does, feeling its squishiness; he squeezes harder and harder until it bursts gently, pulpy wet and slime slithering down his wrist and his arm as he holds it aloft. Pull him off and lay him on the blanket. Cold cold cold rain on his head as it pours. The sweat trickles down his forehead, obscuring his eyesight. All he can see is that biscuit-tin-sized hole in Bob's guts. Nicely down on the blanket now, Bob. It's all for the best. Just shut up while I think about this. I need Martin to blag me out while Bernie catches their attention. One of his off-colour jokes should do the trick. Fucking hell, Bob, why'd you have to go and do that? So bloody cold. No wonder, bleeding hit I've taken. I'm shivering, for Christ's sake. Just get hold of his coat. They'll never know and if they do just say it was the shock. Confused. Not far wrong if truth be told. What in hell's name is going on? Christ, me feet are wet now. It's all that sweat. Are you done yet, Sylvia, my love? He looks down at her in shock. It's the woman from the train. Marlene, he calls her. She shows no signs of life. What you all staring at? I didn't do nuffink. Course I wouldn't do nuffink to a kid. Even a fucking Schröder kid, you know all about them, Herr Weber. Ten a penny, them girls. What you looking at me in that tone of voice for? You and Vincent, the both of you? Got your anxious face on, have you, Vinny? All spectacles and frowns. All right, nice one, but you can can the act now. It's me, remember, not some mark. Give up on your prodding, you fucking Scotch bastard. And stop mumbling among yourselves. Speak up. Whassat?

I don't think we can afford to . . .

Couldn't withstand the . . .

No, the stress . . .

Hmm . . .

In his condition . . .

Could we try . . . Nah, silly idea . . .

Not much we can do about . . .

Better leave it at that . . .

Blah-di-fucking-blah.

Jesus, it's hot in here. Those bleeding lights flashing. You sure you got this boxed off, Martin? What a fucking mess. Couldn't bloody trust you with nothing. Gonna have to make a run for it. Brussels is the best bet. Or Paris. We're staying at the Crillon, actually. His Lordship's favoured establishment when in the city. Actually, he's on the lookout for a little, um, light entertainment. You do understand me? Jolly good. We're prepared to reward you handsomely for the right services and the appropriate, ahem, discretion. Charles? We're on. Nudge nudge, wink wink. You simply wouldn't believe me. You explain, Martin. Ha ha ha ha ha. No, I'm not from Russia. Dearie me. Come from Croatia, proper German. But we can do business, right? Get on with it, lads. I'll just sit here looking wise and mysterious. Wipe the grin off that bastard Karovsky's face. I will have my piece of flesh.

Und Sie, Herr Schröder? Nein. Bin gar kein

Jude, echt deutsch. So cold.

Quiet now, and dark. He can feel his heart flapping like a trapped, dying bird in his chest. The lights come up and a couple take the stage. The man wears a three-piece suit in mustard with red windowpane checks that match his red beard, and a bowler hat which he tips off and replaces with deft dandiness. The woman is silent and superior, a sardonic smirk on her face, in a black evening gown and diamonds. It's Konrad and Renate Taub, the famous comedians!

'Well,' says Konrad, beaming, sweat mingling with greasepaint as it drips from his forehead in the footlight glare, once the audience has finished its introductory tittering. 'Well. Did you hear the one about the German lad who sold his good old mum and dad down the river? Ah, never mind. Thick bastards.'

Tomatoes and eggs rain on to the stage and they shield themselves with their arms. A noose descends from above. The light is cut and again it is silent.

The lights come up more gradually the second time and it is darker. Smoke, delicious smoke whorls around the seedy cabaret club. The announcer takes the stage, his fixed grin flashing malevolence to all corners.

'And now, gentlemen,' he says in German, 'you've met her sisters, all three of them. You've even met her mother. She's young but she'll knock you off your feet — '

'Get on with it, Weber. And get orf the stage.'

Weber pauses and sweats and shines that

379

spotlight white-toothed beam again.

'Gentlemen, for your very great pleasure. May I present? The one and only. Lili Schröder.'

He dances to the wings and there is a hush. She approaches from the rear of the stage, at first in outline, then clearer. She is wrinkled and disorientated. Crimson silken tassels hang from tired old tits. Her knickers slip off her bony hips. She opens her mouth. He is terrified, sweating ice. He can see the outlines of the chimneys behind her, pumping out that gorgeous smoke. There is muted applause.

'Lili,' he cries plangently, though no one can hear him. 'You're just a child. My little Lili. I never meant . . . '

He has missed the act. Somewhere along the way he must have dropped off. Weber is noting, with approval, the honourable lady's speech. As she leaves the chamber she passes the newly ennobled Martin in his ermine, who taps her arm and says, 'Always did have a nice pair on you, Maureen. Should have been with me, not that nobody Roy.'

And dark again, and silent. And now so very cold. The English, they never heat their stately homes. He looks across. There she is, Marlene or whatever she wants to call herself, in a nurse's uniform, giving him an eyeful of that soft peach silk. Must get back on that train, though. Bleeding freezing. Time to go. Everybody gets it in the end. No use crying over spilt blood. Get on with it. Not a propitious time for weakness. His fingers are numb. He can't light his fag. Come on, Bob. Just fucking get on with it.

Sylvia's waiting. Yeah, the ice maiden. No wonder Tommy plays for the other team. He shivers, and sniffs his fingers. A play. That's what Lili called it. And she was right. Time now for the final play. One last hustle. Our Father, Who art in Heaven, Hallowed be Thy Name . . . how does it go again?

Lili
Mother
Father
So cold. So frightened. Forgive me.

★   ★   ★

Ich . . .

★   ★   ★

If anyone had been there to hold Hans Taub's hand and to witness his passing, they would have reflected that he died peacefully in his sleep with a smile on his face. As it was, there was a minor crisis in the ward at the time and not until twenty minutes later was it discovered that the nice old man in the corner bed away from the window was no longer with them.

19

No Time for Profundity

1

Elisabeth's family are by her bedside. At first Stephen feels like an intruder.

She is in a single room, tastefully furnished in modern light wood. She is connected to various pieces of equipment by means of cables and tubes. Flowers in vases all around the room imbue it with a cloying sweetness, but he knows how much she loves fresh flowers so it must be to her taste.

She is conscious and seemingly alert. Her children, their partners and her grandchildren turn to him and he introduces himself. Andrew knows him, of course.

'Now then,' she says brightly enough, though without her normal vivacity. 'Would you kindly allow me a few private minutes with this handsome young man?'

They obey without a word and pass him with expressions that vacillate between weary anticipatory grief and welcoming, downcast smiles. They look bewildered. She beckons him forward and he sits at the chair beside the bed. He takes her hand and she smiles.

'Sweet Stephen,' she says.

'Are you in pain?' he asks.

'A little. But I've asked them not to dope me up with morphine. I've managed to keep my marbles until now, so why should I choose to lose them in my final few days?'

He smiles.

'There's no need for you to cry,' she says. 'On my account at least. For yourself, perhaps. But I died during the war. All those things that happened to me. I became indifferent. Their prophecy had come true. I had become subhuman. I was dead. Then, when I left the camps, I lived again. I've had a marvellous life. Death, then rebirth. That's what my life has been. And who knows, I may yet live again, in another unknown dimension. I doubt it somehow,' she adds quietly, as if considering a conundrum. 'And Hans is definitely gone?'

She knows, but requires confirmation.

'Hans died more than eighteen months ago,' he reassures her.

'Yes, of course. It's difficult to believe, isn't it?' she says in apparent puzzlement.

'What is?'

'That there are people like him in the world. But there are. So many of them. So unhappy. Just be glad you're not one of them.'

They talk for a few minutes longer and he realizes it is time for him to go. If she is to belong to anyone, he thinks, it should be her family.

As he stands, she says, 'Platitudes are best at such moments. Let's not go searching for profundity. It's been lovely to see you again, Stephen. You look so well.'

She nods at him, prompting.

'And you too, Elisabeth,' he lies obediently. 'Goodbye.'

'Goodbye,' she says, and he turns decisively towards the door.

Acknowledgements

I'm never sure about acknowledgements. A large part of me feels that thanking people is an activity much better conducted in private. Public gushing can somehow seem false. But here goes . . .

Deeply felt thanks go to: Chris Wakling, Anna Davis and Rufus Purdy of the Curtis Brown creative writing school for encouraging me to believe I might have this in me, and for guiding me so well.

My fellow students on the CBC six-month online course for bearing with me and for their critiques, many with new insights, all thought-provoking.

The superb teams at Viking in the UK and at HarperCollins in North America, and especially my two wonderful editors, Mary Mount at Viking and Claire Wachtel at HarperCollins.

All at the Curtis Brown Agency who have helped me navigate this (for me) strange new world — above all of course my brilliant agent, Jonny Geller.

And not forgetting my first reader, my first everything: Catherine, to whom this book is dedicated.

I've left out many of those who more generally have been crucial in shaping me and my writing — family, friends, colleagues and others to whom I owe so much, and those who deserve recognition for showing me how not to conduct my life. They are too many in number (in both categories).

It should go without saying that any inaccuracies in this book and its deficiencies are mine alone.

We do hope that you have enjoyed reading this large print book.

Did you know that all of our titles are available for purchase?

We publish a wide range of high quality large print books including:
Romances, Mysteries, Classics
General Fiction
Non Fiction and Westerns

Special interest titles available in large print are:
The Little Oxford Dictionary
Music Book
Song Book
Hymn Book
Service Book

Also available from us courtesy of Oxford University Press:
Young Readers' Dictionary
(large print edition)
Young Readers' Thesaurus
(large print edition)

For further information or a free brochure, please contact us at:
Ulverscroft Large Print Books Ltd.,
The Green, Bradgate Road, Anstey,
Leicester, LE7 7FU, England.
Tel: (00 44) 0116 236 4325
Fax: (00 44) 0116 234 0205

Other titles published by Ulverscroft:

LOVER

Anna Raverat

Home is where the heart is; and Kate, who works for a global hotel corporation, thinks a lot about making people feel at home. She has a happy one of her own, with her husband of many years, two daughters, and elderly dog Charlie — or so she believes. But her home and her heart both shatter when she discovers a series of emails from her husband Adam, a.k.a. 'Prince Charming', to another woman. Probing for answers, Kate realizes this is not the worst possible discovery — in fact, it is only the beginning. As her home life unravels, her job — and her nightmare boss — become increasingly demanding. She wants to protect her young girls, but her own foundations have been knocked away. Who is the man with whom she has lived all these years?